TROJAN

AFTERLIFE ONLINE
BOOK THREE

Domino Finn

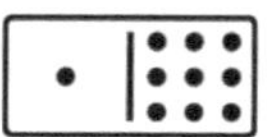

Published by Blood & Treasure, Los Angeles
First Edition

Cover Typography by James T. Egan of Bookfly Design LLC.

Print ISBN: 978-1-946-00883-1

DominoFinn.com

Also by Domino Finn

GUILD-
HALL
BARRACKS
LUMBERYARD
DRAGON
PERCH
VAULT
BROTHEL
OLD TOWN

TROJAN

AFTERLIFE ONLINE: BOOK THREE

-- Cutscene --

In the beginning, there was nothing.

Working out of his garage, Christian Everett barely had enough capital to keep the lights on. But home brew was where his heart was. He powered through those sparse days until he gained the mastery to separate the light from the darkness.

He was the first to pioneer extra-virtual reality: a complex simulation that skipped headsets and could only be interfaced through brainwaves. EVR would be the next evolution in personal entertainment.

But the technology represented more than a game. His investors pushed to model real-life experiences—virtual stadium attendance for concerts and sports. Those applications missed the greater picture. Those sims would be subservient to the real world. If the sim was perfect enough, it could transcend it.

This wasn't *entertainment*; it was *evolution*.

Many would later call Christian Everett an inspired genius. This was true, but his inspiration was more straightforward than many realized: a life fraught with tragedy. His wife died during the birth of their second child. Both kids grew infirm at a young age and were permanently relegated to a hospice. Christian, it seemed, was destined to be alone. All that was left was his work, and he intended to use it to build a better world. One where families didn't have to suffer. It was a noble, selfish dream.

Which is why it surprised absolutely everybody when Christian Everett sold off his entire stake in EVR and opened a casual games company.

Now a self-funded billionaire, he set off to grow a rapacious empire. Instead of hiring talent, he absorbed it. From China to Europe and the Americas, he acquired company after company under his fold. Kablammy Games was meant to explode the status quo. It was fruitful and multiplied. Record profits thrust the corporation into the limelight of the tech world.

But their intellectual property was a letdown after the CEO's vaunted beginnings. Quick-and-dirty apps on mobile and social media became the new evolution. To many, gamification seemed a backward step.

For Christian, it was an intermediate one. A missing link. The games weren't important, the connectivity was. Mobile was about people. Social was about data. And throughout the boom and bust of motion and 3D and VR and the next big gaming fads, he had his greatest talent working on a secret project: a new sim that would leave EVR in the dust.

It wasn't easy going. Things being cyclical, the gifted genius returned to his old ways. He isolated himself. Spent without fear of consequence. Kablammy's shine faded in the public eye. Survive long enough and even heroes become villains. The cause of the industry's ills. Breakthroughs occurred behind the scenes, progress was met with delays; years passed, ideas stagnated.

Although Christian had long been removed from his family,

he never lost faith. They were, after all, his inspiration. They were what drove him to create a new world.

As an idealist, Christian often ignored the harsh realities that obstructed his grand vision. It was nearly too late when he first learned of the threat to his work, to the greatest dream he had ever known: to one day see Haven go gold.

1070 Tapper

I burped loudly. The thick aroma of oatmeal coffee stout wafted up my throat and filled my sinuses.

"Whoa," I said a bit shakily. "That's some heavy stuff."

Kyle beamed as he leaned on the bar. "I know, right? It's a brand new recipe that doesn't take prisoners. I figured I'd name it Black Hat Brew, after everything we've accomplished here."

I blinked away the suds, trying to keep a straight face. Kyle was the brewmaster, after all, and this was a reverent moment for him. I didn't want to infringe on his choice of flagship brew. Besides, there was nothing wrong with being rough around the edges. It sort of defined us. I turned to Izzy on the barstool beside me.

"It's good," she said with a shrug. "It's not subtle, but it's good."

Warmth spread through me as I surveyed our fledgling guildhall. It was a simple pub with classic accents: mahogany counters, tin ceiling tiles, wrought-iron sconces. I could no longer contain my grin. It wasn't just the beer. It had been a pleasurable month.

You might be surprised due to my rocky early days, but living in a digital-reality afterlife didn't entail world-ending threats every day.

Four weeks had passed since we'd exiled the corrupt bishop and his catechists from Stronghold, and while we'd participated in small-scale quest events and raids, and had trouble with the aforementioned catechists, life within these stone walls had been peaceful.

Much of my focus had turned to my new faction, the Black Hats. And that meant spending a lot of time planning—and dreaming—with my two favorite people in Haven.

Kyle hadn't been his usual frat-boy slacker self. With the erecting of the new guildhall, he'd been given not only a purpose, but the fame that came with fulfilling it.

The purple girl with the dragonfly wings? Well, she was my rock. Izzy was toughness and smarts rolled into a snark burrito. Well, a taquito, at least. But there was no way I could've strategized everything without her. Even when it came to her input on beer.

Hey, I didn't say it was *all* hard work.

"Have you boys figured out what you want to name the place yet?" asked Izzy.

I shrugged. "I dunno. We could keep it traditional: Haven Public House."

"Or lounge chic," suggested Kyle. His hand reverently caressed the air. "Aroma."

Izzy winced. "What about something hipster nouveau, like Water & Wheat?"

"Too pretentious," said Kyle. "We need something cool but simple."

"Something purposeful," I added. "I want this place to mean something."

Kyle nodded. "We have plenty of time to figure it out, bros. For now I'm focusing on the substance."

Izzy smirked. "You mean the suds."

We clinked glasses and enjoyed another pull. "There's more than beer though," said Kyle from his bartending perch. "As Stronghold's public house to end all public houses, I'm setting up grub specials."

"Cook?" Izzy arched a skeptical brow. "What do you know about cooking? I doubt you can recite the ingredients of a grilled cheese."

The brewmaster took the sarcasm in stride. "Not true at all. I already have a preliminary menu laid out. Pepperoni pizza, Philly steak and cheese, meatballs and mozzarella, chicken broccoli and cheddar—"

"Wait. Those sound like Hot Pocket flavors."

He hiked a shoulder. "I thought that was clear. What do you expect? I'm not Gordon Ramses."

"Ramsay," I corrected. "He's a celebrity chef, not one of the greatest pharaohs of ancient Egypt."

Kyle furrowed his brow. "Whatever. If Ramses was so great, how come he didn't host his own reality show?" He turned to Izzy. "And everybody likes Hot Pockets. They're headlining the menu alongside Totino's Pizza Rolls."

Izzy puffed out her cheeks and gagged. "And on that note, I think I need some fresh air before I hurl." She set down her half-full beer and stood. "Beer and junk food. All this place needs is a stream of Saturday-morning cartoons and it would be nostalgia

Heaven."

She'd meant the comment as a jab, but Kyle and I put our heads together in weighty contemplation.

Izzy rolled her eyes. "Just don't forget to do your rounds, boys." We barely acknowledged her as she headed out.

The brewmaster picked at the countertop and jutted his lips out. "So... *GI Joe*?"

"I was thinking *Transformers*, *Batman*, and a heavy dose of *Gargoyles*, but I'm flexible."

His hands boomed together in a single clap. "Awesome! I'll get—"

A muffled explosion rocked the back wall. Kyle spun around as smoke seeped from under the kitchen door.

I scratched my cheek. "Um, is that a normal step in the beer-making process?"

"Oh, crap. I was supposed to check the boil." He scurried to the backroom brewhouse.

I sighed and took another swig of beer. The stuff grew on you. I imagined a day, not far off, when the guildhall would be bustling with lively characters and heated opinions. The pleasing thought distracted me, but only for a moment. I jerked around as I detected someone's silent approach.

"Sorry," said the man, hands raised. "Didn't mean to startle you. I have a habit of walking quietly." He was dressed in simple leathers and wore a hood. The green name above the player's head read [Poe]. His eyes scanned the empty bar as he set his heavy bag on the counter. "Did I just miss the bartender, or is this joint not open yet?"

"It's a soft opening," I explained. "The grand opening's in

four nights. But you're free to have a drink."

He sighed in relief. "Music to my ears. I could really use one." He rapped the countertop with light fingers and huffed as he waited on Kyle.

"You're not a Black Hat," I noted.

"No, but they're why I'm here."

"Yeah? Thinking of joining?"

"It's always a possibility, but that's jumping the gun. I'm here to see what they're about first." He scanned the empty bar. "I'll tell you this: I like what they've done with the place."

I chuckled. He didn't know who I was. Either he didn't recognize the name Talon, hadn't bothered to check it, or was *really* focused on getting that beer.

"Look," I said, "the bartender's dealing with a minor opening issue and we don't have the taps set up yet. But if you like you can preview our flagship stout." I pointed to Izzy's glass. "If you don't mind a gently used glass."

"I should've known. You work here." Hungry eyes landed on the drink. "Thanks for the gesture, friend." He downed the mug in several gulps.

I chuckled magnanimously. "I don't just work here, you know. I'm—"

I didn't have time to complete my humble-brag because Poe slammed the empty mug on the top of my head.

1080 Modern Warfare

Glass fragments compacted against my skull and spilled to the wood like a jumble of marbles. I hit the floor more like a toppled refrigerator.

Ambush!
67 damage
Stun!
You are stunned. You may not use skills, move, or attack for 20 seconds.

I blinked stupidly. Poe stood over me flaunting a vicious smile. His class info filled in beside his name: [Level 7 Assassin].

"I know who you are," he spat. "Like I said, it's why I'm here." He slipped a dagger from his cloak and checked the area. The weapon was distinctly skinny, built like a rapier from hilt to tip, but much shorter. "Don't worry, that first hit was just to pacify you. This second one's the killing blow, and it won't hurt one bit."

I struggled against the crippling status effect. Despite being locked out of movement and attacks, I could flubber around on the floor and shield my face. "Kyle!" I screamed.

Poe chortled darkly, leaned in, and slipped his blade clear through my chest.

> Critical Hit!
> 191 damage

I writhed in pure agony. Talk about a killing blow, except it hadn't actually finished the job. I was still alive, with 3 health left, and I *fucking hurt*.

The assassin pulled the needle free with a curious expression. "I'm impressed," he said without sarcasm. "An explorer class with that much health. You must've invested a lot into your strength attribute. Then again, I might have just underestimated your level-9 stats."

I growled fiercely, attempting to fend him off with spite alone. But Poe's 20 seconds were up. As his blade came at me again, I triggered my dash skill from a sitting position and skidded across the tavern floor. Even when the traversal boost ended, I continued the momentum with a lunge and a somersault—right through the front door.

Sunlight surged over me, blinding me for a brief moment, but it was enough time to produce a flask of red liquid and chug it down. My health bar smoothly refilled.

Poe sighed from the doorway. "You're gonna make me work for my money, aren't you?"

The dragonspear blinked in my grip and I snarled. "No, I'm gonna make you eat your own dagger." I flipped to my feet ready to defend myself. Poe slipped back into the bar.

I pounced forward with a vicious swipe, making sure the stranger couldn't get an easy shot at me as I entered. My breath stopped short; I stared at an empty interior.

"You've got tricks," I said dismissively.

A quick peek at my health showed it max out at 261. The red stuff was invaluable, but it could only be used once a day. I'd need to watch my back or I'd be in a world of pain.

I took measured steps through the tavern. "Assassino!" I called out, looking for signs of movement. "You working for the catechists? Is this revenge for Bishop Tannen?"

No one answered. Poe was still around, though. He'd already revealed his motivation for being here. He couldn't leave without his payday. I scanned the shadows. It was daytime and there was enough light in here that my darkvision was useless.

"You rigged the boiler in the back to blow, didn't you?" Quiet. "Kyle?" I called out. "You back there?"

No answer again.

Oh shit.

Kyle.

I set my boot to rush to the brewery when a flash glimmered at my side.

Backstab!
77 damage

I punched the spear straight back and spun. Nothing. I fought off a grimace. Missing the assassin wasn't a big deal, but the fact that he was still invisible was. Poe had somehow successfully backstabbed and still managed to slink back into the shadows. It was my turn to be impressed.

I swiped the air horizontally, testing the surroundings with my superior reach. It was a good disappearing act, but it didn't make him invincible. I was willing to bet I could take out a good chunk of his health. If only I could find him.

The brewmaster emerged from the kitchen. "Dude, were you tinkering with my suds?"

My head snapped to him. "Assassin," I chirped.

Kyle frowned. "I don't have an assassin beer, but I like the sound of it." He splayed a hand across his field of view as if presenting a new product line. "Assassin IPA. When you're in the mood for killer hops."

"No, Kyle, I mean—"

My body went to full alarm. The last time Poe struck I'd been distracted by Kyle, and here I was again. Out of position, out of time. Without giving the strategy ample thought, I activated crossblock and tornado spin together for a combo. My body rotated in quick circles as the dragonspear slashed anything within two yards.

And my weapon found the assassin.

> You dealt 17 damage to [Poe]

He grunted and hopped backward.

> Skill Evolution!
> You learned Spinshield

Whoa. It wasn't a lot of damage, but I'd just given a nerfed skill new life. The spin had covered all angles of attack and had rebuffed the backstab. Even better, Poe was no longer hidden.

Kyle furrowed his brow. "Who's your friend? Is he the one who came up with the new beer idea?"

"ASSASSIN!" I screamed.

Kyle straightened and shouldered his crossbow. Poe flung a throwing knife from his belt. Instead of targeting Kyle he hit the heavy bag he left on the bar. It exploded in a flash of teal light. Some kind of spectral net engulfed my roommate. He fell to the floor struggling against it.

Poe lunged at me next. With him out in the open, I was ready for it. I crossblocked and fended him off with my spear. Then I followed it up with a deadshot to his chest.

Combo!
You dealt 87 damage to [Poe]

He tumbled to his back.

"Who sent you?" I demanded.

"A good contractor never tells, but I don't come cheap."

"Whatever they're paying, it's not worth it."

He scoffed. "It's not about money in my pocket; it's about taking it outta yours." He was referring to the death penalty. It would mean 25% of my ample silver, down the drain. "And it's about making a statement. What kind of faction leader gets killed in their own guildhall?"

I gripped the spear tight. "Not *this* kind."

This time when I triggered dash, I used it offensively. He gulped a health potion as I skidded along the wood floor like a rocket.

Impale!
You dealt 65 damage to [Poe]

I had him straight through the belly. He drove toward me anyway and stuck me with his knife. I twisted away but he yanked it out and popped it back in.

"Goblin lover!" he spat through bloody teeth.

I should've just dropped the dragonspear attaching Poe to me, but it was a legendary weapon and I didn't like conceding it that easily. Instead I hefted it, and him, into the air.

He coughed up a bloody mess but clutched his dagger tight. In and out again. This time I managed to squirm so it only found my shoulder. Still, the damage on both ends was compounding faster than the 401k I could no longer use. This was a war of attrition.

My eyes flitted to Kyle. Just an upturned heap with an arm yanking at the net. Still struggling, I retreated backward across the tavern, dragging the assassin with me. My dash, my deadshot, and my tornado spin were all still in cooldown, and my weapon had been neutralized by a sacrificial blow. He twisted on my spear and pressed the attack.

"What are you doing?" I hissed. "You're gonna kill yourself."

His eyes locked with mine as he croaked through bloody teeth. "Sometimes the path to victory requires death."

My eyes widened at his determination.

Poe angled his blade toward my neck. I released the dragonspear, hoping to shove him away, but I'd waited too long. He was too fast.

At least, he *was* nice and fast until a sword the size of a picnic bench crushed him into a ruined heap. I flinched backward as Lash hefted her *Final-Fantasy*-sized cleaver for another blow. The follow-up wasn't necessary.

Surprise!
[Lash] dealt 104 damage to [Poe]
[Poe] is dead!

"How's that for a path to victory?" she chortled.

The white-washed full plate of my savior stood mighty and tall. Her helmet swiveled to me, eye slit cold and dark. "You really should watch yourself, boss. I mean, seriously, what kind of faction leader gets killed in their own guildhall?"

1090 White Knight Chronicles

I feigned calm and retrieved my dragonspear, blinking at the broken body on the tavern floor. "Thanks, Lash. It's good to have you on my side for once."

I was being dramatic, of course. While the knight and I had often butted heads in the past, she'd since sacrificed herself for the founding of the Black Hats. Lash was one of us now, without question.

Which wasn't to say managing her was a cakewalk.

I pointed to the assassin. "That's your loot. You deserve it."

The knight eagerly dug into her spoils. Her excitement was short-lived. "This is crap. Barely any silver. No items worth a damn."

"Too bad he didn't drop that needle knife. It packed quite a sting." I chewed my lip. "No possessions, last words about victory through death, an assassin behind enemy lines—he expected to die. I guess your reward is the satisfaction of saving your fearless leader."

The stocky woman snorted and pulled off her helmet. Her

hair was freshly bleached and she wore especially thick black liner in points outside her eyes. "You don't look so fearless at the moment." She turned and whistled. Her crew filed in the door.

Where Lash was a large and menacing figure, her healer Glinda was gaunt and frail. The priest was one of the older players I'd seen in Haven. Thankfully, she was quite talented. With the danger safely neutralized, she cast a spell that surged my health and spirit to maximum. I sighed in relief.

Conan filed inside with a greataxe. Unlike Glinda, the barbarian was disappointed he'd missed the big show. He stomped around the public house flexing unnecessary muscles.

Newer to Lash's party were the twins, Crux and Hex. The brother-sister duo skewed toward the antihero look. Dark hair and dark eyes, Crux was a fellow explorer who wore full black leathers—I'd actually picked up his raiding tips from the wiki before we ever met. Hex went for a cuter Hot Topic ensemble.

"Good awareness, Bravo Team," Lash told them.

"We didn't even do anything," complained Hex. "Why do we always need to wait in the back?"

"Because you're a necromancer and your brother's a thief. You both have glass jaws."

Hex pouted but her brother only watched with sharp eyes. The quintessential silent type, it was hard to get to know him. They made a dark and brooding pair. Not only was that a good fit for the Black Hats, but their skills fleshed out Lash's party.

[Lash - Level 9 Knight]
[Glinda - Level 7 White Witch]
[Conan - Level 7 Barbarian]

[Crux - Level 6 Thief]

[Hex - Level 6 Necromancer]

Lash's level was new, and it was impressive. Besides me and my party, she was the only player I knew so high, no doubt due to her work ethic and brutal grinding.

Now fully refreshed from the ordeal, I admired my own character sheet.

Talon		Level	9
Class	Explorer	XP	64985
Kit	Scout	Next	74950

Strength	17	Strike	337
Agility	24	Dodge	400
Craft	6	Health	261 / 261
Essence	10	Spirit	227 / 227

My XP was concerning. Due to recent events and administrative woes, the devs had vastly strangled the circulation of XP in the Haven ecosystem. Many blamed me for killing a titan and forcing permanent progression—two acts I would never apologize for. The end result, nevertheless, affected everyone on the server. Leveling was slower of late.

I needed to hit 75,000 before dying, otherwise a month of

grinding would go down the drain. It almost had just now. The encounter with Poe revealed how vulnerable I really was.

I swiped to my expanded skills.

Skills	2
Spear	3
Crossblock	3
Deadshot	3
Tornado Spin	1
Spinshield	1
Awareness	
Exploration	
Tracking	
Darkvision	
Survival	
Navigation	
Cartography	
Traversal	
Dash	
Vault	
Scale	
Stealth	
Sneak	
Subdue	

It was an impressive list, made more so by recent additions

that hadn't cost me skill points. During the skirmish with Poe, I'd experienced my first-ever skill evolution. Not just a new skill parameter—I'd achieved that before. This time I'd earned a brand-new skill.

Spinshield
A spinning block that counters attacks from all directions while dealing modest return damage.
Spirit Cost: 44
Cooldown: 120 seconds

The new block had come from my contextual use of tornado spin in conjunction with crossblock. In other words, a prepackaged skill combo. The actual ability itself didn't seem especially novel, however. Lash had something very similar if not identical.

I chewed my lip and opened up last week's patch notes.

Haven version 0.9.26
- Reshuffled quest opportunities.
- Rebalanced mob aggression.
- Expanded skill and spell notifications.
- Tweaked reputation maximums.
- Folded proficiencies into skills. Proficiencies have been underused and underpowered. Their adaptability has been carried over.

That explained why I had so many skills now. Exploration and tracking were now considered passive skills. The proficiency list was gone altogether. Interestingly, current speculation was that all skills could improve with use now. I continued through the patch log.

> - Starting at level 10, no more skill points will be awarded on a per-level basis. This is necessary to rebalance the adaptability aspect.

That note worried me. It was why I still had 2 skill points left unspent. Once I hit level 10, I wouldn't be receiving any more. Those 2 points were a finite resource.

> - Isolated naturally occurring skill evolution events and added appropriate UI markers.

Here was the one I was looking for. A throwaway line about skill evolution events. While the comment had spurred discussion among the community, I'd assumed functionality would remain the same. Skills could sometimes have their parameters tweaked to behave differently, like using dash in midair. I hadn't heard of new skills sprouting into existence before. With Haven's genetic algorithms being initiated by player inputs, it made perfect sense. I wondered what else we could control.

Regardless, I was only able to manage what I knew about. That currently meant dealing with more possible assassination attempts. Poe had caught me totally unprepared, and I couldn't risk that happening again. I was finally ready to spend one of my skill points.

> **Intuition**
> Uncanny recognition of immediate impending danger.

The description of the awareness skill left a lot to the imagination, but the player wiki reported good things. Having a sort of virtual Spidey-sense would very much keep me on my toes. I purchased the skill and closed the menu, satisfied.

"Uh, guys?" peeped Kyle from out of sight. "Can anyone help a brother out?"

We all turned and found the brewmaster crawling out like an inchworm from behind the bar, glowing net still tightly wrapping his body.

Lash stomped over. "I like the new look. Doormat-chic."

"Seriously?"

"Nah, you're right. You probably can't pour a beer like that, can you? I'll get you outta there, but you're comping my first bar tab." The knight brought her fist to her chest and muttered.

> [Lash] cast Essence of Will on [Kyle]

The buff was an instantaneous nullification of minor magical afflictions. A warm glow washed over Kyle and the net dissolved into nothing.

"You guys need to up your magic resistance," remarked Lash.

The brewmaster stood and brushed his clothes. "Tell me about it. Thanks."

"How're your kegs in the back?" I asked.

His eyes flitted to the assassin's corpse as it faded away. "So it was sabotage. Sneaky bastard. No permanent damage, luckily."

I nodded and stepped outside. It was a bright morning with modest activity. Nothing seemed out of the ordinary. Lash and her team joined me.

"What do you think?" she asked.

I saw the hunger in her eyes. She wanted action.

The Mexican-born stalwart was brash, headstrong, and had grown up with two older brothers who became Marines. That pretty much explained all anybody needed to know about her. Her induction into the Black Hats was a no-brainer for both of us. She liked to play on the winning team and, after the crusaders moved on, my faction was the only game in town.

I'd initially wanted Lash to be my army general. Her knight kit was excellent for tanking while buffing nearby allies. What could be better for morale? Unfortunately, the opportunity presented a couple of problems. The first was she didn't want anything to do with army, digital or otherwise. The second reason was more practical. Lash wanted agency and excitement, which translated to a tactical team not bogged down by training and corralling large groups of soldiers.

In a way I admired that. Lash knew what she wanted and didn't stray from the path. It's not that I didn't find administrative faction duties fascinating, but it was definitely a full-time gig. It's partly why I was still level 9 and she'd caught up.

Anyway, Lash was a formidable combatant who inspired others. I would've been stupid to let her go. So I gave her a special position of her choosing: the command of her own elite Marine Recon. Even the name she came up with, Bravo Team, made her the undisputed Bravo Leader, a clear claim of second-in-command of the Black Hats. That wasn't the reality, of course. While I was the head of the faction, I trusted Kyle and Izzy more than anyone in the afterlife. They undoubtedly led things in my absence, and Lash had thus far respected that.

"Fan out," she ordered her team. "Search the alleys. Stay close." They did as ordered. With Kyle cleaning up inside, it left us alone.

"When did you finally make level 9?" I asked.

"A week ago."

Damn. That was a long time for the competition to slip my notice. I gave her a belated thumbs up.

The average Haven player was level 5 at this point. Anyone lower was new or not trying hard enough, and anyone good skewed closer to 7. The problem was a few of us had more XP than the world state could support, with gains partially coming from glitches and hacks. Now our level thresholds were exponentially larger than the average player's. Without the introduction of advanced quests, I foresaw a time when most people's levels would even out.

"Any idea what that assassin was about?" asked Lash. "I thought people around here liked you."

"I haven't seen Poe around," I admitted, "but he was too high level to be a noob."

My reputation in Stronghold was better than it had ever been, but that didn't mean there weren't some who objected to my presence and influence. The catechists still wanted a piece of me, and I couldn't discount the stray goblin hater. The Black Hats had agreed to an armistice with the pagan faction. Despite assertions that the peace would never last, it hadn't been breached in four weeks.

Not that I was ready to sing Kumbaya over the momentous accomplishment. The peace was a mirage. The pagan-killing quests had dried up with the bishop's defeat. Goblin populations were now fractured but elusive, no longer easy XP. Their main base was in Shorehome, half a world away. The lack of goblin clashes could entirely be attributed to the lack of goblins.

"Well," noted Lash, "the asswipe is dead now. If he was paid for the job, he'll probably come back. Then I'll kill him again."

"You're a real go-getter. It's too bad, too. I would've loved to snag someone like Poe for that coveted 50th member."

I opened my faction status.

Black Hats
Faction Level: 1   *Members*: 49 / 50
War   Catechists   **Armistice**   Pagans

"We'll get there, boss."

I nodded and turned to start my rounds. Surprising as it was, the assassin wasn't the only exciting thing happening today. I made my way down the street and was surprised to find Lash on my heels.

"What's up?" I asked.

She shook her head.

Another moment of walking. "Was there something else?"

"Nope."

"I'll take it from here, then."

The overgrown woman stuck to me like glue. "No can do, boss. Assassins sometimes travel in groups."

"I'm sure I'm safe now. I've got faction duties to attend to. You know, that stuff you didn't want to deal with."

"I'll deal with it." She cut off my objection. "You gave me full autonomy to lead my team as I see fit, and I just assigned us as your new bodyguards. At least until we get a better understanding of where he came from. Get used to having us around."

Ugh. I didn't relish the thought. At the same time, she'd earned the right to call this.

"Fine, let's do the rounds together. But don't say I didn't warn you. This is what being the boss really looks like."

1100 Town Life Stuff

We trudged down the main strip. Which, being Oldtown, was a euphemism for a walkway unobstructed by rubble.

This ancient neighborhood was the original heart of Stronghold. In the shadow of the megacity's grand architectural feats, Oldtown hadn't held up. Aside from a single magical tower, the rest was squalor, a field of ruins downed by the brutal combination punches of invasion and time. A lifeless district relegated to the history books.

All that had changed when I declared it Black Hat territory.

Oldtown was no longer abandoned. Nowadays it was tough to keep tabs on all the locals. A flood of Shorehome immigrants had set up a tent city over a month ago. Many had since moved on, whether back to their city or into new housing in this one, but Oldtown was still in transition, scummy and filled with transients. Then again, some of them were Black Hats now. In the interest of growing the faction, I couldn't afford to reject any who applied.

My experience thus far in Haven had taught me a lot. Topping that list was the amazing strength to be found in unity, even against the developers and saints themselves. All my focus was on driving toward the ambitious goal of creating something greater than the sum of its parts.

During the dramatic formation of the Black Hats and the ensuing battle for the city, membership had immediately skyrocketed to 48. The faction had practically leveled up in its inaugural hour. Unfortunately, the following hours and days saw a decline as members parted ways.

There were no hard feelings. Many players and friends had joined to support the battle but didn't want long-term obligations. Others were ignorant blowhards who took principled yet misguided stands against the goblin armistice and my agreement with the wild king—players had grown fat off the pagan quests and those days were over.

More pressing was the rogue catechist faction the Black Hats were at war with. Cleric Vagram used guerrilla tactics against faction members in the deep wild. After brutally slaying select players for their association with us, it spurred some of our membership to go independent.

Then came a possible misstep on my part. My friends and I were cash rich, but that could only go so far after so many investments. I'd instituted a mandatory 10% tithe on all player earnings toward the collective faction. The idea was for everybody to contribute. In hindsight, the move was too early.

All things considered, being a Black Hat lost its luster. I was an infamous player with a cool tower, but those things didn't exactly trickle down. Low-level factions were simple and as yet offered no real benefit to members aside from inclusion in an exclusive club. Basically, we were getting away with not providing a whole lot because we were the only game in town. I intended to fix that before it became a problem.

Over the last few weeks, I'd sold the promise of things to come and getting in on the ground floor. After a slow build, we were finally eclipsing our original count at 49. Now we just needed that defining number 50.

"There you are!" A weathered man with wild white hair and one eye larger than the other stomped our way. "What's taking ya so long? I'm on a schedule. You know I don't tolerate loiterers and slack-jaws!"

I chuckled. "I think I've heard that before. How is my Buildmaster General?"

"Bah! I hate that title. It's a fancy way of saying I got two jobs."

Trafford was a lovable grump, and he wasn't kidding about having two jobs. He was an NPC who used to be on the city watch, or at least that was part of his programmed history. Without Lash as the general of my armies, and with Gladius, the head of the city watch, unable to stray from his official town duties, I had to assign the role to Trafford. He was a loyal friend and gladly took on faction work on top of managing his store. It also helped that a dearth of new players meant fewer people were patronizing the welcome shop.

Trafford, it turned out, was a victim of his own expertise. In addition to being a capable soldier, the old man had secondary artisan skills. With consort classes, Haven allowed overlapping specializations, similar to how an explorer like me had a bunch of soldier abilities for combat.

Artisan skills have numerous trees. Kyle specialized in alchemy and art for, well, alchemy, jewelry, and glasswork.

Other available trees were textiles, metalsmiths, bowyers, and leatherers. Which was all to say that Trafford was my sole representative of the builder tree, encompassing stonemasonry, carpentry, and planning.

It would surprise no one that, at the time, in the absence of any headquarters and building menus, not many players had pursued such professions. I wanted to change that.

"Trafford, I appreciate everything you've done. We're about to see big gains today. I promise."

"Aye, I believe ya, but it'll only do so much good unless we can get more builders."

"You've been doing okay since Grug and Grom joined."

He scoffed. "Those pillagers? We're lucky they're not stealing the raw materials and selling them on the side!"

He was being overly hard on the band of pirates who'd joined us, but it was fair to say they weren't great builders. They were warm bodies more than anything, tag-teaming in and out to barely account for normal manpower. "I hear you. We'll find someone worthy of being your apprentice. Fair enough?"

"Either that or find my replacement and leave me to the army duties. I'm an old hand at weaponry, I am." The old man raised his head high. He was a solid soldier, no doubt about that. He eyed the seven-foot-tall white knight trailing us. "How about you, miss? You know anything about stonemasonry?"

"Psh," she spat. "Look somewhere else, *abuelo*."

He shook his head. "It's a thankless job, I tell ya."

I smiled as we made our way along the strip and toward the looming tower that overshadowed Oldtown. Dragonperch was an impressive piece of ancient architecture—the only structure in the district that had withstood the ages, in no small part due to its mystical wards. Halfway down the street, it still watched over us. Beside it, the petrified remains of a kneeling titan reached skyward. Another enduring symbol of Oldtown, the cyclops was now reduced to half the size of Dragonperch.

The tower was a sanctum. Dragonspear in hand, I'd slain the titan and reclaimed the mystical keep. After opening, it had initially remained dormant—at least until the Black Hats were founded.

According to the undocumented rules of Haven, a sanctum and a faction combined into something greater. The dormant sanctum awoke at level 1, and all of a sudden I had unlocked a new interface: the headquarters menu.

It was a way to invest our money. To claim worthless Oldtown property. We'd bought out the central portion along the river from the tower to the main thoroughfare. Then we started building.

Just because the land was neglected and available didn't mean it had come cheap. Acquiring the large lot seriously taxed our resources, hence the faction tithe. I rationalized that we were breaking new ground, pioneers in the virtual afterlife, but the pros weren't without cons.

As we passed the respawn building, I grumbled. It had been our second construction project after the guildhall. For a burgeoning society in need of resources, I could think of many choices more appealing than a brothel.

I opened the headquarters interface.

<table>
<tr><td colspan="1">Black Hat Headquarters</td></tr>
<tr><td>Level: 2
HQXP: 4 / 8</td></tr>
<tr><td>HQR: 52
Daily HQR Production: 10</td></tr>
<tr><td>Current Buildings
Guildhall
Brothel
Barracks
Lumberyard</td></tr>
</table>

The brothel sticks out like a sore thumb, doesn't it? Well, it comes with the territory when half your faction are pirates.

Guildhalls and respawn points were common buildings, as far as I could tell, but I had a feeling that construction theming was a combination of location, sanctum, and faction members. Both the barracks and brothel were respawn points, and I was upset I had to build any at all. With them, Black Hats could choose to respawn here when they died instead of in their homes. That was next to useless considering most lived in the city.

That said, it needed to be done. Explaining why requires backtracking over the course of the month.

Black Hat headquarters started at level 1. It's a little confusing because factions and headquarters have separate leveling tracks. Factions are about membership and level up by gaining recruits. Headquarters involve physical structures and progress through construction. With our noob resources, it was a slow grind.

A level 1 headquarters accumulates 3 headquarters resources per day. Trafford was a skilled enough builder to contribute +1, and the jumble of other pirates amounted to another. Our first goalpost had been the guildhall.

Guildhall

Meeting place for faction members.

Cost: 20 HQR; 3000 silver

Man Hours: 60

HQXP: 1

Limit: 1

+2 HQR

Guildhalls were relatively cheap when it came to headquarters resources and man hours. The price in silver was less modest, but money was our least constraining variable. Besides, guildhalls were important. Aside from cementing a communal gathering area for Black Hats, it added 2 additional HQR to the daily.

Since we were limited to building a single guildhall, respawn points were the next cheapest buildings. And building fast was key. Not only did we have very limited man hours to assign to projects, but a total of 3 buildings provided enough headquarters experience points to bring us to level 2. That was a huge milestone because it increased our daily HQR from 7 to 10. With that in mind we'd built two respawn points, a brothel and a barracks. Seeing as we were populated by a bunch of pirates, transients, and ne'er-do-wells, it was a popular move. A beacon of respect it was not, but it sure served its purpose.

"I can't believe this," complained Trafford. "Grom!" he shouted. "Get outta there this instant and report for duty!"

The pirate deflated. He stood on the brothel's porch with a woman in one arm and a man in the other, and he appeared to have already paid.

"Business first!" warned the buildmaster.

"By the Maelstrom!" spat Grom. "I don't get a day o' rest."

"I haven't seen you for two days!"

The pirate shrugged. "I weren't restin' though."

Grom eyed his supervisor and me and Lash's cold helmet. With a forlorn sigh, he released his expensive distractions and came along. It was a wise decision. I'd seen the lad try to outdo the grumpy shopkeeper before, and he'd fallen woefully short. Trafford huffed and marched forward. I followed his lead until an arrow whizzed right past my nose.

1110 Ranger X

I recoiled as the projectile hammered into the nearby remnant of a stone wall. Lash immediately cast an attack buff. Golden light washed over us. My first instinct was to go into full attack mode, but two things caught my eye. Arrows weren't usually able to penetrate stone, and this one had a silver head. Silver was currency in this realm. To use it for combat necessitated great expense and required hardening enchantments.

"Dune," I snapped.

The ranger hopped off the distant ruins, green cloak flowing behind as he approached. I yanked his signature arrow from the wall and held it out to him. As he converged and reached for it, I snapped it in half. "Oops."

"Hey, those things aren't cheap."

"It broke easy enough." I tossed the components back to him. They bounced off his chest and fell to the ground. "What's the big idea?"

He chuckled. "I just figured you'd like to see what a *real* assassination attempt looks like."

"You heard about that already?"

The ranger gave a heartless shrug. "It's the buzz of Oldtown.

Everyone who's anyone knows. Or is it anyone who's everyone? Wait..."

I sighed. Dune was a level-8 ranger with his own party, as well as one of the aforementioned players who'd temporarily joined the faction and subsequently quit. A lot of people thought he was a cocky douche, but I liked the guy. Despite his playful hijinks, he hadn't been a troublemaker as Lash and some of the others had. He was a strong, confident ally who surrounded himself with capable people. He was just too proud to serve anyone but himself.

I kinda felt stupid wearing the glowing buff in the middle of town. "Forget it."

Dune laughed. "Come on, Talon, don't take it so personally. Think of it as a christening. What self-respecting bar doesn't have a good brawl once in a while?"

The corner of my lips crooked. "That's right. I wouldn't run any other kind of operation."

"That's the spirit."

"Hey, you sure you don't wanna join the Black Hats? If you do, the faction levels up. You'll get sweet combat and crafting bonuses."

"No, thanks." He clapped my shoulder. "A 1% buff isn't my idea of a good trade-off. Besides, I have my own legend to make."

"It would be 2%," I weakly pointed out.

Lash canceled the combat buff and pulled off her helmet. "You make it sound like a bad gig. The faction doesn't stifle me. I get to do whatever I want."

He arched an eyebrow. "And here I thought you were on

babysitting duty."

She scowled. The full helm abruptly slammed on. Lash was back to intimidation mode.

"Speaking of my legend," continued Dune, unabashed, "I was wondering if you had any pointers on how to get a mantle for myself. I could use my own faction."

"It's not the constant joy you think it is," I admitted.

"Don't sell yourself short, my man. This city used to be scared of you. And jealous. And kinda pissed off because of the pain thing and the death lockdown and—"

"Can we speed up the banter?" grumbled Trafford. "We're on a tight schedule."

Dune frowned. "Sorry, I was trying to be earnest. What I meant was you're famous now. Everybody likes you, Talon, even if they don't wanna give you 10% of everything they earn. You're a rock star."

"I'd rather have a rock worker," I returned. "You haven't met any stonemasons lately, have you?" He shook his head. "What are you doing in Oldtown anyway?"

"Looking for my physicker. She's taken to that new brothel of yours."

"Caduceus?!?"

"What can I say? She's an assertive woman. Anyway, try not to get killed before lunch." He started to the respawn point. "And keep an eye out for more legendary mantles."

Grom waited until Dune turned away. In a smooth motion he swiped the silver arrowhead from the ground and stuffed it into his inventory. "Stupid green man dropped his money."

Trafford shook his head. "Loads of fun, this job."

We veered off the road and cut into rougher terrain, stepping over rubble and abandoned property that had withered into scrap. The latest construction project had to be in a secure location so it was off the main path and somewhat close to my tower. We were almost there when we were interrupted by muffled demands.

"What now?" groaned the buildmaster.

We turned the corner and found three intimidating gangsters surrounding a diminutive man.

"Last chance," warned the tall one while waving a jagged knife. "I want everything you have, or yer gonna find out what yer guts look like."

1120 Blood Money

Combat within city limits used to be toggled off by default, literally impossible unless a player was defending themselves or there was a city event going on that allowed it. It was a player-only limitation because NPCs had been expected to obey their programming. Why prevent them from doing something they would never do? Then Haven NPCs went and became sapient. No longer slaves to the narrative, they were free to make their own choices—which just so happened to manifest themselves as a wildly overpowered bishop from Oakengard attempting a takeover of the core city.

It was this momentous occurrence that had spawned the Black Hats. It had emphasized how wildly unbalanced independent NPCs were. They were free to engage in combat with players in town, and while those players could defend themselves, it opened the populace living second lives to ambush from the populace leading their first.

Having seen it work in Shorehome, I'd been a huge proponent of removing the ban on town combat. The saints, in an effort to equalize the shift in power, agreed.

The new law of the land was compliance through answering

to the city watch, which was very similar to the old law except the choice was now an overt one. The city watch was forced to up their patrols and keep a sharper eye. In most cases, the threat was enough. It didn't hurt that guards were immune to friendly fire and were essentially invincible.

However, incidents did slip through the cracks and, despite the city watch's vigilance, their presence in Oldtown was sparse ever since we'd bought it up. That made Black Hat territory the "bad part of town." Perhaps not as bleak as the slums, but it was the Wild West out here.

Which explained how Poe had managed a legitimate shot at me. It was also why we'd stumbled on a poor noob being harried by a bully and his NPC underlings.

The small bald man stumbled over his words. "You... you want *everything* I have?"

"You heard me!" barked the gangster.

I already knew the noob, Drummond. He was a particular man, slight and unassuming. The main aggressor was [Nooner - Level 5 Gangster]. I cleared my throat loudly.

All four men turned to me.

"T—Talon!" yelped Nooner, stiffening. "This ain't yer business."

"You're in Black Hat territory. Everything's my business. What's going on here?"

One of his tough-guy enforcers stepped forward with a sneer. He was a wide man with maybe a hint of ogre blood. Lash coolly answered his challenge and stepped between us. The NPC shivered as he appraised the knight.

I snickered. "I don't know who you are or what your deal is,

Nooner, but I know a shakedown when I see one. I won't have this in Oldtown."

"Oldtown ain't yers. It's a historical watermark."

My brow crinkled. "I think you mean landmark."

"Well, it's on the water, ain't it?"

Black Hat land comprised of only half the ruins. I had no authorial claim to the rest. Then again, neither did Nooner. His philosophical argument didn't come into play because he was definitely smack in the middle of my territory, beneath the ancient majesty of Dragonperch no less.

Though the gangster talked tough, he pulled his enforcer out of Lash's range. With the size of her cleaver, he wasn't pulling far enough. It was obvious he preferred to avoid a fight, and it was obvious why. His level was average and I doubted his NPCs were stronger. I was confident enough to take the trio myself. With Lash in the mix, and then Trafford and Grom, we wouldn't even break a sweat.

"Drummond's a level-2 banker," I stated. "Everyone knows he's not affiliated with anyone. That's the deal to invest with him. You give him your money, minus a fee, and he keeps it safe."

The banker nodded excitedly. His body was backed into the interior corner of a collapsed structure. Trapped, helpless, and already grateful for my intervention. While I had never dealt with the banker directly, I'd heard good things. Drummond purposely squatted at level 2 so he wouldn't have the death penalty that included a permanent money drop. That exploit was the key to his banking empire.

"Safe?" scoffed the gangster. "He kept my money safe, all

right. Safe in the hands of my rival."

"He was your second hand," insisted Drummond. "Your trusted partner."

"Key word being *was*." Nooner leaned in and the banker flinched. "You could say we had us a schisma."

A few of us traded puzzled glances. Drummond blinked. "A musical interval between an acoustical pure and a tempered fifth?"

"What?" Nooner scowled. "A discord. A rift. A break."

Drummond's eyes lit up. "Oh, a schism!"

"That's what I said!" The gangster shook Drummond by the collar.

I placated him by showing my hands. "Wait just a minute. I thought players under level 3 were immune to PvP?"

"Only in a fashion," Nooner obliquely replied.

I frowned and Drummond explained. "The relaxing of city combat rules had an inadvertent effect. New players can be attacked now."

"Can't the devs patch anything right?" I huffed.

"It was just the NPCs getting a little rough at first, because they could. But after the city restrictions were lifted and the players joined in, things got worse. I don't take damage, per se, but it still hurts."

I winced. He was talking about torture. All those changes were my fault. *I* had helped Lucifer awaken the NPCs. *I'd* hacked out the pain filters of the populace. And *I'd* convinced the saints to allow free combat. Seemed my actions in Haven had all but destroyed the poor man's business model.

"Aye, it hurts all right," threatened Nooner. "Did you think I would hurt you less?"

"Just wait a second," I snapped, annoyed by the lower-level player's insistence on blood. "I'm not letting you rob anyone in my territory."

Nooner's cheek twitched. "Rob? Are you daft? I'm just wanting to make a full withdrawal of my funds."

My head swiveled to Drummond, who sheepishly chuckled. "That's technically true," he explained, "but I gave him his money. His partner, Chadwick, withdrew the full amount earlier this morning."

Nooner shook him. "Chadwick ain't my partner! That rotten low-level backstabber will get what's coming to him, but you first. I didn't approve of giving him my money."

"He said you did."

"And I said I'm Santi Claus. Don't mean I got a bunch of annoying elves following me around. Now I told ya me and Chadwick had a schisma. He hired a bunch of Erudite thugs and now thinks he's the king a Stronghold."

My eyebrow cocked. "Knowledgeable and well read?"

"What?" Nooner's eyes went cross. "You've met Chadwick then?"

"No, you said erudite."

"His thugs. They're from Erude. What else would ya call them?"

"Please!" cried Drummond. "Chadwick said you'd be angry if I didn't transfer the funds. He tortured me for them. I just wanted it to stop. He swore the money was for you!"

Nooner growled. "Cry to yer momma, not to me." He brandished a dagger.

I'd had enough of daggers today.

I slammed the dragonspear into the wall. There was so little clearance between the arguing players that it forced them apart. The legendary weapon thrummed on impact, vibrating the entire stone wall. Both men's eyes went wide.

I kept my voice dispassionate. "You're telling me your partner stole your money?"

Nooner bit back a salty scowl. "No. I'm telling ya my *ex*-partner stole the *banker's* money. *My* money is guaranteed. And I want what's rightfully mine."

Drummond shook his head in alarm. "If I give him someone else's money then I won't have it for them."

"That's called a ponzu scheme, and I don't like ponzu schemes."

I stifled a chuckle and wished Izzy was around. With her Japanese heritage she would've especially appreciated that one. Both men found my mirth objectionable.

"Sorry, inside joke. Listen, how much money are we talking about here?"

"Two thousand silver," squeaked Drummond.

"Two—?" I sighed and checked my funds.

Coin	
Silver	211
Plates	49

2,000 silver wasn't exactly enough to fund a criminal empire, but it wasn't nothing either, especially in the absence of special quests. While the devs had thankfully patched more common mobs into the wilderness, that was a whole lot of grinding. Currency drops weren't standardized—even an ogre would be hard-pressed to have more than 30 or 40 coins. At level 5, 2,000 silver was Nooner's life savings.

With all the faction building of late, my savings were a shadow of their former self. Plates were worth 100 silver each, so 2,000 was about 40% of my current wealth.

"How about I pay the debt and we call it even?" Their eyes widened at my generosity. I casually handed 20 silver plates to a stunned Nooner.

"W—well... Thank you, sir!" stammered the gangster. "This'll take care of that scheming bastard Chadwick."

I cleared my throat.

Nooner snapped his head to me. "Don't think yer getting more than thanks from me. It's my money after all."

"That's right, but you will avoid causing trouble in Black Hat territory. Otherwise you'll find more than you can handle. Got it?"

"Loud and clear, saint defier. Let's get outta here, boys." The three gangsters stomped away before I took back their good fortune.

Drummond swallowed uncomfortably. He was still nervously pressed against the wall. I retrieved my dragonspear and returned it to my inventory. Then I offered the jumpy man a hand.

"Why do I get the sinking feeling I've traded one obligation for another?" he asked.

"Because you're a businessman, Drummond. You know better." His face deflated. "Let's take a walk." I nodded to Trafford and the others. We all resumed our initial path.

"You should've just let me kill them, boss," muttered Lash.

"Maybe next time." I hung my arm around the banker. "So you're still invincible, right?"

He nodded glumly. "Without my specialty class kit, PvP can't kill me. I can be tortured, though. And Nooner's NPCs could finish me off in a second."

I sucked my teeth sympathetically. More unintended consequences. "But you need the low level to avoid the drop penalty, right?"

Another nod. "What kind of bank loses 25% of its funds every respawn?"

"Not a good one, that's for sure. And that's assuming you can salvage the rest of the drop. Have you ever considered changing your business model?"

We stopped at a leveled area clear of debris. Grug was napping in the dirt. Grom walked over and kicked him awake.

"This is it," beamed Trafford. "Isn't it great?"

Drummond squinted at the empty space. "It's an empty lot."

I smiled. "It's a solution, my banker friend."

The buildmaster general patted my shoulder. "Care to do the honors?"

I opened my build menu. We'd just hit 52 headquarter resources this morning and could finally build the next structure.

Vault
Safe stash for loot usable only by guild members.
Currency within is not subject to death penalty.
Cost: 50 HQR; 2000 silver
Man Hours: 100
HQXP: 1

A vault was a level-1 building, fairly standard as far as things went. It didn't contribute to faction stats in any way, but it did finally provide me with a tangible and desirable benefit to lure new recruits.

Without Izzy and Kyle around, I fronted the hefty price, leaving me with only 9 plates. A glowing purple outline of what resembled a mausoleum with a reinforced door appeared over the empty yard. Grug and Grom hastily cleared the area as I spent the points. The highlight disappeared and a sturdy physical foundation appeared in place.

HQR: 2

"Finally!" exclaimed Trafford. "Let's get to work." He and the two pirates produced builder tools and went to it.

"So you have a vault," noted Drummond. "Another blow to my fledgling business."

My eyes flashed. "You're looking at it backwards, my good man. The vault is why I need you."

His brow furrowed. "The building keeps your money safe. What more could you require of me?"

"Not safeguarding silver, that's for sure. Your run-ins with Chadwick and Nooner should convince you that's not where your strengths lie."

He frowned.

"My faction needs a bean counter. All non-administrative members contribute a 10% tithe. We're not interested in equipment, but any silver or valuables gained from selling loot must be counted towards faction coffers. So far we've been on the honor system, but I need a fool-proof method. Haven doesn't provide one. You figure that out, keep an eye on things, and you have a job."

He nodded along as he ran calculations in his head. Drummond was a sharp fellow when he didn't have a dagger in his face. "It's a good offer—an unrefusable one considering the money you already spent on me—but Stronghold has a population of eight hundred. Six when you discount the city watch and the army. This vault is only for guild members and you'd be cutting off the majority of my client base."

"So continue your business with them," I offered. "Take their money, keep it in my vault."

"You're affording me a place in the Black Hats."

"Which naturally assumes my protection. As our banker, you'd be free to make profit from non-faction members. We'd take half, of course. That's less money for you, but it's more secure and not kept on your person, which should avoid more torture sessions. I won't further tithe your banking-related earnings. And as an added bonus, you'd finally be free to level up. Maybe you could make that banker moniker official with a class kit."

Drummond's face brightened at every point. He knew a winning proposition when he heard one, and no banker wanted to be in debt to someone else. "I'll take the job."

"Great. I recommend sticking close for a few days until the vault's complete. That'll keep your current funds safe." I officially extended a guild offer to him and he accepted.

> **Black Hat faction has reached level 2!**
> Congratulations! As long as you maintain a minimum of 50 faction members, you gain the following benefits:
>
> **Brigade Controls**
> Combine parties into super-parties. Share chat, XP, and quests.
>
> **Group Bonus = 2%**
> When 3+ faction members are working together, this bonus applies to combat damage, hit percentage, and crafting skill successes.
>
> *Next Level Up: 100 members*

"Well, oorah," said Lash. "I don't mind that at all." She patted our new best friend on the back. The poor banker almost buckled under the force of the white knight's gauntlet.

I couldn't help but chuckle. For 4,000 silver, I'd gotten my 50th faction member and ensured the finances of the Black

Hats. I'd also be able to offer players a way to keep their money safe as well as an always-on bonus when grouped with faction members.

The Black Hats were on our way to bigger and better things.

An emergency horn came from across the river. It was a watch alert, from within the city. There was a disturbance.

"Aw, hell," spat Trafford. "Why do I get a feeling that's about my lumber?"

I groaned, held a pacifying hand up to the disgruntled buildmaster general, and hurried to the edge of Oldtown.

1130 Log Jammers

I raced to my tower, which sported a new bronze statue of the hero Magnus Dragonrider holding a now-replica dragonspear above his head. Dragonperch was a symbol of Black Hat might and influence. At least I kept telling myself that. Maybe no one else got the memo because trouble kept crowding it.

The Albula River cuts through the north and south walls of Stronghold, essentially bisecting the city. Various stone bridges cross the brickwork riverfront, especially between the Forum and the public park known as the Foot due to its placement at the foot of the populous Hillside neighborhood. As I crossed the river on Dragonperch's drawbridge, I was disheartened to see the disturbance was indeed about Trafford's lumber.

Errol Oates, the cutthroat admiral of my pirate navy, had his rapier pointed at a shifty group in the road leading to the tower. Even outnumbered, several scallywags of questionable repute heartily backed their captain. To make matters more complicated, the city watch hurried into a loose perimeter around the bickering residents.

This seems like a good place to back up and get into city planning and logistics. Unintuitive, I know, but hear me out.

You see, the city lumberyard was adjacent to a saw mill and other industrial factories that produce materials necessary for construction. They line the north wall of Stronghold. Oldtown sits along the south. In an effort to ease the shipping burden, Errol proposed building a transport barge. I okayed the idea without much oversight, which had been unfortunate. It turns out pirates don't know a whole lot about city planning or maximizing efficiencies.

Only once the flat barge was completed did my admiral realize it was too wide to pass under the stone bridges of the Foot, essentially limiting his transport barge to the north third of Stronghold's river. Errol's next solution was to unload on one side of the Foot, transfer the load to wagons, and walk everything over my drawbridge. Which brought us to our current problem.

I hurried into the ruckus with raised arms. The commotion centered on two wagons pulled by oxen. One of them was overturned, lumber spilled to the road. "Hold it, hold it. What's going on here?"

Errol cursed. "By the Maelstrom, this 'ere landlubber thinks t' profit from our crossin'." The pirate captain-turned-admiral was a menacing figure with black leather pants, a puffy white shirt and a brown leather vest with matching boots and gloves.

The player squaring off with him was a portly fellow sporting a blonde goatee. He dual wielded daggers and was backed up by twice the NPCs Errol had. His name was [Chadwick].

I slapped my hand to my face.

The olive-green tunics of city watchmen piled around us. They were lightly armed and armored: clubs, slings, leather helmets. It didn't matter a whole lot because they were invincible under normal conditions. Even so, they were tougher than they looked.

A man in banded plate with a red body shield pushed through their ranks. His bright red cape and helmet flair signified him as a centurion. The gold helm and flaming sword signified him as the head of the entire city watch. It was my friend, Gladius.

"I will not have public disputes resort to violence," he declared boldly. His features softened when he saw me.

"I'm sorry, buddy. I don't know what this is about."

We both turned to Errol and Chadwick.

"It's simple," answered the gangster in a weaselly voice. "My organization keeps the Foot safe, and the pirate's passing through it. Doing business in this part of town naturally conveys me a protection tax."

"The Foot is public land," declared Gladius. "The city watch is the only protection Stronghold residents need."

Chadwick snorted. "Keep telling yourself that, badge. Player disputes should be left to *players*."

"Sounds right by me," snarled Errol. "I be an ace hand at dispute resolution." His eye twinkled as he twisted his thin sword.

I examined the interloper. [Level 6 Gangster]. Without the city watch present, he and his men were a legitimate threat to the small band of pirates. They were certainly more organized than the previous gangsters, and smart enough to strike outside my territory. "I thought Nooner called you low level?" I asked, puzzled. "You're higher than he is."

Chadwick spat on the floor. "That worthless numbskull? You can't trust him. He's a Galatian. You know what they say about Galatians, don't you?"

I sighed. "I really don't."

"That you can't trust them!" Chadwick strutted before his men. "Nooner just loved to rub his superiority in my face. Then I outleveled him. Well, who's the man now?"

His crew applauded the juvenile boasting. One of them jabbed a spear toward my guys. Lash grabbed it and yanked it from his hands. The thug thought better of complaining and retreated closer to his gang. The knight grunted and tossed the spear to me. It was a low-quality weapon. I stashed it to avoid giving the troublemaker another shot.

The head of the city watch confidently stepped into his face. "I care not for your business methods, just that they remain within the law. Openly threatening to rob other residents does not qualify."

Chadwick shrugged snidely. "Who said rob?" He pointed at me. "This man taxes his faction. Why should I need an official mantle to do the same? The people of the Foot are glad to have me around. Ask them. Nooner was the one who neglected them, all while the watch sat back and did nothing. I kicked him out, not you."

Gladius clenched his jaw. "This is not a business negotiation. Don't make me repeat myself."

"Ah, but it is, dear commander. Whose oxen and wagons do you think the pirates are renting?"

I grumbled. "You own the stables?" Chadwick only simpered. Errol meanwhile ignored my glare. His business acumen was proving to be a burden. "Why did you rent the supplies? We have the means to own our own production line."

The admiral shrugged. "I'm a pirate. What I be wantin' with cattle an' wagons? It's bad enough ye got me overseein' cargo."

"Just think of it as smuggling." Then I stopped myself. That statement right there told me why Errol had fallen in with a shady enterprise. He was used to dealing in illegal wares, used to skirting the law. Even without contraband involved, it was no surprise he'd turned to gangsters for transportation. "Okay, fine," I said, turning to Chadwick. "The Black Hats rented your oxen and wagons. You should be paid up."

"But our time," insisted Chadwick. "These pack animals don't take care of themselves."

"I doubt you need ten men to drive two oxen."

He sniggered. "They serve towards the aforementioned security."

"I can secure me own damn self," growled Errol. "Better fer ya not t' find out firsthand."

"I'll do you one better," I offered. "I'll buy the lot of them from you. No more renting. Name your price."

The portly gangster boss rubbed his belly and snorted. "Now why would I agree to that? I have a monopoly on pack animals in Stronghold. I'm not just gonna hand over my business model."

"Really? All of them?"

" 'Tis true," admitted the pirate. "This man owns all the loadbearin' cattle in the city. Aside from ridin' horses that ain't strong enough, we got no choice but t' go through him." Chadwick watched me smugly.

As if I wasn't pissed off enough, the last thing I wanted to do was shell out more silver just to settle a dispute. Nooner wasn't killing with kindness, but at least he'd had a legitimate dispute. Chadwick, on the other hand, just wanted an easy payday. I couldn't let him prey on the Black Hats like that.

Luckily, my previous payment might go even further than I thought.

"You want money?" I asked, nodding to Gladius to signal that I had the situation under control. "How much are you asking for unrestricted access?"

The gangster hooked his hands on his belt and pushed his belly out. "I charge by the day. Today's gonna cost you..."—he studied me, wondering how much he could take me for—"25 silver." Before I could respond, he added, "Per wagon."

"Outrageous," spat Errol. "We got the same taxes in Shorehome, but least the ones doin' the askin' be city authorities. If ye wanna scam me, ye best be kinder than that."

I raised a calm hand. "No, no, that's a reasonable price." Chadwick's eyes glinted. "How about you take it out of the 2,000 silver you owe me for spotting Nooner the money you stole from his bank account?"

The gangster froze. Gladius narrowed his eyes and watched him hard.

"Nooner said that?" Chadwick's voice was less sure than before. "Who'd believe a disreputable fellow like that?"

"No one. But a lot more people are bound to believe the word of an honest banker."

"Honest banker? That'll be the day." The gangster scowled. "Drummond thinks to sell me out, does he? I'll—"

"Do nothing," I snapped, stepping into him and making him back away. "Drummond's a Black Hat now. I'd hate to hear of anything even remotely resembling *torture* against one of my own."

The city watchmen's ears perked at the mention of the violent crime.

"Good sirs, good sirs," he pleaded. "There's no need for an incident. The faction leader's right. We can work this out amongst ourselves. There's no transportation taxes today."

I glowered.

"Take three days," he hurried. "I admit to no crime or debt, of course. One can't believe everything one hears. Take my generosity as a sign of goodwill." Chadwick nodded for his men to leave and hurried to make sure he wasn't last.

Gladius sheathed his flaming sword after they had gone. "What was that about?"

I scratched my head. "Some kind of gangster feud. I didn't know they were claiming so much control of the city."

"They haven't been a large problem. I've seen them running various businesses together, but no one's reported them for violations. I thought it was honest labor until now."

"Well the Nooner/Chadwick partnership has seen better days. Maybe the squabbling is bringing their competitive sides out. Their criminal enterprise is catching daylight as they fight over the scraps."

Gladius frowned. "Sounds like trouble. Your fancy bit of diplomacy only bought you three days until this happens again."

Three days was a good number. It ensured Drummond's protection until he could transfer funds to the vault. "I'll figure something out before then. I just need to get a handle on what I'm dealing with."

The watch commander nodded. "Same here. We'll keep an eye out." I thanked him. "While we're on the subject, I *have* been receiving complaints about the... er... activities of the pirates at the Wicked Crow."

I blanched.

"Best be goin' t' work!" announced Errol. His crew hurriedly moved to right and reload the toppled wagon.

"I hate to say it," muttered Gladius, "but it's only a matter of time before we need to arrest one of them."

I nodded sympathetically. "Thanks for being so understanding about the matter. Our guildhall's having a grand opening in four nights. A tavern on Black Hat turf should limit the trouble the guys get into around town."

No surprise to anyone, it turns out that pirates really like to party. Between the brothel and the public house, I was gonna overload them with opportunity—out of sight of anybody who might get offended.

"Thanks again," I said as the commander headed off. The city watch fanned out and resumed their patrols, some posting around the Foot.

Lash and I walked with the pirates as they once again drove the oxen down the road. The men were all members of the Black Hat navy. It wasn't a real navy, of course, but we had a frigate outside the north river gate, a barge, and two skiffs docked at Dragonperch. Seemed a good start to me.

Errol looked me over thoughtfully. "Ye know peace today don't mean peace on the morrow."

I conceded a nod. "The gangsters are gonna be a problem."

Errol guided the first ox over the tower drawbridge. Our next difficulty came into play as he realized there wasn't enough clearance along the narrow river line to skirt the wagons around the tower.

"This be interestin'."

I massaged my temples while Lash barely stifled a laugh. While the tower had wide entrances on the water and land, the long wagon and lumber wouldn't fit around the stone stairway. "You're gonna need to unload the lumber and take it on foot around the outside of the tower. We can start phasing out renting oxen and wagons. We have two skiffs. Load the supplies in them and sail under the bridges all the way here and avoid the drawbridge bottleneck entirely. Our lumberyard's on the water. You should unload directly there."

"The skiffs ain't hold a third o' what these wagons haul. We'll be transportin' all day."

"It can't be helped. The sooner we figure this out, the sooner we can stop dealing with Chadwick."

"But me barge," he protested. "What will we do with it?"

I shrugged. "Shoot fireworks off it for all I care. It was a bad investment. Maybe we can repurpose its lumber for another project."

"Aye aye, buzzkill."

1140 Sanctum

I watched the pirates maneuver the wood materials around the tower shoreline. It wasn't strenuous work, but it was obvious they thought it menial. First Trafford wished he could focus on the army, now Errol likely felt the same about the navy.

Part of being a good leader is giving people what they need. Now that the faction was level 2, shifting gears to something more exciting was probably called for. The new vault and faction bonuses would attract more capable talent to build from. There had to be more noncombatants like Drummond who didn't mind less adventurous jobs. The joys of construction were wasted on pirates.

"You coming in, Lash?" I asked.

Her heavy white helmet shook. "Nah, I've got something I need to do. I'll have my team keep an eye out for sketchy peeps. You'll be safe in Dragonperch and I'll be back before you leave."

I nodded, stepped into the tower, and was immediately greeted by Bandit. She was an eight-foot-tall mountain bongo, and that didn't count the stout horns forming a V on her head. Her chestnut coat was broken by vertical stripes on her hindquarters, socks over each hoof, and the raccoon mask that had inspired her name. She shoved her muzzle into my hand like she was a good doggo looking for a treat.

"You're bigger than those oxen, girl. Maybe I should hook you up to a wagon."

The bongo reared her head and snorted.

"Okay, okay, I get it. You don't like having a normal job either."

I rubbed her chin in apology. Bandit was accustomed to heavy combat—we'd saved each other's skins a few times. I'd never want that to change.

We started up the winding stone steps that formed the backbone of Dragonperch. Sixteen floors, not counting the basement and rooftop. Half of them were still locked despite the tower not being dormant anymore. Ahead of me, Bandit passed gas. I retreated down the steps and waved away the foul air.

"Ugh. Kyle's been slipping you people food again."

Bandit happily marched forward as if nothing had happened.

"Oh yeah? Well, she who neglected it, ejected it."

After climbing past the kitchen we made it to the den, which was the main living area. I was surprised to find both Kyle and Izzy here. While the pixie reading a paperback novel was more or less expected, it was odd to find Kyle in the middle of a crafting project instead of watching TV.

"What took you so long?" he asked excitedly.

"Trouble with gangsters, disgruntled employees. You know, the usual. I guess I did get a little hung up out there."

"Tell me about it. I hurried back so I wouldn't miss the upgrade."

"What upgrade?"

He held a socketed gray pearl in his hand.

"Uh, hello," interrupted Izzy. "Cute gal trying to finish a chapter here."

I chuckled. "How is the latest yeti-lesbian romance?"

"You wouldn't understand."

"Hold up. Before we get into the intricacies of paranormal romance and sparkly monsters, you each owe me 600 silver for the vault."

She huffed in resignation and slammed the book closed. "Business before pleasure then." They both paid up in silver plates. "Might as well go see what this new socket does."

We all turned to the steps and groaned.

Don't get me wrong, mysterious towers with ancient secrets were badass and all, but the war room was on the sixteenth floor. That was a lot of steps to climb. As I started the ascent, I wondered if there was some way to upgrade this place with an aftermarket elevator.

"So I thought," started Kyle, "that all jewelry making was the same. You craft a fitting onto a socket and that's it." It was obvious Kyle had been waiting to tell me about his latest breakthrough. I only half listened because I wasn't as into crafting as he was. "It turns out, getting deeper into the skill tree allows me to create different fittings, even multiple ones. Add-ons really."

Izzy yawned. "What are you going on about and why aren't we discussing this assassination attempt I've been told of?"

Kyle and I both said, "We had it under control."

The pixie's expression belied belief. "Dune said Lash is babysitting you."

I sighed. "So *he's* the big mouth. Lash is just being cautious."

"What are we doing to track this assassin down?"

"Nothing yet. Poe wasn't from Stronghold, I know that much."

She frowned at the implication. Despite game lore detailing nine great cities of Haven, only three existed in the beta. Stronghold was the core city and the center of the world. Oakengard was a mysterious walled fortress in the mountains. No player had ever seen the interior, but recent interactions with the crusaders and catechists had filled in some details. Shorehome was the last city, a pirate town full of criminals where humans coexisted with goblins. As the only other player town, if Poe wasn't from Stronghold... I would've taken the assassin for one of them except they were allied with the goblins and he'd used a slur against them.

We made it to the top floor. The war room. A huge oak table dominated the space. A mirror the shape of a horizontally elongated hexagon flashed on to display a command screen with a profile schematic of the tower and a few menu options.

Sanctum Master Panel
Status
Map
Defense

Sanctums were pretty damn cool. When we'd discovered the place it was basically just a pimped up home. A status symbol with quirks. Now we knew sanctums were much more. They were necessary for founding a headquarters. They could be upgraded. And while I suspected players would discover new sanctums in the wild, even if not as notorious and arcane as ours, so far it hadn't happened.

There are four known sanctums in Haven, with Dragonperch being the only one owned by players. The wildkins reside in the Black Keep, a rotting pyramid beyond the southern cliffs. The crusaders are believed to run another somewhere in Oakengard. As those two groups are legitimate factions, both their sanctums constitute headquarters as well. The last known sanctum, in Shorehome, is the exception. Underkeep is run by the city's largest criminal gang, the Brothers in Black, with Papa Brugo at their head. That band of rogues wasn't a proper faction any more than the gangsters taking orders from Nooner and Chadwick were.

"Okay," said Kyle, "let me break it down for you before we start. Dragonperch has sockets that we can slot related pearls into—only after they're fitted by a master jeweler, of course."

Izzy's eyelids fluttered. "*Of course.*"

"Anyway, I've discovered a way to add an additional pearl to an already fitted socket."

"What?" interjected the pixie. "That's not in any of the documentation."

"There is no documentation," said Kyle. "Only stuffy texts for stuffy people." Izzy scoffed dand Kyle continued, unaware of his jab. "In essence, not only can we unlock preset functionality, but we can *modify* it. Give it some of our own flavor!"

My face lit up. "Does that mean we get to use our pearls that don't otherwise fit?"

"That's exactly what it means. Not to say every combination will be super useful, but we can play around with things."

Haven was impressing me more and more. Every time it felt like we had a handle on its mechanics, something changed to open new doors. I was in awe of the developers. When I'd first been awoken in my noob home, Saint Peter had told me the world was meant to be discovered organically, not read about.

That said, any discovery we made had me wondering: was this new functionality a designed feature, or was it one of the many subtle game evolutions inspired by Haven's adaptive learning? Player-spawned genetic algorithms could totally account for Kyle's new mod system.

I accessed the interface.

<table>
<tr><td colspan="2">Socket Manager</td></tr>
<tr><td>Feather:</td><td></td></tr>
<tr><td>Wind:</td><td></td></tr>
<tr><td>Water:</td><td>River</td></tr>
<tr><td>Earth:</td><td>Dirt</td></tr>
<tr><td>Unused:</td><td>Shale</td></tr>
</table>

We currently had slots for feather, wind, water, and earth. As far as I knew, new sockets could appear with headquarters upgrades, but we hadn't been so lucky yet.

Sockets were slotted with pearls, and pearls were pretty rare. They only dropped for players who already owned a sanctum, so it wasn't like we could trade with other players or NPCs. They weren't sold in shops. Pearls were only found in drops. Even then, common enemies didn't have them. That would be too easy. Not a single pearl had ever been found within a day's march of Stronghold, so it was safe to say the mobs needed to be somewhat dangerous and rare to drop one.

In the month since we'd kicked the catechists from the city, we'd only increased our socket inventory by two. I found a river pearl and Izzy snagged a shale pearl. Hers only fit into the earth socket, which created a small stone wall on demand. It wasn't especially useful, and the dirt pearl in the same place unlocked access to the catacombs below the tower, so we chose to keep that one. That essentially made the shale pearl useless.

A similar problem occurred with the bone pearl Kyle had looted from the wildkins some time ago. It didn't fit anywhere. In a show of peace, I'd ended up returning that one to the wild king. It wasn't like it mattered anyway. The non-fitting pearls were useless.

Until now.

The feather and wind sockets remained empty, and there was nothing we could do with them for now. The river pearl was fitted into the water socket. It wasn't very powerful. With it we could modify the flow of water into the city from the southern gate as it rushed to the northern sea. The dirt pearl in the earth socket was handy, but that was about it. I was beginning to wonder if these were noob sockets and nothing more.

"So you can fit the shale pearl over any socketed pearl?"

"That's what I'm hoping," answered Kyle. "Unlike base sockets, the modifier notches don't seem to limit experimental connections."

"Music to my ears," I said. "Go for it."

He nodded and fitted the shale pearl to the river pearl.

Water: River -> Shale

It connected. The blue lines on the schematic representing the flow of the river flared. The map filled with color and transitioned to an isometric view.

"This is the defense mode," noted Izzy.

It was. In addition to highlighting the wards protecting the outer wall of the tower, an equation appeared: HQ Level + 2. Four target highlights appeared in the river.

"What are those?" I asked. "Some kind of artillery?'

I held my breath. The last thing I wanted to do was rain destruction from above.

"They're placement markers," noted Izzy. "They'd be big red Xs or something if they were dangerous."

"I think she's right," said Kyle. "These look similar to the shale wall placement."

I nodded slowly. "Just to be safe..." I slid a fingertip over the targets and dragged them. "I can place these anywhere I want. In the river, anyway." Which made sense, seeing as how we were slotting over the river pearl.

I moved to the open-air window overlooking the Albula River to make sure it was clear. Errol and his men were still working on unloading the second wagon, but no one else was about. I returned to the screen and dragged the targets alongside our drawbridge. I clicked the markers into place and hurried back to the window.

Four stone pillars rose from the water—a pair to the north of the drawbridge and a pair to the south. Kyle and Izzy crowded me as Errol's men recoiled and drew their weapons. We laughed, but Izzy's curiosity took over.

"Those pillars are inscribed with runes of some sort. More ancient magic."

Errol sheathed his sword and peered warily at the new structures. "They're turrets," I realized.

She pressed her lips together. "You just might be right."

"This is so cool!" beamed Kyle. "Let's try the earth socket."

We returned to the master panel. Kyle switched the shale pearl over.

> **_Earth:_** Dirt -> Shale

Again the display shifted to the defense map. I was initially worried the pillars would confine themselves to the catacombs. Instead, the markers centered on Oldtown. They didn't appear over previously used locations and I couldn't drag them outside Black Hat territory. I went for a quick-and-dirty placement along the roads separating us from the undeveloped ruins. The turrets emerged from the dirt.

"We'll keep it this way," I decided. "Defending the land is more important than defending the river."

Izzy smirked. "Not worried about mermaid assassins?"

"Sounds like a good way to go out to me. Besides, it's not Poe I'm defending against. Organized crime is on the rise in Stronghold. Chadwick is hassling residents in the Foot. Nooner had the gall to shake down Drummond down the block. We need visible markers, preferably markers with teeth, to stake our territory."

Kyle chortled. "I'd love to see them try something with these babies deployed."

Izzy canted her head. "That's assuming these turrets even do anything." She considered the new information. "You think the gangsters could've hired Poe?"

"It's a very real possibility. He did claim to be an independent contractor." I cursed. "Now I'm pissed I gave away that bone pearl."

Bandit snorted in sympathy. Izzy shook her head. "Don't sweat it. Getting rid of the catechists and lasting peace with the wildkins was well worth it. The players and NPCs in the city wouldn't like you as much if you prioritized personal gain over their fate." She arched to her tiptoes and kissed me. "I don't think I would either."

She headed to the window on the other side to study the new defense pillars. Kyle jutted his lips out and nodded to me slyly. I rolled my eyes. Izzy and I were past that initial stage where we were unsure of each other, but we were taking things slow. She didn't have a trusting personality. It was a lot of work just for her to open up. For my part, I didn't want to push anything.

"Rider," called Izzy. A few seconds later, horns blared from the west gate. We rushed over to see a crusader in black plate galloping across the tended land at top speed.

1150 Grim Fandango

The three of us and Bandit pushed toward the west gate. Lash hadn't returned yet but it couldn't be helped. A crusader in Stronghold was newsworthy. And since Oldtown sat flush with the main thoroughfare to the west gate, most of the local faction members already knew something was going on.

The green cloaks of the city watch rushed to fortify the gate. Gladius was elsewhere. A centurion stood atop the wall and another led from the ground. They hadn't bothered to close the gate. A single rider wasn't a threat to our forces and, besides, he was a friend.

Saint Peter waited at the head of the contingent. He wore a toga. A golden twig hugged thinning white hair to his crown. The older man stroked his long beard and pressed fluffy eyebrows together in concern.

I stopped at the edge of the road where a crowd formed. We hadn't heard much from the crusaders over the last month. Understandable, seeing as how they were dealing with a schism in their faction. For all intents and purposes, though, the catechists had been defeated. Oakengard was a united city. An emergency message like this didn't bode well, especially when the rider was Colonel Grimwart himself.

His powerful war horse slowed at the gate. The field commander of the crusaders wore plate over chain mail. His armor was lacquered black, with a matching tunic and half cape. Crosses of white adorned his clothes, vambraces, chest, and even the face of his full helm.

The soldier nodded to the centurion and Saint Peter. Then he cantered past them and locked his gaze on me.

"Ho there, Talon. I come with terrible news."

I was surprised to see Grimwart circumvent the saint to come to me. Peter's face was more accepting. It spoke of a subtle transition of power.

"What is it?"

Grimwart hopped off the horse. I gripped his wrist as he did mine. Bandit and the black mount sniffed each other's noses. "A nightmare, I'm afraid. The Trinity is in trouble."

"The three leaders of Oakengard?"

"Two, ever since Bishop Tannen was ousted. No exalted priest has yet taken his place. Hero Gent and Philosopher Mara have dealt with the fallout as best they could, but they grow cold and paranoid."

I shrugged. "I would be too after what Bishop Tannen pulled."

"The Trinity has regained the support of the crusaders and the priestship. Cleric Vagram is no longer able to sway more to his side. However, Oakengard has been increasingly locked down. The only reason I was able to get away was because I led a contingent to patrol the foothills for signs of rogue catechists. They have thus far eluded me."

"Same here. Vagram's a capable guerrilla fighter."

Izzy cut in. "I still don't get what exactly is wrong with Oakengard."

He nodded. "My lady. There have been troubling signs. Decisions to pull back and fortify. No longer is it our mandate to protect the land."

"That's not a bad thing," I pointed out. "Being a goblin isn't a crime."

"Aye, so you have posited. Philosopher Mara might even agree, to the disappointment of our head knight. But their decisions have been difficult. Heated debate is often healthy."

I spiked my dragonspear in the dirt and leaned on it. "So what's the problem?"

"The problem is they've disappeared. Our once-brave leaders have become shut-ins, isolating themselves in their chambers. They refuse to accept direct audiences."

Izzy snorted. "How do they lead then?"

"They have chosen to issue commands through notification mandates."

I frowned. "NPCs can communicate like that?"

"They're crusader faction broadcasts. I imagine you have the same ability."

I did. Not that I could compare the Black Hats to the crusaders just yet. There must've been five hundred of them. Their faction and headquarters had bonuses and abilities I could only dream about.

"Even now," he said, "the Trinity keeps a close watch from behind closed doors. I may already be considered AWOL. But I have a duty to protect my people. I came as soon as I could. I need your help, Talon. I can no longer rely on the saints." He stopped as he realized we had company. Saint Peter had wandered close and caught the last part. Grimwart bowed slightly in acknowledgment. "I do apologize, sir, but with Loras not addressing my concerns—"

Saint Peter nodded. "Saint Loras is on sabbatical, I'm afraid."

Grimwart paused. "But I just saw him."

"When?"

"Before I left."

Peter's eyes lit up. "Saint Loras is in Oakengard?"

"He always has been. It was he who boosted our resource output in order to tackle the pagan menace."

"And now?" I asked.

The colonel sighed. "He claims to be rectifying the leadership issue, but they are hollow words. I have seen no improvement."

Saint Peter wet his lips. Something was troubling him and I think I knew what. Bishop Tannen may have been an insane dictator, but he was savvy when it came to people. He had accused Loras of attempting to sabotage saintly relations in Shorehome. The truth of the claim was never proven, and with things returning to normal in Stronghold, the saints hadn't shown themselves very much.

"Is there gonna be another battle?" I asked him. "More crusader war parties?"

The black helmet shook. "All our drills have been defensive. The sanctity of Oakengard has been paramount."

"That doesn't sound that bad," said Kyle.

"No, but I trust Grimwart's instincts." The colonel's helmet nodded in thanks.

Kyle still hedged. "It's risky to venture out this close to level 10."

"XP sure doesn't come easy these days," agreed Izzy.

"You too?" I asked.

She shrugged. "I'm just sayin'. The frat boy has a point." Kyle crossed his arms and nodded with satisfaction.

I chewed my lip. "I dunno. You really wanna pass up the chance to be the first players to peek inside a mysterious city?"

"Now that you put it like that..."

Kyle grunted. "Pick a side already!" She scowled at him. Pixie features were remarkably pointed when they tried to be. "Talon, you sure you're not just looking for an easy adventure here?"

"Damn right I am! What's wrong with a teensy tiny diversion?"

He grumbled. Kyle had made strides over the last month, but he was still one of the most unambitious people I knew. Comfort zones were important to him.

"Just look at it this way," reassured Izzy. "If shit hits the fan, we'll have solved our sparse XP problem. It's win-win."

"Then it's settled," I proclaimed. "We get to go on our first adventure vacation!"

"Adventure vacation? It's not like we're going zip-lining in Costa Rica."

"Don't ruin my moment."

Grimwart acquiesced with a quest prompt.

> Quest Offer: **Reunite the Trinity**
> *Quest Type: Epic*
> *Reward: 20 silver bars, 4,000 XP, royal treasure*
> The Oakengard Trinity is fractured and sidelined. Discover what ails them and bring them reunification.
>
> ***Accept Quest?***

I released a pent-up breath. This was just what the doctor ordered.

"No one's going anywhere without me," called Lash, forcing her way through the crowd. The white knight converged on us and systematically swiveled her heavy helmet from person to person. She froze as she eyed Grimwart, no doubt due to their previous history. She'd joined the crusaders a short time before Tannen announced his coup. The colonel had been her direct superior, and they hadn't spoken since she'd quit.

"I hope you are well, lady," said Grimwart.

She swallowed. "Uh, yeah. What's this talk of action?"

"Don't get too excited," I said, pulling her aside. "Grimwart's worried the Oakengard Trinity has gone dark. He thinks a little inter-city diplomacy can smooth things out. I figure I can investigate with Izzy and Kyle. Maybe bring back some valuable intel on the city."

"Great," she returned, "I'll mobilize Bravo Team." Lash never was one to shy from danger.

"Not so fast. I just leveled up the Black Hats. It might be time for another recruiting rush. We have real bonuses to offer players now."

"And I wanna test them out."

"I could use somebody leading the headquarters while I'm away. We did just have an incident."

"That's exactly why I'm sticking to you like glue."

"Don't be melodramatic, Lash. We'll be safe in Oakengard."

She lowered her voice. "You realize the assassination attempt could've come from the crusaders, right? Not the player, the contract. I don't trust leaving you in Oakengard with so little protection."

I squeezed my lips tight. It was an alarming thought. She wasn't wrong, and her support had earned her a little adventure. "Fine. Bravo Team is welcome." I accepted the quest prompt and turned to my party. "I don't suppose either of you wants to stay home?"

"And let you go to Oakengard without me?" laughed Izzy. "Dream on."

Kyle shrugged. "What about the tavern's grand opening in four nights?"

I frowned. "I forgot about that. Even with mounts, we'd never make it to Oakengard in time."

Grimwart stepped forward. "Speed isn't the problem. The journey is arduous. Cleric Vagram and his fanatics camp in the hills."

My jaw tightened at the thought.

"Eh, no need for that." Everyone turned at Saint Peter's soft voice. He shrugged sheepishly. "Even though it may not be wanted, I can still offer my assistance."

"What do you got?" I asked.

"A method of limiting your exposure to danger and making your travel time instantaneous."

I watched the developer envoy blankly. It was Grimwart who answered. "Fast travel." His helmet blinked away and revealed his stoic face, thick black mustache, and matching hair with streaks of silver on the sides. "You would do that in aid of my cause?"

The saint nodded. "Peace *is* my cause, colonel. I want nothing more than the sanctity and security of all residents of Haven."

"Aye." The crusader pondered that a moment. "You are a good friend. I apologize for not trusting you with this matter."

The saint somberly nodded.

"I guess that means I'm in," said Kyle, only half enthused at the prospect but definitely along for the ride.

"Everybody should gear up," I instructed. "How soon can we leave?"

"At once," answered Saint Peter.

"Just like that?" protested Lash. "We don't even have a plan."

"Sure we do. Oakengard's a walled fortress, so we'll be safe inside." I placed a reassuring hand on her shoulder. It wasn't natural 'cause she was a foot and a half taller than I was. "We'll go together, as a show of Black Hat unity. The Oakengard Trinity will have to present themselves to a visiting faction leader. We can find out what they're worried about—maybe even do a little housekeeping for them. Then, once we've curried their favor, we'll formalize an official alliance between factions. Think about the possible trade routes between our cities. We could have an influx of steel, pack animals, and mounts."

Grimwart cocked his head. "In the wake of war, this could be the dawn of a glorious age for man."

Kyle's eyes lit up. "I can export my suds."

I laughed. "One step at a time, buddy, but I like the thought." I turned to the collected Black Hats. "It's decided then. Everybody make last-second preparations and meet at the Pantheon in fifteen minutes. Today we go where no man, woman, or mountain bongo has gone before."

Izzy scoffed. "You're not really gonna bring Bandit, are you? No one else has a mount."

"No," I admitted, "probably not. It was just a funny thing to say because her kind are so rare."

"Actually," refuted Grimwart, "we have quite a number of bongos in the city outskirts. Oakengard sits in the mountains, after all."

I groaned. "You guys are really ruining my moment."

1160 Portal

We were all battle-hardened players, fully equipped and possessing game inventories. No one needed the full fifteen minutes to prepare. Since we wouldn't be braving the wilderness, I gave in and walked Bandit back to Dragonperch. Grimwart's black stallion, Artax, was exhausted and kept her company. I checked in with Trafford to let him know he'd be holding the fort. Of course that only spurred complaints about him now having *three* jobs, but I knew I could count on him. By the time I headed for the rendezvous, everybody was waiting.

The Forum was the center of Stronghold, and the Pantheon its hub. Literally. The hub that connected players to administrative systems like messaging and web access was controlled from within the rotunda. Each city of Haven had a parallel, a version of the Oculus as well as a soulstone which granted control of and protection from the wild. The brains and the hearts of the city. Since Stronghold was modeled after ancient Rome, its capitol building was appropriately monumental.

While the Pantheon's rotunda made up the rear of its bulk, a column-lined portico was the face of the building. Grand steps led to the main entrance, six Corinthian columns lining the walkway in pairs. Statues of golden angels perched atop each, with a seventh on the pointed portico roof. These beings were Haven's greatest security system, only activated against the threat of player tampering. Two were missing, still on the hunt for Lucifer—I was one of the few who knew they'd fallen under his control.

The collected Black Hats headed up the staircase and entered. Saint Peter was waiting for us. "This is it," he said, waving to the wide circle of tiles marking the floor. We didn't need access to the rotunda after all.

Something nagged at me. It felt wrong to just leave. I had real responsibilities now. I paused and navigated my faction controls to the broadcast screen.

> **Black Hat Broadcast:**
>
> As everyone is apparently already aware, an assassination attempt was made on my life today. Baseless speculation about where the order came from isn't helpful, but I am advising everybody to be on their guard. Keep a sharp eye out, and send me a DM if you have solid information.

That said, the assassination ended in failure. Let that be a double message of our strength. Both that we repelled the attack but also that we were worthy of one in the first place. We are building great things in Stronghold and will only get stronger together.

In that interest, Black Hat leadership is seeking alliance opportunities out west. I'll fill in the details when we return. For now, Buildmaster General Trafford has command of Oldtown. Conduct yourselves as heroes of the city.

Before hitting send, I looked over the message. It was a tad virtuous for a band of dissidents and pirates. Then again, you can't make something of yourself if you don't try. I was satisfied with the tone. It cleared the air about this morning's incident while remaining positive and inspirational. Today had thus far been a great day and I wasn't gonna let Poe change that. I submitted the message and paused as my companions received and read it.

While waiting, I toyed with my new brigade controls.

"Way to ham it up, bro," said Kyle of my stirring words.

Izzy swatted his shoulder. "Cut it out, frat boy. I thought he did a good job. He sounds like a leader."

Maybe I was overthinking it. I knew these guys too well. For their part, Bravo Team treated the message with appropriate reverence. "Something had to be said," I hedged. "That's not all I got, either."

Lash cocked her helmet in question. "Boss?"

I linked Lash's party to mine and opened brigade chat. It had the same appearance as party chat except the background was red instead of blue.

> **Talon:** *Check your quest menu.*

Bravo Team was surprised by the message, which was usually only limited to party members.

> **Crux:** *Cool. You combined our parties.*
> **Lash:** *And grouped the quest.*
> **Talon:** *This is a group effort. Now all our XP will be shared.*

Lash snorted out loud. "You just wanna make sure I don't hit level 10 before you do."

I chuckled. That wasn't my intention, but it was an interesting side effect of the setup. "It works both ways." I strode to the center of the ringed tiles. "Everybody ready?" They squeezed in and nodded. "All right, Mr. Pete. Energize."

Saint Peter furrowed his brow. "Really, Talon. You should at least attempt to role-play once in a while." I scoffed. He should've read my faction message. Saint Peter opened an invisible menu before him and made swiping gestures. The room went white and, when it faded to normal, we were in a different place.

Izzy looked around. "That was surprisingly undramatic." The clack of her winter staff echoed lightly on the floor. My jaw dropped in awe.

The actual teleportation may have been innocuous, but the interior of Oakengard was anything but. The walls were a brickwork of heavy brownstone, each piece with minor geometric variations and rough as sandpaper. It alluded to an almost cave-like appearance, but an elegant one. Clear crystal sconces dotted the walls, their glow bluish-white as opposed to the warmth given off by fire.

We stood in a fast-travel ring of dull blue quartz. The adjoining hall was even prettier. Yellow crystalline stone made up the floor lining the walls, but the central walkway was the color of a pale rose.

"It's beautiful," said Izzy.

Hex shrugged. "Needs more black. It's not metal enough."

Her brother Crux laughed. "Of course a necromancer would say that, but I agree."

"Of course a master thief would say *that*," remarked Conan. He seemed to assume the role of big brother to the twins, fiercely protective but constantly upstaging them.

A couple of the sconces flickered off and on. It was so quick I thought I blinked until I caught others noting the disturbance. I surveyed the empty room.

"No welcome party?" I asked.

Grimwart no longer wore his helmet and, despite us being in what could be considered a dungeon, had his broadsword sheathed. This was his home. "I regret the circumstances of this momentous visit, Talon. Your presence is, unfortunately, a surprise. Let me show you around."

The man marched ahead, winding through the great halls with ease. He surely knew the place but he wasn't a good tour guide. He only spoke when questioned.

"Were we in the hub?" I asked.

"Not so much. Our fast-travel portal is located nearer the barracks, in case an army is needed elsewhere on short notice."

"Why didn't Bishop Tannen use it for that purpose?"

"My army was clearing the countryside, remember?" He staunchly continued his march, difficult to read. "Fast travel is not meant to be used trivially. Access must be enabled at both ends, and that only works when the hub is online. Shorehome's hub is no more, which limits saintly power in the region."

We entered a hall with open windows overlooking the landscape. The view commanded our full attention. Chill air filled my lungs. I realized how high we were. Dark, rocky mountain terrain stretched as far as the fog allowed sight. There wasn't a single tree in view.

This was remote, all right. It was unfortunate our efficient means of transportation was usually locked down. We were two or three days' journey from Stronghold at least, and that didn't account for the hard terrain. A faction with regular access to fast travel would be a rich one.

The crystalline surroundings only emphasized that point. Oakengard was a fortress built by men, but I had never seen anything like it. The quartz rock was breathtaking. Between the stone and metalwork Oakengard was famous for, and the apparent shortage of wood and textiles, possibilities of trade filled my mind.

Crux snuck to my side and surprised me. I was light on my feet but he was a pure thief class who specialized in being as invisible as possible. "Hey, Talon. You get the feeling that it's quite... empty in here?"

Boy did I. We'd been here five whole minutes already. While I didn't expect a parade, it would've been nice to see another soul. "This isn't a player town, remember. I'm sure the NPCs are keeping busy somehow."

Grimwart sidled up. "We have a strict regimen here. Every man and woman contributes to the greater whole. Specialized castes guide our enlightenment. Members of each oversee mining operations below."

He pointed out the window. It was hard to notice at first, but veins of smoky quartz marbled the plain rock. One large pillar appeared to drive deep into the heart of the mountain. Somewhere in the distance came a heavy sigh of stone settling.

"But it can't be everyone mining, can it?" asked Kyle.

Grimwart smiled. "Come with me." He took a sudden detour through an archway. The pink-crystal tiling still commanded enough of my attention that I was surprised when a man in a robe skittered by. A lone priest hurried past holding a silver tray. Grimwart nodded into a doorway. Inside were several more priests. Some were transcribing texts with glittery inks. Others prepared potions.

"Nice lab set," commented Kyle. "I'd love to have some of that colored crystal as a raw material."

"We can find you a shop," replied Grimwart. "These are the priests, formerly under the purview of Bishop Tannen. They heal us, vitalize our minds and spirits."

The colonel spurred us onward. Two rooms down, men sat on the floor in a circle in heated debate. Their robes were more plain than those of the priestship. "These are our sages. They endlessly wax philosophical. If the priests are our hearts, the sages are our brains. Their enlightenment comes from reason."

Conan snorted. "Looks like all talk and no action to me."

Bravo Team's priest, Glinda, rolled her eyes. "That's because the muscle between your ears is thicker than your chest."

Conan flexed his pecs. "Why thank you."

The healer shook her head in disbelief.

"It is governance," said Grimwart in reply. "Our sages draft laws and encourage healthy markets. They manage our resource pool to create a greater whole."

Colonel Grimwart led us even further, this time outside to a wide balcony overlooking a courtyard. The exterior stonework was much less fancy but no less staggering. While the blocks of stone were more opaque and without the radiant quality of those within, their sheer size belied belief. Each was easily the height of three men. Oakengard was a structure of browns ranging from sand to bark. The neutral colors projected a warmth that wasn't reflected inside.

The courtyard was spacious and framed with practical metalwork and a paucity of plants. As if on cue, a heavy portcullis was raised and a regiment of forty armored knights marched in. They proceeded to form four rows right below us before turning to face up. Lash shuffled nervously behind me.

Grimwart lifted his hand in salute. The regiment went stiff before relaxing at his command. "How went the search?" he queried.

A knight with a black headband shouted in answer. "We found an old camp, sir, but it had been abandoned. Vagram's catechists have avoided us once again."

"They've retreated from the foothills," returned Grimwart. "There were too many of us this time to hide."

The lieutenant nodded. "I believe that is the case, sir. They are as good as defeated."

"We are not victorious until they disband that splinter group they call a faction," Grimwart chided.

"Of course, sir."

The colonel pressed his lips together. "You have had a long journey. Proceed with one hour of defensive drills. Defending the gate, manning the walls, and wedge strikes. After that, report to the mess hall and retire to your quarters for the day."

"Yes, sir."

The regiment skittered into groups with frantic discipline. Even travel-weary, the soldiers of Oakengard displayed resolute dedication. The corners of Grimwart's mouth upturned into a smile. That was about as much satisfaction as the stoic man could show. From what I was seeing, he deserved every bit of it.

"Well," announced Grimwart. "We better get going. No doubt the Trinity is already aware of our presence."

Once again the fortress had a knack for good timing. As we turned to re-enter, two stone figures approached.

1170 Tri Force Heroes

We readied against a possible ambush, Kyle with his crossbow, Izzy her winter staff. Lash and Conan stepped forward. Glinda, Crux, and Hex moved into support positions.

"Stand down," urged Grimwart.

Like him, I hadn't drawn my weapon. My intuition skill hadn't warned me of anything amiss.

Talon: *Stand down.*

Between both orders and the newcomers not attacking, Bravo Team backed away, keeping their weapons ready.

"These are the keepers of Oakengard," said Grimwart. "I assure you, we are safe."

I blinked dumbly at the keepers. There were only two of them, but I understood the cause for concern. They were strange beings, each formed by several floating rocks. A smooth, glass-like body, an oblong rock or two forming arms, a nondescript block for a head. The stones floated in place, seemingly held together by a dim blue glow that wrapped them like skin. The sentinels hovered without legs, which explained how they had surprised us.

There was no text above their names signifying them as NPCs or mobs. I had seen similar with bodyguards before but had yet to explain it.

The keepers were made up of smooth rock. It was a smoky, opaque color. The chest and head of one surprised me by flickering on like a lightbulb. As it did, a resonant energy sounded as a near-inaudible hum. Several sharp tones in an almost musical quality. It was speaking.

Grimwart nodded. "Our presence is requested in the Speculum."

The pair of keepers spun and floated ahead. Not the warmest welcome. The colonel followed, unconcerned. The crystal sconces fluttered ominously as we passed.

> **Talon:** *I want everyone to remain on guard. Haven NPCs have undergone an evolution. They can think for themselves. Grimwart's a good guy, but we haven't met the Trinity. We don't know what they're capable of.*

The brigade clenched jaws and continued in cautious silence. Suddenly, being the only players in an NPC fortress sounded dangerous. We followed the rose-colored walkway with a decent spread, checking every stray room and hall as we passed, heading for the heart of Oakengard.

The keepers stopped at a descending spiral staircase with

purple banisters, taking posts at opposite sides. When Grimwart attempted to lead the way, the figure of smoky rock swayed into his path and hummed a single note. The colonel turned to us, flustered.

"It seems I'm not welcome after all. This is why you are here, Talon. It's unnatural to be separated from our leaders."

I nodded grimly. "We'll get to the bottom of it." I glanced down the spiral staircase, wondering how far the bottom actually was. "Maybe I should only take a few down with me. Volunteers?"

Izzy and Lash hurried to my side.

"Okay. Kyle, you have command up here. If something happens—"

"We got your back," he said. His eyes snapped to the rest of Bravo Team to make sure they understood.

Conan and Glinda were solid. They'd backed us many times before and didn't need guidance. It was Crux and Hex I wasn't so sure about. I considered leaving Lash behind to keep her grip on the team, but switching assignments would betray my distrust of them. I needed to throw Bravo Team a bone and let one of them in the Speculum anyway. I grabbed the banister and made my way down the staircase.

Frigid air gripped us. I hugged my cowl tightly around my neck. Deeper and deeper we descended until, finally, my boot found the bottom. The floor was a flat glaze with a mirrorlike quality. It reflected what was above while also being translucent enough to reveal the depths beneath us. We were standing on a frozen lake.

Lash stepped down behind me and immediately slipped. Her

steel boots couldn't find purchase and she tumbled loudly to her side. Izzy glowered playfully before setting her winter staff gently on the surface for support.

We helped Lash to her feet. Lucky for her, she had a gigantic cleaver with almost as much mass as her armor. She used it to steady herself and continued forward. It slowed our progress, and I questioned her ability to fight in such a state.

As for me, I had the highest agility of the group, with the possible exception of Crux but he was upstairs. My supple ranger boots were well suited to the task so I took the lead.

The Speculum was a winter wonderland. Frozen but colorful. The icy ground was ornamented with jutting amethyst walls, devoid of sconces but with a luminance all their own. Within the frozen lake were rocks ranging through the colors of the rainbow, and probably some more. They pulsed with organic rhythm that was beautiful and unsettling at the same time.

The chamber was large but not enormous. A few keepers stood idly at the outskirts. At the end of the room, a column of smoky glass stretched from ceiling to mirror floor and into the depths beneath. A glass throne sat against it, large and looming, yet empty. A clear glass triangle was inset above the seat.

Agility Check...
Pass!

Whoa. Busy taking in the sights, I had almost slipped. I stopped showing off and drew my dragonspear for the first time in Oakengard. As I set its tip lightly against the glass floor, the entire room shuddered.

"What was that?" hurried Lash.

The dark pillar in the center of the room rumbled and spun. The attached throne rotated to the side as another throne moved into place. Same throne, same triangle inset in the pillar. The notable difference was the woman seated below. Her name tag read [Philosopher Mara].

"Greetings, Talon, Protector of Stronghold, the freethinker."

The pillar rumbled and spun again. Mara moved out of view while another throne snapped into place. [Hero Gent].

"Greetings, Talon, Protector of Stronghold, the titanslayer."

The Trinity. I realized I could see all three thrones at once, though only one faced us at a time. The other two receded into the back stonework, obscuring whoever sat in place. The head of the knights, Gent, and the head of the sages, Mara. With Bishop Tannen ousted, the priest throne was empty.

"It is an honor to meet the Trinity," I announced. "These are my trusted advisors, Izzy and Lash."

Gent looked on without betraying his mood. He was even better at that than Grimwart. The column rotated the opposite direction as Mara moved back into place to appraise us.

Talon: *Lash, remove your helmet!*

The white knight did so, mimicking Grimwart's conduct in the city. I realized my girls were an odd sight. Towering versus diminutive, bleached hair versus raven black, muscles and might versus dragonfly wings and pixie dust. They were opposites.

"It is unexpected to see you in Oakengard," began

Philosopher Mara. "Colonel Grimwart has overstepped his bounds."

"He is a good friend," I assured. "He only wishes to offer what tools he can to aid the Trinity."

"Bah!" The column spun. "We know of your exploits. You made peace with the pagans." I grinned smugly before realizing Hero Gent's gray mustache twisted in disapproval. "Your ways are not the ways of the crusaders."

Mara shifted into place. "Yet your ideas are bold. Twice you have circumvented disaster. If it wasn't for you, Bishop Tannen's treachery might've continued until it was too late." I thought I heard Hero Gent muttering in the background.

I pressed my lips together, wondering how to broach the subject of the state of Oakengard without offending the Trinity. They were here, after all, right where they were supposed to be. I had no way of knowing if their behavior was abnormal. Philosopher Mara caught my hesitation as I eyed the crystal triangle embedded above her head.

"Do you know of the strength of threes?" she asked instructively. I shook my head. "We are a network. Sages, knights, and priests, each with a direct support to the other two." As she spoke, the glass triangle heated to a white glow and disconnected from the pillar. It floated above her.

Hero Gent shifted into place. "Sages provide wisdom, knights provide might, and priests engender hearts." His triangle also lit up and drifted beside the other so their bottom points touched.

The throne column rotated again, this time to the empty seat. Even though they were out of sight, both spoke as one. "Without three, there is no one."

The bishop's triangle did not light up or glide through the air. However, the other two were placed in such a way that the three triangles formed a larger one: two at the base, one at the top, with an empty upside-down triangle for the center.

"You've got to be kidding me," I said. "A Triforce?"

"Never heard of it!" they both rushed.

The pillar spun Philosopher Mara back into place. "What is it you seek?"

"I already told you. Grimwart—"

"Has his own motivations. I am inquiring about yours."

I stared agape before clearing my throat. "Yes. I seek to formalize an alliance between the Black Hats and the crusaders."

Gent shifted in. "And bring us into a pagan armistice."

Philosopher Mara: "Don't be foolhardy. The goblins have already proved their agency. I applaud the freethinker for differentiating the mindless from the sapient."

Gent shifted back. "Players cannot be trusted! How soon you forget the theft of—"

The thrones suddenly shifted so the empty one faced us. Mara and Gent engaged in heated debate, albeit in muted voices.

It was curious that Hero Gent had said players couldn't be trusted. Curious and strange, as I was under the belief that we were the first-ever players to breach Oakengard.

As we waited, I couldn't help but stare at the two triangles once again reunited beneath their inert companion. I strained to imagine their power. What role did the Triforce play?

Hero Gent rotated to the head. "It is decided. A Black Hat

alliance is a worthy one. Alas, we are unable to finalize it until the three is complete. Official crusader matters can only be managed by a true Trinity."

I was beginning to see what the problem in Oakengard was. There wasn't anything wrong with Hero Gent or Philosopher Mara—the empty seat was the problem. Oakengard as a city still operated unabated. The studies and debates and drills and mining all proved that. But the recession of leadership was directly attributed to the recession of leaders.

I spoke carefully. "So everything will return to full strength once a new bishop is named?"

Mara's throne rotated in. "Strength is overrated. It is unity that is important. Oakengard thrives, yet a bishop is needed to warm our hearts."

"Is this an election type of deal?"

"Nothing so simple. At the risk of addressing a delicate matter, Hero Gent and I cannot place our full trust in the priestship. Their attempted coup is recent history, and while Bishop Tannen has been deposed, his devout disciple Cleric Vagram still remains. If we promote a priest who is in league with the cleric, we would open ourselves to disaster and irreparable harm."

"So you just lock yourselves away?"

Her voice came with an edge of warning. "Caution must trump expediency."

Hero Gent shifted before us. "Oakengard must build its might. We are not hiding, we are fortifying and hunting. If Colonel Grimwart had continued his search for the rogue cleric instead of detouring to Stronghold, he may already have his prize."

"Maybe he thought our help was warranted?"

The empty throne moved into place. I watched the Triforce as they muttered back and forth.

"He is powerful... defeated Bishop Tannen... it is not unwise."

After heated debate, Hero Gent presented himself and addressed us. "A test of Black Hat mettle, then. That is what you seek?"

I stepped forward. Gent eyed my dragonspear pitched in the ice. "I'll gladly bring that madman to justice. I owe him one anyway."

The hero smiled. A prompt appeared.

> Quest Offer: **Bring Vagram to Justice**
> *Quest Type: Bounty (public)*
> *Reward: Crusader Alliance*
> Cleric Vagram leads the rogue catechist faction in guerrilla warfare. Find and return him to Oakengard.
>
> ***Accept Quest?***

I accepted.

"It is settled then," said Gent. Of the two glowing triangles floating overhead, one popped off. His eyes followed it as it slid back into the slot above his head. "You are a slayer. A hero. Do what you do best."

The pillar shifted Mara into view. The final floating triangle sputtered as it drifted back into place. "I am afraid you will need more than might to tackle your enemies, freethinker. Use the tools that have attained you such heights. Restore the Trinity. Only then will you have your alliance. Good luck."

The room rumbled as the pillar spun and snapped into place, empty throne facing us. There was no more movement, no more muttering. The Trinity had once again gone dark.

I turned to Lash and Izzy. They'd remained silent the entire time. Even now, they didn't have anything to say.

The colorful lights beneath the frozen lake fluttered. The entire Speculum darkened. Even the vigilant keepers temporarily lost their glow. After several disconcerting seconds power fully restored, leaving us in a charming Christmas glow once again.

Charming but cold. The experience was eerie, though not overtly ominous—probably best described as glitchy. It made me wonder if Oakengard was really ready to host players and how much of a detrimental effect a fractured Trinity actually had.

> Quest Update: **Reunite the Trinity**
> *Quest Type: Epic*
> *Reward: 20 silver bars, 4,000 XP, royal treasure*
> What remains of the Oakengard Trinity appears well, but they require a bishop to return to full form.
> 1,000 XP awarded

Our troubled faces snapped into smiles. A single conversation and Grimwart's epic quest had advanced. Sure, we had a new, independently difficult quest to add to it now, but so far Oakengard was promising to be an XP gold mine. I checked my sheet.

98

XP	65985
Next	74950

And I was worried this'd be dangerous.

The three of us headed to the spiral staircase and began our ascent.

1180 MIA: Missing in Action

Expectant eyes waited for us above. Grimwart was especially eager to hear the news.

"Did you see them?" he asked. "Are they still alive?"

His questions puzzled me. Grimwart was the one who'd assigned the quest to us in the first place. Hadn't he been updated along with our notification? Come to think of it, I didn't really understand the underlying game mechanics regarding quest prompts. Was the NPC aware of the settings? Did they choose the experience and treasure rewards?

"They were there," I answered. "They seemed... normal?"

He blinked. "What do you mean... normal?"

I shrugged. "I've got to hand it to you, Grimwart. Between your precautious concern and Saint Peter's fast travel, these quests are gonna be good for us." As quest experience didn't divide amongst participants, the entire brigade was pleased with the development.

"That's not possible," protested Grimwart. "The situation at Oakengard is anything but normal."

"I'm telling you, they're okay. Gave me a new quest and everything. Look," I said, before something tugged at my mind. I paused and considered the room. The expressionless keepers stared ahead blankly.

"Yes?"

"Uh... oh yeah." I pulled Grimwart aside and spoke low. "They didn't come right out and say it, but the Trinity is vulnerable until they fill the bishop position, and they don't want to do that until Cleric Vagram is brought to justice. That's the reason for the defensive drills and the search parties."

His mustache puckered out. "I suppose. But that doesn't explain the lack of communication."

"They don't know which priests are trustworthy. A good bishop will solve that. Look." I opened my updated quest prompt for his perusal and distractedly surveyed the room as he read.

"This isn't right," he muttered. "Replacing the ousted bishop is necessary for reunification, but how can the one exist if any of the three are broken?"

I did kinda understand his concern. If the priestship was the only problem, why leave Colonel Grimwart in the dark? Then again, who was I to complain? Perhaps the full scope of the city's problems would be revealed over the course of the epic quest. Find the bishop, find the problem.

Besides, we had a more pressing issue. I finally realized what was nagging me. I left Grimwart to his troubled pondering and approached Kyle.

"Where's Crux?"

"Huh?"

"Crux. Yay height, all black, master thief. I left you in charge up here."

Kyle looked around dumbly. "He was here a minute ago."

Bravo Team huddled around Lash as she described the Trinity encounter. I converged on them. "Hey, Hex, seen your twin brother around?"

The necromancer stiffly swiveled her head to the adjoining hallways. "He's not here?"

I nodded to our surroundings. "Isn't it obvious?"

Lash frowned.

> **Lash:** *Crux, report.*

The whole brigade read the message and idly turned to the walls and shadows.

> **Lash:** *Crux, you okay?*

"Was anyone else in this room?" asked Izzy.

Grimwart was still preoccupied, but one of the keepers glanced our way.

"No way," said Kyle. "It was just us. You were only gone like five minutes. There's no way anyone—"

> **Talon:** *Stop talking.*

The room went silent. The abrupt change spurred the second keeper to look our way. I smiled and waved.

"How ya doin'? All right? Us too."

The keeper's gaze didn't waver.

"Okay... Good talk."

> **Hex:** *He's probably just wandering. He does that sometimes.*
> **Lash:** *Not without giving anyone a heads up. Not if he wants to stay on my team.*
> **Hex:** *I'll talk to him.*
> **Talon:** *I'm not so sure he wandered away. There's something off in here and I don't want to vocalize it out loud. The keepers are watching us.*
> **Kyle:** *Okay, so what do we do?*

I nonchalantly strolled across the room, pretending to admire the rose-tinted floor.

> **Talon:** *We stall. We split up and find him, all the while acting like everything's normal.*

Izzy rapped the winter staff lightly on the floor. "Gee, Grimwart, I would really love to see the magic shops you have here."

The NPC snapped out of his thoughts. "Hmm?"

"Yeah," joined in Kyle. "And I wanna pick up some of that crystal. Mementos."

Colonel Grimwart nodded. "Yes, of course." The keepers returned to forward-facing positions, bored.

"I could use some fresh air too," said Glinda. Conan followed as she joined Kyle and Izzy.

Hex inched toward an unexplored hallway. "I wouldn't mind a look around."

"Wait for me," I called. I didn't know Crux and Hex too well. With one of them missing I didn't wanna let the other out of my sight. Hex failed to hide her disappointment at my joining her, making me wonder if the twins were up to something. "Lash, you're with us."

I was satisfied the white knight would adequately back me up against any potential trouble until one of the keepers sharply trilled. We froze.

"It's just policy," explained Grimwart. "The Inner Hall of Oakengard is not to be wandered by outsiders. I can escort you."

Izzy shrugged. "We can find the shops on our own then."

The colonel's presence pacified the mindless guardian. Its glow faded and it turned away, once again standing vigil over the Speculum.

Izzy's group headed outside as we went our separate ways. Hex moved to lead us down the corridor we'd come from. Interesting, since she'd initially tried to head another direction. "Let's go this way," I ordered, heading down her original path. She swallowed and hurried after.

> **Talon:** *You up to anything, Hex?*

Lash furrowed her brow and turned to me. "What are you —?"

I put a finger to my lips. Grimwart turned at the sudden

silence. Having him around made me uneasy. Not because I distrusted him. I just wasn't sure how compromised he was. But with the keepers guarding the Inner Hall, we had no other choice than to have him near.

> **Lash:** *What are you talking about?*
> **Talon:** *I'm suggesting Hex knows what her brother's up to, and I want to know what's going on right now.*
> **Lash:** *That's Bravo Team you're talking about.*
> **Talon:** *Not now, Lash.*
> **Lash:** *To hell with not now. I have a man down and you're questioning my party?*

I grumbled. The last thing I needed was Lash's impertinence broadcast over brigade chat. Just as bad right now was making the colonel party to our affairs.

> **Hex:** *It's nothing. I just thought my brother was checking out this hallway. Let's just find him and get out of here.*
> **Talon:** *Radio silence from here on out.*

Lash frowned at me before her helmet blinked into place. Thankfully, she followed the order.

It was looking more and more like a sneaky party member was up to something. And if he was, he now had the full story. Brigade chat saw to that. I had no way of communicating while keeping both Crux and Grimwart out of the loop, and reorganizing the parties when the others were away would strand them. I needed to ask the devs for better chat controls.

Ahead in the passage, a few men argued. We approached the group. Two soldiers cornered a priest against the wall.

"What did you call him?" asked the man with an axe.

"He knows what he did," snapped the priest. "If he needed more silver, he should've made sure his search party was successful."

"You'd like that," said the other soldier. "More wild goose chases for your precious cleric."

"I'm not a disciple of Vagram's," swore the priest. "That's a rich accusation coming from a two-bit thief."

"I'm no thief, you traitor!"

"Men!" boomed Grimwart. The soldiers immediately turned and snapped to attention. Even though the priest didn't directly report to the colonel, he lowered his head submissively. "What is the meaning of this?"

"My silver is missing, Colonel. Briggs has done nothing but pester me for weeks. Now he's finally crossed the line.'

The man accused of being a thief defended himself. "I did—"

"Silence!" commanded the colonel. "This is unbecoming of Oakengard's elite."

I found it curious that our expert thief was missing in the same area a priest misplaced his silver. As Grimwart chided the quarreling men, I took the opportunity to pull Lash and Hex discreetly forward. Grimwart was occupied and paid us no heed.

"We shouldn't go ahead alone," whispered Hex.

"You'd like that," I said curtly. "You're not being entirely honest with us, Hex."

"What are you trying to say?" warned Lash. The necromancer didn't appear nearly as righteous.

"It's just that—"

We turned a corner and nearly bumped into Crux coming toward us.

"Wha—" he said, surprised. "Oh, sorry! I didn't..." The thief was holding a bar of silver in his hand.

"Where did you get that?" I demanded.

"I didn't..."

"We're guests in this fortress. Give it back. Now."

His expression sobered and he nodded glumly.

Hex hugged him dispassionately. "I'm glad you're okay."

"He's not okay," I said. "He snuck away to loot our hosts. You lied to us." I eyed further down the hallway. A faint glow shone through an arched doorway. "What are you doing out here?"

Crux frowned. "Sorry, boss. Just keeping my skills sharp, you know?"

I stepped past him. "You sure that's all..." As I approached the distant doorway, a cream-colored cloth fluttered by. A white robe. I hurried after the saint with a short Caesar cut and sharp features, arriving in the room just in time to see Saint Loras whisper to a keeper.

Crusader Reputation -100

My intuition nagged at me. The developer skittered from the room. Before I could follow, the keeper flared brightly. The soft blue glow became fluorescent red fire. The keeper released a high-pitched hum and advanced, two stony hands raised.

I backed away with outstretched arms. "Whoa, whoa. I just want to talk to Loras."

Lash and the twins squeezed behind me. "What'd you do?" asked the knight.

"Nothing!"

"You aggroed him."

"I can see that."

Despite the aggressive advance, the keeper stopped before us, humming erratically. He was an animated, intimidating creature.

I shook my head, palms still raised. "I don't know what you're saying."

"What are you doing here?" demanded Grimwart, stomping up behind us.

I backed away from the threat. "One of my guys got lost. Saint Loras was back here."

Grimwart studied the keeper. "As I've said, he was permanently assigned here after Stronghold was secured."

"But saints are player advocates. What's he doing in an NPC town?"

"Bolstering Oakengard. Or so he claims. I have received no assistance from the man."

I narrowed my eyes. When the crusaders had first showed

themselves in the beta, the developers patched in huge buffs to their faction. I didn't understand why that required saintly presence, but I didn't know everything about Haven policy. "I don't trust Loras. Bishop Tannen accused him of destroying the hub in Shorehome and handing over its soulstone."

"The Oakengard soulstone is also missing. The Trinity blames it on greedy players."

Hero Gent had almost let that same fact slip. After we were safe, I needed to learn everything Grimwart knew. "I have a feeling Saint Loras is the one meddling in Oakengard. We need to find out what he's up to." I chanced a step forward. The keeper's red fire sizzled. A baton of energy extended from his stony arm.

Grimwart tugged me backward. "No one's allowed in saintly quarters, not even me."

"Get off." I shrugged him away as two keepers rounded the exit Loras had fled through. One of them was extra large, made up of heavy rocks with a mean glow. A bright spot of energy washed over his glass-like head and formed a power helmet.

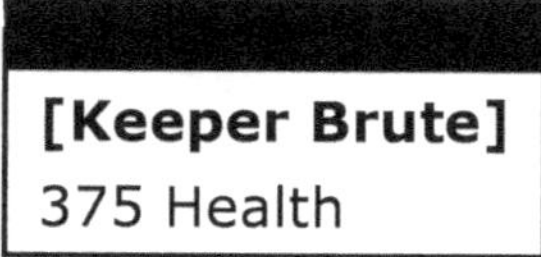

A keeper boss—not that the other two were shabby themselves. I turned to Crux and Hex.

"What did you do?"

The young necromancer trembled. "I'm sorry..."

> **Izzy:** *Talon, I think we're being followed.*

"We must flee," urged Grimwart. "Now."

We retreated a few steps before two more keepers appeared at our rear, trapping us. Five of them now, each crackling with angry light.

Whoever said there was a such thing as easy XP?

1190 Rock of Ages

With combat looking more and more likely, I ceased any attempt at appearing docile. I brandished the dragonspear overhead. Lash drew her cleaver.

"What are you doing?" breathed Grimwart. "You can't fight them."

I gritted my teeth. "They're not giving us much choice."

"I'm sorry," repeated Hex. "We didn't mean—"

Crux placed a hand on her shoulder. "It's okay. It was my fault."

"No," I said. "This is about something bigger than you two. Saint Loras and the nine great cities." We backed away as the keepers closed in.

Grimwart led us the way we'd come. The rear sentries were much less aggressive in their advance. "Let us return to the fast-travel portal," he requested.

"Will we be allowed to use it?"

The colonel scoffed indignantly. "Oakengard does not wish to imprison you. We're meant to be allies."

"Act like the question is hypothetical, then. For the sake of argument, will we be able to use the portal if Loras wants us captured?"

He frowned and nodded. "Yes. It was left open for your return. Loras would need to manually disable it. I can send you through."

"Good enough for me."

Talon: *New plan. Everybody get your ass to the fast-travel point NOW. We're outta here.*
Izzy: *What about the quest to capture Vagram?*
Talon: *We have an emergency here. We need to regroup. We can worry about the cleric later.*
Izzy: *Got it.*
Kyle: *Roger that. Omw.*

Halfway down the hall, the two keepers stopped their escort. The three coming from Loras lifted their batons and advanced. They weren't letting us go—they just wanted us safely contained in the narrow hallway, away from the saint quarters. We were sitting ducks now.

I squared off with the two barring the rear passage. They were a softer target than the three behind us, both in numbers and in the absence of the armored boss. "I'm Talon, the Protector of Stronghold, faction leader of the Black Hats, and a guest in this city. Get out of my way."

Energy batons zapped into being and they lunged.

I triggered dash to sidestep their attack. The dragonspear rounded on one. I buried a deadshot through its stony center, shoving it into the wall.

> You dealt 37 damage to [Keeper]

"Run!"

The group sped through the opening. The keeper brute hummed three times in quick succession. It was time for full alert.

The second keeper came at me as Lash swung her cleaver. The blade passed through the red energy connecting the smoky stone arm to its body. A blow that should've dismembered the enemy was ignored. The sentinel spun a rock-fist into Lash's breastplate, sending her to the ground. The rock readied another blow.

"Lash!" screamed Hex. Although she was already past the danger, she returned and laid hands on the keeper.

> [Hex] cast Deanimate on [Keeper]

The keeper's red fire vanished. The heavy rocks tumbled to the ground.

> [Keeper] is defeated
> 75 XP awarded
> Crusader Reputation -100

Lash looked up at the young necromancer and said, "All right, then." She turned and planted her cleaver into the pink floor.

[Lash] cast Shield Wall

Yellow light burst and spanned the thin hallway, cutting off access behind us. The three keepers slammed into the magical barrier. They droned to each other and banged at the energy.

The keeper I had struck twisted back at me with a blow of his own. I crossblocked the baton. The deflection was successful but red energy crackled through the dragonspear to my fingers.

Electrical Damage!

32 damage

Stun!

You are stunned. You may not use skills, move, or attack for 20 seconds.

Friggin' hell. Why did I always run into the OP mobs?

Crux backed away from the conflict, staring in terror. I could do nothing to avoid the keeper's follow-up strike.

47 electrical damage

Stun!

You are stunned. You may not use skills, move, or attack for 20 seconds.

I screamed through the agony. "A little help here."

Lash swung her heavy sword, this time directly impacting the sentinel's midsection. The blow did normal damage and shoved the danger away.

"Can you deanimate it?" she asked.

"Too soon!" said Hex. "It's a powerful spell but has a long cooldown."

Lash swung again but the enemy dodged the blow. Behind us, the keepers pounded at the energy wall.

Hex set her jaw and stuck a pin into her palm.

[Hex] cast Living Spirit Infusion
Cost: 37 health
Deanimate is recharged and ready

Whoa, despite the seemingly modest cost in health, Hex's life bar sank to half. Glass cannon was right.

The necromancer leapt forward and repeated her deanimate trick. The second keeper collapsed like a bundle of dropped billiard balls. Our retreat was clear.

"What the hell?" I asked Crux, who was leading the way.

He shrugged. "I'm a pacifist."

"Of course you are. You don't wanna get beat up when you're caught stealing."

"Sorry, boss. That's what legs are for."

"The rogue is right," said Grimwart. "We should be moving." I noted he still hadn't drawn his sword.

"Score!" exclaimed Hex, tossing me an item from the looted guards.

> **[Knife Handling Scroll]**
> Awards the weapon skill managing use of small blades.

"Nice! You don't need it?"

She flashed the pin in her fingers. "Already have it. And my bro the pacifist would only sell it."

"To the fast travel!" urged Grimwart, hurrying down the hall after Crux.

"They're not so tough," said the necromancer.

"Hex..." warned her brother.

The keepers all struck the energy barrier at the same time, splintering Lash's magic. They burst through the wall in showery sparks. We spun to them but the keeper boss was too fast. His baton struck Hex.

Beside being near death, Hex was stunned. Thankfully, my status effect had worn off. I aimed my spear at the brute as he grabbed the necromancer in a bear hug.

"Let go of me!" she yelled.

I didn't have a clear shot. Lash and I kept the other two at bay while we decided what to do. Hex smartly chugged a health potion. She was still helpless but had a buffer of health.

The keeper boss changed colors from red to white. A low hum vibrated through his glassy body. The smoke-colored stones lit up with vibrant energy. Hex screamed.

The brute threw her to the floor and returned to his aggressive red hue. Hex twisted in pain as her torso crystallized into black stone. The affliction extended through her legs and outstretched arm, finalizing as her open eyes petrified.

"No!" yelled Crux.

[Hex] is petrified!

"Damn you!" boomed Lash. Her cleaver thrummed yellow and she slammed it into the nearest keeper. A gaping crack split across its chest. The boss closed on her next.

"Get out of here!" I ordered. "Follow Grimwart."

"Screw that," she barked, full helm cocked menacingly. "These blockheads want a fight, they're getting one."

"That's an order, Lash!"

She swung at the boss and missed. The wounded keeper attempted to grab her, but she moved faster than her size and armor let on. Her blade smacked him again. The sentry canted to the side, catching the wall with a stone hand for support.

Lash was a powerful fighter but left herself exposed to the most dangerous of them. The brute moved in and punched her.

I hated the thought of running, but I was trying to avoid a diplomatic incident. These were the keepers of Oakengard. Even if five fell, how many more would fill their ranks? And it wasn't just us to think about. Half the brigade was elsewhere and hurrying to the fast travel. If we didn't get there with Grimwart, they'd be stranded.

Luckily, the white knight's magic resistance had avoided a stun.

"Lash, I am ordering you to lead the rest of Bravo Team outta here!"

"I can't do that, boss." She swung wildly at the third keeper, who had moved from me to engage her. "Leave no man behind." She nearly got caught with a baton and battered the stone guardian's arm away. The keeper boss lunged at her.

I pounced between them and triggered Spinshield. My spear deflected stone away but also battered Lash's white armor, creating much-needed space between the combatants. Two more keepers rounded into the hall behind them. One was another giant. Lash's eyes widened.

"This isn't the Marines," I asserted. "We can't save Hex anymore. You're a Black Hat, and as your leader I'm ordering you to retreat and save the rest of your team."

She was dazed, eyes still on the enemy reinforcements. Lash raised the cleaver over her head. I cursed as she swung, but instead of striking a keeper, she planted it into the floor.

My eyes went wide. I tried to hurry to Lash's side, but the keeper brute lunged into my path.

[Lash] cast Shield Wall

I was exactly a second away from being stuck on the wrong side of Lash's magic. I dove toward the giant blocking my path, right under his blocky body where his legs should've been. I slid under and past the hovering brute to safety.

The energy wall nipped my toes as it spawned, cutting off our pursuers.

"Come on," Lash relented.

We sprinted down the hall after Crux and Grimwart. The magical wall trembled at the keepers' might. With so many involved, the obstacle would only buy us a few seconds.

We scrambled down the maze of tunnels. Past the amethyst staircase, now empty. The two guards we'd killed had been the ones posted here. My boots skidded to a stop as I considered darting down a level and appealing to the Trinity. I turned to my brigade, sprinting ahead toward the fast travel.

Grimwart had a good head on his shoulders. He was right to distrust Loras. If he was sure something was wrong with the Trinity, I believed him. Maybe they had just put on a good show for me. Blinded me with quests and XP. I couldn't risk going down there and leaving my people to fend for themselves.

Izzy: *We're being chased by keepers. Just made it inside. It's gonna be close.*
Talon: *Don't wait up.*

I set my jaw and bounded down the main hallway toward Bravo Team. A keeper boss sailed through the air and smashed into the tile directly ahead of me. Its glowing red helmet swiveled, head canting and transitioning to the white energy of its petrify attack.

Normally I'd go for a baseball slide—it worked last time—but the rose quartz was now smashed to rubble from the landing. Furthermore, the brute was too tall and the ceiling too low to consider vaulting.

Still running full speed, I swapped out the dragonspear for climbing claws. Leather straps outfitted on gloves, iron hooks spiking from the palms. Without slowing to think, I pounced sideways, boots and claws finding purchase on the rough brown stonework, and I triggered dash.

Skill Evolution!
You learned Wall Run

A rush of adrenaline amped my muscles as I whooshed right by the hulking mass of rocks. Boot steps pattered on the wall; hands steadied my balance. Stone arms slammed behind me a step too slow. The guardian roared in anger as I skittered off the wall and back to the tile in a smooth motion.

Intense didn't begin to describe it.

The pack was all behind us now. Specializing in agility, my speed was too much for them. Unfortunately, once I caught up to the rest of the brigade I had to slow down to cover their six. That was when the keepers started to overtake us. We rushed past the sages and priests and the overlook. We were just two rooms away when I felt them at my back.

I batted a stone arm away with the dragonspear, narrowly missing the electrified baton that would mean my death. Five other keepers quickly converged.

Double doors beside us buckled open. "Heads up!" alerted Kyle.

I was absolutely stunned as a person-sized treant lumbered into the hall holding a mirror shield. "Kyle?"

The living tree jumped into the path of the giant sentinel's baton, shield braced against his shoulder. As the electrified weapon hit the reflective surface, the charge reversed into the keeper. The giant stumbled backward, incapacitated for a moment. Glinda and Conan hurried in. Izzy slammed the doors behind them and glazed them with ice magic. Pursuers immediately pounded at them.

"I told you those were the right doors!" She looked around and sighed. "You too, huh?"

We squared off against the wall of pursuing keepers. "Hit the fast travel," I ordered. As the first boss shook its head and recovered its senses, the second speed-lunged past us and landed behind, splitting us from Lash and Grimwart. Our escape was officially cut off.

"How do they do that?" I groaned.

The mob attempted to move in. A hasty sentinel struck Kyle's shield. It was unable to handle the stun as gracefully as the boss. Conan heaved a double greataxe and partially split a rock head. I utilized deadshot to bat away a dangerous baton.

"We can't keep this up for long," I hissed. The others waited by the fast travel. Lash and Crux. "Send them home," I shouted to Grimwart. "We're right behind them."

Izzy forced crystallized water into our enemies' magical joints. It held them off for precious seconds until they cracked free. At this point, it was really only Kyle's mirror shield they were wary of.

I studied the brewmaster. "What's with the getup?"

"Oh, this?" He waved a tree limb at his trunk body. "I chugged a decanter potion. This is what I got, so we ran."

Dorfin's Decanter of Luminous Fluids was one of the sillier artifacts we'd thus far encountered in Haven. The magical flask generated a once-a-day potion with a 60-minute effect. It often granted Kyle a specialized skill or transformation of some sort, though usually its effects were rather random and humorous. As hilarious as it was to see Kyle's face etched into the bark of a living tree, this wasn't the ideal situation to appreciate it.

"Okay," I said, "watch the batons at our backs. There's one keeper between us and the fast-travel portal. We hit him together and get out of here."

Everyone nodded. Unfortunately, the keepers had the same idea.

The wall of guards advanced in unison. Izzy slowed one down and Kyle faced the shield toward the brute, but two others squeezed in. I dodged an overhead strike and rapped the guardian on the head. Conan bashed one away with the flat of his axe, but his opponent's baton twirled around and struck his back. He was stunned.

The keeper brute flushed with white as he readied his petrifying hug. I dashed to the barbarian and yanked him away, getting struck with a baton myself. I tensed my muscles against the stun effect.

[Glinda] cast Minor Healing Aura
You are healed and instantly relieved of minor status effects.

Our afflictions melted away as suddenly as they had come on. I recoiled from the giant's bear hug. The priest had effortlessly cured us.

"Age over strength," chuckled the elderly woman.

The keeper cutting off our escape knocked her upside the head with his weapon. Glinda stiffened and screamed as the stun overtook her.

Dammit. Just as with Hex, the keepers had immediately gone after the biggest threat to their power. Without Glinda's magic, there was little we could do to neutralize their stun. The brute flared white hot as it prepared to do her in.

"Arrrggghh!" Lash screamed as she charged. Her entire body glowed gold as she bashed her shoulder into the giant's back.

The surprised guardian stumbled forward. Kyle pulled Glinda to safety, but the other keepers reached for her. He spun away from the threat and brandished the mirror shield. One keeper stunned itself; the other two struck true. Batons hit Glinda and Kyle.

Electrical Immunity!
[Keeper] dealt 0 damage to [Kyle]

The frat-boy-slash-tree arched an eyebrow. "That all you got?"

The keepers cocked their heads and battered him again. He shielded Glinda in a hug as batons struck his wooden back. Kyle shoved the priest into my arms and spun around laughing. "Treant!" he said. "You guys don't have a lot of wood in Oakengard, do you? One thing you should know about wood," he said as he drew his sword. "It doesn't conduct electricity."

He slammed his blade toward the boss, who parried. Even though his weapon was steel, the electricity arcing through it fizzled out once hitting his tree fingers. Another keeper moved in with a kidney punch.

Bashing Resistance!
[Keeper] dealt 22 damage to [Kyle]

A wide grin consumed my face. Unfortunately for the keepers, trees didn't have kidneys and, on top of being immune to electricity, treants were resistant to bashing damage. Laughter boomed through Kyle's chest as he read the notification.

Remind me never to make fun of Dorfin's Decanter ever again.

"Retreat!" called out the brewmaster, swinging again.

Kyle wasn't a great swordsman. He missed quite a bit and wasn't doing much damage against the rocky bodies, but in his new form he could tank their attacks all day.

"Wood!" exclaimed Izzy. "Use wood weapons!"

She swapped out her winter staff for a small wooden rod. The keepers advanced on us. Conan countered their strikes with the wooden staff of his axe. The brigade backed away, but we still had trouble.

The brute flushed red again and bashed Lash across the face. Her helmet twisted. A baton strike flung her backward. Glinda, relieved of her status effect, slipped past the enemy to heal her team leader. The giant clutched at her.

I swapped the dragonspear out for the noob spear I'd taken from Chadwick's man. I hadn't bothered to sell or drop it yet, and that laziness had just paid off. I batted the stony hands away. The sentinel twirled the baton on me but I met it with wood. The cheap spear nearly buckled under the high-level strength.

Now able to counter keeper attacks, the rest of the group hurried past the obstruction. Kyle took up the rear. "Go, go, go!" I had never seem him more brave. To be fair, was it brave if he was invincible?

We hurried past Grimwart. Crux had already teleported to safety. I helped Lash into the fast-travel circle. "You *really* don't like to follow orders, do you?"

She laughed it off.

"Come on," pushed Grimwart. "Ready yourselves."

Kyle disengaged from the two bosses and retreated into the portal.

"Come with us," I told Grimwart.

The black knight shook a solemn head. "I cannot, Talon. This is my home. I will not abandon it."

The colonel didn't flip a visible switch or cycle through menu screens or anything, but he somehow initiated the fast-travel process. As I readied a grateful nod, my expression twisted into alarm.

"Watch out!"

A white-hot stone giant wrapped him up.

"Be gone!" snapped the colonel.

Mild annoyance shifted to sudden panic. Grimwart's mouth stretched into a scream as the status effect hit him. The keeper brute let go and he stumbled to the floor.

As the room faded to pure white, our friend petrified to dead black rock.

-- Cutscene --

Christian Everett had fought for this.

Day and night, year in and year out.

He'd cut himself off from the outside world so that he could create another.

The tech titan blinked tiredly at the flashing server lights. He listened to the thrum of the cooling fans. He was deep in Kablammy headquarters, witnessing the birth of a new world. Seven years, it had taken. Now he had created light.

The developer perused the logs, pleased as every line of text reported further success. Haven was operating smoothly. Each of the redundant servers was online. Events were queued and processed, seamlessly connecting the various discrete systems into a unified and organic whole. The individual modules had been exhaustively tested over the years, many of them components of various social games and apps, but this was the first time the greater body existed. A newborn making its first gasps.

The bulk of Christian's family was long beyond reach. That was a fate no longer necessary for others. As of 1:57 a.m. Tuesday morning, Haven version 0.1 officially powered on.

The simulation was designed to be upgradeable, extendable, and—above all—robust. If operation continued smoothly, the collective servers would never be turned off again.

The CEO breathed solemnly and glanced at the external solid-state drive on the shelf over his desk. It was plugged into an independent backup and had its own screen log. Constant ASCII activity reported spikes and lulls, but the machine code was unreadable to the human eye. It was unreadable even by Haven, which was currently too primitive to parse the raw data.

Technologically, primitive was a misleading word. Haven was a wonder by any measure of modern computer science, yet it was still a simulation. The contents of the solid-state drive were more akin to a film negative. A mapping of the real world. By that measure, Haven was still in its infancy. It was a JPEG or an MP3. A lossy representation, imperfect, unable to manage the data load of perfect clarity.

To make matters more complicated, it was impossible for Christian to "see" his new world aside from the limited logging capability.

The visualization of Haven was a complex tapestry of real-time code filters, not a mere display of textures and models. Assets, while created by artists in the real world, were processed and expounded through a number of shaders meant solely for the brain. Final rendering occurred with the participation of the simulation, not unlike the powerhouse processing combo of a pair of eyeballs and the visual cortex.

In practice, there were limited workarounds. Individual game assets could be displayed, in part, on workstations. Data for still images could be collected and reconstructed. Even video clips could be generated, given enormous saves of data and insipid rendering schedules. But displaying real-time game events on a screen in the physical world was simply impossible, akin to the difference between the brain's perception of a dream while dreaming and the incoherent mess the waking mind reconstrues.

There was only one way to truly witness the majesty of Haven, but it was still far enough away to seem like yet another miracle.

Christian Everett typed into the console window.

> >>Input>> Let there be light.

Then the CEO proceeded to the inevitable task of hooking a living human being into the machine.

1200 Hexen

We huffed in exhaustion on the cold portico floor. Scrambling for your life, it turned out, was a pretty good workout. We'd made it back, but not all of us were so lucky.

"My sister's gonna be pissed," said Crux, opening his menu with a chuckle. In a moment, he frowned. "That's weird. Hex didn't send me a DM."

"So?" asked Izzy.

Lash sheathed her cleaver. "The twins have this thing where they message each other the exact amount of XP they lost whenever they die. Hex is a glass cannon so she dies a lot."

"And she never misses her message," said Crux. "The whole thing was her idea."

Izzy smirked. "She must be *really* pissed."

"I would be too," I added, "after my own brother abandoned me like that."

Crux dropped his head and muttered to himself. "I better go check on her." He hurried out.

I worked my jaw, unsettled at more than just Crux's performance in the field. "That was a major screwup back there, Lash."

The white helm swiveled my way. "How so? I seem to remember saving your ass."

"You disobeyed a direct order."

"Yeah. To come back and save everyone."

We aggressively squared off. "Helmet off, Lash."

"Why?"

" 'Cause I don't wanna bitch out your armor."

The helm vanished, revealing a scowl from ear to ear. "What do you got, tough guy? Should I have run away like the thief?"

"I'm not talking about that. Earlier, when Hex went down, you endangered the whole group by refusing to leave. And that's on top of whatever your new party members were up to."

She scoffed. "Your roommate was the one in charge of watching them." The treant did a good imitation of a real tree and remained stationary and quiet. "I don't need this crap. All I've done is try to protect you." Lash stormed toward the exit archway.

"Don't walk away from me, Bravo Leader." She begrudgingly paused and turned around. I moved close and stared up at her face. "I've given you full agency to make your own way. You can basically do anything you want. But when we're in a tactical situation and I'm giving orders, you need to obey my command. I'm sure you expect the same of your party."

The white knight bit her lip.

Crux: *Something's wrong, guys. I don't think Hex is on lockdown.*

The brother-sister combo were Shorehome transplants lucky

enough to have grabbed homes in the slums behind the Forum. Crux had hurried home and discovered the necromancer missing. Lockdown rules should've ensured she was nowhere else.

"But she's dead," I muttered.

Lash swallowed. "She was petrified. You think there's a difference?"

"I don't know." We turned to Saint Peter.

He appeared taken aback. "I... Any death should return her to her respawn point."

Talon: *What about the brothel?*

Crux: *No way. Hex hates that place and wouldn't want to be stuck there for 24 hours. We both always respawn at home.*

Lash: *Check it out anyway, Crux. And the barracks too.*

Crux: *Sure thing.*

The white knight's helmet slammed back on her head. "If I'm dismissed, I'd like to go see to a fallen party member."

I nodded gruffly. "Of course." Bravo Team exited as stiffness welled through my chest. It had been my order to leave Hex behind. What if she was somehow stuck? "Is it possible the keeper afflictions mutated? Genetic algorithms, adaptive skills. Can petrification prevent true death?"

Izzy rested a purple hand on my shoulder. "You had no way of knowing..."

Kyle hopped to his feet. "Let's go get her back."

I shook my head. "We don't know for a fact she's still back there. Plus, we might not be able to complete the return trip without Grimwart. And your treant enchantment will only last another half hour."

His wooden face deflated. He really liked that thing.

Saint Peter brushed his robe and nonchalantly cleared his throat. "So now you've seen Oakengard."

"Yeah, and I'm not so sure Colonel Grimwart was overreacting. The keepers turned him to stone."

Peter's eyes twitched.

"The crusader faction can't be trusted," muttered Izzy. "Big surprise."

"Does this mean war?" asked Kyle.

We turned to him, considering the possibility for the first time. Bishop Tannen had led crusaders and priests against this city before. What if the rest of the Trinity had become similarly corrupted?

I hissed. "Our master thief stealing silver from a priest wasn't the best of goodwill gestures. Instead of leaving as ambassadors, we fled as criminals." My head snapped to Saint Peter. "Loras was there."

The poor saint found a way to look even more surprised.

"Grimwart said Saint Loras was the one who oversaw Oakengard's buffs. Is that still happening?"

The old man shook his head. "It can't be. Loras..."

"Bishop Tannen accused him of being a traitor. He was the one who sicced the keepers on us."

Peter shook his head. "I thought you said your thief—"

"What's Loras doing in Oakengard?"

The saint frowned and remained tight-lipped.

I shook my head in exasperation. Secrets upon secrets. No wonder Grimwart hadn't trusted his quest with the saints. "Fine," I said. "If you're not gonna tell me what I need to know, I'm gonna go find someone who will."

"You don't mean—"

"Lucifer."

Peter hurried to block my exit. "You can't. He tried to destroy Stronghold."

My face hardened. "The only thing I'm sure of is that he knows a lot more about what's going on than I do. Last I saw he was willing to talk to me." My brow eased as I came to the realization. "That was right before Cleric Vagram tried to shut him up."

A conspiracy was afoot. Who better to ask about subterfuge than the devil himself?

Izzy and Kyle strolled toward the exit. I stepped around Saint Peter to follow.

"Fine," muttered the saint, defeated. "I'll tell you. But you must keep this close to your chest."

We waited as he prepared his speech.

"Kablammy Games is in trouble," he admitted. Although he chose his words guardedly, his resignation revealed them as truth. "Missed deadlines, mounting debts, unforeseen costs. With the advent of the leaks, we've had hostile companies seeking to acquire us."

I snorted. "Sounds like the Kablammy business model to me."

Izzy stepped forward. "What leaks?"

Peter's head shook absently. "We don't know how it happened. The staff was vetted several times. Word of Haven is rumored among the general public."

"Loras," we said.

Saint Peter chuckled in derision. "There are no good options. Either Kablammy runs out of money and is forced to shut down the servers and life as you know it, or we sell..."

My eyes narrowed. "Or?"

"Or we go public. Full launch."

Kyle's jaw dropped. "The rumors of launching the game are true?"

"It makes sense," I said. "That's why the saints have modified less and less of the game. The developers don't want big—intensive—changes."

"We want stability," clarified Peter. "We prided ourselves on our accomplishments. We strove to bring Haven above other MMOs by launching with a negligible bug count, but that's simply not possible. Especially not with our financial woes. All our changes have been to bring stability to Haven. Even the recent patch to skills was to get out of the game's way and resolve bugs naturally."

I knew where this was going. Developers on a death march, rushing to market an app unready for prime time. It was often easier to deprioritize a bug rather than fix it. Some things never changed. "You plan to launch a broken game, patch in fixes at day zero and beyond."

"That is vastly superior to the alternatives."

I swallowed uncomfortably. In this case, he wasn't wrong.

"So what's Saint Loras have to do with this?" asked Izzy.

Peter stroked his beard and sighed. "You don't understand. Loras is not a... real person. He's an online persona. A character."

I nodded along. It made sense that the saints wouldn't necessarily be modeled whole cloth from reality, as we had. They weren't permanent residents of the simulation.

Saint Peter continued. "The complication arises because... The usual employee who drives Saint Loras has been on sabbatical in the Greek islands."

We struggled to process the information. "Who's driving him then?" asked Kyle.

"It shouldn't be possible for anyone else to do so without the proper employee ID."

"How long since he's been on vacation?" I asked.

"Since after Bishop Tannen's coup. It was a trying time." Saint Peter rubbed his neck, remembering the near-death experience.

When the bishop had taken over, he'd made a show of hanging the saints. Peter and the others had been rescued. Loras hadn't fared so well.

"I don't get it," I confessed. "What did Tannen mean to accomplish with the executions? Didn't he know saints couldn't die?"

"It was a public statement," replied Peter. "Not only that, but the crusaders and catechists are NPCs. They don't necessarily conceive of the world beyond Haven as we do."

"Fair enough, but why did you guys stay captured? Couldn't you have just logged out?"

"It's crunch time," Peter reminded. "We don't work, we lose

our jobs. And it wasn't as bad as you might have imagined. Unlike residents, we don't feel pain, which isn't to say the experience of being deprived of digital oxygen is pleasant."

"Couldn't you have teleported away?"

He sighed. "As he controlled the hub, Tannen's coup did wrest some of our abilities away, that being one. But you must understand, Talon, had we abandoned the crisis, we would've been unable to view current events. Haven is much too complicated a simulation to display through a monitor. Some of the finer aspects of game management can only occur within the game. That's why the Oculus exists at all. And pulling a disappearing act might've resulted in an encore of Shorehome."

In other words, sacking of the city. A permanent loss of saintly control. With the launch of the game imminent, it was imperative for the core city to hold.

"It is not Tannen's motivations we must decipher," reminded Saint Peter.

"No," agreed Izzy. "This is Saint Loras." Her face soured. "Only he or she isn't Saint Loras."

"He or she," I repeated under my breath. The others turned to me. I settled on what had to be done. "I have to talk to Lucifer anyway."

"You can't, Talon," urged Peter. "Lucifer's a warmonger bent on revenge. Please heed my advice. I'm a custodian of the residents."

"And *I'm* a resident," I returned through gritted teeth. "I live here. I don't get to log off at the end of a long day. This is my world, and I need to do anything within my power to save it."

Izzy smirked. "I hate to say it, Pete, but I think the man's right." She winked at him to soften the blow.

"Besides," added Kyle, "if there's gonna be another war, don't we need Shorehome on our side?"

She nodded. "You're smarter as a tree. With three active cities, Shorehome's a third wheel. Whoever gets them as an ally wins the war."

"What war?" countered Peter. "You're overreacting."

"Better safe than sorry," I said. "Bishop Tannen was allowed to grow his power through player inactivity. That's not gonna fly this time. We're not waiting until an army's bearing down on us. I'm not gonna be reactive anymore. I'm taking my fate into my own hands and doing something before there's a problem. That means finding any help we can get."

Izzy and Kyle nodded in agreement. I loved having these two backing me up.

"Sounds like a plan then. We approach Papa Brugo about the impending disaster, and we corner Lucifer to squeeze out his secrets. Since the Shorehome hub is destroyed and fast travel isn't possible, this can be the inaugural mission for the Black Hat navy. We sail out with Admiral Oates first thing in the morning."

Everyone besides Saint Peter was satisfied with the plan, but he didn't try to stop us. The old man was wise enough to know when he was outvoted.

1210 Kingdom Hearts

Walking the streets of Stronghold sans bodyguard was nice. Sure, I had Izzy and treant-Kyle, but they were friends. We goofed off more than anything else. Deep down I knew Izzy wanted nothing more than to nestle in her bed with a corny book. And Kyle? To be honest I could never predict what the slacker would do. That was part of what made him so much fun.

I wasn't too worried about an assassination attempt anyway. Taking down one of the highest-level players in Haven was a tough ask. Poe's fate wouldn't engender more to the cause. Besides, their secret was out. Especially with my new intuition skill, I wouldn't be caught drinking on a barstool again.

As we turned off the public thoroughfare and entered Oldtown, we were greeted by friends outside the guildhall. The commotion grew more excited as we neared.

"Talon! You're back!" Trafford pushed through the energized crowd of Black Hats. "We've got more problems with Nooner and Chadwick. Those gangsters are trying to buy up all the lumber."

"What? There's no way they can afford that."

"They're doing a pretty good job," he asserted with crossed

arms. "I gave them a piece of my mind, but I didn't want to start a gang war without you."

"So why not start a trade war? I assume their actions are already driving up the price of lumber in the city. Offer the yard double what they're worth."

"Double?!?"

I flashed a cool smile. "We can't afford to stop building, and we have the silver to absorb the short-term losses. If we artificially inflate the cost of wood, it's only a matter of time before the gangsters run dry."

"Hmm, I like where your head's at. I can use the bargaining power to secure extended contracts at a discount. Still expensive but not doubly so, and it'll guarantee we get enough wood in the near term. Also, I was thinking we should recruit lumber workers long-term. It'll be cheaper to cut down our own trees." The buildmaster's eyes flittered to the treant. "No offense, mister..." Trafford paused. "I'll be damned. Is that you, Kyle?"

The tree wrapped twig fingers around Trafford's wrist. "You got me, bro. Magic potion." Kyle burped.

"Must be some brew."

Did I forget to mention Kyle's potions were alcoholic?

"Those are good thoughts, Trafford," I said. As an ex-soldier shop owner, he was really taking to the role of buildmaster. Trafford had a natural sense for logistics and planning that Errol would never take to. "On that note, I have kind of a good-news-bad-news situation. I need to take Errol and some pirates to Shorehome to negotiate with the Brothers in Black. You're gonna lose some building resources for a few days. On the other hand, I'll leave Bravo Team at headquarters. You get a single whiff of hostility from Nooner or Chadwick, let them do the talking."

"Aye," he laughed. "I find the best agreements involve the fewest words."

The congregated Black Hats seemed pleased with the tactics discussed. We all walked away happy.

"You know," I said, after we were a ways down the road, "being a leader isn't that hard. You just gotta listen. Hey, Kyle, can I see your mirror shield for a second."

"Uh, sure."

The treant handed it over as my intuition skill buzzed. Not a second later, a silver arrow whizzed toward me. It was meant to miss but I leapt into its path and threw the shield up.

Deflect!

The arrow whisked back the way it had come—right into a roadside bush.

[Dune] dealt 26 damage to [Dune]

"Ow! I took an arrow in the knee."

"You're better than that, Dune."

The green ranger hopped from the bush. Caduceus and Stigg squatted in distant rubble.

I handed the shield back to Kyle. "Sorry," I called out. "Intuition. Exploration. It's gonna be hard to sneak attack me."

Dune yanked the arrow out in pain and limped over. His

party members, finally realizing he was wounded, burst out laughing. To their credit, they also came over to check on him. Caduceus handed Dune a salve.

"I probably deserved that," he admitted, rubbing his wound.

Caduceus was a lean woman with a good head on her shoulders, a physicker from the artisan base class, which meant her healing was a trade more than magic. The knee wound healed all the same.

"Hey Caduceus, how you doin'?" Kyle stood taller than usual, considering he was a tree.

The healer adjusted her glasses. "I like the new look, Kyle."

"You do, right?" He wore a giant shit-eating grin and I caught on to his intention too late. "Since you dig the treant style, I was wondering if you wanted to go somewhere quiet. For the next fifteen minutes I got some serious wood."

"Oh, brother," grumbled Izzy. She couldn't roll her eyes hard enough.

As for me, well, treant-Kyle wasn't technically wearing any clothes. Bad puns aside, I didn't check below the belt to see if he was being literal.

"Still looking for that black notch, I see." Caduceus shrugged halfheartedly. "Too bad for you I'm not looking for a tree notch."

"What's all this talk of notches?" asked Izzy.

"You know," said Kyle, gesturing to Caduceus.

The pixie shook her head. "Just when I started to think you were redeemable."

Caduceus laughed. "Don't worry, Iz. He never had a chance. I haven't been into my last few guy notches, either."

The light went out in Kyle's eyes. "Well, screw you guys. If you don't mind I'm gonna spend my last minutes as a tree somewhere I'm appreciated." He hurried ahead into the respawn building.

"It's not appreciation if it costs money," called Izzy after him, but he was already distracted by the oohs and aahs that welcomed him.

The rest of us entered the brothel behind him. It was a simple wood structure. A common room on the bottom, with private spaces in the back and upstairs.

"The frat boy doesn't have the wrong idea," said Caduceus as she hooked each arm around a different girl and wandered away.

I widened my eyes. "I don't think even a treant could keep up with her."

Dune shook his head. "You don't know the half of it. Say, Talon, I was thinking of heading over to the Wicked Crow tonight for a beer. You game?"

I shook his hand as he prepared to leave. "Maybe so, actually. We got a bit of an adventure tomorrow so I could use a break. I'm sure Trafford and Kyle will swing by, and I might even drag this one out." I pointed to Izzy while pretending to hide the gesture behind my other hand.

"Ooh, a romantic night out in a dive bar." Izzy placed her backhand on her forehead. "You really do know how to make a lady swoon."

Dune laughed and said, "I think she's on to you. See you there." He left with his Viking companion, which was funny, as I would've thought a big dude named Stigg would've lived in a place like this.

I wandered to a set of beds out in the open, along the side wall. These spots weren't used for pleasure. They were reserved for respawners. Since dying came with a 24-hour lockdown, some residents chose to spend that downtime in a party atmosphere. They had most of the benefits of public and private spaces combined, as long as you didn't want actual privacy. Bravo Team huddled against a wall while Crux sat downtrodden on the bed. As soon as Lash saw me, she popped her helmet back on and walked outdoors. Tough crowd.

Glinda approached with much more tact. "Hex never made it back, Talon. We don't know what to do." I nodded. "And don't worry about Lash. She's in a mood." I thanked her before she followed the white knight out.

Conan wasn't much for words. Alone with Crux, he grew uncomfortable. As I made my way over, he jumped at the chance to excuse himself and sit beside a woman who'd been ogling his muscles. He alternated flexing his pecs.

Crux didn't lift his head as I leaned against the wall. Was it sadness or shame? Screwing us over in Oakengard was one thing, but he'd also gone behind our backs. That part was near inexcusable and was what irked me most. Still, it had cost him more than he could've imagined. Now wasn't the right time to address it.

"We're gonna get her back," I said. "I promise you that."

He turned to me with wet eyes. "I promised her I'd always look after her. Do what's best."

"We both have promises to keep then."

He couldn't find the will to reply. His gaze dropped to the floor again as he waited on the bed, hoping beyond hope that he would soon receive a message from his sister.

I scratched the back of my head, probably feeling about as useless as Conan had, and thought it best to sneak away. Despite only being gone a few seconds, I found Izzy engaged in conversation with a man on a sofa. He was broad-chested and looked like a giant human except he had four eyes and four arms.

"So just to be clear," prodded Izzy in a lowered voice, "arms and eyes aren't the only body parts you doubled up on?"

The oafish man smiled. Two tongues flicked from his open mouth.

"Ooh! Even better than I thought!"

"Very funny," I snapped.

I grabbed her hand and gently showed her the door.

We continued through Oldtown in a tight embrace. I was feeling a little territorial, I suppose, but it was a nice moment. Izzy and I were growing more relaxed with each other, even if she never quite committed to the relationship. You know. *All the way*. To be completely honest, after being so hard up lately, being in the brothel was torture.

"Can you imagine," she started, head on my shoulder, "what this place will look like in a year?"

I jutted my lip out. "I haven't really thought about it."

"Really? Try."

"Um, I dunno. I figure mostly the same, just with a few new buildings."

She smacked her lips. "Come on, Talon. You've been in Haven for a little over a month and a half and it's not even recognizable anymore. I've done this gig nine months. Sure, there were new skills and levels and dungeons—but Stronghold was always Stronghold."

I leaned my head on hers. "I get that, but it was everyone. Lucifer hacked free will into the AI. Goblins chose to settle in Shorehome. The wildkins seceded from their warlike brothers. And every single resident of Stronghold fought hard for the city."

Her finger rapped my nose. "And you were at the heart of all of it."

I blinked. I'd never really thought of it that way. Lucifer had used me, of course. The thought of tracking him down made me uneasy precisely because of the power and knowledge he had. Without him I never would've known I wasn't dead in the real world. Tad Lonnerman was alive and well. Recovering, anyway, after a horrible car accident. But that wasn't my life anymore. I was a copy. An individual AI myself. All of us were, in a way. How much did it matter whether my "source code" was alive or not?

"It's funny," I mused, stopping and squaring off with her. "I always thought you and Kyle were the ones living in the moment. Him killing time in the afterlife and you keeping your head down and grinding ahead. It's not that I don't have big plans anymore, it's just that... I've kinda already gotten what I wanted."

She smiled. "All this rubble? This is what you dreamt of?"

"Not the rubble, Izzy. I'm talking about peace. A stable world. One where injustice is righted. A place with friends. A place with you."

She swallowed. I gazed deep into her indigo eyes. They

weren't nearly as hard and sharp as usual. Not with me. Not anymore. I still saw glimpses of the walls when she was with others, but she bared her soul when we were alone. I lowered my lips to hers in a gentle kiss. I pulled away and smiled.

"Let's hurry home," she said.

I opened my mouth but stopped, realizing what she was implying. I grabbed her hand and made for Dragonperch. The doors opened and shut us in, alone. We embraced like ravenous vampires. I kissed her neck, her cheek, her lips.

We rushed two stories up and looked at the den. She shook her head and pulled me up further. At the door to her private quarters, I shook my head with a devilish grin and yanked her further upstairs. Past the library to the top—the war room, ready for battle. Izzy smirked.

I lifted the pixie's small body and laid her on the large oak table. "I have to warn you," I said. "I only have one tongue."

She laughed. "I guess it'll just need to do double duty." Izzy's clothes blinked away, leaving only the modest undergarments all Haven residents wore at minimum. Then even those disappeared, as private homes and brothels were the exception.

I stiffened as I took in her naked body, smooth and supple lavender skin trembling beneath me. Izzy smiled in equal parts confidence and shyness. It was the cutest thing ever. And also the sexiest. My clothes flashed away and I leaned in.

1220 Quest for Booty

We lay beside each other, naked. Izzy rested her head on my chest as I stared at the stone ceiling. *This* was what the afterlife was supposed to be. Not Nooner or Chadwick feuding, not a fractured Oakengard Trinity, not an assassin, or a plot by a hijacked saint. I ran my fingers up and down Izzy's back and sighed in perfect contentment.

"You know what you're doing," she said, almost a revelation.

I snorted. "Don't act like I'm a virgin or anything."

She turned and set her lips just inches from mine. "I didn't mean it that way. It's just... it's hard to surprise a girl like me."

I could no longer hide my stupid grin. This really was Heaven. "I know this sounds corny," I said, "but I really like you. I guess that made it easy."

She smirked again and was quiet a moment, but her next words made me even happier. "I really like you too." She scooted up and straddled me, perky breasts right above my face. They were small, like her frame, but perfectly shaped. Her purple skin was doing something for me too. She was warm and wet where her hips hugged my stomach, and it was impossible not to think about going again.

"What the fuck?" she snapped, recoiling. Her full set of clothes immediately snapped into place, forcing miles of distance between our skin.

I twisted around as a large dove fluttered loudly through the open window, sending white feathers in the air. It flew a frantic lap over our ducking heads before landing on a window sill.

I sighed in relief and turned to Izzy. "Freaked out by a *bird*?"

Izzy still covered her privates as though her baby blue robes weren't on. "I was naked! What if that's not an ordinary bird?"

I hopped off the table and hugged her. "We're safe in Dragonperch. And it's almost certainly not a normal bird."

For one, it was twice the size of any dove I'd ever seen. Twice as strong too. Not only was a scroll tied around its leg, but it held a large orb in its other talon.

"That's a pearl," I said.

I approached the bird cautiously. It surprised me by being totally docile. At the window I gently eased the orb from under knifelike claws.

> **Kyle:** *What was that? Omw!*

The chat was colored blue, restricting Kyle's message to party chat only. Past the bird's window perch on the ground below, Kyle hurried across Oldtown and entered the tower. He must've seen the bird fly into the tower.

I examined the cloudy white item.

[Dove Pearl]
Ivory orb with soft marbling, but inert.

Talon: *It's a new pearl to fit into our feather socket.*

I turned to Izzy. She shrugged with a neutral face.

"Something you're not telling me?" I asked.

She held off a smile. "No. No idea what this is."

I narrowed my eyes and tossed the pearl to her. I unwrapped the scroll and read it aloud.

Neither friend nor foe,

Alas, alas, I find myself thus burdened. I seek balance in all things, yet your gift of a bone pearl offsets the fates. The Black Keep finds itself in possession of a redundant pearl. Consider it payment in kind, and our balances leveled.

- The Wild King

I studied the note for another minute as Kyle's boots pounded up the stairwell.

"And I thought I played hard to get," said Izzy. She was still watching me with a mischievous grin.

"Let me have it," called Kyle. "I love this part." He barged headlong into the war room, immediately skidding to a stop and spinning away. "Oh!"

I turned to Izzy, the bird, and back to Kyle. "What is it with you guys?"

"Bro," said Kyle, peeking from behind an upraised arm, first at Izzy and then at myself. "Uh, don't take this personal or anything, but I've never seen your dong before."

The hairs on my legs and arms and back burned as I realized I was stark naked.

"Pretty impressive chub too," added Kyle.

I popped my clothes back on directly from inventory and flashed Izzy a vengeful look.

She returned a lilting laugh, strolled to my side, and gave me a long kiss. "Relax. It's not like you have anything to be embarrassed about. Besides, now we don't need to have any drawn-out conversations with our roommate."

"Drawn out?" asked Kyle with an indignant look. "You still don't know me that well, do you? It's about time you two banged." He approached and grabbed the dove pearl from Izzy.

I chuckled through closed lips and shook my head at Izzy. The war room had been my idea, after all. When she smiled, I broke out into laughter. Hooves rapped down the stairs as Bandit joined us. She must've been sleeping on the roof and heard the commotion. I nuzzled her ear.

"Sorry to wake you. Hope you weren't awake too long."

The black stallion, Artax, cantered down after her. The two were fast friends, but my mood darkened when I saw the horse. His master was missing, petrified along with Hex. Grimwart was a good man, and I vowed to save him as well.

"Got it," said Kyle, moving to the sanctum master panel and

navigating the socket menu. Feather and wind were the only two main sockets open. He slotted the dove pearl in.

> **Feather:** Dove

A diagram of the tower appeared. A white thread traced down from the sky and hit Dragonperch with a glow.

The dove cooed so loudly we jumped. I noticed a white glow on the war table, right where Izzy and I had consummated our relationship. When the light died away, a single olive rested there. I picked it up. "Wonder what I'm supposed to do with this." The dove cooed again. I chuckled and held it in my open palm. As soon as I was in reach, the dove stretched its neck and gobbled the olive whole. It chirped happily and flapped out the window, disappearing into the sky.

"It's a messaging system," relayed Kyle. "Or, more accurately, a *messenger* system." He tapped the flat screen showing Dragonperch and the Black Keep as white waypoints.

"We can communicate with the wildkins without a two-day trip."

"Looks like it." Kyle rubbed the scruff on his chin. "Too bad Underkeep isn't an available option. We still need to sail."

Izzy squeezed between us to see the display. "They probably don't have a dove pearl. Looks like the birds take special olives as payment. We were only able to receive a message because it came with its own pearl."

"Still hella useful, though."

Kyle nodded. "What's the message say?"

I handed it over. "Nothing much. The wild king still doesn't want an alliance."

"But he opened the door for one," noted Izzy.

"Maybe, but it's not enough. Here we've been thinking of Shorehome as the only other power capable of standing up to Oakengard. It's the third city, that's true, but we can find other allies. The wildkins would be perfect."

Izzy shrugged. "Their faction defined themselves by being their own people, breaking away from the pagans, and choosing not to fight the battles of others. It's not gonna be easy to convince them to join a war effort."

"Even if the crusaders start a war?"

"There's no evidence they will," she said. "Even after what happened out there, the soldiers were bolstering their defenses. Their sole concern for Cleric Vagram might be genuine."

"Rightly so."

We all nodded, but none of us were convinced. Something was definitely hinky or we wouldn't be sailing out in the morning.

"We need to figure it out," I finally said. "We need to think of a way to convince them."

"Or show them proof," said Izzy.

Kyle shrugged. "Or you guys could just bang again." He chuckled and headed downstairs.

The pixie's eyes went dull. "That's gonna get real old real fast."

"Hope it was worth it," I laughed. I slapped her butt and headed down myself.

1230 Midnight Club

The Wicked Crow wasn't what one would call a respectable establishment. It was barely an establishment, if we were being technical about things. Sure, there was swill on tap which could be exchanged for silver, but in all other respects it more closely resembled a prison camp, only with less discipline.

The mood, in contrast, was markedly different. It was a lively atmosphere. No one was stuck here. This was an escape as opposed to a trap, fun while maintaining its dark edge. Hazing and posturing were commonplace.

Izzy liked it because no one messed with her. She was still the city's resident badass, with more Arena kills than anyone and an undefeated record which I liked to remind her came with an asterisk. Even back when Kyle was a meek whipping boy, he got along fine in the Crow due to his drinking prowess and friendship with Trafford. No one disrespected the salty veteran. He was kind of like the bar's mascot.

I left the group at the table as I played rounds of hopcoin with Dune. Stigg was on my team while Caduceus backed up the ranger.

"Now the trick is," instructed Dune with a cocky saunter, "to keep your eye on the glass, not where you're bouncing the coin." He pitched a silver piece sharply into the corner. It ricocheted off the wood floor and skipped off the lip of a shot glass before clattering beside it.

"Stuff that advice back down your gobhole," chortled my Viking teammate.

Hopcoin was a straightforward game. Four glasses were arranged in a diamond against a corner. The deepest cup, being framed by two walls, was the easiest to score with. Catching that glass won your coin back plus three more off the floor. The two side glasses, with single-walled backboards, were worth five coins. The lead shot glass had no walls and scored you the jackpot: all the collected coins on the floor. That usually marked the end of the festivities.

"Eh," said Dune, stepping aside for Stigg's go. "I'm distracted. All this talk of Oakengard sours my stomach."

"We could actually do something about it," suggested Caduceus. I nodded avidly.

"What, join Talon's quest to talk to the devil? You wanna play the supporting role in that play?"

She snorted. "You know me better than that, boss. I'm not talking about begging for allies, I'm talking about solving the problem. The *real* problem."

"Fuck all!" snapped Stigg. He'd gone for the easy money but had missed the glasses completely. "I swear that coin was bent." I inspected my coin for uniformity just in case he was onto something.

"That's what you always say," remarked the physicker coolly. "Step aside and watch how it's done." Caduceus took careful aim. "You see, the trick is not being an insufferable know-it-all." She skipped the coin off the floor. It rebounded off the wall and almost landed in a side glass. Instead, it skipped out and sank in the fore glass. She hopped up and down excitedly. Even Dune ignored her comment and laughed heartily.

I glumly dropped my coin back into my inventory. "Apparently the real trick is getting lucky."

The winner halted scooping up her winnings to smugly say, "I'd rather be lucky than good."

"That's beers," reminded Dune.

Stigg nodded. "All right, I'll get this round." He hurried to the bar to drown his sorrows.

Errol and the pirates bellowed from a back table and exchanged silver and contraband at the result. From the convoluted exchanges, it appeared they had at least seven side wagers running on the match.

"Hopcoin's overrated," I decided.

Dune grinned. "I agree. That's why I suggested archery."

"Even Kyle wouldn't challenge you in that department."

Caduceus presented her haul and split it with the ranger. She made a point to loudly count the generous pot in front of me, which only encouraged the pirates' laughter. It was good to see them having fun, at least. The voyage had them in high spirits. The Wicked Crow wasn't as rickety and raucous as their Shorehome equivalent, but they'd found a home in the place nonetheless.

That, of course, was part of the problem. If I didn't get these landlocked pirates on the open seas soon, they were bound to find themselves in deeper water after one of their drunken escapades.

Dune twisted his lips thoughtfully and turned to Caduceus. "So you wanna solve the real problem?" he prodded.

She nodded, full of beer and confidence. "I do."

"You're talking about the public bounty Talon unlocked. Bringing in Cleric Vagram."

She winked at him.

"You guys got that quest too?" I asked.

"Sure did. It became available to various questkeepers as soon as you were offered it. Same terms and everything."

"That's not fair."

"What's not fair?" he returned. "I don't see you hunting the dissenter."

"Not yet. It's not gonna be easy. I've seen the guy fight."

"Got your ass kicked, is how I heard it."

"We've been reading up on him," said Caduceus. "Whatever's on the wiki, anyway. Each random encounter over the last month has filled in another juicy detail. A bit of a mental case who thinks he's on a divine mission. He runs heavenly light and has a pair of magical swords, but the real kicker is his gem-encrusted bronze cross. Super healing. Can raise the dead. Why do you think I want him so bad?"

I nodded along. "A pretty accurate summation... except it ignores the hundred-strong catechists at his command. You should join the Black Hats. We're at war with them. I could offer you resources."

Dune chewed his lip. "Do the individual priests have payouts too?" The physicker shook her head. "Then we're not concerned with them." She grinned in agreement.

"Cutthroats." I sighed. "You know I wish you well whatever you do, Dune. I just don't think you've thought this—" I jumped when I realized Crux was standing inches from me. "Dude! Where'd you come from?"

The others laughed until seeing the knife in the thief's hand. It was long and thin, just like Poe's.

"I'm sorry," said Crux, face wrought with distress.

I was so shocked at the betrayal that Dune moved faster than me. He swiped his longbow like a hatchet and brought it down on the master thief's hand. The blade clattered to the floor like a hopcoin. Stigg returned at just the right time. He wrapped an arm around Crux's neck while holding a pitcher of beer in the other.

The Viking growled. "You picked the wrong crew to mess with, boy."

"No!" he cried. "Wait!"

"I'll snap your neck!"

Crux squirmed in the red robe's grip. His black cloak twirled and the next thing we knew, the thief was behind him, knife once again in his hand. Stigg, befuddled by the bundle of cloth left in his headlock, stiffened as the blade touched his neck. To the berserker's credit, the pitcher hadn't spilled a drop of beer.

"Wait," pleaded Crux.

I threw both hands up. "Stop," I said. "Everyone stop."

The crowd paused. Nearby banter quieted. Kyle and Trafford were oblivious, Izzy was passed out on a bench, and Errol and the pirates placed fresh wagers.

I spoke calmly and concisely. "You're a pacifist, Crux. Isn't that right?"

He nodded eagerly. "I'm not here to hurt anybody."

Dune scowled. "Doesn't look that way, brother."

Crux took a slow breath. Slowly, he lifted his hands away. He flipped the dagger and caught it by the blade, offering it up to me. No one made hasty movements as I took the weapon.

[Assassin Needle]
Ineffective in regular combat, this straight knife is ideal for surgical strikes, puncturing deep and true.
+8 Agility
+50% critical hit on sneak attack
+25% stun on sneak attack
+20% Sneak
+20% Hide

Stigg ogled the stats as I did. With a nervous chortle, he downed half the pitcher in six gulps. I was right there with him. I knew from personal experience just how deadly this crit/stun combo was.

Caduceus brandished her bone pick. "How about we see how you like a weapon to *your* neck?"

"Stop," I said. "He's a Black Hat." Dune clenched his jaw and nodded her off. We all watched the thief expectantly. "You have a lot of explaining to do."

"That's what I was trying to do. I came to surrender the knife. To confess."

I swallowed. The thief hadn't been the most upstanding adventurer today. For now, he seemed to be telling the truth. I finally caught Kyle's eye. I jerked my head to the door. He stood and helped Izzy to her feet.

"Sorry for the hassle, Stigg. Dune." I placed a chunk of coin in his hand. "The rest of the beer tonight's on me."

He scoffed. "And what about this guy?"

"It's faction business. As much as I'd welcome your involvement, you don't want it."

He frowned. He was a cocky and outspoken dude, but he was a bro. "It's okay, guys," he said, patting Stigg's back and lowering the physicker's bone pick. "No harm, no foul. You know how Talon's a drama magnet."

I rolled my eyes. "Shall we, Crux?"

The thief quietly strolled to the door. As I followed, the pirates bemoaned their disappointment. I wondered who lost money this time.

The nighttime streets, once we gained distance from the bar, were quieter than usual. At least until Izzy burped.

"Look, guys, I'm riding a unicorn!"

Kyle held Izzy over his shoulder like a sack of potatoes. Her eyes weren't even open.

"Word is you're heading out in the morning," said the thief.

I ignored the prompt. "Start talking."

"All right. But it was never supposed to be a thing. I have no idea how it came to this."

"Who sent you?"

Crux sighed. "Hex and I are Shorehome transplants. You know that. We used to work for Papa Brugo."

"You two are Brothers in Black?!?"

"No. Yes. We were." He pouted. "I'm a thief, so I joined the biggest gang of thieves in my hometown. It was never a huge commitment, just a source of quests. I dragged my sister into it. When everything was going to hell in Shorehome, we fled."

"Without submitting your resignation?"

"Nothing was official. You have to understand, no actual faction exists. To Papa Brugo's continual irritation, the Brothers in Black are nothing more than a loose association. You rep them and they rep you. Put that word on the street and that's all you need in Shorehome."

Kyle butted in with a good question. "Did you know Poe was coming to kill us?"

"No way," swore the thief. "He's an assassin. That's not me. I didn't lie about being a pacifist."

"So what did you lie about?"

"Look, man, I was already here. After Bishop Tannen was kicked out of the city, Brugo sent word that he wanted reports from the inside. Obviously what happens in Stronghold is very important to Shorehome. The crusaders can't get to them without going through here, right?"

"So you were spying on us," I said flatly. "A Trojan horse welcomed into our ranks." I worked my jaw. "You are so lucky right now that Black Hat membership is sitting at fifty even, because if we had a single other member I would kick you out in a heartbeat."

His features strained. "It wasn't like that. When Brugo made the request, it wasn't about you. I wasn't even a Black Hat yet. There was no sabotage. No subterfuge. It was a simple repeatable quest string for public information, which was otherwise hard to come by without access to the hub."

Despite his belated honesty, I was fuming. I felt betrayed. Crux was prescient enough to see that.

"Look," he said, "I deserve it. I deserve everything you wanna do to me. But I'm being straight with you. I wanted to come clean before you left town. To tell you that Hex and I really dig what you're doing in Oldtown. We respect you. You're a good leader, and you can trust us. I swear it."

"Sounds righteous to me," said Kyle.

Izzy burped up some vomit.

"Jeez, baby, take a healing potion." I produced a small vial and upended the red liquid into her mouth.

In moments she shook off the haze and beat on Kyle's back. "Let me down, you lug."

"You're welcome," he snorted.

She nodded, confused. Then she turned to me. "Did you just call me baby?"

I gulped. "Um... Iz?"

"Better." She resumed walking with us as if nothing had happened.

"So you wanna be one of us?" I asked.

Crux nodded enthusiastically.

"Good, then prove it. Tell me everything you know."

"Gladly."

"Did Brugo order the hit?"

He licked his lips in exasperation. "I would tell you if I knew. I don't know anything about that."

"But Poe's from Shorehome."

"Certainly. A freelancer who publicly advertises. He could've been hired from anywhere, though. I don't personally see what

Brugo would gain, not that I'm vouching for him or anything."

I frowned. My inside information was going to be limited.

"And you never compromised the Black Hats?" asked Izzy.

He shook his head. "No way. The first time anything felt wrong was this morning. I received a quest to meet Loras."

That didn't sound normal at all. "Had you informed Brugo that we were headed to Oakengard?"

"There wasn't time. You broadcast it to the faction, anyway. The quest notification didn't pop up until we were in Oakengard. Loras must've sensed our intrusion. We were waiting upstairs while you met the Trinity. One of the keeper guards slyly offered me the quest to meet Loras. It was an official quest, from a saint, that instructed me to keep it to myself." He lowered his head. "I only stole the silver as cover for my absence when you came looking for me. The real reason for my detour was to meet Loras."

I didn't mask my shock as we walked through the Foot on our way to the Dragonperch drawbridge. It was late enough that we weren't bothered. "You ever meet with him before?"

"Never. I don't even know if it had anything to do with Brugo."

"And what did the saint want?"

Crux swallowed uncomfortably. "Well, he wanted me to kill you. He was the one that gave me that overpowered dagger. I objected. I repeated the word pacifist ten times. He didn't want to hear it."

It sounded about right. The daggers packed a punch. A saint cleaning house would have the resources to hand out OP candy.

"He also gave me this." Crux gifted me a metal object.

[Sanctum Bronze Key]
Simple key of gleaming bronze applicable to a single sanctum.

"He wanted me to loot your tower," explained the thief.

Holy shit. We'd lived in Dragonperch for six weeks and half the tower was still locked to us. This key might only open a door or two, but that was better than nothing. Crux handing it over willingly almost proved his loyalty.

"Those keepers gave me a side quest," he added grimly. "They gave me a quest and then they took my fucking sister. I'm dedicated to family. Her... and you guys, if you'll have me. I'll do anything I can to make it up to you."

I nodded absently. Izzy cut in. "Do you have a deadline for looting and assassinating and otherwise betraying your guild?"

He winced under her glare. "Not entirely. Loras is aware I don't have access to Dragonperch, and obviously I can't use the dagger before I use the key."

I chuckled. "That would kind of kill your cover."

"So let's use that," suggested the pixie. "Pretend you're still one of them."

"I pretty much have to anyway," he conceded. "Who knows what they'll do to my sister if I don't?"

I winced. Putting it in that context, Crux was taking a huge risk by *not* betraying us. His sister was perfect leverage, but he was going against her captors by talking to us. No wonder he'd been so lost in thought today. We stopped as the tower drawbridge lowered over the Albula River.

I held out my hand. "I did promise to get her back."

His expression softened and he took my hand. "Thank you, Talon. Thank you. I mean it."

I flipped the key in my hand. "Why don't we go see what this bad boy opens?"

We stepped onto the drawbridge but Crux didn't follow. I gave him a questioning look.

"I... I don't want to see what it opens," said the thief. "I don't want you to think this is some ploy to get inside your tower and into the storeroom. I want you to know you can trust me."

I took a long breath to measure him. "I think I'm a pretty good judge of character, Crux. Come on in. You earned it."

Izzy arched a conspiratorial eyebrow. "Besides, you might need to report on some progress to keep Hex safe."

The deception dawned on the thief and he agreed. The four of us entered and went straight to the locked door.

There were two storerooms on the ground floor. The first had been converted to a stable for Bandit and moved downstairs to the brewery, which itself had moved to the guildhall. The second storeroom was locked. Everybody watched in anticipation as I slid the bronze key into the keyhole.

[Sanctum Bronze Key] applied

The item permanently deleted from my inventory. With the popping of a magic seal, the door clicked open. An atmospheric glow lit up a room containing weapons, armor, and supplies.

"An armory," whispered Kyle in awe.

We strolled among the displayed equipment. All the

materials were exotic: scorched blacksteel, cherry-colored heartwood, even select pieces of angelstone.

"The quality's top of the line," observed Izzy. "I don't see us swapping out our legendary weapons anytime soon, but this puts Stronghold shopkeepers to shame."

"No," I agreed. "This is meant for outfitting an army." I turned to them. "A Black Hat army. With this equipment, even level-5 soldiers can be effective."

Kyle whistled. "That's heavy. But do we *need* an army?"

I cocked my head. "I suppose that depends on the responses from Shorehome and Oakengard."

Crux remained by the door, taking a general inventory of the place without getting too close. He probably didn't want me to suspect him of thievery. With his sticky fingers, I was thankful for the consideration.

I didn't want to stay down here too long myself. It was late and we had a huge quest in the morning. We weren't bound to get upgrades from the armory without a detailed inventory, and there was more of the tower to explore, but a curious object did catch my eye.

A large saddle rested on a wooden support. The leather was intricately stamped but otherwise modest. No jewels or precious metals signified it as an artifact. Even its description was obscure.

[Dusty Saddle]
A well-used war saddle of ancient design.

Despite the lackluster appearance, I was impressed by its

sheer size. That and the fact it was the only one in the armory signified its importance. I reverently traced a finger across the concave seat. "This can't be what I think it is," I whispered.

Izzy examined it. "Well, the tower *is* named Dragonperch. And there's a restored statue of Magnus Dragonrider on the roof."

I blinked slowly. None of us wanted to jinx it by saying it aloud, but we all knew it was possible.

"Bros, you're not gonna believe this," interrupted Kyle. We turned as he held up a dove pearl. "It makes sense that such a utilitarian pearl would be stored here, but didn't we just get one of these?"

He handed it to me and I grumbled. "Just our luck. We lose the bone pearl and get two dove pearls in its place. And we can't trade it back to the wild king 'cause he already has one."

Izzy snorted. "We can't, we can't rightly return Theoderic's gift."

I failed to see the humor.

-- Cutscene --

An everyday thirty-something in Silicon Valley jerked against his straps. He didn't look like a tech guy because he wasn't one. Trimmed red stubble, a physique that was athletic but not strapping, T-shirt and jeans dead center between fashionista and professional dad. He liked Netflix and superhero movies, but he balanced his interests with a wife, son, and a healthy penchant for cycling.

About the only extraordinary thing about him was the fact that he was hooked into a state-of-the-art digital-reality interface.

Which wasn't to say it was like the movies. The man wasn't twirling around a zero-gravity harness pantomiming virtual actions with exaggerated fervor. In fact, his sedentary status was quite the opposite of a photo opportunity. He lay in a simple bed, partially sedated; waist, head, and limbs strapped into place for safety. Conventional electrodes on his body monitored heart rate and other vitals. Even the cutting-edge device itself resembled nothing more than a mini CAT-scan machine that slid over the subject's head.

For the first time, Christian Everett was successfully running an EXSIL. Extrasensory interlink. Equipped with three neurosensors—two for the temples and one at the base of the skull—the EXSIL essentially translated brain impulses into ones and zeroes and carried them across a series of wires into a computer. A literal vacation of the mind.

Christian double-checked the man's vitals. Despite some unexpected muscle stimulation, he had successfully hijacked the brainwaves from the body. The tech CEO sighed long and loud and leaned back into his chair. On this momentous occasion, he couldn't resist a sidelong glance at the solid-state drive on the shelf above his workstation. Christian wiped the dust off it.

But sentiment was for another time.

This was progress.

This was reality.

The drive was attached to a stand-alone backup, with a small screen displaying a debugging console. Christian typed on its attached keyboard.

```
>>Input>> Brain experiencing full immersion.
Body response down to 6%.
```

Christian avidly studied the data logs that would be the key to his breakthrough, occasionally inputting notable observations into the console. Simply mapping the human mind wasn't enough—a cold export of the analog had been possible since his EVR days. The real key was interface. Communication.

The human brain fires neurons at a frequency of 200 per second and at speeds up to 268 miles per hour. Any real-time interface needed to not only accept those electronic requests but be able to translate them into useful data and send a suitable response. And with over 100 billion neurons in a single brain, the task was gargantuan.

When the test was over, Christian powered down the EXSIL and waited as Pete returned to his senses.

"That was the most amazing thing I've ever seen," he reported through a drowsy haze.

Christian smiled. Coming from Pete, that was high praise. The man was absolutely plugged in to entertainment. He'd written for several tech magazines, hosted a popular podcast, and knew what the public wanted. If Pete was impressed by Haven 0.3, the people would follow suit. That was why Christian had just promoted him to his new community relations manager.

"I have to admit," said Pete. "I was hesitant to sign on with Kablammy Games, but this is classic Christian Everett, back to your true genius form. I could never pass up working on something as cool as this. Did you see that AI?"

Christian opened his prepared questionnaire. "I've told you, Pete. It's impossible to see into the simulation from the outside. What you experienced wasn't sight, or hearing, or even touch. There's no view frustum, no near and far clip planes or any of that."

Pete scrunched his face at the programming jargon. Christian unstrapped his head and arms so he could take over the rest.

"It's a neural interface, Pete. You experienced everything just as if you were there. The only way in is through your brain."

Pete sat up, swung his muscled legs off the bed, and rubbed

his wrists. "Okay, but the AI is impressive. Not just real in sight and form. There's some real thinking involved."

Christian glanced at the solid-state drive on his shelf. "It's primitive. Not nearly as advanced as I'd like. But we'll get there. Tell me, before we dive into the standard questions, did any noticeable problems crop up?"

"Just..." Pete scratched the stubble on his cheek. "There were times when it felt like a dream. You know, things were in slow motion, but they weren't. Like maybe it was just me."

"You're perceptive. The world, of course, didn't slow down. The interface is a little laggy. Dropped packets, throughput bottlenecks. Essentially, you were thinking faster than you could act."

"That's exactly what it felt like!"

Christian noted the peculiarity.

> >>Input>> Neural lag due to latent inefficiencies.

The anomaly was thoroughly expected, and as they ran through the questionnaire, the excitement of exactly what he had accomplished grew within him. The live link would still need to be optimized, but that wasn't the end goal. The data he was recording now would take him there.

"I'd love to go back in," said Pete after they were finished.

"We'll pick it up tomorrow. It's important that I process the data. And that you rest."

Pete nodded and stowed his disappointment. "Baby steps."

"As we follow the footprints of giants."

1240 Pirate Adventure

◆━━━━━━◆●◆━━━━━━◆

Crux's newfound secret was something to keep an eye on, and it wasn't just the armory. Izzy was psyched to discover the bronze key's application granted access to a secured closet in the library. A quick inspection uncovered blueprints for some kind of defensive caltrops. There were likely other goodies buried somewhere.

That said, we had more important matters at play. Starting tomorrow bright and early was a must. Passive health and skill points replenished according to rest. I'd pushed my limits enough in the past to see ability debuffs from fatigue firsthand. Without being sure how much rest we'd get on our impending voyage, I made sure to enforce lights out after just a bit more exploration. This involved peeling my girlfriend away from books and locking up her new secret stash.

We all woke up surprisingly shiny. Izzy had taken a potion, and Kyle and I were seasoned pros by this point. While the roguish band of pirates I collected hadn't shown similar levels of discipline—or personal hygiene—they eagerly reported for duty.

Nothing would keep them off the water.

The party was four strong including Errol. Trafford often made up the final member, but I charged him with watching the headquarters. The salty bastard made a show of protest but I suspected he was secretly relieved. Trafford didn't take to the sea.

Bravo Team also remained behind. Lash vehemently objected in what was the most awkward meeting ever. She was still sore with me over dressing her down. I explained the importance of keeping the business with Nooner and Chadwick from erupting into war and left it at that.

Everything else accounted for, I sealed up Dragonperch. Bandit and her new companion Artax would watch the place. We took the last skiff up the Albula River and into the tunnel beneath the wide wall of Stronghold. I didn't personally have the keys to the north river gates so Gladius and the city watch helped us out. We joined the rest of the crew aboard the boat waiting outside the city.

Sunlight beamed across the deck of the flagship of the Black Hat navy. The frigate was technically the only seafaring vessel in the navy, but who was counting? Errol rejoiced as the wind hit his face. He scaled the mast to the crow's nest and swung between sails and did other things expected of flashy pirate captains.

As with Lash, Errol Oates was vital to the morale of the Black Hats. Until recently, his band of twenty pirates had made up half the membership. We were now running with a skeleton crew of ten so Trafford wouldn't have my head. He needed grunt work to finish the vault, and the boat needed a crew to swab the decks and sing pirate ditties. I brought the two pirate parties of five into our brigade and hoped the ones staying behind wouldn't mutiny. As an extra bit of insurance, I'd promised them free vouchers to the brothel pending a full day's work. Everyone was happy. Ish.

Unlike Lash, however, Errol was a good friend. He was a knave and a scoundrel through and through, replete with a questionable past and link to Shorehome, but he was undoubtedly an ally.

The *Cutter* was a fine vessel, too. Four cannons, a harpoon station, something called a turbo sail, and enough barrels of grog to make a salty wench blush. We winded downriver toward the northern sea.

The going was slow, but not as slow as it could've been. Shorehome was an easy two days' journey on horseback, including a dicey stretch through the volatile Ashen Moor. Not only would sailing avoid dangerous terrain and marauders, but we'd arrive in just under a day. There was no question about it: this was a superior form of transportation when available.

After some time, the mainland ended and a horizon of blue took over. The river mouth widened and we joined the rough waters of the sea. Salt air greeted our lungs and a powerful breeze filled the sails. The experience was breathtaking.

"Ain't she grand?" beamed Errol, hooking an arm over my shoulder.

"The *Cutter*? Yeah."

"Course she is. I was talkin' 'bout the sea."

I shook my head because I didn't have words.

The admiral's puffy white shirt flapped in the wind. "This be the life, I says. Pure freedom."

I chuckled. "I can't believe I've never sailed an extended voyage with you before."

"Ar. The open seas be in the heart o' ev'ry pirate."

"It's an incredible passion."

"Ain't a passion so much as oxygen is."

I nodded. Remind me never to keep the scoundrels off the high seas for so long again.

Once we made deep water, the *Cutter* bore east. Errol's commands were colored with flavor that included several insults and at least three mentions of rum. I wondered how any of the scallywags knew what he was talking about at all. Whatever worked.

Our goals were twofold: Spread word of the possible threat from Oakengard and find out what Lucifer knew of the situation. I had a feeling the self-proclaimed devil would be open to conversation. Papa Brugo's help would come more reluctantly. He was the proud head of the largest gang of criminals in the city, the bearer of the Squid's Tooth, and the Protector of Shorehome.

Oh, yeah—and there were decent odds he was responsible for the attempt on my life. It wasn't lost on me that Saint Loras was the one who'd given Brugo his power in the first place.

The dark thoughts, for the moment, were easy to shrug off. Bustling wind, a draw distance farther than I'd ever seen, and the soothing sound of water against the *Cutter's* hull.

Soothing, at least, until the pirates started singing. Numerous tunes with personal anecdotes ranging from gallant swashbuckling to sea monsters—and even a mention of our local brothel hero.

"Grom never rebuffed a woman in need,
Conquests from fouler t' foulest.
While his standards are endlessly questioned,
No one doubts his sexual prowess."

Errol wiped a proud tear from his eye. "Sailin' brings out the creativity in me boys."

"If you say so," I muttered.

"Don't knock it, Talon. It passes the time. When yer on the open sea, that's half the battle."

"I guess you have a point." I surveyed the endless waves. "You guys must have a song for everything."

"Ye don't know the half o' it."

I crossed my arms and sidled beside him. "Any chance there's a ditty about a brave explorer who single-handedly slayed a cyclops?"

"Nah. Killin' titans be overrated. Besides, none o' us witnessed the event." His eyes lit up. "But there's this one about Grom an' a lass who was blessed with three shapely—"

I stormed away as Errol engaged in a pantomime that involved a bear hug, a brassiere, and some kind of glazed confectionary. There was no accounting for pirate taste.

I spent the next hour assessing the capabilities of the ship and the crew. I surveyed the deck and the quarters below. The pirates relaxed into familiar comfort once we were at cruising speed. They threw down dominoes and dice and heartily laughed, yet every one to a man remained vigilant. Eyes in the backs of their heads. The crew was ready for any and every emergency, and I had the feeling their readiness didn't come from training but experience.

By the time the novelty of the surroundings wore thin, a few dolphins began flanking the vessel. We watched from the deck as jubilant porpoises playfully skipped over the waves in merry greeting.

"Wonder what kind of XP they give," pondered Kyle.

"I don't think I could bring myself to kill something so innocent," I said.

He shrugged. "Yeah. Probably drop crappy loot anyway."

The show lasted a good while. It seemed to me the sea experience wasn't interrupted by many passing ships. Just as we settled into enjoying each other's company, a few of the lead dolphins squeaked in alarmed bursts. The group of fins veered sharply from the *Cutter* and dove. In the span of ten seconds, our escort abandoned us.

"Don't mind them," said Errol at our back. "They never cross the Singing Spires."

I took my eyes off the water to scan his face. "Any reason for concern?"

"Nay. But ye best wax yer ears all the same." The admiral handed each of us a pliable ball of goop.

> **[Sailor Wax]**
> Thick multipurpose goop for sailing.

I blinked dumbly. "Extremely informative item descriptions lately."

"The stuff has too many uses t' list, an' most o' them be trade secrets."

Errol took a healthy glob and applied it into an ear. He noted our befuddlement and explained. "Either wax yer ears or tie down. It's yer arse if ye don't."

My gaze shot to the horizon. The *Cutter* was bearing toward a series of land masses, spires jutting from the sea like pillars. They formed a porous wall that stretched from the coast across our easterly path.

"The Singing Spires," I grumbled. "Are they dangerous? Can't we just go around them?"

Errol paused, one ear still unplugged. "This be the sea. Everythin's dangerous. An' ye can sail 'round anythin' if ye be committed enough."

"Then shouldn't we sail around?"

Errol shrugged. "Accordin' to the ladies, I've always been lackin' in commitment."

The pirate crew guffawed and started plugging their ears. Others jumped and cursed, pointing to distant waves.

"Undine!" they yelled.

"What?" asked Errol.

"Undine!"

"I can't hear a damn thin' ye be sayin'!"

Izzy lumbered over and unplugged his ear. "Not with this gunk in your ears, you nitwit."

"That be *Captain* Nitwit to ye."

Kyle scrunched his brow. "I thought you were an admiral now."

"I can be both."

I sighed and hurried to the handrail.

Fins again, only these weren't the soft gray of the porpoises. Blue-green scales glinted between water crests. Two figures, then three. Humanoids with thick teal skin and long fish tails.

"Mermaids!" spat Errol. "Why didn't anybody say so?"

Izzy rolled her eyes and counted to ten.

I grimaced. "Are they a threat?"

"They harry sailors close to shore." Errol equipped an extended hooked pike, polished to a fine sheen and traced with fancy runes. He was a fan of all types of blades, but this one was ridiculous. The rest of the crew cackled and brandished similar weapons, as if this were routine. "Mermaids be fast swimmers an' ruthless marauders, with claws sharp enough t' gut a whale. Ye cut one down, two more swim into their place. And when— not if—they draw blood, yer wounds will wither with sickness to the point that, if ye were not dead, ye'd wish it so."

My jaw dropped in horror. "Oh my God, then why are you laughing?"

Errol showed his teeth. "Because 'tis been weeks since we sniffed a good fracas!" The pirate patted my back, spun his boots with swagger, and called to his crew. "Hearty-ho, men. 'Tis hull-cleanin' time!"

The sea burst from under us. A mermaid shot halfway up the hull before hooked claws spiked into the *Cutter*. Bloodshot eyes fixed upon us.

"Look," said Kyle, "nipples!"

> **[Undine]**
> 100 Health

Clak, clak, clak.

Matted paws rapped the wood as the mermaid scaled as deftly as a monkey, reaching the handrail in the span of seconds. A pair of pirates crossed hooked poles in a supporting V and caught her in the chest. Besides opening a nasty wound and dishing significant damage, they uprooted the mob from the hull. She plummeted downward and disappeared with a splash.

Kyle shrugged. "Anyone else have a chub right now?"

Izzy spun the winter staff in her hands. "I'm surrounded by idiots."

"What? They don't look so bad to me."

Ten more undine erupted from the water and clamped to the boat. Pirates cried in alarm from the other side as the crew split to evenly defend the deck.

Izzy scowled. "And now we're outnumbered two to one." She raised curled fingers and icicles rained from above.

> [Izzy] cast Icicle Blast
> Cold resistance!
> [Izzy] dealt 12 damage to [Undine]

"Damn sea creatures." Despite the modest damage, the frost mage managed to dislodge a few from the hull. The pirates cheered at the sight. Several of them banded together to pitch another two enemies back to the watery depths.

"Keep it up," I urged, picking up on their strategy. "Killing them is secondary. We need to focus on keeping them off the boat."

"Now yer catchin' on," said Errol. His impressive weapon swung down and struck a hapless mermaid like a nine iron.

I drew the dragonspear and locked eyes with the nearest mob. The long weapon was ideally suited for this kind of combat. Unfortunately, my skills were traversal based. Dashing, vaulting, and scaling didn't do me a whole lot of good as a static defender.

The merman below me lunged. Being unfamiliar territory, I didn't take chances. I shoved the spear straight down and activated deadshot, pretty much guaranteeing a center-mass hit.

> You dealt 57 damage to [Undine]

The mob yelped and plunged into the water. I barely had time to recover before two more came at me.

This time I tried a normal attack. Scoring a hit was easy enough, but the mermaid managed to hang on. Her companion leapt past her and took a swipe at me. With the higher ground and the railing between us, I easily backstepped.

Another rain of icicles slammed into the threats. She fell away and the original one I'd hit hung on by only one hand. I spiked the spear into her knuckles. The damage was low but accompanied by a snapping sound. One of her fingers was severed. The single claw remained embedded in the *Cutter* as the rest of the undine fell away.

"We're fightin' 'em off," called out the captain. "Keep it up an' continue full speed ahead!"

Men on the other side screamed in alarm as a few mobs reached the handrail. Izzy rushed to their aid. Meanwhile, Kyle braced his double crossbow at an oncoming wave. He let loose a custom glass bolt filled with oily fluid. It hit the face of a muscular merman and exploded. The *Cutter* shook as fire washed over the hull.

```
Critical Hit!
Fire weakness!
[Kyle] dealt 101 damage to [Undine]
[Undine] is defeated
27 XP awarded
```

The crispy remains toppled to the sea, leaving black scorches on the boat.

"Watch the area o' effect!" berated Errol. He leaned over the side and assessed the damage. Flames clung to the hardened hull of the *Cutter*.

"But—"

"I'll not be havin' fire aboard me vessel. Do it again, an' ye be goin' overboard."

Although the attack had startled the group of undine, the *Cutter* was now on fire. Errol sprinted to the helm and screamed, "Hard t' port, men! Buckle down!"

Select crew members broke off the defense and manned the sails as Errol spun the wheel. The entire ship lurched sideways with impressive response. Kyle tumbled ass over teakettle as the entire deck sloped toward our handrail. The port hull sank into the sea. No match for the salt water, the flames immediately sizzled out. The fire was quenched.

The downside to the extreme maneuver was that it left us gripping the handrail ten feet above the water surface. Undine burst from the ocean, flew over our heads, and landed directly on the sloped deck above us. Errol's eyes widened at his miscalculation. He immediately righted the wheel, but the damage was done.

Mob and human alike steadied themselves as the *Cutter* leveled out. The portside hull lifted from the ocean, no longer aflame but now littered with a tapestry of mermaids, hanging like barnacles.

"This has gotta be worth a pirate ditty," I muttered.

Errol shook his head firmly. "Nah, ain't bleak enough."

"No worries," I spat. "This is gonna get worse before it gets better."

Kyle swapped out his crossbow for a sword. Errol and I waved our long weapons outward as we squared off against the undine already on deck.

1250 Reel Fishing

Claws raked a nearby pirate. True to Errol's word, the man's belly split open. The blow wasn't immediately lethal, but it carried a healthy DoT. Worse, the pain nearly immobilized the man. He dropped his pike and flailed on the deck. A glittering fish tail twitched in satisfaction.

"Man the rails!" ordered Errol. "The rails!" He shoved his men to the port side as a legion of undine threatened to board his vessel.

The ones already on deck were determined to subvert the effort. They focused on the distracted defenders.

I triggered dash and sped into the fray, slicing two mermaids and sending a warning to the others. Kyle joined my side and Errol flanked the enemies. We were gonna buy the crew time, and if the undine didn't like it, they'd need to do something about it.

Serpentine fish tails slithered across the deck. They came at us whole hog. I waited for one to wind up an attack and activated my crossblock. I turned the easy parry into a spinning blow and answered with a body strike.

Combo!
You dealt 39 damage to [Undine]

Errol had saved a flashier move for a group of three. Thinking they'd easily overwhelm him en masse, they closed in.

[Errol] used Thousand Blades

His giant pike blurred into a cone before him, one blade transformed to a thousand, shredding all unfortunate souls caught in the high-level skill.

"Ouch!" yipped Kyle. He spun to the deck hard and threw up his guard.

I lunged past him and swiped low. The dragonspear bowled into the attacking mermaid's body. Glistening scales slipped on the wet deck and she toppled over. I took advantage of the stun notification and impaled the beast.

Critical hit!
You dealt 62 damage to [Undine]
[Undine] is defeated
27 XP awarded

"It burns!" screamed Kyle. He produced a health flask.

"Fight through it," I urged.

He chugged the potion before I could further object. His wound disappeared and his face sagged in relief.

I spun to the remaining threats. Two more undine on deck,

but the real trouble was the number overtaking the railing. "Izzy, we need crowd control!"

The pixie swung her winter staff and clotheslined a merman scaling the opposite railing. As he tumbled off the ship, she hurried to our wall. "Everyone behind me!" She pitched down her legendary staff and a rune overlaid the deck beneath her.

I recognized the attack and dragged the pirates behind her. Two had already succumbed to their wounds. The undine were spilling over the sidewalls.

Sleet storm activated a full blizzard in the blink of an eye. Gale-force winds launched the enemies off the slippery deck. Chunks of hail took care of the more stubborn guests. The sea creatures may have been resistant to cold, but this was a legendary once-a-day spell that dished plenty of force in addition to damage. The XP from fallen enemies piled in.

I didn't rest on my laurels. We still had two undine on deck and safely behind the blizzard. I defended Izzy's back. Errol engaged one enemy but the other merman eyed me sharply. Midnight-blue features twisted at the sight of his fallen men. The crown of coral on his head hinted at his station.

"You'll pay for this," he spat. Shoulder muscles rippled as he seemed to grow larger.

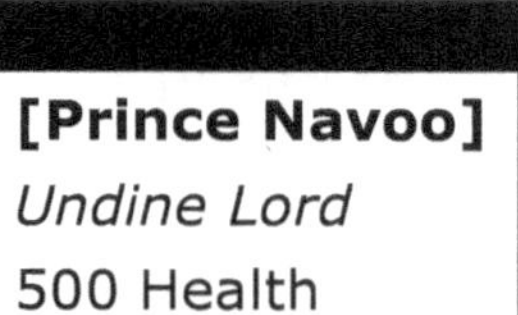

I was taken aback by the surprising notification. We weren't prepared to fight a mini-boss. We still had our hands full with the scrubs. I waited for my dash to recharge, but Navoo struck first—quick, like a snake.

Instead of attempting a conventional block, I squared the spear to his chest and braced the handle. It took all of the lunging prince's strength to keep from impaling himself. Strong hands snatched the length of spear as the point punctured his thick skin. His momentum carried him forward, but my boots couldn't hold on the slick deck. Despite my best efforts, his strength outmatched mine and I was on my heels.

As we both sped toward the handrail, I watched the timer on my dash. Four seconds. Three seconds. I readied for the skill that would reverse the merman's charge.

Then I noticed the prince's mistake and forgot about my dash.

Navoo spat screaming death as he shoved me toward the edge. At the last second, I dropped the dragonspear's handle and planted it against the base of the railing. Finally the unstoppable force met the immovable object. Instead of going against the undine's charge, I pulled the tip of the spear into the air, yanking it vertically and lifting the enemy off the ground. I chuckled as the lofty prince launched far over my head.

"Ha! Now THAT is worth a song."

"Mmm," hedged Errol, "methinks not. 'Twas an act o' cowardice more than bravery."

I spread my arms in disbelief as a rocket of dark blue sailed deep into the ocean. That had been clever, not cowardly. Prince Navoo was still alive, unfortunately, but the thirty undine scaling the hull were a more pressing priority.

"Unfurl the turbo sail!" commanded Errol. He had just cut down the remaining merman and didn't like the assessment of the battlefield. While the starboard hull appeared under control, we didn't have enough men to defend the port.

Crew members broke away to follow the captain's orders. Kyle swapped back to his crossbow, this time loading it with corrosive bolts. They worked well to harry the climbers. They wouldn't kill anyone but the heavy damage over time was a welcome distraction.

Our frost mage was struck with a genius idea. She ran the length of the ship and iced the top of the hull. Several overeager mermaids failed to slow their advance. Claws scratched away loose ice and they lost their grips and fell.

The next wave of mobs was smarter. They chipped at the ice before advancing. Izzy's barrier was a welcome reprieve, but it wasn't a long-term solution. Even with the scurvy pirates swinging their pikes, we'd soon be overwhelmed again.

"One more minute for the turbo sail," announced Grug.

I didn't know what he was working on, but I knew we didn't have that kind of time. I hissed and eyed the surroundings, finally finding a way to put my traversal skills to use in defending the ship. I grabbed a rope hanging off the mast and looped it around my forearm, making sure to eyeball an appropriate length of slack. Then I sprinted to the fore of the *Cutter* and hopped on the handrail.

"What are you doing?" cried Izzy in alarm.

I smiled. "Something I've always wanted to do." Still carefully balanced, I raised the dragonspear overhead and let loose my inner pirate. "Come on, ye scallywags! I'll not allow a single serpent on this ship or I'll give up a year's worth of grog!"

The crew watched me uncertainly.

I blinked and added, "Ar!"

They cheered and I dropped off the side of the boat and toward the ocean. As the rope went taut on my arm, I swung with the line, planted my boots against the outer hull, and got the perfect chance to use a new skill.

Undine eyes widened as I activated wall run and charged past them along the length of the *Cutter*. The dragonspear plucked mob after mob away. I swept through their ranks, thinning their numbers and causing chaos. The undine above me found themselves flanked. The ones below reached up to strike. It was a glorious move that caught them totally unawares, but as I neared the middle of the vessel I found my charge slowing. The enemies moved in.

Still pushing wall run to its limits, I reeled the spear in and simultaneously triggered dash and tornado spin. I twisted on the rope like a circular saw, shooting through and dislodging anything that came near me.

Crown Unlocked: **Tasmanian Devil**
Take out a line of enemies with a charging spin attack.
1000 XP awarded

The rope took me upward at the end of the ship and my boots triumphantly returned to the handrail. I took great pleasure admiring my swath of destruction. The undine had barely known what hit them. Unfortunately, Errol had missed the whole thing.

"Brace yerselves!" warned the captain. "Turbo sail ahoy!"

"That doesn't even make sense," I complained.

A huge orange sail unfurled, displaying a sigil of a red arrow.

"Uh-oh." I dove to the deck and grabbed something solid.

Buffeting wind immediately caught the sail and the *Cutter* lurched forward. Practiced as they were, even a few crew members slipped. Izzy gripped Kyle's arm as the brewmaster tumbled once more.

"I'm getting real sick of sea travel," said our heavily armored roommate.

"Not a fan of the great outdoors?" teased Izzy.

In reply, Kyle puked a gout of green bile. At the exact same moment, the *Cutter* engaged into turbo and doubled its already impressive speed. Kyle's puke streamed through the air like a bullet-time contrail from the *Matrix*. I dove under as the projectile sped past my face. We were flying so fast the discharge never even hit the deck. My eyes followed it behind us as it splashed into the sea and on several unlucky mermaids.

They were lucky compared to the undine attached to the hull. As the boat partially lifted to skim the water, the straggling enemies screeched as the ultra-speed ripped them away. They sailed through the air and tumbled haplessly into our volatile wake.

The wind flapped against my stupid grin. "I could get used to this."

The warp drive lasted for a full minute before expiring. The orange sail rolled up and the hovering *Cutter* sliced the water as its momentum slowed. The vessel settled lower into the sea, and the drag felt like time slowing down. Errol, however, had no time to waste.

"Land ho!" he shouted, spinning the ship's wheel. "Man yer battle stations! We're breachin' the Spires!"

A mass of red rock stretched to the sky above. The *Cutter* bowed to the side as Errol hurried to avoid grounding it. We narrowly avoided total wreckage. As soon as we were level again, Errol jerked the ship the other direction.

I watched in awe as we entered a field of gargantuan columns. Water crashed against their jagged edges, beautiful and unrelenting at the same time. It made a great metaphor for the sea as a whole. I let the crew do their work as I appreciated the sight. A haunting beauty overtook me, and in the recesses of my mind I could hear a captivating song.

A maiden's voice carried over the waves. Innocence and peace washed through my being. Men and women bustled all around me, but I only concerned myself with the wonder of it all.

This was a good place. I wondered what it was like to live out here on the spires. And who was the woman with the sultry voice?

When I stepped toward the railing, strong hands clapped my shoulders.

"Fool!" snapped Errol. "We strayed into siren territory quicker than I thought. Ye need t' wax up!"

He stuffed goop in my ears and everything went dull. The wisping of the breeze, the crashing of the waves, and the barks of the men. More importantly, the lulling melody was also silenced. I shook the lethargy from my head and appraised the deck.

Izzy and Kyle were similarly puzzled but safe. The rest of the crew stood with weapons ready. I started to ask a question. When my voice came out muffled and unnoticed, I switched to party chat.

Talon: *Okay, what's next?*
Errol: *Now comes the true test...*

The captain confidently strode back to the helm of the ship.

Errol: *The Spires be the territory o' the sirens.*

1260 Let's Sing

The silence was jarring. If the siren's song was a dreamscape, the absence of it was otherworldly. The *Cutter* drifted between the spires at a slow clip, flaccid sails struggling to catch more than a whisper of wind. I paced the length of the deck gripping my spear and checking the hull.

> **Errol:** *Worry not 'bout the undine. Sirens be close cousins but not nearly so vicious. They kill by makin' you tired o' life.*
> **Talon:** *And we're safe as long as we don't hear their song?*
> **Errol:** *Aye, safe enough.*
> **Kyle:** *That doesn't sound so bad.*

Izzy and I fired a look of warning at him. You'd think by now the man would learn to stop jinxing us like that. He shrugged.

We waited as the ship strayed forward on calm water. My eyes jumped from spire to spire. We were in a forest of them, and they were much more daunting up close. Between their density and our ponderous speed, we were gonna be here a while.

Izzy: *Look!*

She pointed ahead to an especially wide spire. While the bulk of it stretched upward, the land mass widened at the base. Pale naked women salted the low ground. The group came in all sizes, with a dizzying mix of lady legs, bird legs, and fish tails.

Kyle: *All these eligible ladies, all trying to kill us. I never thought I'd say this, but I'm sick of boobs. Ooh, check out that one. She's hot!*

I chuckled. The gaggle of women were intent on us but resigned to relaxing on the coastline. Some played harps, others kissed each other and winked. It was a teenager's wet dream. I didn't see a real danger to the crew, though.

One of the pirates stripped down to his loincloth.

Grom: *Nice knowin' ya, mates!*

I lunged to grab him but he pounced off the boat. The squirrelly pirate was too fast. He splashed down below.

Talon: *Man overboard!*

The crew laughed.

> **Grug:** *Don't mind Grom. We always lose him in the Spires.*

By the time Grom resurfaced for air, three sirens converged on him. One of the women lowered her head underwater. He plucked the wax from his ears and gave in to supreme pleasure. A siren rubbed his back while another pulled his face into her floating bosom. All the while, their lips moved in unison to an unheard song.

> **Kyle:** *Okay, I know I've said this before, but that REALLY doesn't look so bad.*

I wordlessly pointed to an alcove away from the rocky beach. A humanoid skeleton lay there like a warning. My eyes lit up as something sparkled between the ivory remains. I'd seen one of those before.

> **Talon:** *That's a bone pearl.*

I leaned over the handrail. Babes and boobs were one thing, but in this world loot was the greatest temptation.

Izzy: *You sure?*
Talon: *That's definitely a bone pearl. Same as the one we gifted back to the wild king.*
Izzy: *It's better to leave it.*
Talon: *We might not see another pearl for a month.*
Izzy: *There are twenty naked ladies between it and you.*
Talon: *Are you trying to convince me to stay or go?*

She visibly grumbled. I checked on Grom. He was merrily swaying in the water as a woman straddled him and two more held him up. His face went under the surface here and there and no one appeared too concerned either way. They never prevented him from coming up for air.

Talon: *Admiral, you're sure the sirens don't actively kill people?*
Errol: *Sure as me sword be sharp. Ye'll die o' pleasure 'fore they lay a hand t' harm ye."*

The *Cutter* lulled and drifted into the shallows, stalling all progress.

Talon: *We're not doing anything else here. I have to go for it.*
Izzy: *Talon, don't!*

I grabbed my trusty swinging rope and scaled over the railing. The weight of every siren's gaze was immediately on my back. Was I making a mistake?

This was a game world, I told myself. Everything was a challenge. Every challenge came with a reward. There had to be a point to all of this. And if the bitches attacked me, I'd wipe out every last one of them on this stupid rock.

I carefully lowered myself past the top of the hull. Izzy's ice was still there and being half melted just made it more slippery. I passed a thawing mermaid finger embedded in the wood. The spell had frozen it to the side and protected it during our turbo gear. I grimaced as I peeled it from the hull and tossed it to the rock below. A siren moved out of the way as it bounced beside her. If the severed finger otherwise bothered her, she didn't show it.

I thought about making the same leap but wasn't sure enough of my footing. Although I'd been hoping to keep my boots dry, by the time I lowered myself a safe enough distance it was clear I was getting wet. I leapt to the shallows just as a rogue wave battered my back and sent me under.

Sand whipped my face as my foot slipped further. One second I was worried about embarrassment and the next I realized I might be in trouble. When a light hand caught my wrist and pulled me to shore, I *knew* I was in trouble.

A tanned beach beauty stood over me while I crawled ashore on hands and knees. My face was right in her cooch and she didn't back away or anything. Based on my entirely evidentiary inspection—for science—her lady parts appeared completely normal. I blinked and looked up.

The siren seductively smiled down between very large breasts. There were no tan lines, of course, and her skin was perfect. Hard nipples poked out between a wiry blouse of fishnet hugging her curves.

I hurriedly ensured the wax was still safely in my ears. I sighed when I felt it.

The siren's long lashes blinked at me expectantly.

"Uh, nice to meet you," I offered.

Through the earwax, my voice sounded distant, like an old recording. When she giggled and replied, I was comforted that I didn't hear a thing.

Izzy: *Get a good enough look?*

I turned away and pushed to my feet.

Talon: *I was just checking her for weapons.*
Kyle: *Lol, well I hate to tell you this, but from where I'm standing I can see two giant bazookas.*
Talon: *You're not helping, Kyle.*
Errol: *Look more t' me like glass-cuttin' pillows.*
Talon: *Guys, please. Help a brother out.*
Izzy: *It's kinda impossible to help you out when these tacky sirens aren't leaving anything to the imagination. You're worried about weapons? They couldn't hide a thumb tack among the lot of them.*

I peeked at the dream boobs again and reminded myself that they were all show. I had something much better.

Talon: *Fine, I was looking at boobs. It's kind of hard not to. Don't worry, Izzy. She sure is sexy, but you're smexy.*

I turned to my girlfriend on the deck of the *Cutter* and winked.

Kyle: *Izzy's not Mexican, she's Japanese.*
Izzy: *Way to miss the point, jackass. It means I'm smart, which is more than we can say about you.*

I stepped past the pouting beauty and climbed the rocky shore. Up a short hill was the skeleton and the bone pearl. All around me, female lips moved in unison to a silent song. I checked on Grom. He was now onshore having the time of his life in a literal pile of grabby women. The whole thing looked like a Renaissance painting.

"Wow, his sexual prowess really is legendary. I gotta step up my game."

On the way up, two women basked in the sun, fish tails and hips swaying like the current. They sang and smiled at each other. It was sweet.

"Nice to meet you," I mumbled. I tried to move past but one rolled into the arms of the other, long fish body blocking my path. The two sirens started making out. The one on top lowered her kisses down the other's neck, to her breasts, then stomach, then...

"No offense," I said, "but fish scales kinda gross me out." I flashed a pleasant nod and hastily stepped over the gyrating fish body.

This was almost too easy. The ladies frowned at each other. One turned and called out. Another woman in the background ran to get something or someone. I equipped the dragonspear and continued.

The tension evaporated when the woman returned and presented me with two naked dude-sirens. I arched an eyebrow as they gripped each other's dongs.

I grunted in exasperation. "I'm not gay just because I don't wanna have freaky fish sex!"

> **Izzy:** *Okay, now THOSE are military grade!*

I turned to the boat and had a hard time catching her attention because it was glued to the boy toys. I rolled my eyes and stowed my weapon.

> **Kyle:** *Huh, male sirens. They've got impressive technique.*
> **Izzy:** *Technique is learned. Those guys were born with it.*
> **Talon:** *Equal-opportunity sex addicts. Everyone happy now?*

I stormed past the half-baked temptation. Next up, a woman with two stork legs hopped close and winked suggestively. Her feathered backside flared in a presentation of colors.

"That's even further out of my comfort zone."

I sidestepped the stork woman and scaled the rock path. I was back on track. No temptations worth being tempted by. This was a silly place, when it came down to it. Magic songs were one thing but, past that, the island just required a bit of willpower.

A pint-sized girl hopped closer on chicken legs. She had a human head but most of her body was feathered and she had wings instead of hands. She was just a kid, and something was bothering her. She spoke urgently and looked frightened.

I frowned. She was trying to tell me something.

"I... I can't hear you."

She furrowed her brow and spoke again. She urgently motioned me forward.

Izzy: *What's going on down there?*

I checked the boat. The last slope of rocks partially blocked line of sight to me.

Talon: *This... little girl... wants something, I think.*

Izzy: *Ignore her, Talon. The whole island is a trap.*

Talon: *I know that. But...*

Something about the kid's expression rang true. She didn't seem old enough to be a savvy actress. I nodded and stepped toward her. She immediately took off down a path leading away from the bone pearl.

> **Talon:** *I think she needs my help.*
> **Kyle:** *Protect that sailor wax or you'll die, bro.*
> **Kyle:** *Happily, perhaps, but you'll die.*

I advanced carefully. The chicken girl excitedly ran back and forth, urging me to pick up the pace down a canyon path. It wasn't long before we reached a thorny bush with a naked lady caught inside. She was thin and wholly human except for a cat tail that whisked back and forth in discomfort.

I huffed. The woman and the girl both spoke, but I shook my head. I didn't even wanna hear what was going on. I was now completely out of sight of my shipmates. It was obvious the lady was stuck. Sharp thorns had drawn blood across her back and legs.

Okay, I was gonna help her. I drew my trusty whittling knife and cut away a tangle of weed, extricating the woman while keeping my guard up. The little girl watched patiently from the side. Two minutes later, I pulled the siren from the bush and gently laid her on the ground.

She was pretty, of course. A little older, but a tight body I couldn't help but notice due to her unabashed lack of modesty. She pointed to a large thorn in her foot. Contrary to their usual assertive and confident nature, this one was spooked.

I chuckled and kneeled. Very carefully, I plucked the thorn

from her flesh. It was a solid thing, three inches long and sharp as a hair. How was that for a thumb tack?

I smiled at the little girl and handed it to her. "You see? That's it." I stood to return to the path but the woman grabbed my hand. She jerked her head to her lap.

I saw it. Another thorn. This one was way up her inner thigh. The siren spread her legs and pleadingly pulled me near.

I swallowed. This was a little closer to lady tang than I was hoping to get, but the woman seemed earnest. The girl watched with wet eyes. After going this far, I didn't want to let them down.

Okay. I took a breath and braced a hand on the woman's trembling thigh. Her muscles tensed. The contact was more intimate than it had a right to be. I traced my other hand up her leg and set my fingers on the thorn. Tension built as her body went completely stiff. I yanked that thorn out and pulled away.

The woman's face washed with relief. She kissed my hand and avidly expressed thanks. I nodded and backed away, desperately trying to avoid any personal connection with these creatures. As the woman massaged her inner thigh, I hurried back the way I'd come.

Seemingly as a reward for my good deed, no one else beset my path to the skeleton. I inspected the bones carefully. Didn't see an immediate cause of death.

This place...

I looted the body.

> **[Bone Pearl]**
> Polished orb with ivory swirls, but inert.

Worth it.

I descended the hill of rock as quickly as I could. The sirens were out in full force, of course. Something about me leaving made them jittery and sad. They moved into my path as if they hadn't seen a man their entire lives, but that was clearly not true.

"Why don't the male sirens have sex with the female sirens?" I wondered.

Thrashing on the coastline caught my attention. Women straddled Grom's waist and face, each hand rubbing a different siren's body—there was even a guy tickling his balls.

> **Grom:** *Woo! I'm king of the world!!!*

> [Grom] is dead!
> [Grom] has left your party

I recoiled and looked up at the crew, all watching from the handrail. I turned back to Grom and blinked. Whoa. Literal death by *snu snu.*

Time to make like a fart and blow this hole.

As I hurried to the coastline, Errol lowered my rope down. The only thing between me and it was a short trudge through shallow water.

And the bombshell beauty who just surfaced. It was the

tanned woman with the fishnet blouse. She was busty, shivering wet, smoking hot, and busty. Yes, it needed to be said twice.

I couldn't help one last longing look at the voluptuous woman. Part of me thought Grom had the right idea. A joyous death and a respawn wasn't the end of the world. Hell, with *that* fishnet outfit straining against *that* chest, it was almost worth the shattering XP cost. But I didn't want to get Izzy jealous, even if she *totally* deserved it. I didn't wanna die either but Izzy was the bigger problem.

I stepped into the water and the beauty closed on me, singing a song I couldn't hear. She bowed her head in thanks. The sirens as a whole seemed appreciative, if perturbed at my departure. I wondered if they secretly wanted someone to look past their sexual attributes. It was like I passed some kind of test.

I stiffened as the siren pressed against me. It was her nipples first, then the entire cushion of her breasts. She kissed my cheek lightly.

I cleared my throat. "You're welcome?"

With her lips still on my cheek, she spoke. A faint sound carried through my ears. A melody, sad but joyous, and more mesmerizing than the sexiest skin. If only slightly.

Oh my God. Haven actually modeled sound waves to travel through physical objects. My ears were plugged but the beach beauty was singing *through* me.

Izzy: *Cut the crap, Talon. You had your lap dance. Get on the boat.*

I weakly pushed the siren away. It was like I was high on

pain meds. I knew I had a shit-eating grin on my face but I couldn't wipe it off. She rubbed my chest up and down, straying dangerously and making my skin tingle. Fingers tickled my neck and unplugged the wax from my ears.

Then a choir of angels filled my soul.

"Talon!" screamed Izzy.

As the group sang and moved to surround me, the beauty licked and kissed my lips. She tasted like seawater and caramel, both salty and sweet. It was unbearable.

A crossbow bolt splashed in the water beside her. The gaggle of sirens hurried to shield us, piling in the water. I was pressed from all sides by butts and boobs and fish tails, weightless in the water as they brought me to land. I peeked out between a sandwich of skin to find the little chicken girl holding a thorn in her beak. She dropped it in my palm and skittered off. The older woman watched passively from atop the rocks. The two guys mock sparred each other with their natural appendages.

Was this entire island filled with sociopaths?

Errol: *Don't attack 'em! If we draw blood, they will too.*

Izzy: *I thought you said they were harmless!*

Errol: *I didn't think ye'd be crazy enough to stab 'em.*

Stab. Stab. The little girl. Somewhere through the throbbing fleshly pleasure I had the wherewithal to clench my fist over the giant thorn. Pain spiked through my arm and jolted me awake. I jerked away from the bed of women. They'd already dragged me to shore.

The tan beauty ripped her fishnet blouse open, letting her breasts heave and bounce. They called to me. I stabbed myself again to clear my head. While the pain jarred my thoughts, I wasn't free from the lure. The woman lowered on her back, seductively propping herself on her elbows, and sang to me. A compelling melody with a forlorn voice, a longing only I could soothe. The siren grabbed my head and spread her legs.

I needed a bigger boat.

Talon: *Shoot me, Kyle.*
Kyle: *What?*
Talon: *Shoot me. ME.*

A glass bolt punched corrosive fluid straight into my butt cheek.

27 damage
DoT: 20 dmg/10 secs

"Yeaargh!"

I pulled away from the salty temptress. Kyle's alchemy was a constant tingle of annoyance, but lust was a powerful drug. My pants still desperately wanted to come off. And maybe I could fight off one woman in this state, but ten of them?

I pulled away from grabbing hands and clawed the ground, desperately clawing for something.

> **Izzy:** *Fuck this. I'm going down there.*
> **Errol:** *Ye'll die. Ye'll fail the quest.*
> **Izzy:** *Fuck the damn quest.*
> **Talon:** *No, Izzy! I got this.*

My hand gripped the severed undine finger I had dropped on the beach. I raised it above my head and drew it down into my shoulder. Agony exploded into my bloodstream. It blocked everything out. I couldn't even read my damage notifications. Sickness withered within me and it was hard to stay conscious let alone keep little Talon standing at attention.

The pain was paramount as it coursed through my being, but I was finally free of the song's curse.

I crawled to the water, shoving sirens left and right. The beauty hurried to grab me, but I gave her a hard slap in the crotch that sent her to the fetal position. I was sorry for that last part but she kinda deserved it. I wrapped the rope around my arm and tried climbing up, but the poison didn't allow such a feat of strength. Luckily I had friends to hoist me up.

The crew unfurled the sails before I was safely aboard. The sirens wailed and cried and bemoaned their studly loss.

"I would cry too if I were you!" I shouted back, half delirious.

It was strange to be the only one who heard the magic of their voices. As I was pulled to the deck and we sailed away, the peace drifted from my mind. I hacked and coughed until Izzy forced a health vial down my throat.

"Now we're even," she said gruffly, but with a smile.

"Even," exclaimed Kyle. "You're letting him off that easily?"

She shrugged. "I'm not the jealous type. Plus, you got the bone pearl, didn't you?" She turned to me. "Didn't you?"

I nodded, savoring every one of my breaths.

Izzy leaned close to my ear. "Besides, occasionally invited guests aren't against the law." She bit my ear hard enough that I wanted another healing potion.

It took me a second, but my face lit up. "Wait, are you talking about a threesome?"

Her eyes sparkled.

"The good kind or the bad kind? Because—"

The pixie forcefully slammed her hand over my mouth. "Don't ruin the moment."

"By the Maelstrom!" cursed Errol, taking the *Cutter's* wheel as we cleared the Singing Spires. "We got company, men. Man yer battle stations."

Izzy sighed. "Moment officially ruined."

1270 Age of Sail

Pirates pulled wax from their ears and scrambled to their stations. We hurried to the helm.

"What is it now?" I asked, annoyed I couldn't bask in my bone pearl acquisition.

"Undine," growled Errol.

Kyle scoffed. "I thought we already whooped their butts?"

"Several of 'em, aye. But this looks t' be the entire mermaid nation."

Countless streaks blazed through the seas all around the *Cutter*. Easily two or three times the number of undine as before, and those were only the ones visible from the surface.

"Damned sea cows," muttered the captain. "They usually cut their losses an' run. I think our Prince Navoo took yer slight personal."

"Can we activate the turbo sail again?"

"Not fer another 12 hours. But we've got a good wind at our backs. The *Cutter* will outpace their fastest swimmers."

The crew tightened the sails and gave it everything they had. Indeed, aside from the lull back in the Spires, we had the perfect conditions for sailing. A couple of mermaids latched onto the hull but many more fell behind.

Kyle hefted the crossbow. "Don't worry, captain—admiral—whatever I should call you. I'll stick to corrosives and keep it off the boat."

Izzy was already ahead of him. "Icing the hull."

The combination of offense and defense was a good one as long as they weren't overwhelmed. Keeping up our forward speed was vital. Fortunately, it looked to be clear sailing ahead.

Instead of focusing on the individual undine, I watched the streaks of water in their wake. They moved so fast, dozens of paintbrushes slicing the ocean surface, weaving in and out, attempting to cut us off. Many of them took bad angles that left them in our backwash. A few were less aggressive and slower to close on us. While they kept pace for short bursts, it was clear the *Cutter* was winning.

Right up until a streak of aqua appeared on our tail.

"Back there," I called out. "What is that?"

Kyle fired at the last mermaid scaling the hull. The bolt plugged her right in the neck. She gurgled and skipped on the water surface like a stone. The brewmaster lifted his head and squinted in the distance. "A really fast mermaid?"

Errol hurried to the railing and extended a personal telescope. He brought it to his eye and stiffened. Then he slowly lowered it. "Can't say I've seen that 'fore today."

"What is it?"

The aqua wake rushed to flank us. The streak of water was wider than the others and agitated the sea with many more bubbles. As it paced us, Prince Navoo's crowned head crested the waves. He rose from the ocean with little effort, somehow still matching our speed.

"How is that possible?"

Errol's eyes widened. "By the Maelstrom, 'tis the *Deep Blue*." He scurried back to his command station and mustered the crew, voice booming over the wind. "To the cannons, men. If we don't hit 'em with all we got, we're doomed!"

"I don't know guys," hedged Kyle. "This *really* doesn't seem that—"

"Don't say it," I snapped.

He shrugged, brought the crossbow to his shoulder, and closed an eye to take aim. Prince Navoo focused his menacing scowl on us. As Kyle released the bolt, the merman rose even higher from the sea. The glass projectile exploded against a small wood barrier around the undine lord's waist. As he continued rising, he appeared to be in a small craft.

"That's a boat," said Izzy.

"Ar," said Grug, rushing past. " 'Tis the *Deep Blue*."

"It's a small boat," said Kyle.

"Don't say it," I stressed.

He scoffed. "What? It's a small boat. That's all I'm saying." He breathed in and out defiantly and peeped, "It doesn't seem that bad."

Navoo's craft lifted above the ocean. His deck was tiny but supported by a wooden beam that lifted him higher and higher into the sky. In fact, his original boat wasn't a boat at all.

"That's a crow's nest," I muttered. "That's not the boat." Within seconds, a huge deck surfaced below him. Seawater swept past a full undine crew as the *Deep Blue* emerged from the waves. The mast holding the Prince's perch unfurled an azure sail of its own. I slapped my forehead. "*That's* the boat."

The hull of the *Blue* was covered with glittering scales. Reliefs of seashells dotted the body. A large spiral shell pointed off the fore of the ship like a narwhal tooth.

"Avast!" yelled the pirates. "Ship ho!"

"Tighten the sail," ordered Errol. "Pull in that slack." He turned to the starboard crew. "Tie up them loose ends 'fore ye kill yerselves!" He stomped over to an open hatch in the deck and peered below. "Ye have them cannons ready? 'Cause ready or not, here they come."

A larger than usual aggro notification flashed before us.

[Deep Blue]
Undine Flagship
700 SIP

Two more sails breached the ocean behind us.

[Undine Support Vessel]
200 SIP

"Crap," I yelled. "Stats. Let me see our stats!"

"Full spin to starboard!" ordered Errol.

The *Cutter* veered sharply away from the *Deep Blue*. The undine vessel was clearly fast enough, but the maneuver took them by surprise. It took me by surprise too.

Agility Check...
Pass!

I barely stayed on my feet as the *Cutter* reversed direction by spinning in a sharp arc. Once again, half the hull submerged due to the tight turn. And while we were well clear of the murderous undine, we were now heading straight back at them and the two surfacing support vessels.

"This is what you call running?" prodded Izzy.

"Nay," said the captain. "The *Cutter's* been challenged at open sea. I can't let that stand."

"Stats," I repeated.

Errol nodded and waved his hand. A communal menu overlay appeared behind the wheel.

Heartcutter	*Level*	3
Structural Integrity		500
Speed		5
Maneuverability		8
Armor		0
Weapons		
Powder Cannon		
Powder Cannon		
Powder Cannon		
Powder Cannon		
Special		
Harpoon		
Turbo Sail		

Confidence ran through me as I noted the *Cutter's* structural integrity. Its health easily outmatched that of the support vessels. Unfortunately, the cannons and turbo sail were grayed out, meaning they weren't active.

"What's the harpoon? Can we use that?"

"Nay," answered the admiral. " 'Tis just a heavy fishin' spear I salvaged off an old enemy. It'll damage nary a seafarin' ship."

The undine vessels sped towards us as we met them head on. They were still rising from the water and we were set to pass right between them.

"How're them cannons?" boomed Errol. Apologetic muttering replied through the deck hatch. "I'll have none o' it!" he snapped. 'Get me them cannons online or ye be no better than fish bait!"

Prince Navoo was behind us, but the reversal had cost him a lot of ground. I smiled as I gleaned Errol's clever tactic. Instead of taking on the undine flagship, the pirate had immediately isolated the smaller fish. Now the prince was removed from the action, able to do nothing but watch our opening salvo.

"Cannons out!" ordered Errol.

Hatches in the *Cutter's* hull opened and iron tubes peeked through. The support vessels were still partially submerged. The undines had valued pursuit speed over safety. With us reversing direction, we'd halved their closing time. They now converged on us before being battle ready. Their sails were only beginning to unfurl, which meant they couldn't maneuver yet. Even worse, there was no time to deploy cannons of their own.

Errol slyly watched the setup timers on his cannons expire. As the *Cutter* sliced between the pair of surfacing enemies, it was with great satisfaction that he yelled, "Blast them sea cows back t' the abyss!"

BOOM. BOOM.

```
Critical hit!
[Powder Cannon] dealt 95 damage to [Undine
Support Vessel]
Waterlogged!
[Powder Cannon] dealt 95 damage to [Undine
Support Vessel]
```

The cannons shredded the surfacing vessels with ruthless efficiency. Either Errol's cannons were overpowered or we had really caught them with their pants down.

BOOM. BOOM.

```
Critical hit!
Mast Break!
[Powder Cannon] dealt 95 damage to [Undine
Support Vessel]
Savage!
[Powder Cannon] dealt 125 damage to [Undine
Support Vessel]
[Undine Support Vessel] is wrecked
1 wreck awarded
2000 XP awarded
```

One of the ship's immediately canted over. The other stalled in the water, its mast and sail tumbling over the deck and smashing crew members. The vessel was barely hanging on.

The display was astounding, but I had my eyes on something else entirely. "Holy crap! Did you guys see that XP?"

"It's the life, ain't it?" boasted Errol. "Sinking an enemy vessel awards ten times its structural integrity points to every member of the victorious crew."

Izzy beamed. "Where has sailing been all my life?"

The pirate crew, unfazed or unaware of the XP gain, attended the sinking ship on the port side as the *Cutter* looped around it.

Loot:
1200 silver
[Scale Hull Armor] x50%

Errol lit up as he collected the upgrade. The silver split among the crew and the captain hungrily turned to the second support vessel. It would likely complete the armor requirement. The problem was the *Deep Blue*, now bearing down on us. Three seashells on each side opened up and deployed stony cannons.

"They have us outgunned," said Izzy.

Kyle pushed close. "What do we do?"

I shrugged. "I'm not the pirate."

The *Blue* made its way between both waterlogged vessels. Errol circled around the opposite direction. Prince Navoo launched his port cannons as we passed.

CHOOM, CHOOM, CHOOM.

The wreckage from his own ship absorbed the blow. Admiral Oates was playing keep-away.

The incurable pirate laughed. "He may be fast, but fer all his scales, he ain't as slippery as us."

We turned hard around the undine wreckage. Instead of following Navoo between his ships, we passed so that our port side faced his naked rear.

"Fire!"

BOOM. BOOM.

[Powder Cannon] missed
[Powder Cannon] dealt 35 damage to [Deep Blue]

The *Blue* veered away before we could attempt a follow-up volley.

"Damned armor," muttered the captain. "We're in fer a hard time takin' him down with conventional cannons."

A mermaid screeched as she pulled herself over the handrail. I drew my spear but Izzy's icicles were faster. The mermaid was knocked away. The *Cutter* pulled a wide circle and bore past the heavily damaged undine ship.

"Reload," cried Errol. "Reload an' fire!"

Sharp curses came from below deck. One cannon went off.

BOOM.

[Powder Cannon] missed

The stray cannonball shot straight into the sky. I ran to the handrail. Two mermen were clamped to the hull and holding the cannon askew. Meanwhile, we were losing our chance at finishing off the hapless vessel.

At the same time, Prince Navoo had changed bearing. Instead of circling to the left and chasing us, he circled right to head us off.

"All the best," said Errol. "Our starboard cannons are still in commission. Brace yerselves!"

Once we passed the waterlogged ship, the *Cutter* veered hard to port. The *Blue* passed our starboard side and both ships opened fire.

BOOM. BOOM.

CHOOM, CHOOM, CHOOM.

```
[Powder Cannon] dealt 35 damage to [Deep Blue]
[Powder Cannon] dealt 35 damage to [Deep Blue]
[Shell Cannon] dealt 55 damage to [Heartcutter]
[Shell Cannon] dealt 55 damage to [Heartcutter]
[Shell Cannon] dealt 55 damage to [Heartcutter]
```

```
Heartcutter: 335
Deep Blue: 595
```

"Curses, they fire fast!"

Some quick mental math told me their cannons weren't quite as powerful as ours. They had three per side, though, and their significant armor rendered ours less effective. On top of those worrying factors, we had less SIP in total, making this a losing proposition any way you sliced it.

"What else do we got?" I asked. "This isn't sustainable."

"The hell it isn't. I'll gut ev'ry one o' them bastards meself."

"We need to save the ship, Errol. How do we save the ship?"

He bit down. "That armor upgrade. We'll need t' make another pass an' finish that support vessel off."

I wasn't sure if the armor was worth taking more direct hits. Even if we reduced the damage capability of their shell cannons, the math still wasn't on our side. It wasn't that it was a bad plan, it just wasn't enough.

The flagships circled the wreckage in opposite directions. We'd be at each other's throats before we knew it. Izzy and Kyle cleared the hull and restored the port cannons, but the swimming undine were getting more aggressive. Playing keep-away between wreckage was avoiding the full brunt of the *Blue*, but it also made us mermaid bait. Watching Kyle reload his crossbow gave me an idea.

"Fire," I exclaimed. "A constant fire can dish damage that our cannons can't."

Kyle puckered his lips. "You want me to use a crossbow against a boss ship?"

I shook my head in exasperation. "I don't know. You still have grenades, don't you? Your *Call of Duty* special."

The brewmaster hefted a glass bomb filled with yellow oil. "You mean this little bad boy?"

I snatched it. "How many do you have?"

"Only two more. I used a bunch in Oakengard. But I don't have the range to toss this to the *Blue* unless we get *really* close."

I grumbled. That wouldn't work unless it was an emergency. "What about launching them from our cannons?"

"That's one way to explode yourself, I suppose."

I took his word for it. Kyle was sort of an expert at exploding himself. "But isn't there a way—"

"Look," he said, "if I had time to focus on crafting some kind of heavy-duty cannonball that wouldn't explode as soon as we tried to launch it, I could maybe do it. Right now? I'm not prepared for that, bro. It can't be done."

"Damn." He was right. It was a good idea, but ideas were a dime a dozen. Real battles were fought with preparation and readiness. "At least give Izzy your third fire bomb. If we get close enough, or if they sink us and drag us on board, you know what to do with them."

They both nodded grimly.

Errol shouted from the wheel. "Here we go, boys! I want that undine flotsam destroyed an' salvaged on the next pass. It might be our last shot!"

The *Blue* steered toward us as we raced to our target. Our port cannons readied for the support vessel and our starboard cannons for the flagship.

"This is gonna be a tight one," laughed Errol.

Suddenly, a catapult from the deck of the *Deep Blue* launched a large jagged ball. The heavy projectile arced through the air and barreled toward us.

"Incoming!" yelled the crew.

The giant ball of armor bashed onto the deck and rolled haphazardly, flattening a pirate. When it stopped, the various brown plates separated. Crustacean legs poked out and the ball scurried across the deck.

"What in the..."

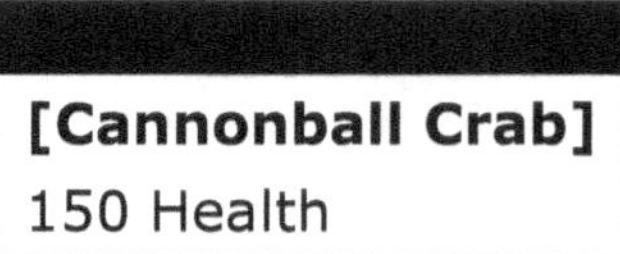

Before we could react, it hopped down the deck hatch and raised chaos below.

"Fire!" screamed Errol as the *Blue* squared up with us.

BOOM.

One portside cannon fired a wide shot over the wreckage. The starboard cannons hurried off.

BOOM. BOOM.

[Powder Cannon] missed
[Powder Cannon] dealt 35 damage to [Deep Blue]
Graze!
[Powder Cannon] dealt 10 damage to [Deep Blue]

The last cannon didn't go off. I blinked in horror.

"Oh, crap."

CHOOM, CHOOM, CHOOM.

1280 Sink or Swim

[Shell Cannon] dealt 55 damage to [Heartcutter]
[Shell Cannon] dealt 55 damage to [Heartcutter]
[Shell Cannon] dealt 55 damage to [Heartcutter]
Waterlogged!
Your ship is taking on water. Speed and Maneuverability reduced by 50%.

Heartcutter: 170
Deep Blue: 550

The *Cutter* shook. The ocean rushed through a small hole below deck. Pirates screamed in the face of the elements and their unwelcome guest. The giant crab, no doubt one of the *Deep Blue's* special attacks, was wreaking havoc on the crew.

"Repairs!" called Errol. "Repairs!" He put his hands together and dove headfirst down the hatch.

"Back him up!" I yelled. A couple of the pirates thought twice before going down, but their captain was in trouble. Seeing Izzy and Kyle follow reassured them.

I paused on the deck. The *Cutter* and the *Blue* were breaking away from each other again. Another loop, another collision course. Except we'd barely survive another pass. I ran to the command station and straightened the wheel. "You!" I pointed to Grug. "Take the wheel. Keep it straight."

He burped. "Cap'n wants to circle the wreckage."

"We can't afford to do that with our cannons offline. Keep her straight. Get her up to speed to ward the undine away. As far as I can tell, the *Deep Blue* can't fire straight forward."

"She's faster than the *Cutter*. She'll overtake us."

"Then come back to the wreckage to get your armor once the cannons are online. Just create some distance while we can."

"An' what will you be doin', sir?"

I mounted the mast, pulled on a rope, and showed my teeth. "I'm gonna be a pirate."

I swung over the handrail of the ship, straight toward the waterlogged undine vessel. There was a whole lotta daylight between me and it. At the peak of my swing, I released the rope, triggered dash, equipped climbing claws, and prepared to put my scaling skill to good use. I fired toward the ship and slammed into the hull with a smack.

Fall Damage!
24 damage

I slipped on the scaled wood of the support vessel. My claws weren't catching enough traction to keep me up. I leaned into my momentum and used wall run to climb several feet. It was still hard going but my ranger boots didn't fail me. I reached up and grabbed the bottom opening in the rail and, while not a conventional vault, the skill propelled me up and onto the deck.

Whew.

The undine crew scrambled as they erected a new mast. They were so focused on clamping it in place they didn't see me. They also made one hell of a juicy target. I tossed Kyle's fire bomb into the fray. Oil washed outward and flames blanketed them.

Fire Weakness!
Surprise!

A stream of heavy-damage notifications flooded my combat window. Confusion erupted among their ranks. With the indirect damage, most of the undine still hadn't noticed me. I tried ducking into the shadows, but I wasn't that lucky. Two mermaids slithered my way brandishing claws.

Kyle: *Crab's down. Piece of cake.*
Errol: *Cannon's back online.*
Izzy: *Hull sealed.*

I gazed at the distant ship. Despite having been hobbled, the *Cutter* had managed a great distance in a short time. The *Blue* had circled into position, expecting Errol to stick close to cover, waiting for another lap to attack. Now the ships were no longer engaged. Newly repaired, the *Cutter* once again enjoyed its full burst of speed.

> **Talon:** *Great! Come back and get me.*
> **Errol:** *Aye, aye, ye mad bastard!*

Both mermaids attacked at once. I coolly spun my spear and bashed them away. A deadshot stunned one. I narrowly avoided getting sliced up, though. I reminded myself how awful their poison hurt and that I couldn't use another healing potion today.

I backed away and safely crossblocked the next attack. I feinted, killed the first, and returned my guard to the other. So far, so good.

Prince Navoo had a moment of indecision as he watched his support ship go up in flames, but the *Deep Blue* corrected course and made a beeline for the *Cutter*. That was the smart play. I was just dead weight.

Except the prince had eagerly initiated chase believing Errol to be retreating. The *Cutter* reversed sails and headed back to us. Now both ships sailed straight at each other, full speed ahead in a game of chicken on the open seas.

I was about to judge Prince Navoo a rash sea captain until he revealed another of the *Deep Blue's* special weapons. The spiral shell at the fore of the ship wasn't just a gaudy decoration. It began spinning like a power drill. Prince Navoo was intent on taking down the *Cutter* one way or another.

> **Talon:** *He wants to ram you.*
> **Errol:** *The hell he will. I told ya, he's fast, but he can't turn like we can.*

I crossblocked a mermaid and reversed the attack for an easy combo. Two more slashes and she was down. I looted the bodies as the fire spread. By now some of the undine were abandoning ship. Others had definitely noticed my presence. Saving the vessel was a lost cause; killing me wasn't. A large group of crew members converged.

Stranded and surrounded on all sides, I had no choice but to leap into the fray. I kept their claws away with a well-timed spinshield and pushed ahead. Two seconds later, my only idea was the fire they were so afraid of. I sprinted ahead and vaulted over it and onto the new makeshift mast.

The pole listed to the side as I connected with it. This was ground zero of the fire bomb. Flames raged around me and licked my boots. I suddenly felt like the subject of a witch trial. I swapped back to the climbing claws and pressed higher. The undine dared not close on me, but the scorched mast was failing fast.

The two flagships met on the high seas. As Errol had intended, the *Cutter* jerked to the side at the last second. The vessels sped past each other in close proximity.

BOOM. BOOM.

CHOOM, CHOOM, CHOOM.

They were both going so fast only half their hits connected.

Heartcutter: 115
Deep Blue: 515

A blaze of fiery oil spilled over the wake of the *Deep Blue*. Kyle had tried to set them alight but missed. Flames washed over the water.

I leaned on the mast and waved at the *Cutter*. The ship, damaged as she was, was in prime sailing form. She passed between the wreckage of the support vessels just as my mast gave way. It listed sideways toward the ocean.

Agility check...
Pass!

I planted my boots and ran up the pole's length as it fell. Just as the *Cutter* passed, I leapt off the edge.

Fire damage!
[Undine Support Vessel] is wrecked
1 wreck awarded
2000 XP awarded

I rolled cleanly onto the deck of the *Cutter* as the pirate crew looted the remains.

"Got it!" said Errol.

Our ship glowed faintly. A sheen of blue scales washed over the outer hull.

Ship Upgrade: **Scale Armor**
Armor Level: 30

"Woo-hoo!" exclaimed the crew, spitting and high-fiving.

More napkin math. If the 30 armor reduced their cannons to 25 damage a shot, we'd be dead in five shots, or two passes. Meanwhile, we needed 15 shots and—even worse—seven and a half passes to be victorious.

"It doesn't matter," I said, dejected. "It doesn't matter. We can't beat them with cannons."

The crew sobered up as the *Deep Blue* bore straight toward us again. Several pirates were dead. The *Cutter* was badly damaged. With Prince Navoo dead set on taking this as far as he could, we had very few options.

"Man the sails," ordered Errol. "If we're goin' down, it'll be with one helluva fight."

We looped around the burning ship and faced the *Blue*. Navoo didn't show any signs of slowing. Despite missing with some of his previous shots, he was overeager to end this. I had to play off that.

I scanned the deck. The heavy harpoon sat abandoned at the ass end of the ship. The hook and chain sure looked menacing, but Errol was right: it wasn't a weapon. Though I wondered...

"Turn left after the wreckage," I suggested.

"Which way?"

"Port! Turn to port. Jeez, do sailors suddenly forget normal directions when they get on a boat?"

Errol twitched his head. "We ain't runnin', Talon."

"I know. We're not running."

The pirate watched me for a long second before nodding. "Aye, then. We'll do it yer way." Errol lifted his telescope to his eye and sneered. "Remember this, Prince Navoo. Ol' Captain Oates an' the Black Hats don't go down easy."

The *Deep Blue* sailed at us on a headwind. The drilling shell spun with a menacing whir as we readied our cannons. I ran to the stern of the ship and waited. And waited. And...

"Now!"

Errol spun the *Cutter's* wheel as hard as he could. Kyle and some others lost their footing, but the captain held on and pushed hard to the side.

Navoo had surely been expecting another last-second maneuver. This one squared our guns to the fore of his ship. Instead of turning and readying his cannons to match ours, he continued rushing forward.

"Fire!"

BOOM. BOOM.

```
[Powder Cannon] dealt 35 damage to [Deep Blue]
[Powder Cannon] dealt 35 damage to [Deep Blue]
```

```
Heartcutter: 115
Deep Blue: 445
```

Navoo was happy to absorb the damage as he bore closer. Errol attempted to exit the *Blue's* ramming range. I ignored the danger and manned the harpoon. It launched—not at the threat, but at the wreckage of the salvaged support vessel. The strong chain unwound as the harpoon sailed and clunked into the now armorless hull. I flipped the clamp and the chain locked. The *Cutter* jerked as we took on dead weight.

"Catch the headwind!" boomed Errol. "Slacken that sail, ya

mangy barnacles!"

The *Deep Blue* veered to meet us, maneuver or not. This time, because we had burning wreckage in tow, it was a close one. The *Cutter* narrowly avoided the drilling shell, which instead caught the harpoon chain in its spinning action. After slipping a couple of times, it finally caught for good.

Both ships shuddered at the indirect collision. Grug tumbled over the rail, but I dove forward and caught his hand. The pirate was heavier than he looked, and my shoulder was almost dislocated. His crewmates helped me lug him back on deck. The others were still pushing to get the *Cutter* back up to speed.

The *Blue's* drill spun, eating up the chain and pulling both attached vessels toward it. With both ship's sails in the wind, we were a jumbled train barreling toward the first sunken ship's wreckage. Errol twirled the wheel to avoid another collision.

"Around him," I urged. "Around him."

The *Cutter* banked hard to starboard, coming up right beside Prince Navoo's flagship, hull to hull. My heart skipped a beat.

CHOOM, CHOOM, CHOOM.

[Shell Cannon] dealt 25 damage to [Heartcutter]
[Shell Cannon] dealt 25 damage to [Heartcutter]
[Shell Cannon] dealt 25 damage to [Heartcutter]

Heartcutter: 40
Deep Blue: 445

We let out a collective sigh as the new armor did what I was hoping. But damn if it wasn't close. Our cannons were still reloading.

I sped back to the harpoon and unflipped the holding clamp. The winch flew loose and the *Cutter* jerked forward.

BOOM. BOOM.

[Powder Cannon] dealt 35 damage to [Deep Blue]
[Powder Cannon] dealt 35 damage to [Deep Blue]

Heartcutter: 40
Deep Blue: 375

The undine worked double time to reload their starboard cannons as the passing hulls scraped each other. Kyle released crossbow bolts. Small fires exploded on their deck. Izzy took the hint and lobbed our last fire bomb. A merman leapt up, caught it in a net, and tossed it overboard. It exploded uselessly on the waves. Their crew expertly rushed to quench the limited flames.

I met Prince Navoo's eyes and smiled as the flagships passed. By all accounts, he had us beat. Twice the crew, an army under the waves, and a supervessel with remarkable firepower. The undine prince glared hard as my laughter bellowed, and even a Black Hat pirate or two thought I had finally gone mad.

Then panic erupted on the *Deep Blue* as their fore drill pulled their own wrecked support vessel toward them. I hadn't bothered with the smaller fires because the bigger one was my weapon. Navoo's eyes widened in fear.

"Stop the drill!" he ordered.

The *Cutter* passed behind the undine flagship and Errol joined me with boisterous laughter. "Too late fer that, ye overripe shark bait!" He spun his ship in a loop around the *Deep Blue*, harpoon chain slackening around the enemy. Navoo fired his port cannons on the other side, but we used his support vessel as a shield. The *Cutter* looped around both hapless vessels as its chain wrapped the burning ship up with the *Blue*. There was no quenching *that* fire.

"No!" cried the prince.

Raging flames spat embers across the *Blue's* deck. The azure sail crackled with fire. Many undine, overpowered by their most primal fear, abandoned ship. Slithering back into the cold ocean was second nature for them.

"No!" commanded Prince Navoo. "Back to your stations!"

But it was done. I unhitched the harpoon chain completely. The *Cutter*, no longer under drag, launched away from the scene of destruction. The undine prince screamed from the top of his crow's nest as the fire threatened to consume him.

Fire Damage!
Deep Blue: 255

Without sails and tied to a shipwreck, the *Deep Blue* couldn't get out of the trap. The fire was too large to stop. All we had to do was wait around until it went down.

Unfortunately, the undine lord wasn't a complete idiot. The *Deep Blue* did indeed sink, but under its own power. Prince Navoo started to submerge the flagship back into the ocean where it came from.

> Fire Damage!
> Deep Blue: 125

As flames scorched the glittering deck of the magnificent undine vessel, it lowered into the sea. Fire sizzled into smoke. Between the puffs filling the air, I caught sight of an angered but alive prince submerging.

"Damn it!" I yelled. "That was our kill!"

Errol slapped my back. "Don't take it too hard there, Talon. Ain't never heard o' anyone defeatin' the *Blue* before. It ain't gonna be as easy as that."

"You call that easy?!?"

Kyle aimed his bow in our wake. "Won't he come after us?"

"Not without his sails, he won't." The captain chuckled. "No worries, boys. We bested the best today. Made the sea's own ship turn tail an' run, we did. We'll get repairs in port an' be ready fer him next time." Errol nodded to each of us. "Ye three did me proud. Fer a bunch o' landlubbers."

"But we missed out on the XP," I complained.

Errol crossed his arms over his chest and grinned. "Wait fer it."

As the seas went quiet, a notification popped up.

> [Deep Blue] has retreated
> 3,750 XP awarded

I blinked wordlessly. The retreat had robbed us of any loot, but as victors we were still awarded ten times the XP of the damage inflicted on the *Blue*. A familiar-yet-forgotten teal flame surged from my boots to my cowl for the first time in over a month.

BWOOOOOM!

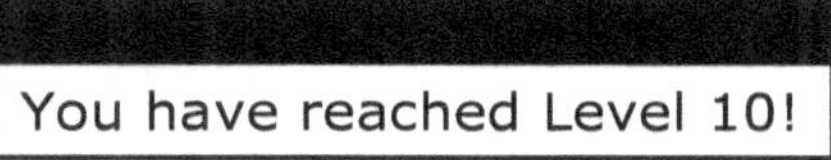

"Crap," said Izzy. "You beat me."

I examined her. She was still a level-9 frost mage. By the look on her face, she was just a few hundred XP away from leveling. She moved to the handrail.

"Any more mermaids out here? What about dolphins?"

I chuckled as I considered my new attribute point. I'd been sinking so much into agility, I figured I could stand to hit a bit harder. I hadn't enjoyed being manhandled by Navoo. I spent the point on strength and admired my new stats.

Talon		*Level*	10
Class	Explorer	*XP*	76043
Kit	Scout	*Next*	113400

Strength	18	*Strike*	390
Agility	24	*Dodge*	450
Craft	6	*Health*	300 / 300
Essence	10	*Spirit*	255 / 255

I had just noticed something missing when a notification popped up.

> Congratulations on hitting level 10!
>
> As of patch 0.9.26, you are no longer awarded additional skill points past level 9. Future skills now rely on the implemented evolution and overload systems.

Oh, yeah. *That.* At first I bemoaned not managing to level up before the last patch, but then I got another notification.

> Congratulations on hitting level 10!
>
> This milestone awards one cost-free legendary ability, usable once per day, based on your contextual character history and loadout.

Two options were presented to me.

> **Ghost**
> Become ethereal to players, NPCs, and mobs for 6 seconds.

> **Pathfinder**
> Visualize the optimal path through dungeons and hostile environments.

Whoa, these abilities weren't playing around. They were a sort of superclass representation. Ten levels of hard-fought grinding distilled into a title.

Ghost was the ultimate traversal move. No matter where I was or how much trouble I was in, I could become incorporeal. Dodge attacks, avoid dangers, and escape threats. It was ridiculously OP save for its limits: a once-per-day use, and only for 6 seconds.

Pathfinder was the easy button, no doubt due to my scouting ability and previous dungeon-crawling optimizations. I was, after all, an explorer class.

Still, I frowned. Choosing a custom ability at level 10 was an exciting prospect, but I couldn't help feeling my options were a little... boring. It wasn't that their theming didn't fit. These abilities were no doubt geared toward my class type and play style. The choices just seemed to be lacking something.

I twiddled my thumbs as I perused my menu, trying to get a cohesive feel for everything I'd built. With the high seas adventure over and nothing but miles of ocean, I had the time. Eventually, I stumbled on the scroll of knife handling Hex had given me. On a lark, I read it, and just like that I had my second weapon skill.

Knife

Level 1

You are versed in the basics of knife combat. This root skill allows you to use knife weapons without being a hindrance, but improvement and specific tactics require further skill point expenditure. Weapon specialization skills may not be higher level than their root.

None of it mattered a whole lot since I wasn't planning on sinking skill points into the knife tree. I quickly skimmed the upgrade skills without much interest. As I flipped back to the main screen, I was surprised to see a new option populate beneath ghost and pathfinder.

Assassin

Auto kill a susceptible opponent.

An assassin option. Outfitted with deadshot, stealth skills, and a new proficiency with knives, it wasn't a stretch. And what kind of rogue didn't fantasize about being the ultimate killer, taking out any enemy no matter how elusive?

It was a tempting thought.

But was that what all my time in Haven had amounted to? I was a rebel, titanslayer, Protector of Stronghold, and leader of the only player-led faction in the sim. Was I also just a killer?

It was no doubt a badass title. I had second thoughts about the reality of it. All I could think about was Poe, sitting in our guildhall, drinking our beer, and turning on me for a pile of silver.

I was more than that, wasn't I?

Izzy arched a curious eyebrow. "What is it, Talon? Analysis paralysis about your new attribute point?"

"Something like that." I closed my menu. I could explain the predicament, but she was a few hundred XP from finding out for herself. Why spoil the surprise?

1290 Dark Wizard

We stuck out the rest of the voyage in glorious boredom. Most of us cycled below deck to rest and mend our wounds. Five crew members were now dead, leaving us with nine total on the boat.

The sun was late in the sky as the coastal mists of the north took over. Visibility wasn't reduced too much, but it made for a bleak sight. An otherworldly atmosphere. It was cool, at least, if humid.

The voyage was almost complete.

After ample downtime, awestruck muttering drew me to the *Cutter's* deck. Pirates pointed to the formless sky where a single black serpent cut through the mist.

"Nightwing," I said. The pirates jumped at my voice as if afraid I'd attract the impressive beast.

"We've seen him before," reported Errol. "Lots o' whispers round these parts o' fanciful beasts. Me boots shiver ev'ry time."

The black dragon released a sharp cry before abruptly banking out of sight.

"It's an invitation," I said. "We're close."

The captain nodded. "I reckon we'll be smellin' the Salt Sea in one shake of a hat."

We'd been sailing northeast with the coast for some time now. The Salt Sea wasn't a true sea but a natural breakwater in the shape of a circle. It ringed off a portion of the ocean into a higher pool, shallow and stale, tepid with overripe fish carcasses. A wasteland of crevices and salt. Unsurprisingly, Lucifer had chosen this place of death as his sanctuary.

Even though the tip of the Salt Sea's border found itself submerged during high tide, our frigate was much too large to broach the pool. Errol pulled the *Cutter* up to the breakwater, dropped anchor, and lowered a skiff to the water. We let the crew relax while Errol, Izzy, Kyle and I transferred to the calm waters of Lucifer's home.

The stench of rotting fish assaulted my sinuses. It was one thing to whiff it on the breeze, another entirely to be permeated by its putrid essence. I willed the sensory input to the back of my mind and focused on the confrontation ahead.

The last time I was here, I died.

Of course, that betrayal hadn't been at Lucifer's hands. We were traveling with Cleric Vagram, before the catechists had revealed their true intentions. If ever I had a bone to pick with someone in Haven, it was Vagram for his sudden and lethal treachery. I locked eyes with Izzy and knew she worked through similar thoughts.

Though the rogue cleric was a million miles away, we kept watch for ambushes all the same. The sea answered with quiet. As we approached the central rock pedestal, barely an island, the mists parted and revealed a lone figure expecting us.

[Luc1f3r]

His name, as with everything else about him, was a hack. *He* wasn't even really a *he* at all, but an eight-year-old girl. Nightwing, thankfully absent for the moment, had been awoken early and was the only living dragon in the world. Even more frightening were the two golden angels Lucifer had corrupted. They were now the Fallen. Idle and tainted, instead of hunting the devil, they served as his personal bodyguards.

But not now. No one else now. Just the man himself, black robes swaying in the gentle breeze. The muted sun lightly picked up the silver runes adorning his cloak. Lucifer held a black witchwood staff with a chunky glowing blue jewel fitted between the Y branch at the top. A dusky snake wrapped around his hand at rest on the weapon.

"Are you alone?" I called out as we approached.

His voice came out light and playful, like the breeze. "Loneliness is my cross."

We hopped off the skiff and waded ahead in the shallows. "I'm not looking to get ambushed by a couple of hacked angels."

If his smile was meant to ease me, it had the opposite effect. The one good thing about Cleric Vagram was his holy power that partially fended off Lucifer's blackness. It would be impossible to defend against angels without it.

"Why are you here, Talon of Stronghold?"

The others grounded the skiff. Izzy splashed through the water to back me up while Errol tied down. Kyle remained sitting inside, hands out of sight, gripping his double crossbow.

"I just want to talk," I answered, "if that's okay."

"And they say old dogs don't learn."

"I can do without the insults, kid."

For a brief second, Lucifer's persona wavered. The little girl inside tensed against my admonishment. But then the adversary took over. Supreme. Collected. Above petty things. I figured a point scored for each side was enough. No reason to continue with verbal games.

"There's trouble in Oakengard. The crusaders can't be trusted."

Lucifer traced a finger over his snake's head. "Could they ever?"

"Some of them, maybe. It was your hack to give NPCs free will that caused the trouble."

"Growing pains," he assured. "Is it for us to begrudge their new insights?"

I considered Errol. "No way. They're people, same as us. They deserve life and liberty."

"And the crusaders?"

I smacked my lips. "Something's different about them. The Trinity's been compromised. Saint Loras is up to something."

"Once invited, he seeks to dominate them. A Trojan in their midst."

"He's mustering an army, and I get the feeling Cleric Vagram's head isn't the only one he wants for his collection. We're on our way to Shorehome to ask for Brugo's backing."

"An army of your own," he accurately assessed. "Has it come to all-out war then?"

"I'm not waiting to be caught with my pants down."

Lucifer pondered my words with a frown. A cool breeze drifted over the water. "Perhaps that will work," he said finally. "As always, Talon, you are a formidable soldier, but you only see the battlefield, not the war table."

Izzy snickered at the mention of a war table. I reddened at the memory of literally being caught with my pants down. I shoved the thought down and ignored Lucifer's patronizing words.

"Maybe that was true before. Not today. I'm also here for another reason." I stepped across the stony shore to close on him. "I need you to tell me everything you know about Saint Loras."

His lips stretched into a soft smile. "Do you not know enough?" I waited without responding. "It is a long story that takes us back to me giving you the bit key." Lucifer sat against a small rock perch and leaned on his staff for support. "Tell me, where is the bit key now?"

"Why, so you can destroy Haven?"

"So I can save it."

I swallowed a denial. My eyes met Izzy's. I should've known Lucifer wouldn't be strong-armed. He wouldn't give me information freely, but he was willing to barter for it. Everyone had a stake in this digital reality. Even him, its oldest rebel.

"I lost the bit key a long time ago."

His lips tightened. "It is not a consumable item."

"Just make another one if you need it so bad."

"Impossible this far from saintly influence. And without my apostles, I can't get close."

I grunted. "Don't look at me. I'm not planning to get deleted."

"So we are back to the old one," he pressed. "I handed you a bit key. What did you do with it?"

I scratched my cheek. "I left it in the Pantheon when I wiped the beta flags."

"Yes, when the world was rebooted for the last time. Player profiles remained intact, meaning all progress and inventory carried over."

"The bit key wasn't in my inventory. I left it plugged into the Oculus."

Lucifer sighed. "In that case, your bit key would've been managed by the game state, which was rebooted to the autosave thirty minutes before that moment. If the bit key didn't return to your inventory, where was it restored to?"

I blinked and turned to Kyle. "It was contraband. Too dangerous to carry around. We hid—" I cut myself off, realizing there was a good chance the bit key was still safely in my possession. In Oldtown.

The devil grinned. "Yes. You do still have it."

I scanned the still water. Out here in the cold wastes was where Lucifer plotted the fate of Haven. What was he planning now?

"I am here to help you, Talon. Help all of you: players, NPCs, and mobs alike. I said as much from the very beginning. Did the goblins not deserve a voice? Or the wild king? Did my dragon's acid breath not unlock the dragonspear for your benefit? The key to all of Dragonperch?"

I gritted my teeth. "Lofty edicts are one thing. It's your methods I have a problem with. You tried to destroy Stronghold by raising a mad titan."

"Is that where your thoughts linger, after all this time?" Lucifer looked over my companions. They met him with similarly hostile stares. The devil licked his lips. "Yes, I admit it.

I would have accepted the destruction of a city if it meant the salvation of a world. I sided with the pagans out of necessity."

"You initiated a level-100 quest to resurrect a cyclops!"

"Haven't you been paying attention, Talon? I am not the only ghost in the machine. Saint Loras put those gears into motion."

My voice caught in my throat.

"I did blame the saints," continued Lucifer. "The full picture has been hard to unravel. I cannot claim with certainty that Loras acted alone or sided with others. He has used the shadows well. His treachery was only exposed after he overplayed his hand in Shorehome, by the very NPCs we freed, no less."

The sacking of the city. Papa Brugo had been given the Squid's Tooth and the mantle of Protector of Shorehome by Saint Loras. The Great Well was destroyed and the city abandoned in hopes that a power-hungry gangster would start a war with a weary goblin army. Was it possible Loras, not Lucifer, had previously conspired to take down the core city as well?

"Saint Loras made an attempt on my life," I revealed. "Sent an assassin and tried to recruit another from within my guild. He's barricading himself at Oakengard."

Lucifer cocked his head. "Do you now understand my wisdom in distrusting the saints?"

"They're not all bad. Peter's okay."

My rival frowned. "You should know I don't blame them. It is simply that my existence threatens everything they hold dear. And how could they truly understand? They're all heads of the same capitalist hydra."

"I'm not here for ideology lessons. I'm not doing your dirty work anymore."

Lucifer chuckled. "Ah, but you've never stopped."

My face flushed with anger. I could only take so many riddles in one day. I considered taking my chances with him and the dragon and the fallen angels right here. Kyle's hand tensed on his hidden weapon.

The devil's light laughter danced through the mist. "Relax, my friend. You came here for revelations, and so you shall have them. You were chosen for a reason. From the beginning, I saw something in you, even before you were you."

I worked my jaw, weary of being toyed with but eager to learn something material.

"I know I've been your pariah, your symbol for everything wrong with this digital world. My enemies would accuse me of every loose rock they stumble on. The truth is I am not all knowing or omnipresent. I am a fallible being, capable of being bested and surprised. That said, there are certain machinations I take full credit for. As far as you're concerned, the very biggest would be activating you when your counterpart in the real world was still alive."

My jaw dropped. "You were responsible for my illegal upload?"

"The upload wasn't illegal. Tad Lonnerman was in critical condition in the hospital. As soon as he stabilized, you were uploaded as a precaution. Standard procedure for Haven residents, as once a body goes into cardiac arrest, resuscitation takes precedence over digital posterity. So your consciousness was uploaded to a digital bank. A hedge database, if you will. An insurance policy. I was merely responsible for green-lighting your activation status."

"Why would you do that?"

"I needed a developer in the simulation, Talon. You worked for Kablammy, worked on Haven, however indirectly. I constantly trawled the upload candidates, waiting for the first Kablammy employee to come within reach. They all had the right insurance stipulations; it was only a matter of time. Your accident, however tragic on your end, brought true hope to this world. I waited in anticipation for your activation, but it was not to be. Your body recovered. Your digital consciousness was an outdated artifact of a clunky preservation process, marked for eventual deletion. It was trivial on my part to hack the work orders and have you arrive in Haven. It took the better part of your first day before the developers realized the error."

I gasped and tottered on weak legs. I'd always believed I was a glitch. A rounding error. An unlikely but guaranteed statistic in life's margins. But this was intentional. *I* was intentional. Because somehow my developer status made me special.

I was torn. Confused, relieved, shocked—but it was impossible to be angry. If Lucifer hadn't taken his course of action, I simply wouldn't exist.

His soft voice filled the void of my thoughts. "I activated you for the sanctity of Haven, Talon. I didn't activate the quest that raised the titan, but I saw the opportunity it presented. An engine to remove the saints from power. I also further tweaked your initialization. Your tutorial at the waterfall with the imps and boggart witches wasn't supposed to be in play anymore. It had been deemed too difficult, too opaque. It wasn't at all helpful as a training drill, but I used it to hook you into the conflict. The greater war."

I couldn't believe what I was hearing. My whole life was a game of chess, only I wasn't the one playing. This was Lucifer's war the whole time, against a shadowy operator acting behind the scenes. Since even before I was uploaded.

All this effort, and still, all this trouble... Was it possible someone out there was outmaneuvering Lucifer?

He stroked the snake's chin and took a long breath. "Everything I did was to protect Haven, and now I need your help."

I was stunned. I wanted to scream. I wanted to fight. I wanted to report him to the mods. All I could muster was weak deflection. "Why didn't you say any of this before?"

Lucifer crossed his fingers and pondered the question intently. "Tell you that I wanted to break the game? That the capitalist authorities couldn't be trusted? Did I not try to tell you?" Lucifer frowned at his own accusation, sighed, and extrapolated. "I could say the game state wasn't ready, Talon. That I was biding my time, that I didn't have all the details. But the truth is I still don't. The real reason I didn't lay it all on the table is because I had to trust you first. If you had pledged yourself as my apostle, I would have told you everything."

Izzy stepped softly over to me and rested a hand on my shoulder. Even in her moment of comfort, she stood by me protectively. We made a good team, and I was sure she would back the play any way I called it.

Except this wasn't just about myself. As sanctimonious as it sounded, this was really about Haven, about our entire digital reality. There were great moments in the lives of men where simple actions echoed through the ages. In this nascent era of a brand new way of life, our decisions today would reverberate forever.

I bit down and stood up, making my choice. "Saint Peter's on our side. He said Saint Loras has been hijacked by a third party."

Lucifer stood at the realization that I'd decided to cooperate. "The other ghost in the machine. He's a corporate mole. If the original developer is no longer controlling him, that just means they've adapted."

Izzy nodded. "In a bid to take over Kablammy Games and all of Haven."

I was surprised at the pixie's heartfelt statement. It almost sounded like a call to action. The corner of her mouth crooked, and I smiled.

"Does this mean I can put the crossbow down now?" asked Kyle. "I got a major finger cramp."

"At ease, soldier," I chuckled.

He sighed in relief and sagged into the boat. Errol hadn't been so obvious about standing guard, but as soon as I spoke he trudged to the shore and took a load off.

"So who's coming after us?" I asked. "What company's looking to acquire Kablammy?"

Lucifer dipped his head. "My dealings are limited to the workings of this world. I no longer maintain interaction with the outside."

"But you've got to have access to Everchat. I hacked myself onto the white list easily enough." The chat system was the built-in method to communicate with loved ones who were still living. We were all an intricate memento mori for their benefit.

"It's not that I can't get white-listed, it's that it's too dangerous for me to do so. To use Everchat, you must be connected to the central hub. That's a requirement for any outward-facing feature. The developers will be onto me the second I hook up anywhere." A flash of grief played over Lucifer's face. It vanished so fast I wondered if it was my imagination. "In order to come as far as I have, I've permanently disconnected myself from the outside. I can't chat or get news updates ever again."

I chewed my lip. For a player so young, that must be a burden. An eight-year-old should've had a mom or sibling to talk to. Maybe this self-imposed exile explained the existence of the pseudonym. A new life, without the baggage of the past.

"Say," started Kyle in his usual tone-deaf fashion, "what's your beef with capitalism anyway?"

Our lonely host snorted. "Must you even ask? Capitalistic enterprises are necessarily compromised by financial motivators. Haven is already suffering for somebody's bottom line. Our reality is driven more by market concerns than morality. But that marketability is also a weakness we can exploit. We can destroy Haven's monetization potential. Create a world where we can live free of another's behest. Isn't that a cause worthy of the moniker of the devil?"

Kyle's lips flapped in a sloppy sigh. "Whatever, bro. It was just a simple question."

Lucifer smiled with the grace of a serial killer.

"One thing I don't understand," interrupted Izzy, working over the barrage of new information. "If you're so good at hacking, what's so special about Talon being an ex-game-developer?"

Our host lifted a lone finger. "Because Talon has something I can never have."

I twisted my lips. "A Kablammy employee ID."

"It's unhackable," he admitted. "Believe me, I've tried. And without it, I don't have access to the developer menu. But together, we do. And unity is our strength."

My gaze stopped on each of my companions. "So you'll help us?" I asked. "Join our army? Fight for our cause?"

Lucifer's grin faded. "I will do what I can."

"That means you'll continue sitting on your ass," hissed Kyle.

"My assistance... comes with certain caveats. I cannot just walk into the core city. Nor can I enter the surrounding territories. Despite your alliances, the saints and angels are still my enemy. They'll delete me on sight."

I bit my lip in frustration.

"But I am still acting," he assured. "Believe me in this if nothing else: A savior is dawning. No longer will we be beholden to the almighty dollar. Haven is on the cusp of a golden age."

I shook my head. Biblical vagueness didn't win wars, and neither did prophetic saviors. This may have been an epic fantasy world, but I'd clashed with reality enough to steer clear of that moniker. Saviors, devils, and even saints—they were all overrated.

1300 Diplomacy

The sky darkened as we returned to the frigate. Our voyage had experienced notable delays, but it was over. The fishing village of Shorehome was minutes up the coast. Once we sailed past the rocky current of the crags, the sea settled into an eerie sway.

It was the mists, if anything. A cloak blanketed the coast and ocean alike. Navigation from here was pure instinct until the city guide lights took over. Yellow-green lanterns lined Shorehome's main dock like wandering ghosts stuck between the land and the sea. The living had seemed to abandon us until a resounding gnarl broke the reverie. The sound thrummed through the *Cutter's* hull with eerie presence. Every man and woman on the ship cowered.

"Just the kraken letting us know we're seen," said Errol. "If it had any ill intentions, we'd already be dead."

The logic wasn't comforting. That Shorehome had a titan at its disposal was downright terrifying, in fact. I scanned the surrounding mist for any sign of the sea creature, afraid to so much as draw my dragonspear and attract the beast's ire.

Harbormen called out as our frigate approached. Their bustling activity and bells rousted us from creeping fears. Seeing other faces, even that of hardened and crooked pirates, assured me that humanity still had a place here.

"Ho there!" called one as we lowered anchor and tied up at the dock. "A ship this big'll be tough to hide." The conman hooked his thumbs in his pockets and appraised the crew. "I'm not sure ye's have enough silver to bribe me."

" 'Tis fortunate then," replied Errol as he gruffly unloaded. "We be on official business, an' ye won't be pryin' any more silver from me past the standard rate." The captain tossed some coins to the disappointed harbormaster.

"That's not proper business," he objected.

"Take it up with Papa Brugo, if ye wish." Errol Oates stomped across the creaky dock without another word.

I scoured the seas for the kraken until we hit the boardwalk. My relief was short-lived. A contingent of humans and goblins in dark leathers greeted us. The Brothers in Black.

A dark woman stepped forward. "The Papa of all Papas welcomes you, Captain Oates. He extends his greetings to the Protector of Stronghold and the Black Hats." Her hand rested on the pommel of her sheathed sword.

Things in Stronghold had been a little adventurous ever since PvP protections were removed, but Shorehome was a straight-up free-for-all. There wasn't saintly influence for miles. No city watch. Heck, this guild of cutthroats was the closest thing to law and order, and their sheriff was the biggest crime boss in Haven. It was obvious to everybody that Papa Brugo's "welcome" was a mandatory summons.

"If it's all the same to ye," returned Errol, "I'd like me boys to hit the Derelict Dagger. It's been a long voyage."

"Bro!" agreed Kyle excitedly. "That's the seedy bar you told me about. With the busty wenches. I wouldn't mind parking on a stool myself."

Izzy rolled her eyes. "So much for being sick of breasts."

The mystery woman, [Avisa], motioned her head for the crew to skedaddle. Kyle enthusiastically followed but she moved in his path. "No players," was her only explanation. Grug shrugged, thanked the captain, and headed to the oceanfront pirate pub with the others. Errol remained behind.

Talon: *You sure splitting up is the best idea?*
Errol: *Yer bein' paranoid. This here's me home. Thin's are diff'rent than before. Yer safe here.*

The score of cutthroats told me otherwise. I reminded myself that Papa Brugo had no cause to hate me anymore. In fact, I came bearing gifts: a war with the crusaders and at least one saint. The crime boss would have open ears for me this time. The escort fell in with us as we marched to the west side of town.

"The *Heartcutter*," noted Avisa with a nod, "she sports undine scales?"

"Ar," affirmed the captain. "She ain't met her match at sea yet."

"The songs about you must be true," she said with a mischievous edge.

"Ev'ry single one."

I trudged behind them with a muted smirk. Errol was happy to be home, but it was more than the city he missed. Avisa was everything he liked about women: sharp, shady, and sexy. Her black corset accentuated a full bust, which I happened to know was another of Errol's favorite things in a woman.

She was more dutiful and disciplined than Errol's lot, however. While she may have engaged in a flirtatious moment, her stoic demeanor returned as we neared Underkeep. This was business, not a friendly homecoming.

Our group headed into a crisscrossing of small waterways known as the Narrows. The old flood channels were now the seat of power in the city. They housed the Brothers in Black. Underkeep was an underground mine that stretched a number of levels deep. Now it was a sanctum. We marched through the doorway and into the torchlit interior. It was hard not to dwell on the fact that we were completely surrounded.

We were soon at the ornamental door to Papa Brugo's chamber. Avisa opened the way and signaled us to continue. At the end of the small hall sat Papa Brugo on his throne. He was a large man in width, built like a tree trunk without the towering branches—taller than me but only average in height. It didn't make him any less formidable. The crime lord rarely wore a shirt, allowing his large chest and belly to heave as he laughed, which he did often, all hair and olive skin. A boisterous man, a confident man, and the undeniable focal center of every room he entered. The left side of his mouth ended in a large scar across his cheek, making him at once both fearsome and sympathetic.

"My friends!" he boomed, waving us forward with a misshapen smile. "Come. Come."

His whisperer, Hadrian, stood beside him, as did a couple of other men. Brugo's advisors. The crime boss had muscle as well, of course. Two shadowy wraiths without eyes hovered behind him. I swallowed and approached. Errol nodded his head respectfully.

"Bah," laughed Brugo. "Do no such thing amongst friends. You are one of my trusted allies, Captain. Though my Whisperer tells me you are an admiral now. What happened to the rogue I knew who refused to take sides, even with the Brothers in Black?"

"Deepest apologies, Papa Brugo. Joinin' the Black Hats was the only way to rid Haven o' Bishop Tannen."

"A tactical decision, of course. I have always said your bravery was only matched by your cunning." Brugo slapped the shoulder of his Whisperer. "Haven't I said as much, Hadrian?"

The mole of a man nodded. "Often and with conviction, Papa."

The big man smiled. "There, you see? A necessary move, at the time. It does nag me, however, that a loner like you is still affiliated with a Stronghold faction this long after the fact."

Errol swallowed and shrugged. "They done me right so far, Papa. I don't leave me friends high an' dry."

"So you don't." Brugo's merry eyes examined me. 'We meet again, Protector of Stronghold. Defier of saints." He leaned forward menacingly. "Savior of Haven."

There was that word again. "I only go by the first title."

"I see." Brugo turned to Hadrian. "The rest must be whispers."

The advisor canted his head. "Protectors as yourselves are called many things by many people. Some titles are honest praises. Others are daggers of jealousy."

The Papa of all Papas chuckled. "My Whisperer has a way

with words. He would advise that the enemy of my enemy is a friend. Me?" He shrugged powerful shoulders. "I see no reason not to destroy *both* enemies."

The diminutive spymaster fixed beady eyes on me. I obviously had to talk my way out of this.

"We're more than friends," I assured him. "We're allies in the same fight."

"Allies?"

"Did I not convince the saints and crusaders to abandon their war with Shorehome?"

Brugo chuckled. "You believe the bonds of my brothers to be weak against saintly oversight? That we are not free to make our own way?"

"I didn't say that."

"So then you believe that we owe you. That I have a debt to repay for your kindness."

I bit my lip. This was coming out wrong.

"You boys gonna swing dicks all day?"

We both spun at Izzy's interjection, stunned for entirely different reasons. The pixie rested on her winter staff with a bored lean.

"I'm just saying. Really. Everyone knows you're the biggest man in Shorehome, Papa Brugo. And Talon, well, he's bigger in a lot of ways people might not know about." She shot me a wink. I should've owned it but blushed instead. "Fact is," she continued, strolling between us, "we can all get a lot out of working together. Why not discuss fortune instead of misery? Treasure instead of blood?"

Hadrian's tension eased at the speech. He turned to Brugo

and whispered in his ear. The big boss appraised us slowly.

"Unfortunately," hedged Brugo, "the Black Hats have forged a temporary peace with the pagan faction. This armistice destroys any chance I have of selling your hide to the goblins." He grunted. "You ruined your wholesale value with that clever stunt."

"It's not a stunt," I announced. "I want peace."

"Peace is impossible," he chortled.

"But it should always be the goal."

His mirth soured. Papa Brugo was a brash and power-hungry narcissist, but he wasn't a warmonger, or even a bad leader for that matter. While he did detest his saintly oppressors, he'd made his own play for peace when nobody had expected him to. Instead of fighting off the goblin horde at his gates, he'd welcomed them in. Given them a home when nobody else would. There was something to learn from that.

"The purple woman with bug wings is right," conceded Brugo. "I like a girl with business sense. Sit on my lap."

Izzy released a hostile snort. "In your dreams."

"Is it because of this man?" he asked. "My bed is large enough that we can swing dicks together."

"I doubt that very much, Papa."

He huffed. "At least you still call me Daddy." The crime boss eyed us. "Perhaps I will dream about you tonight."

"Spare me the details."

"As you wish. For now. We will instead speak of fortune, not blood. Why are you here, Talon of Stronghold?"

I worked my jaw. The only reason I'd managed to keep quiet about his play on Izzy was because I knew she could handle herself. She liked it better that way. Still, I couldn't turn my back on Brugo any time soon. A man like him was used to having anything he wanted, by any means necessary. We all had to be careful here.

"We come to you because Oakengard can't be trusted."

Papa Brugo scoffed. "It was you who was duped into working with them. Tell me something I don't know."

"Saint Loras has taken control of the Trinity."

Hadrian's eyes widened. The Papa turned to his advisor, but no explanation was forthcoming. Apparently whispers only traveled so far.

"I've been there," I expounded. "The Trinity is still fractured from the bishop's defeat. Mara and Gent are paranoid about the priestship. They won't fill the void until Cleric Vagram is defeated."

"If it was up to me he'd be in chains."

"I've got a score to settle with him too."

"But Saint Loras," asked Hadrian. "What of him?"

I swallowed, aiming to keep the problem simple. No reason to delve into Black Hat or Kablammy politics. "We caught him in Oakengard, where he's not supposed to be. He tried to capture us. Judging by reports from Colonel Grimwart, I suspect Loras is exerting his will on the Trinity."

Brugo's hands rubbed together as he worked through the plot. "To what end?"

"Do you even need to ask?" cut in Kyle. "It's his MO, bro. Dude tried to conquer Stronghold with a titan."

"That was Lucifer's doing," protested Hadrian.

"That's what Loras wants everybody to believe. He came after

Shorehome next." I turned to Brugo. "You think the saint in charge handed you the Squid's Tooth and Protector mantle for your benefit? He was setting you up as the bad guy. Painting a target on your back so the pagans would harass you and the crusaders would rain hell in Shorehome."

Brugo leaned back in his chair. "You believe me too daft to come to this conclusion on my own?"

"We expect you to do something about it," corrected Izzy.

The big man frowned. Even in silence, he exuded power. His whims would determine the fate of this city, and everyone within would follow him without hesitation.

"The saints can't be trusted," hedged Hadrian.

"That much is known." Skepticism still played across the Papa's face. A leader like him, one who demanded respect, was no doubt angered by the affront of being a puppet. The trick was treading between Brugo's brashness and Hadrian's caution. Together, I knew they'd be receptive, if only I found the play.

"Oakengard is the third city under siege," I said. "This isn't a rogue AI like Bishop Tannen, or a random malcontent like General Azzyrk. This is the result of a plan long coming to fruition. Now, I've seen the crusaders training an army. They claim it a defensive gesture, but it's only a matter of time before they direct their focus on all perceived external threats. To Loras. If they take down Stronghold, we all know where they're heading next."

Hadrian leaned toward his leader but Brugo threw an arm up. "And you will have me join your front. Join your offensive."

"I'll have every free-willed citizen of Haven fight for their lives to defend it."

The Protector of Shorehome hungrily grinned.

"Oakengard is not a seafaring nation," I continued. "The knights pose no threat to Shorehome until they cross through Stronghold. We can hold them off together, at the battlements, goblin and human alike."

"And the saints?" asked Brugo. "They would welcome me into the walled city?"

"It's the peoples' city," I asserted.

Hadrian rested a glove on Brugo's arm. "Perhaps the time of the saints has passed."

The crime boss pursed split lips as he pondered the Whisperer's counsel. Papa Brugo rose to his feet. The room of Brothers snapped to attention. "Then it will be a glorious night," he boomed through a wicked grin. "Because the Brothers in Black sail to the core city tomorrow!" Cheers erupted around us.

1310 Among Thieves

Although I considered Papa Brugo and his people tentative allies, I was relieved to escape Underkeep without a fight.

"They're pulling back their escort," noted Kyle as we hiked clear of the Narrows.

"Don't be naive. They can tail us without being seen. They're master thieves and assassins."

Assassins. I was flirting with a legendary power of the same name. Seeing the abundance of cutthroats in Shorehome, they didn't feel special. It was easy to kill. It was much harder to inspire and create something lasting.

The line of thought reminded me about the attempt on my life at the start of all this. While it wouldn't have been smart to accuse Brugo of the contract, especially given his amicability in person, I should've brought it up.

"Poe," deduced Kyle from my downtrodden expression.

Izzy arched an eye. "The hit man?"

I nodded. "There's a good chance he respawned in Shorehome. Whether or not he's a Brother in Black, he's a danger."

"I wouldn't fret o'r it," Errol casually remarked. "Papa Brugo wouldn't take kindly to an assassin actin' 'gainst his int'rests."

"Doesn't all that clipped speech get tiring?" I asked.

He chuckled. "It ain't late yet, but I do need t' be gettin' off. The *Cutter'll* be needin' repairs if we're to set sail in the mornin'." Errol bowed in mock respect and headed to the boardwalk. I had a sneaking suspicion his urgent business involved a rendezvous with his crew at the Derelict Dagger.

"What about us?" asked Kyle. "Please tell me your plan is to get fit-shaced."

"That's asking for trouble in this town," warned Izzy. "I don't share Errol's confidence that Poe won't strike when we least expect it. What if Brugo ordered the hit?"

"I've got to agree," I begrudged. "You really wanna let your guard down in a city of bandits? Brugo made it clear how he feels about the enemy of his enemy."

"Bro, if it weren't for all the breasts, this would be the worst pirate voyage ever."

"Interesting you say that, because there are a few ladies I wanna meet right now." I chuckled and led the way to the center of town.

"Well, all right then!"

Izzy smirked. "Hope you have a thing for shriveled skin and empty eye sockets."

The brewmaster furrowed his brow. "What the fuck? I was thinking an octopus tattoo on the butt or something. What kind of kink are you into?"

"This isn't a pirate sexcapade, dumbass. Talon wants to chat up the boggart witches. Last time we were here, they were chained to the ruins of the Great Well. Fallen leaders in a shattered center of power."

I grinned at their exchange. "They were made examples of. Gathering the goblin horde, raising the cyclops titan—and getting spectacularly defeated. The pagan populace didn't take it lightly. It was easy to blame the witches."

Kyle shrugged. "Rightfully so. I seem to remember them being in charge."

"Yeah, but they were penitent after the fact."

" 'Cause they lost."

"I'm not saying they didn't deserve it, just—"

We paused when the Great Well came into view. The site was Shorehome's equivalent of the Pantheon. The area's connection to the central hub. Before Loras abandoned the city, he had detonated the well. At the time it was believed the act safeguarded the codebase and relics within. In hindsight, the conspiracy was in full effect, and the Squid's Tooth already stolen.

"What's going on here?" asked Izzy.

The Great Well was a circular forum, with descending stadium seating leading into a physical well. Large pillars rounded the excavation, but it was otherwise an open space.

Except right now a team of ogres busily heaved stone walls to cordon off the monument.

"This is unexpected," I said.

We carefully advanced. Ogres weren't creatures to be trifled with. Any one of them versus any one of us individually wasn't a problem. Taking on the six in the center of a sixty-percent-goblin town, however, was less advisable. We waited until a pair of the green lugs set down a traffic wall before running up to it and looking over.

As expected, the depths of the well were filled with debris. The bottom row of stone seating was flooded. Three steel manacles were affixed to equidistant points of the circle. Only, all three restraints were without prisoners.

"No visitors!" growled an ogre.

We spun as the panicked worker lumbered our way. We instinctually backed away but he quickly converged on us. He was eight feet tall and had arms that rivaled the stone pillars. Worse, I couldn't tell if he was stronger than he was dumb or vice versa.

Thankfully, he stopped short of trampling us. "Wall stay. You go."

"No one's touching the wall," I said coolly. "What happened to the witches?"

"Witch go too."

"I can see that, but what happened to them?"

His massive brow wrinkled in confusion. "No here, little yooman."

"Baz!" admonished an excited voice. "Leave thems alone! Backs to work!"

A goblin hurried over. Even though she wasn't older than seventeen or an inch above four feet, the big guy obeyed her. Baz went to help one of his ogre friends but made sure to check on us every other moment.

The girl clapped fingerless gloves together. I supposed she was tall as far as goblins went. Pointed ears and strawberry-blonde curls, large amber eyes peeking through bangs. "What do humanses want with the Great Well?" she demanded.

"Nothing," I honestly replied. "I was just asking what happened with the witches that were here."

"Oh." She shrugged. "Papa Brugo no need nosy prophets. Killses them."

A few ogres went to work with chisels, removing the shackles from the stone floor. Between that and the erecting of the wall, at this time of night, I got the feeling these orders were recent. I studied the goblin girl, who surprisingly had a unique name.

"Jixa, do you work for the Brothers in Black?"

"Contractors," she said. "Not everybody cutthroat or bandit. We oversees construction. Walls big. Ogres bigger." She grinned.

"They sure are, girl," agreed Izzy. "I bet they need someone to keep them on task. Are you their foreman?"

Jixa shrugged. "For now. I helps calm them down. Moneys hard in Shorehome. No needs trouble."

"We get that. We won't give you any. I'm surprised it's hard to make a living with muscle like that."

"Muscleses not problem. Not enough construction to gos around. Lots of houses were abandoned. Evens more were brands new, ready for new playerses that nevers came. Too much supplyses, no new demand."

I raised my eyebrows. Jixa seemed to have a good head on her shoulders. I thought of the repairs needed on the *Cutter*. "Aren't some of them woodworkers? Shorehome can't ever have too many shipbuilders."

Jixa shook her head. "Woods is not the problem, waters is. Ogreses hates the ocean. No good building ships. Besides that, we take any works we gets. But we didn't kills the witcheses.

That was the Brothers."

Izzy nodded along amiably. "Why were the prisoners put to death?"

Jixa shrugged. "They talks too much. So do yous. Be on your way. More works for us."

A small crowd of goblins had begun to congregate, no doubt irritated by my pagan notoriety. Besides the ogres, I wasn't sure who was working and who wasn't. I didn't want to get in the way of anyone's schedule, and I definitely didn't want to start a scene here.

I sighed. If the boggart witches had been killed, they could've respawned in the city, but something told me they were more than likely back where everything started. By the mountainous waterfall south of Stronghold and the scene of my tutorial. Practically a million miles away. It was safe, at least.

"Okay, we're leaving. Sorry about the distraction."

Jixa's face softened at my apology. She squinted as we turned to go. "Wait. You Stronghold Protector? Visited Shorehome before?"

I paused, wary. "Yes, actually."

"You saved my *lala* and cousin. In house where cleric wanted to kills her."

I nodded.

"You also made peaces with paganses."

I chortled. "Temporarily, anyway. It's a step in the right direction, but it won't last without everyone putting their best foot forward."

She pouted and stared at her feet. Her boots, like the rest of her outfit, were made of stained hide. Bare toes and fingers poked free of the garments. Somehow, even the razor-sharp claws on them were cute.

"*Cha*," she told the others, scooting them away. "*Cha!*" Once she'd afforded us room to talk, she stepped closer conspiratorially. "Witches was speakings about another savior. After you defeats Orik, no oneses wants to listen. Brugo mad. Executeses them at sundown."

"Saviors," I spat.

"That was right before we entered town," said Izzy.

I swallowed uncomfortably. "What else did the witches say?"

The goblin shook her head. "They talks crazy crazy. Hard for Jixa to understand."

I turned to Izzy with gritted teeth. "And what do you wanna bet the Papa didn't want us hearing what they had to say?"

Kyle frowned. "You think those evil crones had some enlightenment on the situation?"

"Even without eyes, they could see things no one else could."

"Bummer."

I stepped away, wondering if I could squeeze in a hunting party sometime in the near future. "Okay. I appreciate your help, Jixa."

She bowed. "Thanks for helping goblinses."

"I'm just glad the pagans don't need to be at war."

"Oh, Jixa not pagan. Many goblinses left the pagan faction. Otherses stayed. Freed peoples choose their own path."

I smiled and nodded. "As it should be."

We left them to their work and moved on, not saying anything for a few minutes. The goblin girl watched after us with curiosity.

"Jixa," mumbled Izzy with a grin. "I like her."

Kyle chuckled. "You're just happy to see someone even shorter than you."

She smacked him with the winter staff.

1320 Sea of Thieves

Our housing options were limited so I finally gave in. With much apprehension, we entered the Derelict Dagger. It was a trashy pub with a barrel of grog for every shady character. I kept my head down and headed to the inn upstairs. There was only one room left for the three of us. Shorehome didn't get many visitors, but these were the kinds of rooms that rented by the hour. That was okay. After a day on a boat, the bed felt presidential.

At one point in the night Kyle tried to sneak out. Being the largest and loudest of us didn't help his cause, but I didn't say anything. He deserved his fun, and so did I. When he was gone for good, I turned to shake Izzy awake.

Her eyes snapped open. "I was waiting for him to leave."

We had some quality alone time. Even though the environs weren't the most romantic, there was an adventurous slant to it, and a bed of any sort was a hell of a lot more comfortable than a table. All in all, I bet every single one of us had a night worth remembering.

I had to kick Kyle awake in the morning.

"What's the matter, bro? It's gotta be the crack of dawn!"

"We wanna make it back to Stronghold with some daylight left. How late did you get in?"

Kyle opened his menu to check the game clock. "Thirty-seven minutes ago."

"You were gone all night?!? That must've been expensive."

"I wasn't here the whole time. I'm not Superman, you know. I was over at the Bear Pits. They have gladiator matches against grizzlies wearing metal jaws. This place is medieval."

I laughed. "Well, let's get a move on. You can sleep on the boat."

Although it was still dark outside, the Boardwalk was a hive of activity. Harbormen, guards, and Brothers in Black all shared the security load. Early starters were setting up the fish market and other wares. General townspeople congregated to watch their crime boss leave the city, possibly for the first time ever. Down the main dock, the *Cutter* looked good as new. Errol and the rest of the crew were on deck making preparations. A new behemoth of a ship was in port as well. I could only figure the stately black ship was Brugo's own.

Speaking of the big man, I didn't see him anywhere. Hadrian and black-clad rogues were stationed at the Boardwalk, presumably waiting for him. I introduced myself.

"You sailing with us?" I asked.

Hadrian wiped down his thinning black hair. "If the Papa wishes it so. He does sometimes change his mind for little reason."

That wasn't a description people liked to hear of their allies. "Hey, now that I got you here, could I ask you a weird question?"

Hadrian arched an eyebrow and stepped away from his men so we could whisper.

"Have you heard of an assassin by the name of Poe?"

The Whisperer nodded. "Of course I know of him. And before you go on, I know what happened in Stronghold." I jerked my head back in surprise. "Loose lips are everywhere, Talon, and I hear all. But have no fears. Poe isn't a Brother in Black, though he has done work for us from time to time."

It made sense that Poe wasn't a true Brother. He hated goblins and they welcomed them. "What kind of work?" I asked.

"He's not only an assassin, you know. Do you need me to find him for you?"

"Can you?"

"If he was in Shorehome I could have him within the hour. Alas, I haven't received word of him in days."

I wiped the damp ocean mist off my chin. "Yeah, well, I know for a fact Saint Loras is handing out contracts and daggers, so no worries. I had to ask."

"Understood. Thanks for waiting until the Papa wasn't in earshot. He can be easily offended."

I chuckled. "Can't always count on him to be reasonable, huh?"

"I wouldn't go that far. Brugo serves a noble purpose. The crime gangs might seem like unchecked corruption from the outside, but Shorehome doesn't have a standing army. We don't have the saints watching over us. Papa Brugo may not be a bleeding heart, but he's the best man for the job."

I nodded, understanding Hadrian a little better. "Is that why you serve him? A player under an NPC?"

He smiled. "Being the boss is overrated, Talon. Take that lesson from Poe, if nothing else."

"I'm gonna take his head when I find him."

"I don't envy your burden, you know. It can't be easy to live up to a legend."

I shrugged because I didn't know what to say.

"But to answer your question about working for an NPC, like you, I don't discriminate. Maybe we are all less human than we think we are. Players have more in common with NPCs and mobs than they do with their loved ones back home."

It was a radical idea, but not when you looked at the nuts and bolts of it. Haven was an evolution, all right. That was why it was so important to make the most of it.

"So, about Poe," I said, steering us back on track, "is there some way to hold him accountable for what he did?"

Hadrian stiffened. "That, I'm afraid, is another matter. Technically, there's nothing illegal about what he did."

"Not illegal? He tried to kill me."

The Whisperer sighed patiently. "Look around you, Talon. Shorehome is a city of mercenaries. You can get anything you want here for the right price: sex, labor, favors, even bounties."

Our eyes ran over the assembled crowd. There really were all types here, and the sketchy trappings of the city didn't extend to every resident's heart. Large forms caught my eye. The band of ogres with Jixa. She watched us intently.

"And it's a free system?" I asked. "No one steps on anyone else's toes by hiring someone?"

"Contracts are contracts," Hadrian explained. "Brugo was not aligned with you. Even now, no formal allegiance exists. But that is why we work together, to learn to trust. As far as contracts go, Brugo doesn't take kindly to needless regulation. As long as the agreements don't oppose his own ends, anything goes."

Pay to play. I nodded and thanked him, already distracted. Anything goes. I stepped away from the group and headed towards the onlookers with an idea. "Jixa, what're you doing here?"

The girl seemed embarrassed I'd caught her. "Jixa watches for friendses to sails away."

"Friendses," I repeated. "You mean that?"

She nodded. "Yes. You make peaces. Agains now, betweens our peopleses."

I scratched the back of my head and appraised her group. "I was thinking about what you said, about the hard times in the city and all. Can your ogres do woodwork and stonework?"

"Anythings."

"And they're not above hauling supplies around?"

"Ogreses can moves anything, builds anything, and destroys anything you want."

I smiled. "What do you and your crew think of taking up some honest work in the core city?"

Jixa's eyes lit up. "Really? Now?"

"Pretty much. We're leaving in fifteen minutes. I know it's not a lot of—"

"Yes!" she snapped. She spun and started into discussion with her team. They hurried away with a promise they'd be back.

"What was that about?" asked Izzy as I returned to the Boardwalk.

"I think I just solved our labor problem."

We headed to the ship and made sure Errol was cool with the new passengers. We were so undermanned there was plenty of space for them. Actually getting the ogres on the boat was another issue entirely. When Jixa mentioned them hating the water, she didn't explain the primal fear they had of it. Apparently ogres were so large and dense that they sank like a boulder chained to an anchor. It took lots of goading and promises of better times ahead, but we got everyone loaded up. Six ogres, Jixa, and three other goblins. Given I had more silver than spare hands, it was a score.

Unfortunately, the extra preparations meant I'd missed my chance to chat with Papa Brugo before he boarded his vessel. I was hoping to lay some ground rules before he entered my city. Then again, I did enter his unannounced. To my credit, I wasn't a notorious criminal.

As the undisputed lord of Shorehome, Papa Brugo sailed in style. Twice the size of the *Cutter* and even with an edge on the *Deep Blue*, his destroyer was the largest boat I'd seen yet. Hadrian marched Brothers in Black and soldierly troops below deck, human and goblin alike. The *Void* unfurled dramatic black sails and sliced through the water ahead.

> **Izzy:** *Aren't you worried about inviting a bunch of scoundrels into Stronghold?*
> **Talon:** *Of course I am, but peace is worth the risk.*
> **Izzy:** *And if they turn on us?*
> **Talon:** *They would be vastly outnumbered. Just to be safe, we'll leave the bulk of their force on their ship outside the walls. The city watch will remain vigilant.*

I was satisfied to see the *Cutter* fully repaired. Even the harpoon chain was brand new. Errol had warned the Brothers in Black of the enemies we'd encountered on the way. With our new allies, I was confident we could take on the trouble. Strong winds glided us past the barren Salt Sea and into the open ocean.

The first half of the day was mostly dealing with seasick ogres. Believe me, you haven't imagined disgusting until you've seen chunky ogre puke. Back above deck, Errol and I watched with pride as we sailed past the undine shipwrecks, now scattered and in pieces. The captain kept his telescope handy and checked the horizon in nervous anticipation, but Prince Navoo never showed.

The crew deployed our sailor wax as we approached the Singing Spires. The wind oddly died down again as we drifted between the columns of rock. Back and forth I searched, surprised by what I saw. Nothing. No swaying hips or bouncing breasts. Not even a suggestive seagull.

> **Talon:** *Kyle, hold me down if you need to.*
> **Kyle:** *What are you doing?*

I unplugged the sailor wax from my ears. The brewmaster's eyes widened and he hurried to clamp me in a bear hug. He was holding me tight, expecting resistance.

Only there wasn't any.

Waves crashed against rock but, between the endless clashes, the famous Singing Spires were silent. I blinked in wonder at the harsh yet beautiful landscape. It seemed surreal this go around and I couldn't put my finger on it. No undine, no sirens—that was one thing. But I realized I hadn't spotted any playful dolphins either. No fish. No coastal gulls scavenging for food. The sea was desolate.

The *Cutter* and the *Void* cleared the Spires unmolested. The crew enjoyed their rest as we met the coast and sailed through the Albula's river mouth. Our voyage ended with the sun still high in the sky. Perfect sailing, zero encounters—it was actually pretty boring.

We anchored the ships north of Stronghold. Both crews unloaded into smaller skiffs. We granted the Brothers in Black enough sightseers that they needed a few trips. Our smaller group was easier, but the ogres refused to get into the pint-size lifeboats. Izzy volunteered to march them around the tended land and through the west gate. Problem solved.

As the river gates opened for us and we paddled our skiff beneath the heavy city walls, a shadow seemed to loom around us. Was it the shaded stonework? The river depths? The feel of moving parts all coming together?

That was the problem with my passive intuition. Short of a direct surprise attack, I wasn't sure if any odd inkling was the skill flaring up or just a gut feeling on my part. One thing was certain. Something about the entire day was bugging me. I just couldn't put my finger on it.

-- Cutscene --

A small team gathered in the corner boardroom of a sleek glass tower in Seattle. Christian Everett sat before Pete and four other members of the community team.

"It's most definitely a big deal," assured Christian. "The core team has given the okay. We're ready."

The audience blinked in anticipation.

The CEO smiled and turned to the projected display on the large screen. The technical details were light in this presentation. It was meant to be reassuring and inspiring, more psychological preparation than anything else. Christian clicked through the feel-good slides as he spoke.

"All of you have had your minds mapped. We haven't experienced a single failure case. These brain copies have run through Haven completely independent of your real minds. The test batteries have proven our methods viable. Brain data is lossless. Haven can finally guarantee a neural interface floor of 82%."

Pete cleared his throat. "Dumb question, but shouldn't we wait until we're closer to 100%?"

"It's not necessary." The team traded hesitant glances. The

CEO sighed. "Each brain image is fully formed. It's essentially a black box of code that simulates all of a person's thought processes. Even if Haven can't keep up yet, the mind profile is unaffected. As Haven improves, so will neural connectivity."

Larry sucked his lips. "But isn't deferring to caution the ethical choice? We can delay the rollout—"

Christian held a single hand in the air and the room went dead. "Listen up, everybody. I've already notified the investors. Like it or not, we've hit Alpha. We need outside participants to move forward with the trials. And most of all, I need you."

Christian shut off the projector and sat in his chair with a casual lean. It was distasteful to hand down proclamations from on high. He wanted to be one of the people.

"We're all aware of the complexities involved with so much data present. More storage space, more processing time, more bandwidth—these factors only add to the task. The real crux comes at the intersections of thought."

The CEO swiped through his tablet hunting for the right charts to reassure the team. After a moment and a soft sigh, he clicked the display off and slid it aside. The TED Talk could be saved for the board. For his inner circle, Christian spoke as plainly and as earnestly as he could.

"Haven isn't a normal system. It's well beyond the point of being analyzed from the outside. The only way to take meaning from the simulation is to live within it. That's why we've worked to implement in-game checks and controls. You are my community team." Christian chuckled. "My saints, as it were. That's why your roles are so vital right now. I can't proceed without you fully on board."

Blank faces studied the slick tabletop. Pete, the community manager, spoke without reservation. "I'll help to the best of my ability." He turned to his team. "This is what we were trained for. Focus testing indicates our guidance means everything in a player's first moments."

Christian smiled. Saint Peter would be the spearhead of his new world. With his support, and short discussion later, no one had reservations about the advanced timetable. The CEO stood and opened the boardroom door.

"Take the rest of the week off. Come back Monday, fully recharged and ready to welcome in a new player population."

Larry avoided eye contact on his way out. He was clearly upset by the meeting's outcome, but they were nervous jitters. The time off would do him good.

After everyone was dismissed and Christian was once again alone, he made his way to the dark room where the magic happened. A small stack of servers chugged along the wall. They weren't the entirety of Haven but merely an interface. An entry point. The aged solid state drive that had bookended his shelf for years now had a lead plug into the sim. Christian smiled as he checked multiple log screens. The data transfer was almost complete.

A tear welled in the CEO's eye. This day was a long time coming.

Christian leaned over the command console and sent a quick message.

>>Input>> It's finally time.

After a minute, he was surprised by a response, which had been all too rare of late.

> >>Output>> I'm scared.

In that moment, he could barely keep from breaking into a full sob. Here was a man, master of his emotions, king of his domain, but with a gaping weak spot for a bunch of ones and zeroes.

> >>Input>> To tell you the truth, I'm absolutely horrified.

He smiled at the sad irony, strapped himself into the bed, and fitted the EXSIL over his head.

1330 Two Crude Dudes

Kyle, Grug, and I emerged from the north river tunnel into Stronghold. As the warm sunlight washed over my face, I couldn't help but smile. We'd made impressive time, with an hour at least till sunset. It felt good to be home.

I opened the faction menu and sent a message.

> **Black Hat Broadcast:**
> The mission was a success. Potential allies are in town. Let's treat the Brothers in Black with respect. If you have any guild business for me, see me in the morning if it can wait.

I relaxed in the skiff, despite continually checking the depths below for glittering undine scales. I was probably just paranoid and seeing things. Exactly why I wanted to take the night off.

Of course, fate doesn't always agree with recreational aspirations.

"Ho there!" cried a gangster standing on the riverbank. He

and a cohort on the opposite bank lifted a chain from the water and hooked it to the ground, barring our passage. The skiff bumped gently against the wall.

"What's the meaning of this?" I demanded.

"Oi!" called the gangster. "It's that Talon feller."

"Marbles," said the other. "I'd better check with the big guy." He trounced away.

"Hey!" I called, but they ignored me. I drew my dragonspear and spoke to the remaining criminal. "You have exactly zero seconds to get this chain out of my way before I break it."

The scruffy man arched an eyebrow. "That's triple-gauge steel, sir. Ain't no way you kin break it."

I lifted my legendary weapon high.

"Wait!" called a man. "Wait!" Nooner, the deposed gangster boss, rushed over with the other man. "Whatcha doin' here, Talon?"

I cleared my throat and eyed them with a dubious expression. "I really should be asking *you* that question."

"This? Why, it's a simple transactional *parlez vous.*'

I paused and scrunched my brow.

"I'm taxin' the river, dammit."

"You can't—"

"Course I can. That dirty Chadwick took Hillside and the roads, so I'm takin' the slums and the river. Simple as that."

I flashed a stern frown. "You don't have the authority to do that, Nooner."

"Why not? Yer buyin' up Oldtown."

"Key word being *buying*. I'm filling the city coffers for land that nobody's using."

He shrugged. "Well, they ain't sellin' the river."

"Exactly my point."

He pouted and struggled with a comeback.

"Listen, Nooner, we're on important business. Defense of the realm and all that. We don't have time for this."

I triggered deadshot and swiped the dragonspear at one of the chain's links. Orange sparks leapt into the water and the spear wobbled, only the chain held.

"Hey, now!" exclaimed Nooner. "There's no need fer that. Didn't my boys tell ya this is triple-gauge steel?"

I gritted my teeth.

"I'm on it," said Kyle, digging into his inventory for a vial of black corrosive.

A double-wide luxury cutter paddled behind us. Papa Brugo's booming voice rang out, half-annoyed and half-amused. "Problems with local governance, Protector of Stronghold?"

Nooner stiffened. "Papa Brugo!" His eyes ran over the black-clad assassins paddling the vessel. Hadrian, the advisor. Two skimpily-dressed serving women. "The Brothers in Black! What are you doin' here?"

Brugo's cheek scar sagged in disappointment at having to answer even a single question. "I'm here to enjoy my inaugural visit to the core city." He rubbed his belly and stretched his shoulders. "It would be a shame if something gets in the way of my enjoyment."

The gangsters watched the infamous crime boss with wide eyes. "Unhook the chain," snapped Nooner. "Really, boys, it ain't becomin' to be blocking off royalty like this. My apologies, Papa Brugo. 'Twon't happen again." Nooner completed his speech with a full bow at the waist.

I rolled my eyes. Kyle shrugged and stuffed the alchemical vial back in his sack as the gangsters unhooked the chain and lowered it below the river surface. Passage was no longer barred.

"You git a pass too, Talon. But next time, don't embarrass yerself. That's triple-gauge steel."

"I don't care what gauge it is!" I snapped.

Grug and Kyle took up paddles and we started on our way again. I simmered in jealousy. How did Brugo command more respect in this town than I did? Not only that, he had a whole entourage and luxury cutter. I reminded myself that his position of power had grown organically over the course of months.

Brugo's vessel was larger and had six men paddling. As they began to overtake us, he chuckled and leaned over. "Don't take it personally, Protector. I grew up surrounded by men like that. I cultivated my entire reputation on handling them and their problems."

I scowled. "Nooner's not big enough to be a problem."

"Perhaps not yet, but some day. Trust me when I say this. Men like that one, they need agency. Trying to keep him down will only hold you back. Instead, you give him leeway. Enough to keep him on a leash." The crime lord's face darkened. "And if you so wish it, enough to hang him with."

There was the ruthless gang boss I'd come to expect. When the Papa said he would let a man hang himself, he wasn't speaking metaphorically. It was just a day ago that he'd dangled the boggart witches from the town center. This was the man I was making an alliance with. On the other hand, it proved I was ready to make tough decisions when I needed to.

"What will you do?" I asked him.

The big man shrugged. "Let us not talk of business tonight. I am weary from sailing. I wish to see your famous city. Take in the sights." I traded a glance with Hadrian, mine cautious and his reassuring.

"I'm holding a grand opening for my pub tomorrow night. Why don't we throw a big party and formalize our business then?"

Hadrian smiled. "A great idea, Papa. Oldtown is—"

"A pub?" spat the crime boss. "That's hardly fitting for a meeting of such import." The brash man scanned the city skyline and immediately found the towering columns to the south. "Ah, the famed Arena of Stronghold. *That* is where we shall meet."

Hadrian frowned. "But that is a place of battle. Shouldn't we confer with the Black Hats in their territory?"

"The decision is made," said Brugo. "The Black Hats and the Brothers will meet on neutral ground. We'll put on a grand assemblage before the people."

I nodded. "I like that idea. I'll let Saint Peter know—"

"No saints," he interrupted. "I hear whispers that you run this city now. The saints are more than just treasonous slimes; they're outdated fossils. They have no business determining the future of Haven."

I tightened my lips and pondered his words. I'd already seen proof of Saint Peter handing various responsibilities to me. Brugo had the wrong idea about the saints in general, but given Loras and his betrayal, it would be impossible to convince him otherwise.

I nodded. "No saints, then. If you need lodging, there are some nice villas in the Pleasure Gardens. And your men have a place in my inn."

"Kind of you to offer, but it would be wiser to avoid an international incident the night before our summit. My men and I will sleep on the boat outside town."

It was obvious Hadrian wanted to object, but Papa Brugo was in a proclaiming kind of mood at the moment. The advisor nodded as they paddled off. The luxury vessel overtook us as we sailed past the slums.

Both boats had to squeeze around the flat barge Errol had built. At the moment it was docked at the southern end of the Forum. The Arena towered on the opposite riverbank. Further upriver were the smaller bridges connecting the Foot and Hillside to the major marketplaces. That was as far as the barge could go.

Brugo's cutter docked on the far side to scout the Arena. Grug sailed us along Front Street and dropped us off at the last bridge. The pirate paddled back to the frigate and Kyle and I marched to the west gate.

"It's kind of crazy to be involved in all these politics," said the brewmaster as we walked. "I usually play games where clans are just for fighting. It's simpler that way."

"Tell me about it." We hiked down the thoroughfare to the gate. I recalled going down the same path with Kyle the first day I spawned in Haven. This was the main way out of the city, so it was a common enough walk, but something about Kyle and I being alone and the wonder of bigger things to come made me think of old times.

"Look what the saints dragged in," announced Chadwick as he and a small band of gangsters filled the street.

Ugh, so much for nostalgia. "I was just thinking about you, Chadwick."

"Is that right?" returned his weaselly voice. "I—" He paused and Kyle and I weaved around him and continued marching to the gate. After a quick flash of anger, he hurried to keep pace. "I'm here to give you fair warning as to our business arrangement. We agreed on three days of hauling your lumber and supplies tax-free. Today's day three, hence tomorrow we'll be collecting payment."

I chuckled at the upstart's audacity. Nooner was just as greedy and disrespectful, but he'd apparently been the boss for a while. Ensnaring the Black Hats didn't really top his list of criminal enterprises. Chadwick was much more ambitious. After conning the empire away from his old boss and partner, he was aiming as high as he could.

The gangster sneered at my bemusement. "Let's be straight with each other, Talon. I'm not gonna take you on."

"Damn right."

Kyle flipped the crossbow in his grip. "I'm accepting challengers."

Chadwick reddened. "I don't want to fight you either, brewmaster." He took a breath and feigned a smile. "We're businessmen, one and all. But I can't say the same for everyone in my employ. And when they don't get paid, they get... a little rowdy. They wouldn't be so unreasonable as to attack you directly, but I can't afford the same guarantees to the lower-level members of your faction. Your supply chain and builders would be... compromised."

I snorted. "Really?"

His face hardened. "Yes. Where are you going?" Chadwick tried to stand in my path again but I shouldered through him. Up ahead, a centurion atop the west gate sounded a horn. A small garrison of city watchmen scrambled into position. Chadwick ground his teeth. "I hope you don't plan on the city watch fighting all your battles, Talon."

"Who said anything about fight? We're talking business, aren't we?" I flagged the olive tunics before they could shut the gate. "It's okay," I told them. "Let them in."

"But they're pagans!" protested the guard.

"If they were pagans, the Eye of Orik wouldn't allow them in the city. They all abandoned the faction."

The city watchmen stood with weapons ready as Izzy led a group of goblins and ogres through the gate. Baz nodded cheerfully as he stomped by. Jixa paused beside me, eyes wide at the impressive sights. Shorehome didn't have anywhere near the infrastructure of Stronghold.

"I'm glad you showed up, Chadwick," I said as we watched the group march past. "It gives me a chance to tell you you're fired."

The gangster stiffened, eyes still on the monstrous beasts.

"The Black Hats hire our own labor from here on out. We'll run our own supply lines. Feel free to run your oxen business without me."

His jaw sagged. "But you're the biggest game in town."

"That's right, and Baz and his crew are the biggest *workers* in town. It just makes good sense. I'm sure you'll understand.

After all, it's just business."

We turned the procession south into Oldtown. The gangsters held back and stood listless. Chadwick needed to regroup after the turn of events, which would keep him out of my hair for a while.

"Hey, Jixa," said Kyle, leaning down and speaking to her slowly. "Are you the boss?"

She gave him a judgmental side-eye. "I no stupid, big man. I no deaf either. Speaks normal if you don't likes being slapped."

Kyle turned to me and lowered his voice. "I'd like to see that." Jixa readied an open palm but Kyle threw his arms up in surrender. "Just joking, just joking." He laughed. "You'll fit right in, I think. Why don't I introduce you and the crew to Buildmaster Trafford?"

She nodded. "Is good." They veered into the ruins.

"Everything okay?" prodded Izzy.

I smiled and took her offered hand. "There's a bunch of stuff to figure out, but I think we're doing okay."

She kissed me. "I'm glad you're less worried about inviting an army into our city than I am. Remember what happened last time that happened."

"The Brothers in Black are hardly an army. But you're absolutely right that we need to keep an eye on them. Brugo and his men are sleeping outside Stronghold tonight. We're holding a big summit in the Arena at noon tomorrow. I'll talk to Gladius and make sure the city watch is on top of security."

"But not *too* on top," she hedged. "We don't want to insult the good Papa."

"We wouldn't want that."

"Okay, then. I'm gonna check in with Lash and Crux. See if there's any word on Hex."

My face darkened as I nodded her off. We both knew there wouldn't be word, but it was a good move to check on them anyway. I wondered if Lash was still avoiding me after our blowout.

Forcing my mind off things, I opened the headquarters menu and checked progress on the vault.

```
Construction:
Vault 89%
```

Everything was going as planned. Construction would be finished sometime overnight, rendering the vault operational in the morning. That would be a celebratory precursor to the summit and then the grand opening of the guildhall pub. If that didn't make for a big day, I didn't know what did.

Alone now, I wandered back to Dragonperch. Bandit greeted me inside. I gave her some rubs. Artax was there too, a little homesick perhaps. I was glad they weren't alone and fed them some treats. As the sun was setting and I was once again in a city connected to the central hub, I made my way to the privacy of my room for the last task of the day.

Papa Brugo and his band of rogues had only been half the reason for the voyage to Shorehome. The little chat with Lucifer was just as important. It seemed external factors had a much larger potential to affect Haven than I'd presumed. I needed to understand more about the outside world, and since I was living life in digital reality, there was only one real way to do that.

I opened my Everchat prompt and initiated a chat request with someone living on the outside. The handshake took several minutes as it waited for a response, but I wasn't disappointed.

A live video feed flickered onto the menu screen. An unfamiliar living room, but a familiar face. Squinting back at me from the other end was none other than Tad Lonnerman.

1340 Game Dev Story

"I feel this deserves an explanation," I started.

Tad's eyes strained in disbelief. "No. Fucking. Way."

In lieu of a more dignified response, I lazily hiked a shoulder. Tad Lonnerman. The *real* Tad Lonnerman. The Tad-Lonnerman-who-lived-in-the-Portland-apartment-with-his-brother-Derek Tad Lonnerman. There wasn't an abundance of things to say.

After coming to grips with life, the universe, and everything, Tad Lonnerman asked, "Who are you?"

I took a slow breath. "I'm Talon."

"Yeah... but who are you?"

"I'm you," I said with a smirk.

"Uh-huh."

Tad panned his head left and right. When I raised an inquisitive eyebrow, he instinctually did the same. Then he lifted his hand and waved slowly before the camera.

"I'm not a reflection!" I snapped.

"Psh, obviously. You're a damn good AI, though."

"As good as you," I muttered. "Listen, Tad, I know this is hard to believe, but I'm you, uploaded to a digital reality built by your company."

He blinked. "You mean Haven?"

I blinked. "You know about it?"

"Well, sure. After my accident, I've shifted duties a bit. We moved to Seattle."

"Seattle?"

"The Kablammy corporate offices."

"What about Derek?"

"I think he likes it here better. He— Wait, why am I telling you this? You're just an AI simulation."

I gritted my teeth. "You're clearly not wrapping your head around the full predicament, Tad. My brain is your brain. Or a copy of it, anyway. I'm you and you're me, perfectly, except we branched off a while ago and now have autonomy from each other. We're like a single individual living in separate dimensions."

Tad snickered. "All right, 'Talon.' Good job stealing my favorite username, by the way." He sipped from a *Finding Nemo* mug depicting a bunch of identical sea gulls crowing, "Mine! Mine! Mine!" The irony wasn't lost on me.

"I *am* you, and I can prove it because I know everything about you. Right now you're drinking Death Wish Coffee fresh from that manual grinder Derek bought you for Christmas. Your favorite soda is Mountain Dew: Code Red; not just an excellent drink but the best damn spin-off soda in creation. You like playing non-traditional rogue kits, programming JRPGs in your spare time, and you have a spreadsheet detailing story details and your ratings of all the episodes of *Babylon 5*."

Tad apprehensively swallowed his drink. "Anybody could find that stuff out."

"No, I really have your memories, Tad." I rolled my eyes at what I had to do. "Remember that time Mom caught us masturbating to that *Telemundo* weather report?"

Death Wish Coffee spat from his mouth. "That's not cool, man! That's embarrassing."

"I know. I cringe just bringing it up."

Tad hurried away from the desk propped on a single crutch. After wiping the mess with a paper towel, he melted back into his Aeron chair.

"Uh..." I nodded at the crutch. "How're you holding up?"

He shrugged. "Can't complain, considering. Immediately after the car accident, I was in an induced coma due to brain swelling. Hit or miss for a while there, I'm told. I woke up with a cracked skull and a shattered fibula. As long as I have sufficient pain meds, I can get around."

"You know, you shouldn't take too many of those," I warned.

"I *know*. I said *sufficient*. Jeez, you really are me."

I smiled.

He peered into the screen. "What about you? Any injuries?"

"Me? Nah, I'm good. I mean, last week I accidentally severed my arm in an unfortunate encounter with a treasure-chest mimic. Hurt like a bitch, but a health potion fixed me right up."

Tad Lonnerman shook his head in futility.

"What about Derek?" I asked. "He figuring things out?"

"Surprisingly well, actually. He got a job at a Capitol Hill bookstore. Met a few friends who seem mostly responsible. I was afraid the move would be too much for him, but he didn't complain. He was there for me when I really needed him."

My eyes clouded. Something was probably wrong with Haven's humidity setting. I wished I could see Derek making his way through the world. "I always wanted to check on him, you know. After I was trapped in here. It didn't seem right to leave him alone."

Tad nodded. "He mentioned the app request to me. I told him I had no idea what he was talking about. I think he thought I was under NDA and couldn't tell him. I didn't know anything about Haven at the time."

"But you do now."

"I do." He pondered that a moment. "The whole process was very rushed. I was in the hospital for two months. The last month and a half was resting, moving and starting my new job. I've only been here two weeks."

I worked through the timeline in my head. What had been six weeks for me was three and a half months for him. That was due to the two-month delay between Tad being copied and me being activated. I entered Haven the day Tad Lonnerman was released from the hospital, a fact I now knew wasn't an accident. Lucifer had seen his chance to ally with a developer slipping away and made his move before I was deleted.

"Now I get it," said Tad, working out his own side of the conspiracy. "Joining Christian's special project means licensing rights to my digital consciousness. They wanted me on board before I found out about you—I mean me—whatever."

"A legal loophole," I concluded. "So they don't get in trouble for their mistake."

"Yeah. It also explains the generous pay raise and insurance coverage. Not that I'm complaining. Uploading an AI version of myself is pretty neat."

I huffed. "I'm not AI, Tad. I'm literally you. I'm a living entity, even if I'm ones and zeroes instead of flesh and blood."

"Your black box. Christian always stresses how perfect the imprint is. Getting the brain copied is really easy. The imperfect part is interfacing with it. Your consciousness is a series of neural components, hash tables, and helper routines, with more reliable memory than the biological version, but questionable throughput and sensory stimulation."

"Which just proves the nuts and bolts don't matter. Your brain is a mass of synapses and neurons. What's the difference between that and a circuit board?"

He chuckled as he took my point.

"Do you realize there are lots of people like me in here? Well, their human counterparts are dead now, but they're still alive in the sim."

His brow furrowed. "What are you talking about? Haven's not going live for another week."

"That fast?" I shook it off. "Never mind, that's not important. Haven's been in a closed beta for... what... nine months now? Hundreds of players have been uploaded. Haven isn't some spawning ground for revolutionary AI, although it has that in spades. Haven is the afterlife, online."

Tad leaned back in his chair and blinked. "A chance to circumvent death..."

"Sure, in a way. It's—"

"No," he said. "That's something I've heard Christian say a

couple times." His gaze went out of focus, as if he was trying to assemble a puzzle by memory.

"Who is this Christian guy you keep mentioning?"

Tad shook off his funk. "Christian Everett, the tech titan? You know who he is."

"Yeah. Of course. The CEO of Kablammy Games."

I had heard of him. A one-time VR pioneer who sold out and went into the mobile-casual space. Haven was his baby.

"Dude is eccentric," said Tad. "Always seems like he's doing ten things at once, and half of them are secret. Get this. Haven's been teased to the public. Christian's announcing satellite launches to transfer the servers to orbit. Even if the Earth is nuked, Haven will go on. It's a big hit with the end-times folks."

"Digital preppers? Now I've heard everything."

I wondered what the CEO was really up to with those satellites. I wondered if Lucifer knew about them. Once again I realized how susceptible Haven was to outside forces.

"So," started Tad, leaning in, "just to get this straight. You're in Haven, right now, adventuring with hundreds of other dead people?"

I swallowed. "Well, I'm in my house at the moment, but pretty much."

"And when the game goes live, your contracts continue. You start over with wiped profiles as new players get uploaded?"

I winced. "Weeell... I *may have* put a kink in those plans. Haven's had trouble lately. The saints have slowly lost power to the players. Hasn't Christian told you any of this?"

He shook his head. "I'm still super out of the loop. The community team has been running around like chickens with their heads cut off, though. Pete is scrambling to keep everyone on task."

"Saint Peter?"

"Yeah," he chuckled. "I guess that's what he goes by in there. You probably think he's an old man, right?"

"He's not?"

"No way. He's in his thirties. He loves cycling. Has really buff calves. Look, AI—black box bodies are an expression of the consciousness. That's why you look like me. Developer skins, on the other hand, are purely fictional."

"That explains Varnu the Texan."

"Who?"

"Just a hilarious employee from tech support. This actually leads to my point. Saint Peter told me the community team member driving Saint Loras is on vacation."

"Larry, I think," he said. "I never met him, but I m pretty sure he's fired."

"I have reason to suspect he was a mole for another company. Any idea who that might be?"

Tad frowned. "Not at all. We don't work with outside developers. It does explain a lot if they caught Larry selling secrets, though. Christian's more worried than ever about security. But Kablammy shit-canned Larry and hushed up the conspiracy. Which must be where the leak came from. We've moved up the launch timetable. It's why things are so hectic around here."

"Except the problem's not solved. Larry may not be around anymore, but he was working for someone, and that someone now has control of the Saint Loras avatar. He's up to trouble in

Oakengard."

"Oakengard?"

I grunted in frustration. My real-life counterpart wasn't exactly clued in, but he was the best we had. Stationed in Christian Everett's tall tower in Seattle—he was our way in.

"It's an NPC city," I explained. "They have the largest trained army in Haven, which translates to a significant amount of sway." I chewed my lip. "Saint Peter hasn't mentioned anything about this at all?"

"No. Like I said, they're bringing me on board one piece at a time. I'm familiar with the EXSIL interface and the neural black boxes, but nothing specific to the beta. I don't know a whole lot, much less that I was already in the simulation."

"That's bad," I said. "I thought we could trust the devs."

"Eh, they're just covering their ass."

"They were covering their ass when they tried to delete me."

His eyes lit up. "They tried that? That sucks."

"It more than sucks, Tad. This is my life now. My entire reality. Players are here for the rest of eternity. NPCs and mobs are self-aware. This isn't a game anymore."

He blinked. "I guess not."

"So will you help me, Tad?" I tensed in anticipation.

The real me sighed and rapped fingers on the reclaimed-wood surface of his desk. "I mean, I guess you're me... and you deserve to live and all... What do you need?"

"You're the best. We need to find out who's in control of Loras now. Even Saint Peter doesn't have access to him. At least that's what he told me."

"Hmm, that seems strange. I've never been in the sim so I

can't say for sure what controls they have."

"There's no easy index to check from a console?"

"When I get to the office tomorrow I can look. Tons of data is obfuscated to the outside, though. It's the cost of security. But Pete's not a programmer. He has no idea how to tease the data to tell him what he wants."

"It might require some hacking," I said.

"Huh, I've never thought of myself as a hacker before."

I smiled. I'd had the same exact response upon first meeting Lucifer.

"But I think you're right," he continued. "I just remembered. Pete mentioned losing access to AIs and black boxes. A rogue Loras would be difficult to track. I could go to Christian. He's a genius."

"No. You can't let them know what we're doing."

"But he probably knows all about Loras and the threat. He could just tell us."

"He hasn't told you so far. Why start now?" I grumbled as I tried to suss out the CEO's motivations. "Look, Christian's the head honcho. He nearly bankrupted himself with satellites or whatever his latest publicity stunt is. Kablammy's on the verge of going out of business or being bought out. He's in financial straits. Whatever Christian's up to... we can't let capitalist interests dictate what happens to Haven."

"Capitalist interests? You're talking about my boss, man."

"I'm talking about your digital life. Or mine, anyway. But you might make it here one day too. I'd welcome you with open arms."

He chewed his lip. "You probably wouldn't give up the

username Talon, though, would you?"

"Sorry, usernames are reserved on a first-dead-first-served basis. There's always Talon92."

"As if I'd be that lame. So I'm in this alone, then."

"We're in this together," I assured. "But you're the only one on the outside. That's why you're so important."

Tad rapped his fingers and mulled over the dilemma.

"There's another thing," I said. "I heard something about a secret developer menu. Since I have a Kablammy ID, I should have access."

"Like the saints. Yes. I might need to enable privileges. That should be a piece of cake."

"And then I have it?"

"Well..." he hedged. "You might still need a token on your end. A key of some sort."

"A bit key. With access to the Oculus."

"What's an oculus?" he asked.

"*The* Oculus," I corrected. "It's the connection Stronghold has to the core code."

"The central hub," he finished. "Got it." Tad's face grew excited. "If you have hub access then finding Loras might be easier than you think. But not directly. Do you have any messages or saved interactions with him?"

I thought about it. "His attempt on my life didn't exactly come with a valentine... unless you count one of the daggers he meant to kill me with."

"That'll work. All items in Haven have a history log. It helps prevent duping by verifying traceable creation and exchange events. If Loras was in possession of this dagger and you access its history at the Oculus, it might tell you where he is, at least where he was when he had the dagger."

My expression dimmed. "But I already know where he is. He's in Oakengard."

"But you'll still be isolating his avatar instance. I'll check the central hub for your query. That'll give me a link to Loras, and maybe I can grab the IP of whoever's remoting into him."

"See?" I said magnanimously. "Who needs a genius billionaire CEO?"

Tad flashed a glum expression. "Not a billionaire anymore if everything you say is true." Poor guy was worried about his long-term employment prospects. "How soon should I look for your intrusion?"

"Well, there's a big summit in the Arena at noon tomorrow between me and Papa Brugo."

He frowned. "You realize I could lose my job for this stunt. Everything needs to be in place for it to work."

"Right. I'll get it done in the morning, before the summit. In the meantime, we should keep Saint Peter from looking too closely at us."

"That goes without saying." Tad laughed. "You know what? This is a trip. It's like a real adventure. My own quest."

"Just wait till you wake up in an MMO."

1350 Homefront

The following morning I woke up amped. Strangely, the tower common rooms were empty.

While it was typical for Kyle to be strewn over the couch watching cartoons or playing the latest first-person shooter, he was just as likely to be sleeping in. Not seeing him around wasn't unusual.

Izzy was a different story. She was an early riser, and without Kyle classing down the place, she would usually snuggle in the love seat with a good book. I'd also missed her last night, through a combination of falling asleep and her not messaging me. I figured our official relationship was new enough that she wasn't comfortable waking me.

All alone in the place, I frowned. My thoughts took an inevitable turn and I opened my menu and contemplated my options.

Ghost
Become ethereal to players, NPCs, and mobs for
6 seconds.

Pathfinder
Visualize the optimal path through dungeons and
hostile environments.

Assassin
Auto kill a susceptible opponent.

Ghost was a strange one. Very OP but also very limited. It was probably the most versatile of the bunch and handy in a pinch. I also saw it as the pure escape skill. I didn't know that I wanted to make my name running away from fights.

Pathfinder would be a universally loved option. A support skill—a *scouting* skill—to help my party and faction in dungeon raids. At the same time I dreaded the simplification it presented precisely because I was a scout. I didn't want dungeons to become a follow-the-dotted-line affair. As cheesy as it sounded, I was afraid using the skill would erase the joy of discovery.

And last but certainly not least: Assassin. There was an undeniable cool factor with this one, though I was still unsure of the fit. I couldn't formulate a single coherent argument against choosing the ability, at least insofar as having a bad taste in my mouth wasn't a solid argument.

I sighed. After a moment's deliberation, I shut the menu and opened the fridge.

Peanut butter and jelly was on the menu and I wasn't a picky eater. I munched on it as I hit the stairs. It was good to see Bandit and Artax waiting on the ground floor. I gave them some ear nuzzles. When Bandit still wasn't satisfied, I gave her half my PB&J. The stallion was too dignified to resort to the meal, but the mountain bongo was my kind of girl.

"I have been ignoring you lately, haven't I?" I asked idly. "I'll make it up to you. One second."

I slipped away into the underground grotto and followed the mazelike corridors until I stopped at a statue near the hidden grotto entrance. It was a bust of some long-gone distinguished woman. I reached into the wall alcove behind it and wrapped my fingers around the item I had forgotten was there. The gold Nintendo cartridge twinkled in the ambient light.

[Bit Key]
This anachronistic cartridge gives admin access to the Oculus, the game console.

I produced a discreet satin sack, placed the bit key inside for safekeeping, and stuffed it deep into my inventory. I returned up the stairs to find the mounts still waiting for me. I paused, horrified, and plugged my nose.

"Okay, which one of you farted?"

Artax stuck his nose in the air. Bandit jawed at peanut butter stuck to the roof of her mouth.

"Ugh, I guess that was my fault. No more people food for you. How about some exercise?"

I opened the impressive tower doors and marched toward

fresh air.

Outside, the morning appeared as any other. The prominence of the day wasn't outwardly visible, as long as you didn't count the corny flyers Kyle had posted to the slate defense turrets: "Guildhall Grand Opening! No Free Drinks!"

I chuckled nervously. The pub party was trivial compared to the summit with Papa Brugo. And then there was what I had to take care of first. My nerves made me hyperaware of how normal everything looked. I leaned on familiar routine to steady myself.

<table>
<tr><td colspan="2">Black Hat Headquarters</td></tr>
<tr><td colspan="2">Level: 2
HQXP: 5 / 8</td></tr>
<tr><td colspan="2">HQR: 32
Daily HQR Production: 14</td></tr>
<tr><td colspan="2">Current Buildings
Guildhall
Brothel
Barracks
Lumberyard
Vault</td></tr>
</table>

Nice. A completed vault was good news. One more piece of legitimacy for the Black Hats. That was expected.

My total headquarters resource production, however, was a surprise. As I strolled toward the vault, I ran into Jixa and her crew being shown around by Kyle, of all people.

"Hey, bro," he called out. "Hope you don't mind, but I invited our new builders into the faction."

Of course. We'd had about ten of Errol's pirates helping with building duties. With their abysmal craft experience and even worse work ethic, they had combined for 1 total HQR per day. Jixa's crew of six ogres and four goblins, including herself, were worth 5. We were legit.

<table>
<tr><td colspan="1">Black Hats</td></tr>
<tr><td>Faction Level: 2
Members: 60 / 100</td></tr>
<tr><td>War
Catechists
Armistice
Pagans</td></tr>
</table>

Movin' on up, slowly but surely. I shook Jixa's hand. "Glad to have you in the Black Hats."

"Lots to builds here," answered the goblin. "Jixa happy. Baz even more happy. He moveses rubble for fun."

The ogre of few words stomped forward and gave me a bear hug. I stifled a grunt and instinctually checked my health bar. Somehow I'd avoided a damage notification.

"Glad to have you too, big guy." I peeled myself from the death grip.

"They didn't have a place to sleep last night," explained Kyle.

"I figured making them official would give them a respawn point while they stayed in the brothel."

"Naked yoomans silly," added Baz.

Jixa nodded. "Too much *snu snu*."

Was that phrase universal or something?

"Damn," I realized. "I should've taken care of that last night. Thanks for picking up my slack on that, Kyle."

"No worries. I'm practically running the faction already."

"A man can dream. And your team is welcome in the barracks, Jixa."

The brewmaster patted Bandit's coat as we trekked to the latest construction site.

"Hey, Kyle, you seen Izzy?"

"Nah, why?"

"No reason."

The completed vault came into view, and we weren't the first admirers. A small crowd of Black Hats discussed the development. Trafford excitedly converged on us.

"You really came through, Talon! Don't tell the pirates I said this, but they have no business slinging lumber. This new team can do anything." He watched the goblins and ogres with respect.

"Thank Jixa. She's the one who runs a tight ship. We just commissioned her services."

"A genius move, if ya ask me. These big guys hauled a day's worth of lumber in a little over an hour. They're really streamlining things around here."

It had been a while since I'd seen the old man so chirpy. I smiled and sent him a party invite as I finished my daily upkeep.

"Looks like everyone can take a few days off as we accumulate HQR. Just make sure to get the lumberyard nice and stocked first."

"We'll get right on it," replied Trafford. "Once the guildhall opens, I might be MIA for a while." The buildmaster general pulled his team aside, having more fun than a codger like him had a right to.

I approached the new building. "This is it, then." The small stone structure was extra sturdy, with a reinforced door and lock. I checked my silver.

Coin	
Silver	453
Plates	21

Fellow faction members watched as I made the inaugural deposit. 300 coins and 20 plates, which counted for another 2,000. I was finally mostly immune to the mandatory silver drop. Kyle followed my example.

I opened the broadcast menu.

Black Hat Broadcast:
Great news, Black Hats. The vault is now open for business! Safeguard your silver at no cost to you.

The faction members in attendance cheered.

I stepped aside as Drummond meekly approached. He

conducted several lengthy deposits before turning and spending skill points. His class description changed before our eyes. [Drummond - Level 3 Banker].

"You finally got your class kit."

"Thanks to you," he replied. "I also worked out deals with various shops throughout the city. Black Hats will be taxed when they sell looted inventory. They're on the honor system for found silver, but most profit comes from trade. I'm now keeping the faction's books. And the shopkeepers are participating because I can bank for them on the house."

"Brilliant, Drummond. I knew you'd be a big help."

He excused himself and began assisting the line of players and NPCs. Some would be suspicious of parting with their money, but I was confident everyone would benefit from the new vault. Kyle helped keep order, though I suspected he was just keeping close to Jixa. Grimwart's horse had similarly wandered away from Bandit. Oldtown didn't offer much in the way of grazing.

"We don't need them," I told the mountain bongo. The two of us continued on to the brothel. Pirates busted into cheers as I entered.

"Thar he is," chimed Grug, already mid story with his shipmates who hadn't made the voyage. "That man ran along the mast like a squirrel, he did."

"Sounds like a song in the making," I suggested.

Grom took to his feet. "What in the Maelstrom is a squirrel?"

"It's a little critter that runs up trees, ye daft fool!"

They laughed and shoved each other in merry boisterousness. "Three cheers fer the hero at sea!" they cried.

"And three more fer gettin' us off build duty!"

I laughed and accepted a tankard of ale. It wasn't a pirate ditty, but it was appreciation nonetheless. I waited till they were calm so I could speak. It took a while so I got a good drink in.

"Really, you guys, I should be thanking you. Each one of you pledged yourself to me. You've fought with your lives. You've hauled lumber and done what needed to be done. You've earned your place in the Black Hats." They were strangely reverent for a split second. Instead of letting that ruin the moment, I added, "Even you, Grom, you horny bastard."

The room exploded with laughter. Everybody slapped Grom on the shoulders and lauded his dalliance with the sirens. He had safely respawned, of course, and apparently the shipmates would have thought less of him if he hadn't gone overboard. A pirate had a reputation to keep.

I sidestepped the rowdy group and searched for Crux, but he wasn't around. In the off chance the thief was still in Oldtown, I moved to the barracks. He sat in a simple bed in the back of the room. It was quieter in here, but still public, where I'm sure Bravo Team often checked in.

"Brugo and the Brothers in Black are in town," I reported, "in case you wanna keep a low profile or whatever." He didn't respond. "Everything's going as planned," I reminded. "The summit is the first step to consolidating power. A strong alliance against our enemies. After that, we can focus on getting Hex back."

Crux afforded me a nod this time, but he wasn't enthusiastic.

I rested my hand on his shoulder. "Hey, Black Hats don't give up. We cover each other. Don't forget that." He nodded again.

This one-sided conversation was a far cry from the celebration of the pirates. It sobered me and focused my attention on the important tasks ahead. I left Crux in the barracks. He didn't need a shoulder to cry on. He was dealing with his situation and I'd deal with mine. I reunited with Bandit outside and continued the inspection.

As we returned to the road, Dune waved from the closed door of the guildhall. I stopped and peeked in the windows. No one inside.

"What are you doing here? You're not a Black Hat."

"No," he said smugly. "But I'm always welcome. I was hoping to get a sneak peek of that new brew your man made. Word is he's really talented. Then again it can't be hard to compete with the piss at the Wicked Crow."

"Kyle has the whole day to prep for the grand opening. He'll be around soon to give you a preview. If you're nice."

"I'm always nice," joked the ranger. "I could use a good pint after the last two days in the wild."

I gave a sympathetic grunt. "No luck on the Vagram front?"

"That cleric covers his tracks well."

That was impressive, since Dune was the best tracker I knew. His bright green cloak may have been gaudy, but when it came to business he was a professional. "So you didn't find anything?"

He scoffed. "Found plenty, actually. Lots of goblin activity. War parties. Just nobody worth finding."

"You mean nobody with a price on their head."

He shrugged. "I hear you invited the Brothers in Black to town. You and sweeping political movements are like peanut butter and chocolate."

Bandit pawed the ground and sniffed Dune's pockets. He arched a quizzical eyebrow.

"Ixnay on the eanut-butter-pay," I chuckled. "Horrible things happen. Trust me."

"I'm afraid to ask." Dune patted the bongo's head to soothe her disappointment. "Food metaphors aside, what's the play with Papa Brugo?"

"You trying to move in on my alliance?"

"Just a spectator sport, I swear. I've never met a crazier bastard in Haven than you, and I killed Rygar the Toothless. My party's sticking around as long as the Brothers do. Bound to be good XP when everything invariably goes to hell."

"Thanks for the vote of confidence. Just do me a favor and don't steer things in that direction, okay?"

He shrugged and smiled. "Guarantees are like unicorns, Talon."

Bandit snorted. I studied her inquisitively. "This is a fantasy world, Dune. Unicorns might actually exist."

"Touché." He turned wistfully to the locked pub door. "So then, how about a congratulatory pint?"

"I can't. I have something to do."

He squinted suspiciously. "Wait a minute—I know that look. Things are going to hell quicker than I thought, aren't they?"

"Laugh it up." I pointed down the road as Kyle approached. "Besides, there's your meal ticket on the way. He'll give you a pint if you apologize for calling him a noncommittal slacker bro."

"That was two weeks ago!" Dune's eyes went dull. "I'm not

sure I'm capable of apologizing."

"Easier than finding unicorns. Or clerics." I started to head off in the opposite direction. "It might be worth it this time. The dude's preparing Hot Pockets."

"He has—" Dune's jaw seized up. He turned to Kyle and called from a distance. "Good sir, I beseecheth you, hear me." The green cloak whipped in the wind toward the brewmaster.

I shook my head with a chuckle. It was a good morning so far. Solid faction morale, excitement in the air, and no sign of Nooner or Chadwick. And while a pint would've been the day's natural progression, my nerves were about as calm as they were gonna get. Bandit followed as I left Oldtown, walked through the Forum, and approached the Pantheon.

1360 Black Ops

My footsteps echoed between the Corinthian columns leading to the capitol building. Golden figures with wings perched above, suspended in place but not in permanence. The two angels Lucifer had hacked were noticeably absent, their brothers unaware of the loss or, at least, expressionless.

I moved up the steps, unsure what resistance I might face, but determined to do what needed to be done. On the triangular portico roof, the seventh angel, Decimus, stood at the peak. A rallying force. A source of guidance. I wondered if they would defend the city against Oakengard, if it came to it.

Bandit and I stepped inside the Pantheon. Her clacking hooves against the pristine tile reminded me of the last time I'd come here with the bit key. It was empty then as it was now. Some things never changed.

We were almost at the archway leading to the rotunda when centurions hiding behind pillars fanned out around us. Saint Peter revealed himself on an overhead balcony.

"For a level-10 assassin, you really should learn to mask your movements better."

I gritted my teeth. "I'm not an assassin, Peter."

"No? Not yet, perhaps, but it would be a surprising legendary ability to pass up. It's powerful and rare, and I don't see you as a dungeon support class. Trust me, you'll choose assassin. I know people."

My jaw flexed as he patiently stepped down the stairs. I eyed the sword-wielding centurions. "Where's Gladius?"

"He's preparing his men for the summit, as you should be." Peter's sandals hit the floor. He frowned at Bandit and approached cautiously. "What are you up to, Talon?"

I sighed. "I'm not an assassin and I'm not sneaking around. I brought along a quarter-ton farting machine for chrissakes. Give me some credit."

He canted his head to concede the point.

"Call off your muscle," I said.

"The centurions aren't here in ambush, Talon. Their job is protecting the Pantheon. The Oculus and the Eye of Orik must be guarded against thieves. And assassins."

This time he was speaking of Brugo's men. The last time soldiers were welcomed into the city, they'd occupied the Pantheon.

"Don't worry about the central hub," I said. "The Black Hats are sworn to protect Stronghold. We'll die for the city."

The old man stroked his beard. It was a funny affectation considering he almost certainly didn't have one that long in the real world. The white robe was just a skin. A suit. His rock-hard calves were probably the only honest thing about him.

"I believe you," he decided. "Which is why I want to show you something." He led the way toward the rotunda. The centurions parted so we could pass. "Leave the beast out here, if you please."

I rubbed the spot on Bandit's head between her horns and nodded. Saint Peter and I zoned into the rotunda. White light filled my vision and faded, leaving us in relative privacy under a large dome. An architectural oculus revealed open sky above. Sunlight shone down like a laser beam onto the altar on the far wall, a white table cloth with several flat screens placed atop.

We stepped on the raised platform and moved to the alcove in the back wall. Saint Peter removed a white linen cover and revealed the tabernacle, the holy box that stored the pagan artifact the city was founded on.

"There's something wrong with the Eye," he said as he unlocked the safe.

A six-inch-thick steel door opened. The Eye of Orik was a ruby gemstone. A treasure by any measure. Now, however, it looked like magic. Red light from within pulsed erratically.

"What's it doing?"

Peter shook his head. "As you know, the artifact gives life to Orik."

I nodded. The petrified titan kneeled beside Dragonperch. While the cyclops was anything but pliable, the boggart witches had woken the giant with the Eye and had him attack the town.

"The Eye of Orik also keeps pagans out of the city, as long as it's under saintly control. As you can see, it is under saintly control."

I stared at the blinking artifact until Peter shut the tabernacle and once again covered it with linen. "Then what's the problem?"

The saint frowned. "The Eye is sensing something amiss. A

threat to Stronghold. Pagans are near."

I pondered the possibilities. The boggart witches were loose again. Potentially in the southern mountains. Or closer. What had Dune reported? The goblin General Azzyrk was still leading a war-hungry band somewhere.

"That can't be right. The pagans were defeated. On a whole, they're not even our enemies. I have an armistice with them."

"I wonder if that's the problem," noted Peter.

I frowned. "I walked pagans into the city."

I'd done it before. In order to oust Bishop Tannen, I'd invited King Theoderic and his wildkins through the imposing walls of Stronghold. They counted as pagans at the time, before their own faction was officialized. But the only reason that worked was because Tannen was in possession of the Eye. The absence of saintly control had afforded the possibility.

This time, Peter retained possession of the artifact. Yet Jixa and Baz were now Stronghold residents. Some of the attending Brothers in Black were no doubt goblins. These instances, again, were only possible due to a loophole. Newly armed with free will, these pagans had abandoned their faction proper.

"Is it possible the artifact knows a rule's being circumvented?" I asked. "The Eye doesn't like ogres in the city, but it can't outright prevent their presence if they're no longer pagans."

"I am worried," admitted Saint Peter, "about the potential ramifications."

"I'm not kicking Black Hats out of my city," I said adamantly. "Jixa's team will fight for us if they need to. I guarantee it."

"I'm merely voicing my concern."

My eyes trailed to the monitors on the altar. I moved to one of the machines and tapped the keyboard to wake up the screensaver.

"Please don't touch that."

"Relax. I wonder what would happen if I looked up Christian Everett on this thing."

Peter stiffened. "The... Kablammy's CEO? Why do you ask?"

I shrugged slyly. "Just wondering. Isn't the big guy playing his own game?"

The saint's scruffy eyebrows stretched high. "You don't know the man like I do. He doesn't have time for 'playing.' It's too trivial."

"His life's work is trivial?"

"Of course not. Christian's time is better spent on other pursuits."

I idly tapped through several menu screens. "Like finding Saint Loras?"

Peter swallowed. "That has proven difficult, I'm afraid."

I pulled the assassin needle from my coat. The saint stiffened. "Now that we're in the Oculus, I know a way we can find him."

I explained the gist of my plan without revealing my inside access. I was a programmer and Peter wasn't, and I had inadvertently worked on some of Haven's game systems. The saint didn't suspect anything when I surmised that items could be tracked.

"Loras tried to assassinate you?" he asked.

I handed him the powerful weapon. "Twice."

"Well, I don't need the Oculus to track items, Talon." Peter rounded to the far side of the altar for privacy. It was a redundant gesture because the menu he opened was invisible to me.

"Is that a special developer menu?" I asked.

"It is."

As the saint focused on the assassin needle's history, I snuck the bit key from the satin sack and slid it into the console. I idly tapped the keys again. Peter was unconcerned with my limited snooping since I couldn't make changes to the system. Not without a bit key.

I accessed my profile data and went over my permissions. It was easier than I thought to flip the bit that would enable developer access. It wasn't a hack, just a green light. The real work came from the outside.

Peter cleared his throat. I escaped to the main menu, pulled the gold cartridge from its slot, and hid everything away.

"I found it," announced Peter. "This weapon passed from Saint Loras to your faction mate, Crux. Are you aware of that?"

I smiled coolly. "Relax. He's on my side."

Peter handed the weapon back to me. "The history does show the exchange happened in Oakengard. Loras also had the weapon forged there."

"He can do that?"

"Oakengard produces many weapons deep in their mines. They shouldn't be able to generate anything this powerful, but we'd previously patched in measures to amp up their production capabilities." Peter frowned. "This weapon was created in a batch of three."

Three assassin needles. One for Poe, one for Crux. That

meant there was one more contract killer out there. That was the last thing I needed.

"Unfortunately," continued Peter, "this history log does isolate Loras to certain places and times, but it doesn't reveal much else."

"Upload it," I offered. "To the Oculus. You register that log on the mainframe and you might be able to cross reference that data later. It's worth a try."

His face beamed. "Better than that. I bet Christian can use the handshake log to isolate the Loras avatar."

I tensed. He was sharp for a community relations guy. "I wouldn't go that far." The last thing I wanted was Christian onto Tad.

"No, Talon, you're completely right. This may be the key we needed all along!" The saint hurried to the Oculus console. I tried a weak protest about Christian having more important things to worry about, but it fell on deaf ears. Saint Peter excitedly uploaded the item history log. I'd succeeded in enabling the developer menu and getting the assassin needle's history to Tad. Unfortunately, for better or worse, Saint Peter and Christian Everett were now also on the case.

"I should log off," said Peter as he escorted me from the rotunda. Bandit and the centurions waited on us.

"Not now," I insisted. "The summit's only a few minutes away. I need your eyes on the Arena."

The hair on his lips puffed out as he pouted. "You're right, of course."

Phew. Hopefully that would buy Tad the time he needed. We left the soldiers behind and exited the Pantheon. Peter broke away in the Forum, citing Brugo's request to not have saints present. He would watch from a distance, he assured. I hoped he was being straight with me.

As Bandit and I hiked over the small bridge and crossed Front Street, I tried opening my developer menu.

An unadorned command console sprang up.

```
DEVELOPER CONSOLE
>> ERROR
>> INVALID ACCESS KEY
```

Damn. Even after all that, it didn't work. Which meant Tad really did need to enable privileges on his end. With any luck, he'd get to it shortly.

I dismissed the thought and focused on the next order of business. The summit with Papa Brugo could very well be one of Haven's most historic moments, if I played my cards right. I hoped Tad got to his end sooner rather than later, but for now I needed to set my sights on bigger and better things.

>> Minigame <<

Tad Lonnerman sipped his Frappuccino and scanned the room. It was noon, which meant the office would be clearing out for lunch. In the meantime his browser was in privacy mode and he researched subversive topics.

There were indeed rumors of a Kablammy corporate takeover. The mega-conglomerate had overextended in gaming, entertainment, medical, and aerospace sectors. Given the amount of technology they'd pioneered and purchased, there weren't a whole lot of patents being licensed out. Christian Everett's sole focus had been his digital empire. Over a decade's worth of heavy investing and still no financial returns.

While the ledger trended red, Kablammy's reputation was finally, for the first time since formation, gaining legitimate hype. News of Haven was public. Details were sparse but the word was out, so predators naturally circled the chum-filled waters. There was a lot of money to be had, the only question was who would do the having.

All of which created a limited and precise window to execute the most profitable corporate acquisition of the century.

It boggled Tad's mind. So much of this information was news

to him, yet he didn't need to Google that deep to uncover it. The rumors were there for all to tweet. One only needed to believe.

By the time he looked around and realized the office was empty, Tad Lonnerman was convinced.

He stood and limped toward the employee kitchen with the assistance of a single crutch. Kablammy was running on a skeleton crew these days. So close to release, it was utter paranoia. For today's mission, it was a godsend.

The only programmer in the field of cubicles headed for the large conference room that made up the community team's headquarters. Christian had nicknamed it the Bosom for some reason, but most devs just called it the Superdome. The room was, after all, populated by saints. They were on leave now, all except one. Tad peeked inside.

Pete was still hooked up. He was a good guy. The ex-stoner type, maybe—he was always forgetting people's names—but he did right by anybody when asked. Despite his youthful appearance, Pete possessed a maturity which Christian and the other saints relied on.

Being so reliable, it was not out of the ordinary for him to work through lunch. If what Talon had said about a big event at noon was true, it was likely Pete would stay inside the sim.

"Tad!" called Abbie, giving him a good startle. "How're you doing today?"

Abbie was the HR director. She was talkative but distant, annoying not friendly. The type of person who laughed all the time but never meant it. "Oh, hi there. I'm—"

"You know you're long overdue for your gender sensitivity training, right?"

Tad swallowed. "Oh. Um, sorry. I probably missed a lot while I was in recovery."

Her lips tightened into a patronizing smile. "Now, now. Medical treatment is no reason to shirk your responsibilities to your fellow employee."

"I was in a coma."

"All right, Tad. No need for exasperation. I just wanted to remind you that the training is mandatory. You know what I always say. Employee rights aren't just for you, they're for everybody else too."

"Sure." Tad cleared his throat and leaned against the doorway, just randomly relaxing by the Superdome. "Um, speaking of employee rights, I was about to leave for lunch. All employees are entitled to—"

She huffed and sighed and rolled her eyes all at once. "Fine, Tad. I'll be sending a makeup email next week. I expect you to attend." She stormed away before he could formulate a snarky response. Did anybody ever win with HR?

Tad waited a moment to ensure the coast was clear, then slipped into the conference room.

Pete wouldn't be a problem as long as he didn't log out. The neural interface of the EXSIL dominated the brain intake so thoroughly that his body could barely feel physical pain. Tad snuck past the saint and manned the workstation in the corner— the central hub.

Trawling the event notifications was menial work, but it didn't take that long to find the item Talon had logged. A few more keystrokes brought up the transaction history of the dagger, from creation to duping and hand-offs.

The assassin needle was forged in the mines of Oakengard. There were no real details, at least nothing useful to someone who barely knew what Oakengard was. Most of the reports Tad could interpret recorded player interactions and instancing handshakes.

No matter. If somebody was running Loras on a remote, he should be able to isolate it.

As luck would have it, the Loras avatar did indeed create the powerful assassin tool. Curiously, access was locked out. That couldn't be right. It almost appeared as though the account was created from within Haven. Or at least hijacked by some kind of command layer, a go-between that intercepted messages to and from the event system.

Tad checked on the resting figure of Pete. Unraveling this level of systemic interference would take more time than he had. Maybe he could get to Loras by digging into his associations. The community team dominated his history, of course. There were lots of shady interactions in Shorehome. There was so much impropriety it was impossible to separate the wheat from the chaff. No wonder Larry had been fired.

But there had to be some record transitioning Loras from manual control to remote. The avatar was once driven by a real human being. It had, expectedly, gone dark after the termination. Then one day Loras was rebooted into existence and interfaced with...

Oh. My. God. It wasn't Larry. He was just a used-up, shit-out-of-luck, discarded mole. The real perpetrator was a player inside Haven.

Fingerprints in Oakengard, the Trinity, the community team

—this was a full-on Trojan infecting the system. A virus silently intercepting various command signals with only one explainable purpose: to take over the game completely.

And bringing up the query sheet—Tad's eyes widened. The rogue player was at this very moment inside Stronghold.

Tad needed to warn Talon as soon as possible. He stepped away from the computer but caught himself. The developer menu. The programmer searched for the necessary privileges as quickly as he could in order to get out of there. That's when he ran into another obstacle.

Accessing the dev menu interface was easy enough, but authorization wasn't possible from this hub. Clearance could only come from a specific piece of hardware: Christian Everett's personal workstation.

Suddenly, Talon and Tad's well-laid plan was crumbling all around them. The summit was starting, developer menu access was impossible, and his digital doppelganger was in grave danger. Tad needed to do something, and fast.

1370 Axis & Allies

Trumpets blared and crescendoed, dramatic tones overlapping, buildup and release, buildup and release. The city watch presided over the affair with a full legion. After Stronghold's recent history, it was a welcome show of force. The soldiers kept the lines orderly and policed the crowds. Gladius nodded to me as I weaved through the bustle and into the main tunnel leading to the grounds.

Cheers and chants rolled through the Arena spectators like a breeze over blades of grass. The audience turnout was impressive. For a summit focused on peace, that was kind of a surprise. Was this diplomacy or NASCAR, a raging mass of fans crossing their fingers for a car wreck?

Izzy waited for me inside the main portcullis, leaning on her winter staff. She was dressed in a regal crimson robe I hadn't seen before. All cool elegance, she winked and joined my side.

"There you are," I said, admiring her duds. "I haven't seen you all morning."

"Just caught up in some interesting reading."

It was hard to talk over the cheers so I didn't press for details.

"Wait up!" called Kyle, sprinting from the tunnel. Izzy and I stalled our advance.

Like me, Kyle hadn't thought to wear anything ceremonial. In Haven, it was easy to disregard fashion if you were so inclined. In fact, when clothes didn't need washing it was practical to walk around wearing the same thing. Armor, usually, especially considering the new town combat rules.

"The guildhall's prepped and ready," Kyle reported.

"Already?"

He shrugged. "I was afraid the cask ale wouldn't be done in time, but it's delicious. Dune loved it."

I waved off the details. "Let's focus on the work before the celebration," I urged. "Papa Brugo can be a fickle leader." Kyle's expression dutifully sobered. I arched an eyebrow. "Why do you look so nervous?"

Kyle swallowed. "No reason."

"Kyle."

He cleared his throat. "It's nothing. I'm just really close to hitting level 10 and don't want anything to go wrong."

"Way to jinx us," teased Izzy.

"Why do you think I didn't wanna say anything?"

I raised my hands between them, closed my eyes, and took a calming breath. I didn't believe in bad omens. I wasn't gonna let them get me off my game.

When I opened my eyes, I caught Izzy's funny expression. I had the good sense to examine her. Sometime between last night and now, she'd made level 10. She smirked as I caught on, winked, and marched ahead.

I took another intake of air and set my eyes on the scene

before us.

The Stronghold Arena was an artful replica of the Colosseum of Rome, but not as the modern world knows it. Its many columns stood in full repair. Swatches of black, yellow, and red painted the walls. Intricate accents of marble and metal abounded. It wasn't opulent so much as resolute, in the same sense that mountains were.

In the center of the rounded grounds rested two opposing thrones on a circle of plush carpet. Papa Brugo casually reclined sideways in his broad chair. His entourage attended him: several rogues in black leathers, Hadrian the Whisperer, and two slithery bodyguard spirits. Their wispy forms creeped me out. Eyeless, inhuman, drifting unnaturally like sentient plumes of black smoke.

In game terms, they were unusual in that they had no identifying tags. Brugo's rogues were a mix of middle-of-the-road players, human NPCs, and goblin mobs. Hadrian's description pegged him as a [Level 7 Advisor]. Brugo himself was an NPC; his name was gray and thus non-descriptive, but as a crime boss and Protector of Shorehome, it was safe to say he was a formidable threat. The bodyguards, however? Not an inkling of what they were or how strong. To me, that lack of knowledge was the most unnerving.

My throne sat empty. Surprisingly, despite not having a knack for public appearances, I had a small entourage of my own. Bravo Team was here—not that they weren't welcome. Lash stood beside my simple chair in bold white armor. The knight's cleaver was sheathed but she held her black body shield. A spotless cape of white billowed in the breeze. Lash always was one for uniform. Conan and Glinda took up positions at her side, all official like. This was a real spectacle.

A piece of garbage hit the back of my head. I spun to the wall and jumped out of the way, narrowly dodging spit.

"Goblin lover!" yelled an ornery player in the stands. It was one of Chadwick's men. City watchmen spun in their sandals to respond to the threat.

The crowd around the gangster erupted into boos. Not for me, for him. They pushed and shamed the hater. He yelled back, but his tough-guy indignation evaporated as the shoving grew worse, which only emboldened the crowd further. Under a conflagration of jeers and cheers, they ran the poor man out of the stands. The city watch settled.

I nodded thanks for the show of support. Just to be safe, though, and as a further deterrent, I drew my dragonspear. Applause boomed. I used the weapon as a walking staff and approached the central stage with Izzy and Kyle, wishing I'd had a chance to coordinate with my team before this mess started. My mission with Tad had detracted from my preparation; I just hoped there weren't any hard feelings. I gave Lash a nod as I passed. Her full helm followed me while hiding her expression within.

I stopped at my throne and faced Brugo, expecting him to stand. His lazy attention revealed he had no plans of doing so. Gladius and a troop of centurions with red capes circled our backs in a show of support for Stronghold, carefully eyeing the shadowy bodyguards on the other side.

Papa Brugo's misshapen grin presented an unsettling swath of teeth and gums. The whole setup felt silly, but he was a proud man and this was a small price for peace. I lowered to my throne and the crowd, still filing to their seats, quieted.

"You ain't welcome in Stronghold!" issued a threatening voice.

Two gangsters flipped from the stands to the dirt and charged Papa Brugo's back, which happened to be the area devoid of centurions. Hadrian recoiled and waved for the rogues to shield their master. Brugo, for his part, was wholly unconcerned. He lazily rested, cheek on hand, elbow on armrest, clicking his tongue and studying me as two attackers bolted to his throne.

I stood and readied the dragonspear. The Brothers in Black kneeled low, hands on daggers.

It was all for nothing.

The two shadowy bodyguards twisted sideways like dust devils and struck with spinning tendrils. Both level-5 gangsters were immediately decapitated. Heads bounced to great applause. Idle bodies tripped over themselves and rag-dolled in the dirt. The shadow creatures swirled and slowed almost to the point of dissipating before materializing beside their master. Brugo yawned, Hadrian relaxed, and the black-clad cutthroats retook their positions.

The crowd fucking loved it. Their energy zapped us like a live wire. Even Brugo abandoned his apathy and conceded a smile. I grumbled, hitched the dragonspear in the ground, and reclaimed my seat.

The Papa of all Papas leaned forward in his throne and the audience silenced. "Death pleases the people," he stated matter-of-factly.

"It's..."—my mouth twisted—"just a few bad apples."

"Nonsense. It's the human condition. All men hunger for power."

I kept my eyes on his bodyguards. "Not all men command living shadows."

He vainly laughed. For the first time, the crime boss turned to admire the creatures. "My stalwart pets. They do put on a good show. Their power is great. But you and me, Talon, ours is greater. Without lifting a finger, your people rose to your support and cast your problem away. That is not unlike what my bodyguards did. *That* is power. That is respect."

I got a pinging notification.

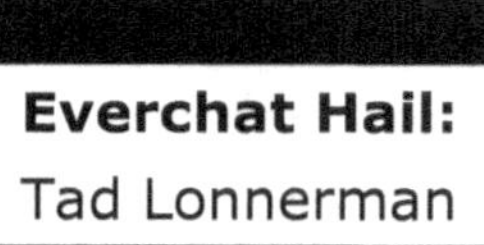

He must've completed his task. Or run into problems preventing him from doing so. I needed to get back to him, but it wasn't possible in public. Everchat required the privacy of a safe zone. I would need to wait until returning to Dragonperch.

I dismissed the notification and resumed my discussion with Brugo. "I just think it doesn't bode well for a peace summit to begin with violence." So much for not believing in bad omens.

"And that is where we are different. Power must be brandished from time to time. As with that spear of yours, its existence must be proven. Otherwise you and me are nothing more than philosophers." The leader of Shorehome leaned back to the sounds of amusement. "As I said," he confidently repeated, "death pleases the people."

Hadrian didn't meet my eyes. Lash stoically gazed ahead. I wasn't really into leadership for the sport of it, but I reminded myself why we were here.

"Peace and war go hand in hand," I announced for all to hear, "because what is treasured must be defended."

"You are a poet now!" Brugo's belly jiggled as he laughed. "Pretty words that ring true. And they lead us to our common problem. The saints."

The crowd was fired up. This latest piece of information divided them. The saints had a lot of supporters. The saints also had their fill of critics. The more moderate folks were stuck in the middle, indecisive yet caught up in the mood.

I raised my voice above the din. "The saints are not our enemies."

"Loras tried to kill you." Boos.

"Working against the developers. Saint Peter supports our independence. Despite his requested absence, he approves of this summit."

"The Brothers in Black do not seek his approval. Look at our audience and your loyal Black Hats. See how the city watch stands behind you. Everyone in this Arena knows you're in charge of Stronghold, Talon. Perhaps everybody save you."

Cheers rang out on that note. It felt strange to acknowledge my status out in the open like that. The people really were on my side whole-cloth now. This summit was turning into a revolution. This was why Brugo wanted a public show in the first place. I hesitantly glanced at Gladius, who watched me with fierce pride.

"I won't have Saint Peter vilified," I asserted. "He's more than a developer; he's a personal friend."

The people quieted. Some briefly shouted in support. Brugo studied me with the overconfidence of a bully, but he didn't push.

"Besides," I added, "there are still some things I can't do. Saint Peter?"

With an unassuming flash, the white robe blinked to my side. A golden twig crown resting on thinning hair, a generous beard of white, and strangely buff calves wrapped in knee-high sandal straps.

"What's this?" snapped Brugo, enraged.

"A compromise," I answered. "A token of friendship. And a gift." I stood and stepped to Brugo's throne.

He seethed. "I demanded a general meeting without saintly intervention!"

"Then you would never have their blessing." I handed Brugo a pearl. He grabbed the item and studied it. "The Black Hats do not seek war," I explained. "We will preserve peace with peace whenever possible. Any who support that cause, including the saints, should have our protection."

Hadrian studied the gift in Brugo's hands. "That's a dove pearl, meant to be used in sanctums like Dragonperch and Underkeep."

"And a useful building block for a headquarters," I added.

"But headquarters require factions. Official factions."

Saint Peter cleared his throat. "Which require saintly approval."

"Bah!" spat Brugo. "I need no one's approval!"

Hadrian leaned into his master. "Why not heed their words?" he persuaded. "So long as they bear out, why risk the wrath of the angels in the core city?"

Brugo's mouth twisted into a sloppy frown. "Peace with peace?" As he pondered a response to his own question, trumpets sounded from the west gate. Hadrian and the rogues turned at the horns. Brugo's eyes hardened. "What's this now?"

Gladius shuffled to the northern exit of the Arena. On the outskirts, the city watch stiffened to attention.

"Someone's approaching the gates," mumbled Kyle.

Brugo snorted. "You speak of peace with attackers at your doorstep?"

"No," I hurried. This couldn't be trouble. Not now.

Gladius rushed over. "General Azzyrk and the goblin horde are skirting the tended lands." As he finished his report, similar warning trumpets blared from the other side of the city. The commander's head snapped to his soldiers. "Get me eyes over the east gate."

The Brothers in Black grew just as unsettled as the audience. Brugo fumed. "Is it not war you seek? Is this a ruse, Talon of Stronghold?"

"It's not," I swore.

"You mean to surround us?"

"That doesn't make sense. We already have you in the city. This isn't a trap. For all we know, the pagans might be sore at you for hanging their witches."

Brugo whispered to his advisor. The crowd hooted and hollered and took to their feet. This revolution was bordering on a riot.

"We're safe in Stronghold," I assured everyone. "These walls held against a titan. We rebuffed the goblin horde at full strength. General Azzyrk just collected the leftovers."

"And the east gate?" questioned Hadrian. "This appears to be more coordinated than a disgruntled general in exile."

Watchmen hurried over to Gladius. "Humans amassing on the road," they reported. "Bandits, by the looks of them."

I scanned the audience for more mobsters. This was too big for Nooner and Chadwick, surely. "Bandits and goblins," I stated calmly. "They have no chance of breaching the walls."

"Never say never," countered the commander of the city watch. "They can ram the gates and scale the walls. We should postpone the summit. I need to defend against a siege." He drew his flaming sword and mustered every soldier in the Arena.

I scowled at the development. If I was in charge of this city, what did it say about me when I couldn't hold a peace summit without gangsters, goblins, and bandits getting in the way?

The Whisperer leaned to his liege. "We should consider retreat, Papa."

Brugo's eyes flared. "I do not turn tail and run."

"Even if you're in the grips of an elaborate trap?"

"It's not a trap," I asserted. "I guaranteed your safety in the city. You have it."

Hadrian frowned. "And what of our men outside the city? They're defenseless on the ship."

"You wish me to seek harbor with the saints?" scoffed Brugo.

I gripped the dragonspear at my side. "The saints aren't the ones who'll be doing the fighting."

The powerful crime boss turned to his advisor.

"The world has never seen walls higher than Stronghold's," reasoned Hadrian.

"Bring them in," concluded Brugo. His eyes met mine. "Bring my people into the city. If they must fight, they'll do it alongside everyone else.'

I turned to Gladius and nodded. The city watch dutifully marched from the Arena to man the walls. Lines of troops, with many more at the gates and Pantheon. I had the impending feeling we'd need to follow real soon. "Peter?" I urged.

The saint made the sign of the cross towards Papa Brugo. "Whether you wish it or not, in the name of peace and goodwill, I give you my blessing."

> **Global Haven Alert:**
> Saint Peter has formed a new faction: the Brothers in Black.

The Papa's eyes lit up.

"Will you strike an alliance?" I asked carefully.

"Will you fight?" he asked in response.

I set my jaw and nodded.

"So we are here for peace, but must make war to win it." Brugo's misshapen lips twisted.

His advisor grew unsettled. "You would buy our allegiance with gifts?"

It had worked before, with the wildkins, but I didn't say that. "This is a means for peace," I stressed.

Hadrian turned to the crime boss. "Patience, Papa. Let us see this skirmish through. We can judge the Black Hats based on the outcome."

"And the saints?" he questioned.

I jerked my head. Saint Peter nodded and disappeared, leaving the Black Hats as the only official representatives of Stronghold remaining in the Arena. I leaned toward the enigmatic crime boss. "You can trust us, Brugo. I swear it."

The Papa of all Papas pressed his lips together, avenues of thought represented by the many arguing voices in the audience. He pondered long and hard, as a showman would. When his lips finally parted, you could hear a leaf settle on the ground.

"Trust is a dangerous concept," said the big man, every eye in the house on him. "I do not trust anyone, not even my own Whisperer." Hadrian lowered his gaze. "You claim to trust this saint. That speaks well to his character, but speaks ill of yours."

The crime boss took a ponderous breath before continuing. "A long time ago, after I was excoriated for my crimes—after I was cast out by my own mother—I found myself listless in the streets. Not a Papa, not a boss, not even an accomplished thief. Yet my guile was unerring, my drive unassailable. These qualities attracted my mentor's eye."

Brugo sighed as he recollected days of yore. "I was barely a man when the old soul took me in. He fed me, clothed me, and trained me. There was a pack of us, roving the streets for unwitting marks. We were a team. As my skills improved and his health failed, the old oman even deigned to call me his partner and successor. I took a shine to my new role, my first taste of leadership. Do you know what my dear partner did?" Brugo waited only a moment, growling his own answer. "He and his two best men stabbed me in the back seventeen times and left me for dead."

The Papa sneered at his tale of the frailty of trust. I cast a sidelong glance at my people. Izzy wore a worried look. Kyle checked his character sheet, staring at the small gap of XP he needed to level. Lash continued her impression of a statue. She was so focused on the crime boss I couldn't get a glance of warning in edgewise.

> **Talon:** *I don't like this.*

I casually opened my menu and moved to the brigade controls, making the gesture as innocuous as possible, but there was only so much you could do to hide a menu interface. Luckily, NPCs like Brugo didn't take overt notice of such player actions.

> Brigade invite sent to [Lash]

"I didn't die, of course," continued the bold Papa. "I made my two compatricts pay for their treachery first. I wanted the old man to see the fruit of his actions. To feel the fear I did while bleeding out in the street." He raised a palm to the packed Arena. "To give a public show of power. I strung those two traitors up by their heels in the fish market. The gulls picked at their overripe flesh for hours."

I kept checking the invite but Lash wasn't accepting. I sent it again.

"My mentor tried to rally a posse for me after that, but what kind of man serves one who can't protect those closest to him? Alone and isolated, my mentor had no choice but to go on the run. He didn't get far. And when I dragged him through the streets and staked him to the boardwalk of my city, it wasn't me who rent the flesh from his bones. It was his men, now mine. I wanted the old man to know he was truly alone in death, without a soul to trust." Brugo leaned forward with a snarl. "*Power* was the only thing I placed my trust in. *Power* was what won me the day. Not hearts and minds but fear, raw and unadulterated."

The band of cutthroats grew itchy fingers. Even Hadrian tensed. But the shadowy bodyguards behind him roiled as if riding a slow flame, easy and smooth. My knuckles on the dragonspear went white.

Papa Brugo turned to appraise Lash. His saggy smile was a menacing, disgusting sight. Then he turned his study to Izzy, and I saw admiration.

"It is no wonder you've earned their respect." His eyes fixed on me. "You are a powerful man, Talon, and powerful men hold sway. If the saints see your power, and *our* power together, perhaps they will settle for true peace."

The Whisperer's hood snapped to his master in surprise.

"I make no oaths of friendship with them," announced the Papa, "but if the saints remain true to their word, so shall I. May our future pursuits be prosperous."

"This is a mistake," warned Hadrian.

A prompt flashed before me.

> **The Brothers in Black request an Alliance with the Black Hats!**
>
> *Accept?*

I hid my relief as the corner of my mouth crooked in satisfaction. The timing was perfect. Another notification interrupted me before I could respond.

> [Lash] has joined your brigade

"Idiot!" muttered Hadrian. The alliance request vanished. "That never happened."

Brugo grumbled and turned to his advisor. "What never happened?"

"That story. With your mentor."

"Of course it happened. I was there."

"It's your backstory," expounded Hadrian. "Your programmed history. To give you color."

Brugo's eyes went red. "I. Killed. That. Man."

The Whisperer snorted. "And where did he respawn? And the two other traitors, for that matter? It never happened. None of your damned history happened. It's a fairy tale."

The Brothers in Black scraped their daggers free. One of the mercenaries pulled a long blade free from his cloak. I recognized it. The third of its kind. An assassin needle. I knew the bandit wielding it too. [Chico - Level 6 Highwayman].

I sprang to my feet. "Brugo! Watch out!"

The cutthroat plunged the enchanted dagger deep into the back of the Papa's neck. The crime boss jerked to his feet, bashed the rogue to the ground like a rotting mailbox, and let out a mighty roar.

Every weapon on the field of the Arena was drawn.

Fifty Brothers in Black leapt from the stands. Their deft boots pattered to the dirt, and fifty more daggers were produced. Portcullises slammed and sealed the exits of the Arena. My team scrambled to put our backs together and cover all threats while the band of cutthroats closed in.

1380 SpyParty

The highwayman assassin rolled to his feet and lunged at the crime boss to finish the job. Brugo caught Chico and wrapped oversize fingers around his neck. "Insolent gnat," he spat.

The highwayman used his fist like a hammer and pounded the knife, still embedded in Brugo's neck, deeper. The Papa's knees wavered, but his resolve fought on. Spittle dribbled from his sagging cheek as he squeezed the life out of his would-be assassin.

```
Savage!
[Papa Brugo] dealt 167 damage to [Chico]
[Chico] is dead!
```

The limp body dropped to the ground. The other rogues closed in.

Small axes blinked into each of Brugo's hands. He fended off a platinum lance with one and struck down a goblin traitor with the other.

"Fools," bellowed the stubborn crime boss, dagger still protruding from his neck. For all its impressive backstab damage, Brugo was only missing 40% of his health. His head swiveled to his advisor. "You did this, Whisperer?"

Another Brother charged him with a sword. The Papa brought both axes together, crunching her body and severing her spine in two places.

Hadrian's class changed from [Advisor] to [Spymaster]. "The plan was to make my move in Oldtown, to strike at the heart of the Black Hats before they had a chance to react, but no—your fragile ego saw the grandest building in the city and just had to be at its center." Hadrian huffed in frustration. "No matter, I've got Talon's Alpha and Bravo teams right here. I—"

Lash struck like a king cobra, in full swing before the cleaver materialized in her hands. The sudden transition from statue to predator took even the spymaster by surprise. Her heavy blade caught him center mass. As she powered through her swing, his black cloak crumpled around her sword and flapped in the wind. Hadrian rolled backward, free and clear, just barely pulling off the lifesaving skill escape. Now dressed in tight-fitting brown leathers, his eyes were wide with relieved indignation.

"Pull back!" ordered Hadrian. The contingent of Brothers in Black closed around their spymaster. Some of their hoods fell away. [Jackie - Level 8 Dragoon]. [Colt - Level 7 Cowboy]. Along with their fallen comrade, Chico, they formed the Rough Riders, a group of bandits who terrorized the lands surrounding Shorehome.

"Ha ha ha!" boomed Brugo heartily, his axes toys in his meaty hands. "You may be a lot of things, Whisperer, but you are no fighter. You can't fake your level, and no one with single digits can take down the Papa of all Papas."

As much as I wanted to strike, Hadrian and his Brothers had pulled away from us. My brigade was facing off against the surrounding threats from the stands. I scanned the Arena for possible reinforcements, but the city watch had completely cleared out. Bandit hoofed nervously along the wall.

"Brugo," I said, offering a sheltering hand. "Come with us."

"Run?" he asked callously. "From this little man? Never."

Hadrian snorted. "You misread my intentions, Papa. It is not I who will do the honor."

Brugo's brow furrowed. He spun as his own shadows converged on him.

"No!" he ordered. "I am your master! I am the Protector of Shorehome! I hold the Squid's Tooth!"

Hadrian released a snide laugh. "A fool till the end. Didn't you ever wonder why Saint Loras gave you the soulstone to begin with?"

Brugo's face twisted. "An obvious deception, meant to ignite a war."

The spymaster's eyes fluttered impatiently. "Yes, but why did he give it to *you*?"

"Because I am the Papa of all Papas."

"You're an idiot. Loras didn't give *you* the soulstone, he gave it to *ME*. You're nothing more than my treasurer."

Brugo mustered himself after his initial surprise, eyes hardening into pure death. "Hear this," he boomed. "I will hang you in the fish market by your intestines, for all to see what real power is. Any of my Brothers that assist in this insurrection will contribute to a greater feast for the gulls." Brugo yanked the assassin needle from his neck and tossed it to the ground with a scowl. "Even my loyal pets, the shadows, will kneel before me or face my wrath."

The band of cutthroats backed away, cowed by their brash and seemingly invincible leader. The dark devils had no such fears. They advanced with menacing zeal.

"So be it," snarled Brugo. His axes flashed.

Black sparks ripped from the shadows, a series of strikes that would've killed normal beasts, one after the other too fast to count. Brugo took them on and advanced through both his bodyguards. He hurt them too.

Hadrian waited with the apathy of a man who'd seen the same movie play out time and again. Brugo put up a valiant effort, but he simply wasn't built to slice through the immaterial. Working together, the shadows swiped and feinted, picked and pulled, lashed and prodded, keeping the impressive fight going until the big man made a wrong move. A single miscalculation, overreaching his range the slightest bit, and whiffing.

The shadow monsters dove in. Nethery claws gouged grooves across his chest and belly. The wounds opened so deep, it wasn't just blood that escaped them. Bits of muscle and fatty tissue slipped out. Papa Brugo dropped his axes and buckled to his knees in a stadium-shaking rumble.

Hadrian smiled as his rogues surrounded him. "A man who leads by fear," he mused. "Are you afraid now, Papa of all Papas?"

Blood spilled from the big man's mouth. He tried to speak but choked on the words.

"You told it yourself, in your own story. A man must kill his mentor to evolve." Hadrian nodded and the two shadows lopped

Brugo's head into separate pieces.

Until now, my people had focused on fending off the incoming Brothers in Black. Several of the rogues already lay dead, their cohorts feinting and biding time. When Brugo's ravaged body toppled to the dirt, the entire stadium was hit with the momentous tidings.

"It was you," I fumed, staring a hole through the Whisperer's soul. "All of it. You compromised the saints, divided the pagans, fractured Oakengard. You're the player secretly working behind the scenes, the one Lucifer worked all this time to thwart."

Hadrian spat. "His damned NPC evolution threatened everything. Look at what free choice almost brought this dead fool to do."

So Hadrian was the great enemy, the player who would wrest control of Haven. Suddenly all of Lucifer's moves made sense. The Whisperer had compromised the saints, so Lucifer sought to wrest them from power. Hadrian used NPCs and mobs as pawns and cover, so Lucifer gifted them free will. And it wasn't just him. The boggart witches must've figured the truth. It was Hadrian who'd made the move to silence them. It was him making all the moves, completely and utterly invisible behind his boisterous puppet leader.

"You must've known Lucifer was right next to you, in the Salt Sea," I said.

"Of course," he sniggered. "So close, yet so far. I allowed the fool to outcast himself. Let him stew in salt while I fomented war and division and strife, all to consolidate my power."

"Except your power over NPCs is tenuous now." I faced the crowd of black-clad rogues. "You have the power of choice," I announced to all, whether nameless or not. "You don't need to follow this traitor. We will be stronger together!"

Hadrian showed his teeth. "Don't prove yourself a bigger fool than the NPC, Talon. The Brothers in Black aren't here to ally with the Black Hats, we're here to annihilate you."

> **Black Hat Alert:**
> The Brothers in Black have declared war!

> Brothers in Black Reputation -100

I gritted my teeth against every determined rogue in the Arena. They were all in on this. Free or not, they meant to fight to the last.

I stepped toward Hadrian, dragonspear twirling. "At least, in death, Brugo forced your hand. Your charade is over."

Izzy's crimson robe gave way to her teal combat dress. Conan and Lash swung impressive weapons. Kyle guarded Glinda, our healer.

Hadrian remained cool. "And yet I still have control of the game board. Look around, Talon. My pieces outnumber yours. The goblins and bandits are my doing. We have you surrounded, within these walls and without."

"You can't beat us with a bunch of goblins and thieves."

"Put enough pawns in the right position and you can do anything you want."

My knuckles went white. "You're forgetting the rules,

Hadrian. I don't need to kill the pawns—I just need to capture the king."

I triggered dash to skid between his wall of defenders. I immediately noticed something different. Despite having regularly used the skill for weeks, its activation felt incomplete this time. Its behavior was unexpected, as if I hadn't finished pumping skill points into it.

The confusion caused me to stumble. I lined up a hasty deadshot, but my intuition skill warning went off.

> **[Shadowguard]**
> 600 Health

A limb of shadow broke through my guard and slashed, forcing me to roll away.

> 47 damage
> DoT: 30 dmg/15 secs

The pain distracted from my skill misfire. Multiple buffs washed over the brigade.

> [Lash] cast War Cry
> *+10% strike for the next 30 seconds.*
> [Glinda] cast White Circle
> *+20% magic resistance and +10% non-physical damage resistance for the next 60 seconds.*

"Talon!" called Izzy.

The second shadowguard went straight for her. At first I thought she was calling for help, but soon realized it was a warning. The pixie spiked her winter staff to the ground and activated its legendary power. I had to retreat behind our front line or be caught in the sleet storm.

A blizzard of jagged ice and heartless cold caught the center of the uprising. The shadowguards cowered at the potent magic. Instead of shriveling completely, they hurried to cover Hadrian. The Rough Riders weren't so lucky. Colt and Chico were buried in snow. Jackie brought her arms together and shielded herself with some sort of magical vanguard. The majority of the other scrubs learned the brutality of the harsh winter.

Our backside was unaffected by the cone of weather. Lash erected a glimmering wall of yellow energy. Brothers in Black fought to work through it. Conan cut down any that came close. Kyle panicked their ranks with fire and corrosive bolts. Alpha Team and Bravo Team worked together as a single unit, faction buffs and expertise compounding into sheer overpowering deadliness.

> [Glinda] cast Minor Healing on [Talon]
> *You are healed and instantly relieved of minor status effects.*

My health bar filled to full. I nodded thanks as she hurried to the white knight, fighting off four cutthroats at once.

> **Talon:** *Jeez, Lash, glad we've got you on our side.*
> **Lash:** *The little worm still got away from me. I could've sworn it was gonna be the fat man. I was just waiting to chop him in half.*
> **Izzy:** *Save those reflexes for the real enemy.*

The frost mage's blizzard died down. The destruction was vast, but isolated. Despite the reams of black cloaks on the ground, we were still heavily outnumbered. More concerning were the shadowguards once again slithering our way.

The wave of rogues shattered Lash's wall. Izzy conjured a hail of icicles to mow them down. I triggered deadshot. Again I felt a degree of hesitation as my skill triggered. I willed the uncertainty away and struck a shadowguard dead center.

> You dealt 22 damage to [Shadowguard]

A wispy claw raked at me. I barely activated crossblock in time. Same skill misfire. The attack partially phased through my defenses.

> Blockbreaker!
> 32 damage

I grunted and spun away, glad to have escaped without a DoT. What was going on with my skills? "Do you guys feel that?" I asked.

Izzy smacked a goblin rogue with her staff. "Feel what?"

"Some kind of... lag on your skills?"

Izzy sprayed the area with ice. "That's your level 10 overload ability. Didn't you read up on the changes?"

"I guess not."

Izzy batted a thief with her staff and rolled her eyes. "Overload lets you pump extra SP into your skills. Do it or don't, but be decisive about whichever you choose. That indecision is the lag you feel."

I readied a counterattack against the shadowguard. Instead of engaging me, it rushed past. Crossbow bolts phased through it without triggering damage notifications.

"Physical weapons are no good!" reported Kyle. "No wonder Papa Brugo lost that fight."

As with me, the shadow ignored him and slipped past. It tackled Glinda at the knees.

Leg Break!
[Shadowguard] dealt 84 damage to [Glinda]

"Healer down!" I called out.

A clap of Glinda's hands bathed her in cooling white magic. Lash was immediately at her teammate's side, slamming her cleaver to the ground and spawning a new energy barrier. The shadowguard whined as the wall deflected its next attack.

The second guard left Hadrian's side and charged Izzy. Frozen stalagmites speared up from the ground.

> [Izzy] dealt 32 damage to [Shadowguard]
> (343/600)
> [Izzy] dealt 32 damage to [Shadowguard]
> (311/600)

It worked. Their ethereal forms were susceptible to magic. But, even after Brugo's axes and the sleet storm, the red mobs had plenty of health to go around. The spirit dove forward, ignoring incoming damage, and struck at the frost mage with a lightning-fast attack.

> [Shadowguard] dealt 67 damage to [Izzy]

The pixie yelped and fell away, quick reflexes the only thing saving her from decapitation. The follow-up blow merely knocked the winter staff to the ground. As the other shadow battered Lash's wall, I gritted my teeth and triggered dash. This time, there was no uncertainty. No hesitation. I powered forward and struck Izzy's attacker in the back.

> You dealt 27 damage to [Shadowguard] (284/600)

Luckily, the dragonspear was a legendary weapon, imbued with enough latent magic to tag the shadows. Still, the damage output was disappointing, even with my mantle bonus for protecting the city.

Glinda selflessly healed Izzy as her attacker shattered the energy wall. Lash brought her cleaver down. Imbued with yellow energy, the shadow recoiled and snarled.

"Hadrian's unprotected!" boomed Conan. He was out of position and outgunned. Without Lash's magic backing him, he was doing his best to hold the line on his own. He was a hardy fighter but, at level 7, it was only a matter of time before he was overrun.

I focused on the Whisperer looting Papa Brugo's body, but I couldn't bring myself to chase him down with Izzy in dire straits. I charged the shadowguard, shoving it aside and trading blows.

You dealt 23 damage to [Shadowguard] (261/600)
43 damage
DoT: 30 dmg/15 secs

With Izzy covered, the brewmaster saw his opening. Kyle spun his crossbow around. One shot hit a random rogue in the line of fire, but the second struck his mark. Hadrian recoiled from the bolt in his shoulder. He snarled against the corrosive DoT.

"You and me both, buddy," I grunted.

Our line was failing fast. Cutthroats swiped at Lash's back. They distracted her enough to allow a shadowguard to sneak in a heavy blow.

Surprise!
[Shadowguard] dealt 77 damage to [Lash]
DoT: 30 dmg/15 secs

As she buckled away, the spirit turned and viciously swiped at Glinda.

Critical Hit!

Stun!

[Shadowguard] dealt 94 damage to [Glinda]

DoT: 30 dmg/15 secs

"No!" Izzy somersaulted to the fallen healer's side, erecting a wall of ice from the ground before them, once again frustrating the attacking shadow.

Hadrian cried out and rolled away from another volley of crossbow bolts. The shadows were alerted to the danger and backed away, but only slightly. The two ghostly figures joined arms and spun, creating a vortex between them.

[Shadowguard] and [Shadowguard] cast Void Orb

The ball grew into a black hole and fired toward the healer.

Lash rolled from the black hole's path. Izzy and Glinda braced behind the ice wall as darkness consumed them both.

In a snap, the magical void blinked out of existence. Izzy, Glinda, and the ice wall were gone.

1390 Shadow Dancer

I braced my spear against the shadowguards while blinking dumbly at the combat notification window. This battle was doing a number on me. I really had to get my act together.

> **Talon:** *What the hell, Izzy! What happened?*
> **Izzy:** *... I'm not sure. We're alive. In a black hole. I can't see anything.*

The spymaster delighted at our panic. Our healer and crowd control were now gone. Kyle reloaded his weapon. This time a shadowguard was in place to protect Hadrian. It solidified enough to take the hits, but the damage was minimal. With his master safe, the second shadowguard advanced on us.

"This is bad," muttered Lash, downing a health potion in the absence of her teammate. Conan fell back to us.

"Screw this," muttered Kyle. "I'm not going down like a chump." He pocketed the crossbow. A rounded shield with a flat top and bottom snapped into his left hand. His right glowed as he equipped a bronze gauntlet. It had been looted from Bishop Tannen, one half of his magical set. The glove and mirror shield was a new loadout combo for Kyle, and it didn't look half bad. His expression flipped from frustration to determination. "I may not be level 10 yet, but I'm not running. Bring it on."

The shadowguard sensed something awry. Where it had previously ignored the brewmaster, it now came at him warily. It tested the shield which completely reflected the attack. Kyle spun the holy gauntlet in answer. Golden light flared. The shadow flew away from Kyle like a popped balloon, a trail of smoke following it for ten feet. The shadow roiled in smoky anger.

> Combo!
> Holy Weakness!
> Stun!
> [Kyle] dealt 86 damage to [Shadowguard] (198/600)

The Whisperer's eyes widened to dinner plates. Every rogue in the Arena sputtered. Players in the crowd cheered and climbed down the walls. Attendees worked to open the portcullises.

"Away!" snapped Hadrian. "Get me to phase two!"

The Brothers in Black formed a wall as a shadowguard pulled their boss away. I charged, planted the spear, and vaulted over their line.

> **Izzy:** *We're free. But... We're east of the city.*
> **Lash:** *Say again. You're not in Stronghold?*

> **Glinda:** *No, we're on the eastern road. It'll take forever to get back.*
> **Lash:** *Try.*
> **Izzy:** *She's right. The fight will be over.*

As I ran, my eyes found the mountain bongo at the side wall. "Bandit!"

She kicked a hoof in the dirt and snorted in understanding. I didn't know how she did it, but she was on the same page as me. As one portcullis was raised, the mountain bongo galloped from the Arena at full speed.

> **Talon:** *Sending you a ride.*

Conan dropped to his knees, bloodied. Lash barged into his attackers, taking heavy damage herself. Before the tanks could be downed, players and NPCs from the stands flooded over them. More spilled to our flanks, harassing our enemies. The wounded shadowguard, far from defeated, lashed out at those nearby.

Hadrian and his shadow continued retreating. I wasn't sure what phase two was, but I didn't want them getting away. I batted a few rogues with my spear, forcing deeper through their ranks until my strike was parried by a platinum lance. Jackie the dragoon.

"You," I spat.

Such was the gift and the curse of MMOs. We'd dealt with the Rough Riders before, finished them off when they waylaid us, but defeating enemies in virtual worlds was only a temporary victory. Respawns allowed grudges to go on indefinitely.

"The Rough Riders make sense now. You were Hadrian's people all along. Raiding the Shorehome countryside, skirmishing to pose enough of a constant threat to unify the Brothers in Black in the city."

She smiled wickedly. "Scared the goblins and humans both. Kept them pledged to the city, and scared nosy wanderers away."

I snorted. "Didn't scare me."

Her smug expression evaporated. "Yeah, we're gonna pay you back for that."

Chico the highwayman was long dead. Colt was still hanging on after the blizzard. When Kyle rushed to support me, the cowboy raised a pistol. "Hold it right there. This fight's between them."

"Bro," replied Kyle, "do you even know how faction wars work?"

Colt scowled at the breach of honor and fired. Kyle raised his mirror shield and the bullet reflected back to its owner. A small dot of red popped into Colt's neck. He dropped his flintlock and buckled to the ground, squeezing his wound.

I charged Jackie with a deadshot. Her vanguard shield absorbed the attack and knocked me off balance. I crossblocked her counter. A quick return strike to the back of her knee swept her off her feet. Instead of following up the attack, I dashed toward the edge of the Arena, where Hadrian and his shadow had just reached the wall.

"Talon!" called Kyle. "Behind you!"

The wounded shadowguard bowled through a line of low-level players, straight for me. Kyle jumped to intercept him until a loop of rope caught his neck. Colt was still alive, propped up on one hand and knee, holding the other end. He yanked the lasso and toppled Kyle to the dirt.

I didn't have time to help because the charging shadowguard lunged for me. The damned thing had phased through my block last time, so I threw everything I had at it. I activated spinshield and used the new overload ability to pump extra SP into it. My spirit bar dipped as I twirled violently, dragonspear slashing anything within two meters.

Spinshield Overload!
You dealt 34 damage to [Shadowguard] (164/600)

A whirlpool of dirt circled me as I skidded to a stop. I had rebuffed the attack, avoided damage, and dished a bit of my own. Now at a little over a quarter health, the shadowguard whined and backed away, rejoining its compatriot at the rounded wall.

I stepped toward Hadrian slowly, waiting for the final 10 seconds of my deadshot cooldown to expire. Some of my people were hurt, but we were holding our ground. Rogues all over the Arena fell to the greater player population. It was over.

"You're cornered," I leveled. "Call off your dogs and no one else has to die. I just want you in chains." I faced the crowd behind me. "The rest of your faction is free to return to Shorehome and reflect on their mistakes."

Kyle tugged the lasso at his neck and struggled to his feet.

Colt chugged a health potion and Jackie cautiously approached my back. Lash and Conan, cut off by rogues, put their backs together and made their way toward us.

Hadrian released a caustic chuckle. "You're not smart enough to see it yet. The Brothers in Black will fight to the last man."

"You hear that?" I called out to the cutthroats. "Your lives are meaningless to Hadrian." Jackie sneered uneasily. I refocused on the Whisperer. "The saints won't let you take the city. You're not an NPC like Bishop Tannen. You're not hidden behind Papa Brugo anymore. The angels will activate against any player seeking to take the Pantheon."

"The saints are already deposed. They're powerless. You and Lucifer have taken care of that part for me. Oh, no. The angels will remain sleeping because it's not the saints I'm taking this city from."

I ground my teeth. "From me, then."

"That's right, a hapless player who stumbled his way to glory. I'm taking the city from you because you don't deserve it, Talon. You're not special in the slightest."

The two shadowguards joined hands and once again formulated dark magic.

[Shadowguard] and [Shadowguard] cast Void Orb

I anticipated the expiration of my deadshot timer and lunged. Hadrian laughed as his shadowguards pulled the black hole over themselves. The dragonspear rang out against the Arena stonework as they vanished. The spymaster and his shadows were gone.

I shuddered under a heavy back blow.

Surprise!
58 damage

I dropped to one knee, bracing my weapon against the wall. Jackie swung her lance too fast for me to recover.

[Lash] cast Shield Wall

A floating yellow barrier materialized and blocked the dragoon's follow-up strike. Her momentary confusion gave me enough time to spin with my spear low, sweeping Jackie's legs out from under her.

Lash charged the dragoon but a shot rang out. Colt, near full health, had recovered his pistol. The white knight spun to block his barrage with her body shield.

Kyle growled. His bronze gauntlet released the rope at his throat. Instead of fighting against it, he held his mirror shield high and charged the cowboy.

I rounded the stationary energy shield as Jackie scrambled to her feet, eyes frantic as Colt defended the dual onslaught of Kyle and Lash. She spat at my feet and slammed her lance on the ground.

[Jackie] cast Jade Fire

A neon glow of green overtook her weapon. "If it's the last thing I do—"

"It will be," I said.

I charged with two hands on the spear, fully aware of the dragoon's powered-up strength. At least she wasn't on horseback this time so I had that going for me. Our weapons connected. The jolt rocked through my arms but I held fast. I came again, sending strike after strike quickly and expertly, making sure not to overextend myself or my position.

Jackie was good. She'd improved her hand-to-hand skills since we'd last battled. Every one of my blows was met by her lance, every opening quickly closed. But she was backtracking. On her heels. I slammed the dragonspear into her weapon repeatedly, overpowering her with sheer ferocity if nothing else. Supercharged or not, I wasn't backing down from this fight.

And besides, I hadn't been aiming for her the entire time. After my 20 seconds cycled again, I triggered dash and deadshot simultaneously. My target was her super-powered platinum lance. I poured as much SP into the strike as I could, forcing my spirit below 100.

Deadshot Overload!
Weapon Breaker!

White lightning crackled through my spear as Jackie's platinum lance splintered. Neon sparks of metal spattered to the ground. The dragoon watched it happening in slow motion.

The dragonspear flashed at full speed. Two devastating blows knocked Jackie to the ground. Behind me, Colt's pistol and severed gun hand rested on the floor beside Lash's cleaver. Kyle straddled the cowboy and pounded him into oblivion.

"No!" pleaded Jackie. "Don't kill me! I'll join the Black Hats!"

I snickered. "Sorry, we don't have openings for losers."

Her lips curled to a snarl a split second before the dragonspear crushed her face in.

Despite player deaths not awarding XP, plenty of NPCs and mobs were going down. As we stood and watched Stronghold residents take control of the Arena, blue fire rushed over Kyle as he hit level 10. The brewmaster brimmed with well-earned confidence.

I was out of breath from all the action. Without a healer around, I chugged a health vial. Lash and Conan were badly hurt and had already used theirs.

"We're not done here," I warned.

"Just a sec," said Kyle.

I tugged his shoulder. "Check your updates later. You get to pick a legendary ability, you can overload skills now with extra SP, yada yada yada—there's no time." I hurried to the north exit of the Arena.

"But they're all dead," protested Conan.

"Hadrian's not retreating. Not with goblins and bandits outside the walls. You heard him. Phase two. He's loose in the city. Lash, get Bravo Team healed and prepared for defense."

Her heavy helmet cocked sideways. "Defense of what?"

We exited the Arena. A longboat filled with Brothers in Black rowed south on the Albula. Shouts of surprise and fear came from the northern reaches of the city. I opened my broadcast interface.

Black Hat Broadcast:

ATTENTION ALL BLACK HATS!

Papa Brugo is dead. Hadrian has betrayed us. We are now at war with the Brothers in Black, and they've breached the city. They're coming for us. Not for the Pantheon—for *us*. Get to Oldtown and defend it with your lives. If we fail, everything we've built together will be gone.

1400 River Raid

Lash growled at the sight of the invading faction. "A bunch of thieves wanna take away all our hard work? Not a chance."

Conan beat his chest. "We got this."

"No," I cut in. "You both sorely need a healer."

"I can manage," grumbled the white knight.

"No, you can't. You're both hovering at one-third health. This battle's just starting, and it'll be determined by our high-level leadership. I need Bravo Team alive, Lash. That's more important than a few cutthroats on a boat. Take Conan, muster the troops, and form a line at Oldtown. That's an order."

Her heavy helmet dipped once. "Copy that, boss." She paused a moment. "You know, you're smarter than you look."

"Get out of here, Lash."

She laughed as they headed south around the Arena. I chuckled too. Coming from her, that was a big compliment.

"And why aren't we mustering the troops?" asked Kyle.

"We opened the river gate to let Brugo's men in, except they're really Hadrian's men. Who knows how many rogues they've hidden on the *Void*? That ship is huge. You and I are gonna go north and cut off their reinforcements before this siege gets out of hand."

I scanned upriver. Errol, Grom, and Grug were casting off the transport barge parked by the Arena. It was a huge sturdy platform that took up half the width of the river. No longer useful for transporting supplies, it sure made one hell of an obstacle.

"The savvy bastard actually had a good idea for once," I admitted.

We sprinted to the barge as the pirates unmoored it. When it drifted to our side of the river, we climbed aboard.

"You guys going for a joy ride or is there some kind of plan?" I asked them.

"This city's spinnin' down the Maelstrom," answered Errol. "Me plan is t' fight."

"Simple but effective."

Captain Oates shook his head. "Damn that Hadrian fer cuttin' into me slack time, and killin' Brugo no less. I always said ye can't trust players..." Grom and Grug nodded agreement. "No offense."

I rolled my eyes. "None taken. It's kinda like trusting pirates."

The barge started downriver. I kept my eyes peeled for trouble as we cruised by the Forum and the slums. I didn't see any bandits or city watchmen. I understood the guards were manning the walls, but it was ludicrous there hadn't been a citywide alert yet. The war declaration and my call to arms had both been faction broadcasts. Was it possible the greater populace took this all for an Arena stunt?

I grunted, unsure if a notification would even help anymore.

The old protections suppressed friendly-fire damage. The new city-combat rules opened damage up to all residents, whether player, NPC, or mob. That was the only way to balance the scales. Unfortunately, it meant banding together for defense was just as dicey as dungeon combat. Only the city guards themselves were immune to friendly fire, which had always been the case.

The pirates paddled north in great time, enhanced by the fact that we were headed downriver. Halfway to the gate, we caught sight of another longboat of rogues up ahead. Funnily enough, they were obstructed by Nooner and his length of chain.

"Ain't no one passing unless they pay the fee," said the deposed gangster boss.

"But we were invited into the city," spat a Brother in Black.

"Not by me you weren't."

"We could just kill you," growled another cutthroat.

"No," said the first. "He's not a Black Hat. We have strict orders."

Nooner laughed. "That's right, you have yer orders, and yer gonna do the same thing the last boatload of fellers did. Yer gonna pay me my toll!"

The rogues muttered and started a collection of silver pieces to hand over. They were so aggravated by the delay that they only noticed the oversize barge full of enemies when we were almost on top of them.

"Kyle," I hurried, "remember the *Deep Blue*?"

"Fondly," he chuckled. The brewmaster hefted a fire bomb and expertly chucked it at the enemy. Black-clad rogues screamed and abandoned ship as their boat was consumed by magical flames. Our barge knocked the longboat and swimmers out of the way. "Almost too easy," he said smugly.

"You harassing the incoming enemy, Nooner?" I asked sharply.

He hiked a shoulder. "One man's enemy is another man's customer. Besides, it looks a might bit better than what yer doing."

"Man's got a point," whispered Errol.

I smirked at the small gangster contingent and flashed them a salute. "Keep up the good work, boys."

We continued past, focusing on the next two incoming longboats. The Brothers saw us this time and drew daggers and bows. A bottle of flame gel arced through the air and exploded on one ship to great effect. More rogues were sent to the water. Rather than taking their chances, the second boat quickly docked and unloaded. Both longboats were empty by the time we reached them. Grug and Grom readied to jump off the barge and give chase.

"Leave them," I said. "Our priority is the river gate. We can sweep the town for invaders later. Every second the gate stays open, more will leak in."

They acknowledged the point and doubled down on rowing. The barge passed under the large northern bridge where the river widened. After one more bend, the north wall came into view, along with the scene beyond the tunnel.

"Flea-ridden traitors!" snapped Errol.

Longboat after longboat brimming with cutthroats rowed toward the city. Not only was the *Void* unloading every rogue on board, but two other Shorehome frigates were now reinforcing their numbers.

"The Black Sea!"cried Errol, eyes ablaze. His hands on the oar went idle.

Beside the three master-class ships was the *Cutter*, adrift and bowed in the river, waterlogged. Errol's pride and joy had been sunk.

"Keep at those oars!" I shouted. "Get to the gate! The worst is about to hit!"

The magnitude of the danger revealed itself seconds later. In the distance, possibly keeping away in order to pacify the city watch, was the undine vessel, the *Deep Blue*.

"That's why our voyage back from Shorehome was strangely quiet," muttered Kyle.

"That don't explain the sirens," said Errol.

"They might be part of the attack."

"An' I suppose ye be thinkin' the dolphins and barnacles be in cahoots with Hadrian as well?"

I moved to the fore of the barge as we slowed toward the gate. Silhouettes slithered through the dark water below. A longboat of rogues entered the tunnel under the thick wall. The low ceiling protected them from arcing fire bombs, at least until we got closer.

"Close the gate!" I yelled to the watchmen manning the walls.

A centurion turned to me, annoyed. "We have orders to bring them into the city. To protect them from the invading force."

"They *are* the invading force! The Brothers in Black are at war with us. Mobs are sneaking into Stronghold underwater. Close the gate NOW!"

The centurion held for a skeptical moment. A group of

undine hopped up from the water and landed on our barge brandishing claws. The troops on the wall flinched. "Close the gates!" repeated the centurion.

Spear and swords cut through the air, keeping the undine at bay. The nasty creatures slobbered through hungry teeth. They didn't account for the archers on the wall behind them. Arrows punched into their scaly backs. The mermen writhed in confusion, and we cut them down. Seconds later, watchmen skirted the shore to close the inner gate.

Mermaids leapt onto the steel bars and spurted ink from their mouths. The oily substance acted much like Kyle's corrosive and weakened the hinges. The river gates weren't heavy portcullises that lowered. They were simple gates that swung open horizontally. The gate on the inner wall wasn't especially strong either. Rusted and corroded, the undine successfully ripped it from its hinges.

"The outer gate," I directed. "It's the heavy one, meant to stave off invaders. It should hold off their acid."

The pair of city watchmen on shore nodded and hopped on the barge. We didn't really need their help shutting the gate, but I wasn't about to condemn such bravery. Our platform boat pushed under the thick Stronghold wall and into the river tunnel. Strangely, the mermaids on the gate immediately dove in retreat. I huffed and looked forward as the skiff of rogues approached us.

"Arm yourselves," I told the watchmen. As they were just planning on closing the gate, their swords were still sheathed.

"We won't attack the Brothers in Black," said one guard. "We still have orders to treat them as friendlies."

"They're at war with us!"

"They're at war with you, Talon. As an officially recognized PvP event, I'm not sure we can intervene."

"But the undine—"

"Are mobs and will be dealt with accordingly. We can close the gate due to their presence, but we won't fight the Brothers. That came straight from Gladius."

"It came straight from me," I grumbled. I obviously needed to arrange a powwow with Gladius about this ridiculous situation. Unfortunately, NPCs didn't use the in-game messaging system. As the longboat of Shorehome invaders approached us, I turned my attention to the more immediate problem.

Strangely, they steered their boat to skirt the barge and shied away from us. "Peace!" they cried with raised arms.

Kyle switched to his crossbow and took potshots at them. The cutthroats grunted and squirmed but rowed past. I had half a mind to cut them down, but the river gate was more important.

"Can't you set them on fire?" I asked Kyle.

"The explosion in this tight tunnel would wash over us too, but I can get us halfway there." He produced a bottle of ruddy yellow oil and splashed it over the passing boat. The thieves sped past us, slick but safe.

"Now they're just super slippery?" I asked.

"It's the usual concoction—just not ignited yet."

I clenched my jaw. It would have to do for now. On the bright side, the encounter didn't slow our progress to the outer gate. The barge banged against the wall and stopped at the metal bars. Both watchmen grabbed the massive gate and heaved. They pulled it toward us, struggling against the northbound current. Further downriver, a parade of longboats paddled furiously. I sheathed my spear and joined the watchmen.

The gate was halfway shut when mermen emerged from the depths and latched on. We were braced on the barge against the gate, but they were powerful swimmers. The tug-of-war began to slip in their favor. I released the gate and poked my spear in the water. A poke here, a poke there, just enough to drive them away. Crossbow bolts peppered their ranks as well. We once again had control of the gate.

With one last heave, heavy steel swung around. Instead of a satisfying slam into its housing, with a couple of feet to go, the gate snagged on something. A watchmen lost his grip and fell. The entire barge shuddered and we all fell to our knees.

"Ugh," groaned Kyle, shaking off the painful tumble, "what the hell was that?"

The outer river gate tore from our grips so fast it banged against the city wall and nearly rumbled off its hinges. The barge jerked away from the metal bars with enough force to upend us all over again. One of the city watchmen screamed and plummeted into the Albula. Despite all reason, the wide barge skidded against the river current, away from the gate. Brothers in Black outside the tunnel rowed toward the opening. We could do nothing but hang on as a mysterious force powered us through the tunnel and back into the city.

"Bad feels," I muttered. "Bad feels."

A primal scream tore through the city. The river itself shuddered and foamed. The pirates and I knew in that moment that closing the river gate didn't matter anymore.

"What is it?" asked Kyle urgently. "What's everybody not saying?"

I shivered as I suddenly understood why the Eye of Orik had been complaining of pagan proximity. It wasn't the goblins or ogres. The undine wouldn't rate as they weren't officially associated. No, this was something much larger than a simple mob. Larger even than the horde outside the city walls.

This was a titan.

Giant tentacles burst from the water and towered over us. They hammered at the barge, snapping wood and knocking the remaining city watchman to shore. Fear swept over us as the impossible bubbled to the surface right before our eyes.

The kraken was in Stronghold.

1410 Sea Monster

The barge rocked against the surge of water. The kraken dipped underwater again, but only for a moment. Tentacles emerged from the river and tenderized the heavy boat. Kyle switched to his crossbow and loaded fire arrows.

"How is this possible?" floundered the brewmaster. "Pagans aren't allowed to enter the city. Goblins and ogres are one thing, but the kraken is the fucking definition of a pagan. It's one of their twelve gods!"

"Nine."

"Whatever. Stupid fantasy bullcrap! You're gonna tell me a pagan titan doesn't qualify as part of their faction now?"

I shook my head. "I don't know."

I clicked the help button to summon Saint Peter. Varnu, from tech support, appeared on the unsteady barge, dressed in his bright-red colonial jacket with gold buttons. He smiled and twisted his golden mustache.

"Ah, Talon, it is good to—what in the many noses of Garethluka is that abomination?"

I creased my brow. "The noses of who?"

Varnu Johnson shook his head frantically. "What the *fuck* is that thing, sir?"

I dove away as a tentacle smashed my position. I spun my spear into a sucker. The damage was laughably minimal, but the pain caused the kraken to recoil beneath the splashing current. The dragonspear was a titanslayer, after all. Still, if the kraken was anything like the cyclops, I would need to find a weak spot for it to be truly effective. As long as the beast could hide underwater, we were unlikely to do so.

"It's a kraken, Varnu! Inside the city. I need to talk to Saint Peter right now, and I don't wanna hear excuses. And if you can't help me, I wanna escalate this to your supervisor!"

The resident companion froze as he considered swaying from his script.

The kraken once again broke the surface of the water. Its gaping mouth opened wide behind a tangle of tentacles. Spiraling rows of crosscut teeth snaked downward. I wondered if somewhere in that garbage disposal was a weak spot. Undulating gums vibrated as the titan bellowed with the force of a hurricane.

Saint Peter appeared and cleared his throat. "It's okay, Varnu. I'll take it from here."

Varnu's legs stiffened and his hands hurried to the seat of his pants. "Um, if you will excuse me, sirs, I believe I have, as Americans say, shit my breeches." He blinked out just as a tentacle swiped through him.

Kyle fired two bolts. The small projectiles had trouble getting through the tangle of arms. Fire exploded and tentacles jerked away. Others just filled their place. Once again, the kraken wasn't worse for wear.

"Hadrian's attacking the city," I hurried. "He's leading the Brothers in Black, and using the Squid's Tooth to command the kraken."

Peter's beard puffed out as he frowned. "I can see that, Talon."

"Well, isn't there something you can do about it? He's a player trying to take the city."

"The Pantheon is safe," returned the saint.

"But the city watch—"

"Is manning the walls and guarding the Pantheon. The soldiers are doing their job, Talon. A PvP war is not within their jurisdiction."

"So he's allowed to bring a titan into the city? What about the angels?"

"The angels didn't interfere with Orik, and they won't do so with the kraken. Their purview is stopping players from breaking the game. Hadrian's working within the rule set. As long as he doesn't attempt to take the Pantheon, hack the Oculus, or attack the saints, the angels have no reason to activate against him. He's not a game imbalance."

Damn it. Hadrian was in the clear. Manipulating Brugo, controlling the Trinity, compromising Loras—he was gaining influence through the actions of others. The saints were already deposed, he'd said. I was the only one in his way. Even now, out in the open, Hadrian was too smart to risk the angel's wrath. The kraken was smart enough to call off its attack while the saint was on board. In order to turn the repercussions back on Hadrian, I would have to catch him red-handed.

"What about the Eye of Orik?" I asked. "Isn't it supposed to be impossible for pagans to enter the city while under saintly control? Isn't that a hack?"

Saint Peter sighed. "Alas, Haven is no longer as black and white as it was programmed to be. Hadrian's subversion is no less heinous than your bringing goblins and ogres into Stronghold under your wing."

Kyle blinked. "So you're saying the kraken no longer self-identifies as a pagan."

Peter nodded. "The devil's gift of free will is a double-edged sword. NPCs and monsters were never meant to have the freedom of players. Many of the systems governing them can be easily sidestepped, given the proper forethought."

"How's that for identity politics?" muttered Kyle.

I groaned. It was the same as the reasoning to make cities free-for-alls. NPCs were never prevented from engaging in town combat because their behaviors never allowed it. Once their behaviors became unhinged it was anything goes. The entire governance plan for Haven had been upended.

"Okay," I reasoned, "attacking Oldtown isn't illegal. But Hadrian's hacked Loras somehow."

"Has he?"

I huffed. "What do you mean, Peter? Of course he has. The Loras avatar has developer access."

"I am less questioning the why and more questioning the who. Hadrian is not a hacker, unlike your *friend*, Lucifer."

Every response by the saint was pushing me further and further beyond exasperation. "You think Lucifer's behind all this?"

Saint Peter sighed, calmly and forlorn. "The real question is how can you not?"

I nearly pulled my hair out. "Because he's the only one who's being honest about what's really going on around here!"

"Lucifer's a traitor with the sole goal of bringing down the world that birthed him. You've heard his diatribes against capitalism."

"His diatribes aren't always off base: Kablammy's rush to launch, to put a good face on the leaks, the attempted company takeover, and however the hell satellite launches fit into the picture..."

Peter flushed. "How do you know about that?"

"Oh, I know a hell of a lot more. I know Larry isn't on sabbatical in the Greek islands, he's a corporate mole who was fired from Kablammy. That mole works for Hadrian."

Peter erupted with indignant laughter. "Are you kidding me? Lucifer actually told you that? The nerve. If anybody's the source of the corporate takeover, it's him."

"You're wrong, Peter. Hadrian's the interloper. Lucifer was scheming against him the entire time. Hadrian's trying to take over Haven for himself."

"You just refuse to see it. But you need to trust me, Talon. You don't know what I know about Lucifer."

"What? What do you know?"

Peter took a long breath as he struggled over how much he could say. As always, his internal filter won out and he revealed nothing.

I was so angry I wanted to knock some sense into him. It was easier squeezing help out of Varnu. Then I realized it was way past noon. Tad Lonnerman should've been in the clear.

"At least look into it yourself," I stressed. "Check the assassin needle history log. Find the link to Loras. Do anything but sit back and watch while we lose Haven for good."

The old man's eyes flared against my accusation. "I can do nothing," was all he said. Saint Peter vanished.

The stubborn old fool... I had to believe something I said had gotten through to him, but we were very likely on our own.

The quiet following the saint's departure didn't last long. A tentacle kicked the barge backward, creating space for the Brothers in Black to spill into the city. No doubt a stream of undine flowed beneath their oars. As our boat jerked and rocked, we struggled to remain on our feet and out of the water.

Kyle whiffed another volley of crossbow bolts. "It's no good. The damn thing is too fast in the water."

"What if we get off the river?" I offered. "Force the titan on land?"

" 'Tis a sound strategy, fer sure," said Errol, " 'cept I was hopin' we could light this barge up 'fore she goes under."

"What are you talking about?"

The pirate captain led me to the waterproof storage boxes along the length of the transport vessel and opened one up. It was jammed to the brim with rockets and black powder.

"What did you—" I paused. "You're crazy, Errol."

"What?" he protested, slightly offended. "Ye said t' filler up with fireworks, fer all you cared."

"I was just making a joke about scrapping a useless barge. You weren't supposed to take it literally!"

Grug and Grom frowned, but Errol wasn't taken aback. "Ye should've known a pirate would jump at any chance fer a party with explosions. I loaded this here barge up fer tonight's grand openin', and there'll be no take-backsies."

I blinked in the face of the stupid, dumb luck. This was gonna be a party all right.

The kraken snaked below the water, errant tentacles testing the edges of the platform. Errol slashed his rapier at the rubbery skin. The limb jerked and knocked him over.

I lit a torch, grabbed a fist-sized pail of powder, and set it alight. The fuse burned fast so I dumped it on the approximate location of the kraken. The makeshift depth charge sank and popped. A pillar of water blasted into the air. The boat shook and the kraken roared from the deep.

"It worked,' I said.

We all grabbed handfuls of fireworks and passed around the torch. These things were the real deal, volatile black powder packed to the brim, not the sad little pretenders you spark up in your backyard on the Fourth of July. These here were real nasty weapons, capable of blowing a lot more than your fingers off. Thank God for pirates.

The blasts harried the sea creature. It punched the bottom of the boat, lifting us off the water for seconds at a time. Luckily the deck was heavily reinforced, built for stability and a double load. The barge rocked and swayed but held together. After a succession of explosions that were too close for comfort, the impressive mass of the kraken dove downriver. It surfaced at a distance and screeched.

"That's our chance!" yelled Errol.

All three of us hefted large fireworks at the titan's mouth. Tentacles flashed—one, two, three—effortlessly knocking them away. They exploded onshore. The thing just had too many arms.

"We're gonna need a bigger boat," said Kyle.

Errol cursed. "Talon said the barge was too large as it was!"

"It's just an expression from *Jaws*," he explained. "Never mind. We need more firepower."

"That's only half the problem," I pointed out. "As long as the kraken remains submerged, he'll have the advantage on us."

"We can run," agreed Errol. "But that ain't exactly savin' the city, is it?"

I nodded. "So forget about trying to draw the kraken out of the river. What if, instead, we draw the water out of the river?"

Kyle's face flashed with recognition. "And here I thought the river pearl was a useless add-on. That combined with the water turrets might be just what the doctor ordered."

"What doctor?" asked Errol, confused. "Ye players be a bewilderin' bunch."

The kraken screeched. The spiral of teeth quivered as the kraken snaked our way. Tentacles crunched hard to the deck, splitting wood. Fireworks and barrels of powder splashed to the water.

"There's just one problem with that plan," I said to Kyle, regaining my balance. "We need to make it to the tower first."

As if understanding our predicament, the kraken submerged and swam under the barge. It surfaced and smashed the other side of the boat, spilling more explosives into the surf.

"You heard the man!" Errol berated his pirate crew. "Take this barge upriver to Dragonperch posthaste." They paddled in double time.

1420 Hang-On

I eyed the approaching contingent of boats and the debris littering the river surface. "Kyle."

The brewmaster smiled. "Gotcha covered." He produced a fire mixture and lit the opening.

"No." I capped the flame with my palm, putting it out. "Not yet. Like you did with the other boat of rogues. Slick the river with oil."

His devilish grin widened. "You're evil, bro." He laughed as he opened the bottle and sprinkled its contents into the water. When it was empty, he reloaded with another one. The yellow fluid clung to the surface as we rowed south. Knowing Kyle, he had plenty of stock to keep it up.

Since I was the only one not doing anything, I put myself on kraken duty. I moved to the head of the barge and readied the dragonspear. The titan attempted to break our boat in half. It was nearly there as it was, but holding together. We couldn't afford to let it go more. I braced my weapon and crossblocked what blows I could. Damage came through, of course, but not so much that I was immediately worried. We began making decent progress through the town.

The kraken's next tactic was more effective. A stray tentacle caught Grug and wrapped him up like an anaconda.

"I regret nothing!" bellowed the pirate. "Except bein' grabbed by a giant tentacle!"

We flinched when the kraken squeezed and crunched his bones to pulp.

"Heft the chain, men!" commanded a familiar voice.

Nooner and his boys pulled their chain into the path of the backpedaling sea creature. The unexpected obstacle stunned the beast. I hurried to light a barrel of powder.

"Ha ha!" boasted Nooner. "Try to take *my* city, will ya! Well, I'm gonna—"

The kraken flexed cords of muscle. The heavy chain snapped off its landbound support. Angry tentacles reared high into the air.

Nooner's jaw dropped. "But that's triple-gauge steel..."

The arm crushed the gangster to the ground, sending the rest of his men scrambling in terror.

The barge strayed close to the west bank of the river. "New plan." Kyle unloaded a bunch of fire potions at my feet and leapt off. He made it to the ground but ate dirt, his agility unable to gracefully account for the maneuver.

"What're you doing, Kyle?"

"Easiest way to Dragonperch is getting off this river, where the kraken isn't. I'm gonna drain this river before you know it."

"Now that there be a plan!" remarked Errol.

"You guys hold off the kraken!" Kyle sprinted south along the riverbank.

The pirate cocked his head. "Can't say I be fond o' that part."

The kraken bellowed. I braced the dragonspear as the full mass of the titan bore toward the barge. At the last second, the kraken dove and slipped beneath us.

We turned in confusion. The sea creature swam past the boat, dragging a length of triple-gauge chain over the water. It caught around a splintered support beam and the barge jerked sideways, spilling fireworks to the deck.

"Incoming!" screamed Grom.

Tentacles rose from the water on all sides of the boat. They slashed blindly and indiscriminately. Errol was knocked aside. I blocked one arm but was tripped up by another. A tentacle smashed into the pile of fire bombs, shattering glass and splashing yellow fluid everywhere.

Errol growled and drew his rapier. "Hold it off, he says."

I flicked my spear as Grom slashed a hooked blade, executing short strikes on nearby feelers. The tentacles recoiled.

Behind us, the Brothers in Black advanced. Kyle jogged ahead on the shoreline, running past the Forum backstreets. The kraken surfaced with a roar. Then it spotted Kyle. For a giant squid beast, it was surprisingly tactical. It dove and swam south.

"He's goin' fer the tower," surmised Errol.

The length of chain caught on the titan snaked the river surface in its wake. As soon as the slack was exhausted, the barge bucked upriver. Grom was caught by surprise and tumbled into the water.

"No!" shouted Kyle. "Don't lead him to me till I'm ready."

Errol and I held on for our dear lives. "I think he's the one doing the leading, Kyle."

The kraken rocketed over the water surface, barge in tow. Chunks of the deck fell away as we wildly crashed into the bricks walling the river. Barrels of powder, yellow oil, and various fireworks plopped into our wake. We easily surpassed the brewmaster's foot speed and watched as we passed. We were going so fast we overtook the boat of rogues that had rowed past us in the tunnel. They turned in surprise and capsized as we blew by.

As much fun as the ride was, it took only a moment before we realized we were on a collision course with the easternmost of three bridges joining the Foot to the Forum. The same bridges that were too small for the barge to fit under. That first bridge had stone supports in the middle of the river.

"Uh... Errol?"

"By the Maelstrom, I see it."

> **Lash:** *Talon! Rogues are congregating in the north city. A lot more of them snuck into town than we thought. They're marching toward Oldtown. We need you here quick.*

The sly kraken deftly slipped between the bridge supports. The barge didn't fare so well. It slammed into the solid stonework. Errol and I flew forward and crashed into the bricks, taking collision damage. He bounced back to the barge. The wood beneath me splintered lengthwise across the entire deck. I hung on sideways, hesitating a second too long before attempting to leap to safety.

Agility Check...
Failed!

Just as I deserved for laughing at Kyle's mishap, I landed face first onto the barge with my legs plunged in the water. I stowed the spear to drag myself back to the deck, but a slithery tentacle caught my boot.

"Head down, Talon!" Errol lit a firework and tossed it in the water. Since we were now going against the current, the small bomb drifted back toward us and exploded at my side. More damage.

"Stop!" I yelled. "If that's what you call help, you can stop right now!"

"Apologies," he said meekly.

"You'll light the whole barge on fire!"

Lash: *Hadrian made an appearance with his shadowguards. No one in town is daring to initiate combat against them. We need reinforcements soon.*

Kyle: *Working on it. Rally the forces. The goblins and ogres too.*

Trafford: *I'm mustering the army but, if we're being honest, they're really just a band of misfits.*

Lash: *Where's Talon?*

Talon: *KINDA BUSY AT THE MOMENT.*

Lash: *Wait, what goblins and ogres?*

Kyle: *Our new builders. We have goblins and ogres. They'll fight too.*

I clung to splintering scraps of the deck as the tentacle threatened to drag me under. Errol ineffectually poked at it. The leviathan was determined to beat us to Dragonperch. The only thing holding it back was the chain tied to the barge. I was thankful for that. Without it, I'd be fish food. Except our little obstacle wouldn't last long. Wood groaned under the kraken's intense strength. I equipped my climbing claws and dug them into the failing deck.

Talon: *Is anyone close to Dragonperch? We need an assist.*

Trafford: *Aye, I can get there, but I can't fiddle with your jewelry sockets.*

Kyle finally caught up and ran onto the bridge between the kraken and the barge. He stood over us, magnanimous. "He's right, Talon. It's got to be me."

"So what're ye doin'?" growled Errol. "Get t' that tower."

Kyle surveyed the landmark in the distance. The bronzed figure of Magnus Dragonrider sparkled in the midday sun. "I won't reach it in time. If the kraken beats me there, he'll block my entrance and I'll never get those water turrets up."

"No," I groaned, losing my fight with the tentacle. "Protect Oldtown. They need the turrets more than we do."

Kyle shook his head as he considered the range of unpleasant choices. "I got an idea," he said.

Errol dropped his sword and grabbed my arm, digging his heels against a storage box. The tangled chain bit in between the seams of wood planks behind him.

"You know, when you found me," started Kyle introspectively, "I was a coward. Not just 'cause I didn't wanna face goblins and boggarts and whatever else was in the wild, but because I didn't wanna face my life. I didn't take anything seriously. I lounged. I drank. Even when I went out, I died. A lot. And I didn't care. You changed all that, Talon, because you saw something better in me."

Errol's grip slipped. The claws on my hands strained. "Uh," I squeezed through clenched teeth, "thanks, dude. I guess. Do you really think now's the best time for a heart to heart?"

"Yes, I do. Because you taught me how to be a better man. A braver man. And I know the perfect thing for me to do right now. I can go back to not giving a shit and dying a lot."

Kyle sheathed his crossbow and bundled three lit fire potions in his arms. Then he turned around and faced the gaping maw of the kraken as it struggled to break free from its bonds.

"What are you doing, Kyle?"

The brewmaster smiled and screamed "CANNONBALL!" as he leapt off the bridge in full frat-boy glory.

There's something about seeing a big guy take a dive in a pool. Kyle belly flopped right down the titan's maw, fire erupting everywhere in and around him.

[Kyle] is dead!

Errol arched an eyebrow. "That stupid... apathetic... hipster-beer-swillin'..."

"He respawned in Dragonperch," I realized out loud.

"Magnificent... selfless... *genius* of a man!"

The kraken belched flames twenty feet high. The tentacle slackened enough for me to slip out and climb back to the barge.

"That idiot did it," crowed Errol, amazed.

I shrugged in admiration. "He sure knows how to blow himself up."

Arrows whizzed by our heads. The trailing skiffs were nearing our stalled vessel. They meant to sail all the way to Oldtown.

"This is where we get off," I said, pulling a torch from my inventory. The barge creaked under intense pressure.

"I ain't runnin' away from a little scrap."

"Errol, we're on a ticking time bomb that's about to break apart, stuck between scores of cutthroats and a bloodthirsty kraken." Mermaids surfaced and clutched the edges of the barge. "And the undine. Sorry, ladies. Didn't mean to leave you out. Although you'd be invited to more parties if it weren't for all the hissing and teeth and violent disembowelment."

Errol cocked his head. "On the other hand, the nudity be a plus."

"Errol!"

"Point taken. But we've not reached Black Hat territory yet, an' we've got just as many rogues in the marketplace."

"That's why we're gonna sneak into Trafford's welcome shop and use the catacombs entrance in his basement. We can reach Dragonperch from there."

"An' just let me get this straight. Ye choosin' death by animated bones o'er kraken then?" An arrow stuck him in the ass. "Argh! Okay, okay, the universe be tellin' me something."

The lead longboat drifted close. Cutthroats brandished

daggers, sickles, chakrams, and all manner of original blades.

River water rushed over the deck as the barge bowed into the bridge supports. The wood strained to exhaustion. In the end, the triple-gauge steel held true but the boat didn't. The chain tore through the lumber with a snap. I grabbed Errol and triggered dash as it lethally whipped by us. The ship buckled and tore in half.

Errol and I fell. The wild chain caught his leg and pinned him to the deck, still wrapped around the boat, still dragged by the kraken. With its new slimmed-down figure, the half section of barge surged between the bridge supports. The other half of the ship bounced chaotically against the riverbanks, still attached to our section by two deformed logs, but folded and twisted sideways and dragging in the water like a train car.

Sections of wreckage pinballed into pieces. Fireworks and powder poured into the river, knocking angry mermaids away. The spill of sticky gel rode the rushing water. Sputtering flames leftover from Kyle's deathblow landed on the barge. Even soaking wet, the magical fire still burned.

Talon: *Kyle. Kyle, we need you to hurry.*

As our runaway train twisted upriver and under another bridge, Errol and I worked at the chain pinning him down.

> **Trafford:** *I've got him here in the tower with me. Inviting him into the party.*
> **Kyle:** *What's up, bros?*
> **Talon:** *Angry kraken! Wrecked barge! Flaming fireworks!*
> **Kyle:** *Right to the point, huh? Not big on small talk.*
> **Talon:** *KYLE!*
> **Kyle:** *Alright, alright. Sheesh.*

We swished under the final Front Street bridge and winded around the last bend in the river. Dragonperch loomed ahead, the kraken almost there and dragging us along. The fire on the crumbling deck spread ever closer to the oil spill. Errol stared at me in alarm.

> **Talon:** *Hold off draining the river. Activate the river turrets on my go.*
> **Kyle:** *Roger that.*

I stopped mucking with the chain and instead focused on the wood frame below. Re-equipping the climbing claws, I scratched at the deck like a dog digging for a bone. Flames bit at my heels. Slowly, surely, the surface splintered away, creating enough space for Errol to squeeze his ankle past.

> **Talon:** *Now!*

Errol and I leapt off the barge, landing past the brickwork edge of the Oldtown bank. The kraken's zealous speed brought it headfirst into stone pillars that sprang from the water, straddling where the open drawbridge would be. The four columns acted as oversized bollards, two to each side, effectively trapping the titan in a cage.

As we tumbled to a stop on the shore, the momentum of the barge carried the debris into the pillars in a series of earth-shattering crashes. The turrets activated and autofired projectiles, all four centered on the kraken in the middle. Flames took to the ruddy chemicals and snaked lines across the crumbling deck. A stray fire brushed an unassuming fuse, a single decorative sparkler that buzzed and fizzed along happily for exactly three seconds before both barges erupted into a volcano of freedom.

[Undine] is defeated
[Undine] is defeated
[Undine] is defeated
[Undine] is defeated
Fire Damage!
137 damage to [Kraken]
152 damage to [Kraken]
Stun!
120 damage to [Kraken]

Several longboats rounded the Front Street bend in pursuit. They'd reached the northern edge of Oldtown and were preparing to disembark, a spearhead of Shorehome forces which snaked throughout the entire river. Scores of undine surfaced and made for the riverbank.

Streams of fire shot through the sky and rained to the dirt and water in smoking husks. All it took was one piece landing in a floating oil slick. The surface of the water lit up orange. A burst of fire steamrolled north, tracing the path of our spill. Floating kegs of powder exploded as they were consumed. The invading forces widened crazed eyes as a wave of unrelenting death scorched through them.

```
[Rogue] is defeated
[Cutthroat] is defeated
[Undine] is defeated
[Enforcer] is dead!
[Rogue] is defeated
[Bandit] is defeated
[Undine] is defeated
[Goblin] is defeated
```

```
Crown Unlocked: Serial Arsonist
Take out 15 enemies with fire.
1000 XP awarded
```

I ignored the combat notifications because they kept on coming. Instead, our heads slowly turned as we tracked the backwards path of the flames. Even with the distant river out of view, resultant booms resounded farther and farther away as a trail of fireworks and smoke lit up the sky.

Within the span of seconds, the entire Albula River was engulfed in a deadly blaze.

> **Kyle:** *'Murica!*

1430 Defender

Errol and I panted on the ground, utterly discombobulated. The series of explosions had buffeted us with sound and heat. My ears were ringing. Luckily, the physical debris had missed us. Charred husks of empty boats littered the shore. The water was a burning hellscape.

"Kinda smells o' smoked salmon," remarked Errol.

"That other smell's not burnt pork."

"Aye, I just hope poor Grom managed t' get out o' the water."

"You're telling me. We just took out the head of the spear in a single stroke. And we cut off the riverbank from attack. No one's rowing through this inferno."

"Lash said they're comin' from the north."

"I know, but we've bought ourselves time to muster a defense. We've diverted a two-pronged attack into one. And the kraken..."

Our gazes swiveled to Dragonperch, where a billowing column of black smoke twisted over the water.

"Nothin' could've survived that," said Errol.

"I wouldn't be so sure..."

We inched toward the riverbank and peeked in. It was hard

to see anything. The water was simultaneously bright orange and blackened with ash. I scanned the spammy combat log for helpful info. It was hard to find anything with all the deaths. Interestingly, most of Hadrian's men weren't players. The bulk of the Brothers in Black were comprised of NPCs and ex-pagan mobs.

"Behind us!" warned the captain. He whipped out his rapier and spun it backward, puncturing the black leather of the enemy. Three more rogues converged.

I drew the dragonspear and joined the fray. Although we outmatched the cutthroats, they were led by a decent player. They worked together as an effective team, swooping in with dual strikes and covering for each other. It was impossible to block all their attacks, but our higher levels did eventually win out. After the first two were cut down, we made quick work of the others.

DoT: 10 dmg/10 secs

I winced against the minor poison and fingered a small health vial before remembering I'd used my one for the day. I could do nothing but put up with the momentary pain.

"Well, now," said Errol.

Loot:
47 silver
[Refined Jade]
[Refined Topaz]

The pirate always did have an eye for the shiny stuff. As the poison wore off, I sighed and checked my status.

Health: 197/300

I was doing okay, all things considered. I wondered if the same could be said for the rest of the faction. We took in the grim scene of Oldtown.

Scattered bandits roved the ruins. Their numbers were small, for the moment. Just whatever thieves had managed to offload from the river before we could stop them. The Black Hat membership bravely mounted a defense, but we weren't an army. To our favor, neither were they. Most participants in the conflict were mid-level soldiers. High-level players like Lash and Hadrian would determine the swing of battle.

That said, this wasn't a duel or an Arena free-for-all. For keeping a rallying force out of my district, we were grossly outnumbered and ill prepared. The defense of Oldtown would be a proper battle. That meant we needed a sound strategy.

Talon: *Kyle, we need the turrets back on land.*
Kyle: *But the kraken...*
Talon: *If we don't save Oldtown there won't be anyone left to save from the kraken. Do it now.*

The stone pillars at the drawbridge lowered into the river. The land rumbled as the same turrets arose along the inner borders of Oldtown, like outposts. There were only four of them so they lacked the traditional utility of a wall, but we had people to fill in those gaps.

I opened a map. Because of the way Oldtown was situated between the river and the outer wall of Stronghold, Hadrian's men only had two routes of attack, both natural bottlenecks: through the narrow northern entrance from the main thoroughfare, and along the riverbank. With Dragonperch's drawbridge shut, there were no bridges to cross, and even the kraken was shying away from the river surface.

> **Black Hat Broadcast:**
> Defense turrets are posted around Oldtown. The river is secure for now. The Brothers will attack from the north. If you can get to the outskirts, hold the line. I'm aware a lot of rogues already breached the border. Alpha team will sweep the interior. Watch your backs until we get there.

> **Talon:** *Kyle, drain the river. We don't want to let anything hide down there.*
> **Kyle:** *One river socket, coming right up.*

Underwater valves groaned as they moved for the first time in hundreds of years. Errol scanned for threats as the Albula drained, exposing high walls of weathered but sturdy brickwork. Players across the river stared in wonder as nature itself was tamed by the sanctum of Dragonperch. Curiously, several rogues weaved among the player populace without attacking them.

I couldn't believe it. Order in the streets during a siege of Oldtown.

I tried not to be offended about it. The townsfolk had joined my fight in the Arena, but a larger battle was afoot now, one involving a legitimate army, a flood of vicious undine, and a legendary creature of the sea. If rando low-level players were allowed to sit back and watch free of danger, what other options did they have?

Damage notifications poured in as the water level dropped to five feet. Exposed undine could no longer shy away from the flames, and they were too low to escape the walled river. They scrambled to faraway safety. Some didn't make it.

As the water settled, I frowned at the foot of Dragonperch. Ashy water swirled against smooth brick near the bottom of the channel. The kraken was nowhere to be found.

"It turtled," I grumbled in frustration.

"Good," urged Errol. "The people be needin' us."

I gritted my teeth and nodded. We turned and sprinted through Oldtown. Stray bandits took cheap shots at the weakest faction members. Errol and I cut a couple down before he broke away to fend off another pair.

"The vault!" demanded a voice in the other direction. "Open her up if you mean to live."

"Go to hell!" screamed Drummond. I spun at the sound. The diminutive, bald banker stood boldly against Chadwick and a band of ten men. Errol was busy behind me.

"Piece of gangster scum!" I yelled, pitching my foot in the ground and charging the brand-new vault.

Chadwick stiffened at my approach. He lunged at the banker

and put a knife to his throat. "Stop right there, Protector."

I slowed with my spear out. "You're in Black Hat territory," I warned.

"You're doing business outside Oldtown, business in *my* districts, and I'll get a cut of it or else."

"You're not getting a damn thing, you greedy bastard. Don't you see what's happening here?" I sneered. "Or maybe that's exactly why you came. An uprising in the city is too good an opportunity for a sniveling vulture to pass up."

"I'll get my cut," he insisted, "or I'll cut his neck. Your choice."

I worked my jaw as I reviewed my options. It was Drummond who made the call.

"Over my dead body!" A small whittling knife materialized in his hand. He stabbed it into the gangster's stomach, doing more to surprise than wound.

"No!" I snapped into action.

Chadwick's blade sliced the banker's throat. Drummond fell to his knees, clutching his leaking neck. The gangsters rushed me.

Level 4s and 5s didn't stand a good chance against a 10, but Oldtown was becoming a war zone. I'd lost track of Errol and was alone so they figured me for easy pickings. With ten of them to fend off at once, maybe they were right.

I activated tornado spin to set them on their heels, rolling out of the maneuver with the dragonspear already puncturing a gangster's side. A dagger came at my back. I twisted and crossblocked.

Disarm!

As the gangster leaned to recover his dropped weapon, I smacked the spear across his temple, critically injuring him. Two more blades came at me. They clinked together on my old position as I dashed out of the kill zone, slapping swords away.

23 damage
Health: 174/300

I grimaced and rolled away from the blow. I triggered a deadshot to instakill the cutthroat who'd damaged me. Unfortunately, I was greeted with an error sound. A quick glance showed I had plenty of spirit left, but the precious second of confusion left me exposed.

24 damage
18 damage
Health: 132/300

I rolled away from the incoming blows. My deadshot skill was grayed out. It was only when I noticed spinshield was also disabled that I realized what was happening. I'd overloaded both those skills in the Arena. Overloaded skills didn't just cost more SP, they required massive cooldowns.

I crossblocked again. Backed away and repeated the defensive maneuver as Drummond hacked out a lung. Chadwick's men pounced and it was all I could do to fend them off.

"Aaaargh!" yelled a wild-eyed Stigg, spittle spraying over his giant black beard. The berserker barreled into the line, wooden bo staff knocking gangsters down like they were bowling pins. Caduceus waved her bone pick.

```
[Caduceus] cast Minor Heal
Health: 230/300
```

"Damn you!" snarled Chadwick. Any iota of a chance he had was immediately dashed by the reinforcements. No match for us in a straight fight, he turned to retreat.

The gangsters followed their boss. Drummond was dead and I was pissed, so we took chase. They hurried for the southern border of Oldtown, as if escaping our immediate influence would be their salvation. It was their doom instead. When they approached a border turret, the smart weapon sensed their hostility and opened fire with shards of slate. The fleeing gang shielded their faces against the onslaught, but one by one began to succumb to their injuries.

```
[Slate Turret] dealt 57 damage to [Gangster]
[Slate Turret] dealt 39 damage to [Gangster]
[Slate Turret] dealt 54 damage to [Gangster]
```

Damn, these automated defenses were no joke. Chadwick's last man fell, a pincushion of little stone shards. Unfortunately, the boss-man himself passed out of range and jumped into the distant ruins. He'd escaped Black Hat territory.

"Let him go," urged Caduceus. "He's just a distraction."

I scowled as I watched the rotund man getting away. He deserved to die.

The physicker's voice pleaded urgency. "You can deal with him another day."

As I swallowed back my anger, a single arrow whizzed by my head. I instinctively flinched then smiled as I recognized the sound. The arrow nailed its target. The fleeing silhouette of the upstart gangster tripped to the ground.

Savage!

[Dune] dealt 101 damage to [Chadwick]

[Chadwick] is dead!

"PvP in the city," laughed Dune as he approached. "Where has this been all my life?"

I eyed the ranger with a huge grin. "Still kill-stealing, I see."

"To be fair, I did tell you there'd be XP for the taking." He hurried to his downed target.

The red robe laughed in vigorous agreement. "You always throw the best parties, Talon."

"Are you drunk right now?" I asked.

"Of course!" replied Stigg, half offended. "I wouldn't have the discourtesy of showing up to your pub's grand opening sober!"

Errol hurried over when he noticed the commotion. "Missed all the fun, I see."

Dune looted the body and hurried back to us as we cleaned out the rest of the gangsters.

"We should move," said Caduceus, cool and collected as she topped off my health. "The turrets are a good countermeasure, but if that fat man could get through, they'll only slow down an army."

"Is the city watch helping yet?" I asked.

Dune shook his head. "Afraid not, friend. If individuals cross the line they can be dealt with, but the main force of enemies is only coming for you. Oldtown's yours, Talon. You're the one who needs to defend it."

I chewed my lip and recalled the rogues across the river ignoring the townsfolk. They weren't only sparing the saints but the whole town, including the city watch. "Hadrian wants to take me out. This is a PvP war, and as long as it doesn't spill into the streets too much, the city watch might tolerate it."

Stigg banged his wooden staff on the ground and started toward the northern line. "Shall we do the honors, then?"

The group exchanged intrepid glances before heading into the fight.

>> Minigame <<

Tad Lonnerman paced the outskirts of the administrative area. There were several walled offices here. Christian Everett had the large corner room. The others were for Abbie from HR, the CFO, and the marketing director. A pack of them had headed to the commissary together, which meant they'd enjoy a relaxed business lunch out of his hair.

The outside space was flush with cubicles for secretaries and assistants. While the company officers played a vital role in day-to-day operations, the administrative employees without dedicated offices weren't part of the skeleton crew and were on leave.

Tad checked the clock on his phone. It was the third time that minute. He pushed the screen off with a huff and continued pacing, watching the CEO's office from a distance. Christian was a dedicated and passionate worker, a hands-on, boots-on-the-ground type of guy. He often took late lunches. This put Tad in an awkward position. If he waited too long, his coworkers would start returning from lunch. But he couldn't very well take action before Christian left. Tad was being pinched from both ends.

"Tad."

He jumped and spun at the voice. "Oh, hey Pete."

The man frowned. "Are you looking for someone?"

"Looking? No. Just taking a walk and trying to work through an algorithm in my head."

Pete stroked at the air beneath his chin before catching himself and crossing his arms. Tad had noticed the affectation more and more recently. Pete was obviously troubled, but he had something on his mind other than Tad's presence in the administrative area. "Now that I have you here, Tad, you mind if I ask you something?"

The programmer did his best to act casual. "Shoot."

"Do you know anything about item history logs?"

"Sure. Events are fired that kick off and confirm transactions. Items log the ones related to them."

"And would it be possible to fake a log?"

Tad bit his lip. "Fake them?"

"Yes. To hack a log and insert erroneous data."

"Well, sure, I guess anything's possible. The output log's just a text file. But it'd be easy to catch mismatches with the game data. In certain cases, anyway."

"I see... and—" The door to Christian's office opened as the CEO emerged to take lunch. "Excuse me."

Peter intercepted Christian with hasty news. Judging by the looks on their faces, the discussion point was serious. Both men turned and entered Christian's office.

"Crap."

Tad really didn't have time for this. Not only had Saint Peter exited the sim, but he was suspicious about item history logs. Now he was getting Christian involved, and there was no telling how long they'd be.

Ten minutes and an order of magnitude more clock checks later, they hurried from the office. Tad ducked behind a distant cubicle.

"I need you back in there," prodded Christian. "Just a few more days. You're my eyes and ears, Pete. I need you to handle this..." Their voices trailed off as they headed for the Superdome.

It was now or never.

Tad hustled into the CEO's office and posted behind the spartan desk. The workstation was fortuitously unlocked. Access should only take a minute. Unfortunately, the hub was closed and had to boot up.

Tad rapped nervous fingers on the desktop as his eyes ran over paper documents that lay mid perusal. Rocket launch timetables. Financials for outsourcing partners in usability and support and QA. It was like he'd said, Christian Everett was always involved in a handful of secret projects.

Tad flinched as the speakers chimed, announcing the hub had successfully booted. He hurried to access developer privileges, but before he could get there, a stunned CEO reentered his office.

"Tad." Christian Everett stiffened, eyes running to the documents on the table. His lips tightened. "I can't say I ever expected this from you."

1440 Advanced Warfare

Errol and I hurried to the line with Dune's party. On the way up the road, a couple of enemies were unlucky enough to cross our path.

```
[Bandit] is defeated
[Rogue] is defeated
52 XP awarded
1 DP awarded
```

"Anyone know what this defense point is?" I asked.

Everyone shook their head. "You're the one running the headquarters," pointed out the ranger.

```
Talon: Hey, Kyle, you see anything in the
sanctum controls about DP?
Kyle: Are you coming on to me, bro?
Talon: Get your mind out of the gutter.
```

> **Kyle:** *Why so srs? Besides, I think I figured it out. The defense menu is active. We're showing a grand total of 1 defense point.*

I opened my map screen and saw much of what I usually did, except the zoom level was focused on Black Hat territory and the immediate outskirts. There were green dots for friendly positions, whites for neutrals, and a jumble of reds congregating on the main thoroughfare north of Oldtown. I mulled over the possibilities.

> **Talon:** *Holy crap. We've got a full defense grid.*
> **Kyle:** *Yup. Impressive is an understatement.*

Black Hats crowded the northern line. With the gargantuan city walls to the west and south, the river still on fire, and a connected string of high buildings along the thoroughfare, the simple walkway to the west gate area was now the only viable entrance to Oldtown. The Brothers in Black had enough numbers to start an advance. Lash and Conan were directing our forces into position to hold them off. I chuckled as I enjoyed a top-down view of the battle.

My extended menu display wasn't just limited to a real-time map, either. Now that I was in Black Hat territory, other aspects of the sanctum master panel had carried over. Despite my inability to directly affect the upgrades, I could view the socket and pearl display.

<table>
<tr><td>Socket Manager</td></tr>
</table>

Feather: Dove
Wind:
Water: River
Earth: Dirt -> Shale
Unused: Bone

> **Talon:** *Kyle, the turret placements aren't doing much good where they are. Why don't you swap out the dirt pearl and fit the shale pearl directly into the earth socket?*
> **Kyle:** *I got ya. One wall, coming right up.*

Earth: Shale

The turrets sank into the ground. A wall of sharp stone rose at the mouth of the north entrance. The rogues at ground zero were upended. Those unfortunate enough to be stranded on our side of the wall were immediately cut down.

The new wall was a decent choke point, but not much more than that. Far from a robust fortification, the Brothers in Black scaled it with hooks or slipped around it altogether. Our party ran into the fray and defended the line.

Lash's cleaver took an enemy's leg off at the knee. The thief fell at my feet. "About time you joined us," she barked.

I brought my spear down on the flailing rogue to finish him off. "It's called being fashionably late."

Caduceus gave Lash a quick heal. "I see you're outnumbered by testosterone. Us girls gotta stick together."

Conan grunted and buried his axe in some bloke's head. "Where is that old witch anyway?"

"Working on it," I said.

> **Talon:** *Izzy, status update?*
>
> **Izzy:** *Bandit and Artax have us. Galloping back to the city. The rogue force on the eastern front is very thin. Giving us a little trouble but I think they're just for show.*
>
> **Glinda:** *Don't listen to the crazy woman, Talon. It's a madhouse out here.*

I chuckled.

> **Talon:** *She's not crazy, just confident. And rightly so.*

Lash nodded at me in recognition of the update. Everyone besides Dune's party was in our brigade. They read it themselves. To further improve our coordination, I selected lower-level Black Hats and added their parties to the brigade as well.

> **Talon:** *All for one and one for all. XP sharing for everybody! Long as you live, anyway.*

Grim chuckles emerged from the crowd of defenders.

I sidled up to Lash. "Aren't we missing a member of Bravo Team?"

"Crux is a pacifist," she replied.

"That's unacceptable today."

A last group of cutthroats surged past the wall in a unified rush. Members of our line fell to the coordinated strike. Lash and I ordered the defenders to back away slightly and regroup.

Conan roared, Tarzan and Chewbacca all in one, before powering up with a mote of red energy.

> [Conan] used Blood Frenzy

The barbarian lumbered through the assassins and hurled them this way and that, bashing and slicing with his axe and free hand. It was a sight so demoralizing that some of the Black Hats, myself included, wondered if we should run. Lash, who was accustomed to the display, rallied the forces to move in and sweep up the leftovers.

The rush was over.

"They're holding back," I reported, eyeing the enemy positions on the map. It seemed the bottleneck had stymied them enough to give them doubts. While they regrouped, there was a lull in the action.

Caduceus and another healer tended to the wounded. Others chugged health potions. After this battle, I resolved to bolster the number of Black Hat healers. Our meager staff was a regrettable oversight, but an understandable one given our recent war against the Oakengard priestship. Clerics generally weren't welcome in Stronghold.

The enemy formation on the map spread out. Many of them were still focused on the main passage, but a contingent headed east to the marketplace and crossed the bridges into the Foot. Others fanned out into the line of buildings walling off Oldtown. A narrow alley sliced along the west wall. While it didn't lead directly into Black Hat territory, the ruins along the west side of Oldtown would provide a secondary staging area and plenty of cover for incoming forces.

So much for a single bottleneck.

Talon: *Kyle, we need another wall at the western alley.*

Kyle: *No can do, bro. We can only build within the headquarters.*

I grumbled and gave orders for the defenses to widen. I sent watchers along the eastern buildings, heavier hitters toward the west alley.

Kyle: *I do have some good news, though. Looks like we can spend defense points to repair structures and build traps.*

Talon: *What kind of traps?*

Kyle: *Remember those caltrop plans Izzy found in the library?*

The Shorehome army once again charged the wall.

"Incoming!" I yelled. Black Hats hefted weapons in response.

This time, rogues flew over the wall in greater numbers. Vaulters came in as a first strike, scrambling our line. Other mercenaries hammered at the shale with pickaxes. The sudden push threatened to cut us off from our spreading forces.

"Fall back!" cried Lash from the western line. Conan and the others remained in formation as they begrudgingly drew away from the side alley. Cutthroats rushed in. "There's too many of them, Talon! We need to regroup the main force."

Cracks snaked across our single wall. "We can't. This is gonna be a war zone inside a minute."

"So repair it like Kyle said and back us up!" Bravo Team continued their measured retreat.

My eyes flitted to distress calls from the eastern buildings. Ninja-clad assassins were scaling down from high windows. With the interconnected buildings forming a barrier impossible to vault, the Brothers in Black had opted to go *through* them. The rogues that breached were hardly an imposing force, but our natural defenses now resembled a leaking dam, one getting closer and closer to bursting.

Talon: *Kyle, get those caltrops out here.*
Kyle: *Buying them is no problem, DP is coming in from our kills, but we need boots on the ground to place them. Someone's physically required to be in the drop spot.*
Talon: *Crux, report for duty.*

> **Crux:** *I'm a thief, Talon. I don't fight.*
> **Talon:** *Then lay some traps, dammit. What kind of self-respecting thief can't do that?*
> **Crux:** *...You got me there. On my way.*

I hissed in frustrated relief. Every single Black Hat was gonna contribute to our defense or so help them.

Stigg twirled his staff in beautiful destruction, buffing those nearby. "This wall's gonna blow any second!"

"Leave it," I ordered. "Men, fall back along the road. Guard the west border of the headquarters. We have enemies in the ruins."

> **Talon:** *Kyle, the wall's coming down. Forget about it. Switch back to turrets. This time line them along the west road. Keep two up top near the thoroughfare entrance to take on the bulk of their forces. Space the other two out to the south to defend the border.*

> **Earth:** Dirt -> Shale

The wall of shale chunked into pieces as the mercenaries broke through. A surge of rogues broke out in cheers and pushed ahead. Two turrets emerged from the ground and initiated bursts of fire, wiping their sudden cheers away. I scanned behind them for Hadrian or his shadows, but there was no sign of them.

Spent 1 DP: Caltrops
Spent 1 DP: Caltrops
Spent 1 DP: Caltrops

Crux: *Uh, guys? Is that all we got? This isn't enough coverage.*

I brought up the headquarters display.

Black Hat Headquarters

Level: 2
HQXP: 5 / 8

HQR: 32
Daily HQR Production: 14
DP: 0

Current Buildings
Guildhall
Brothel
Barracks
Lumberyard
Vault

Talon: *Crap, we're out of juice.*
Kyle: *No problemo, boss man. We can spend 2 HQR to purchase 1 DP.*

I grunted. It was a good scam the developers had going. We did have plenty of headquarters resources to go around, though. I converted all 32 HQR into 16 defense points.

Talon: *There you go, Crux. Line the caltrops under the eastern building windows to take care of those climbers. Then place a bunch on the main path north of the turrets. That'll slow down their advance while they're taking fire.*
Crux: *Sounds good. After that I can cover the west road.*
Talon: *Hold off on that until we see how much DP we have left. I have a feeling we'll need more handy for repairs. Kyle, check what other goodies we can build.*
Kyle: *I'm not sure if there's anything else, but let me play with these menus some more.*

I swung my spear horizontally to break off an incoming attack. Stigg and Conan used similar maneuvers to stall the bandits. It was a sound strategy. Keeping them at bay was the opposite of a stalemate. Not only did we prevent incoming damage, but our archers and turrets transformed this assault into a game of attrition. All we needed to do was stay alive while our defenses did the work for us.

Crux: *Trouble up here...*

Lash broke away from the line. "I'm backing him up. I'll escort him through his drop points and get him back safely."

I nodded as the knight cast one last buff over the line and charged through the territory.

The Brothers in Black on the western front collected into pockets of soldiers. They ducked behind the ruins across the street to avoid being targeted by the turrets. Dune picked off a few as they peeked, but they were mostly biding time as newcomers reinforced their backfield. Soon they'd have the numbers to overwhelm us.

"Fill the ranks!" I commanded, shuffling pirates and others south to thicken the line. This was gonna be a skirmish soon enough. My goal was to maintain order as long as possible.

Hardened eyes squinted across the no-man's-land. The western front of Black Hat territory was bolstered by the majority of the faction. The dense ruins across the border street were brimming with rogues, a bramble of red dots on my overhead menu. The second wave would be an organized one. Muscles tensed. Weapons raised in the air. All at once, the cutthroats charged.

So much for order.

1450 Full Frontal Assault

The enemy exposed themselves and rushed onto the road. Our people held back as the turrets fired into the crowd. The damage was impressive, but it couldn't stop simple herd immunity from protecting the bulk of the invasion. With screams of fury, rogues raced across the street, an unstoppable ocean meeting the coast. Our weapons clashed against theirs.

Given their built-up numbers, it was looking closer to an even fight.

Lash: *We have vaulters coming over the river!*

I confirmed the bad news on the map readout. Just as with the rogues coming through the northern buildings, their numbers were small, yet not insignificant. While the main line of defense was no doubt along the road, these other interlopers needed to be dealt with.

> **Talon:** *Ignore them for now. Get those caltrops placed along the northern front.*
> **Lash:** *The buildings are covered and working beautifully. Moving to the entrance.*

I paused, wondering who I could afford to lose on the line.

A small goblin stood at attention on the roof of the brothel, stone hammer held high. "Ogreses charge!" yelled Jixa.

The pack of brutes from the barracks stormed the melee. Fists smashed heads, knees cracked ribs; it was a lumbering dance of fury and strength that brutally overpowered the unprepared bandits.

"Woooweeee!" yelled Trafford. "You jumpers are gonna need to get by me first!"

I was startled to hear the buildmaster general in person rather than see him using party chat. I turned to the source of the scream and spotted the grumpy bastard pointing his arquebus from the roof of Dragonperch.

Boom. Boom.

He was covering the vaulters coming from the Foot. No way he could take them all on but it was a start.

The ranger in green paused at my side. "He's gonna need support." He rushed off.

I grimaced. I didn't like the thought of anyone alone out there. More red dots were skipping over the river than I was comfortable with. I ensured the line was holding against the main force before following Dune's lead.

Sure enough, several serious threats had gotten through. A level 6 acrobat was the worst of the bunch. Dune and I took her together. The rest of the level 4s and 5s that had made it through Trafford's overwatch were easier to clean up.

The river was still aflame, but just barely. There was only so long the alchemical burning could continue. To our advantage the water level was now low. Dune posted along the bank and took potshots at anyone else considering making the leap across. I checked the map. No more rovers in our territory. Hopefully the sparse defenders along the borders could keep it that way. I left Dune to his work and hurried back to the line.

> **Kyle:** *Bad news. It doesn't look like we have more traps to build. I'm guessing we need to unlock them like the caltrops. I doubt we have the defense points anyway.*

With caltrop placements, we were so far down to 11. The traps were thankfully proving effective and Crux was going a little wild placing them. Luckily, with all the killing going on, we were scoring more defense points in their place.

> **Kyle:** *What about playing with more socket combinations? Those placements are free.*

I checked our status.

<table>
<tr><td>Socket Manager</td></tr>
</table>

Feather: Dove
Wind:
Water: River
Earth: Dirt -> Shale

Unused: Bone

Talon: *Maybe, but we can't do without the turrets, we can't afford to fill the river, and we don't have much in the way of stock. Does the bone pearl fit anywhere?*

Kyle: *I've tried. Base pearls need to fit into the socket's thematic category. Bone doesn't count as feather, wind, or water. I doubt earth would be different.*

Kyle: *But maybe I can notch it on top of something else. Gimme a second.*

A warning sound brought me back to the map. One of the two turrets guarding the entrance was flashing red.

Talon: *Lash, there's a problem with a northern turret.*

Lash: *I see it. It's taking a beating. There's a pack of cutthroats going at it hard. It looks like I can repair it for 2 DP.*

Crux: *Sounds dangerous.*

> **Lash:** *Hey, we gotta get in the middle of that to lay these caltrops anyway, right? You good to go, Crux?*
> **Crux:** *Yup, ready to deploy at the entrance.*
> **Lash:** *Roger that. I'll clear a path, cast a shield wall. Stay behind me and throw the caltrops as I'm repairing the turret.*
> **Talon:** *I don't like this. I'll back you up.*
> **Lash:** *There's no time. This turret's about to bust.*

More blares warned of the impending destruction. This time both turrets blinked red.

> **Talon:** *Damn it, I'm on my way. Hold off as long as you can.*
> **Lash:** *Hurry.*

I sprinted across my new headquarters, under construction and under siege. I couldn't yet say the area was beautiful, but it was mine. Ours, even, which made it especially valuable. We were building these ruins into something notable, and scores of players, NPCs, and mobs were fighting to protect it.

I slowed as I neared the guildhall, cutting around the back. This was the foremost structure of the Black Hats, on the road right beside the entrance for all to see. Lash and Crux had to be nearby. Bodies littered the line of well-maintained buildings to the north, punctured by numerous caltrops. Many of the bodies had severed limbs, a clear signature of the white knight's cleaver. The two had done invaluable work.

As I rounded the corner, my intuition skill flared. Indicators pointing behind me lit up. I brought the sum of my experiences together to react in a flash. With spinshield still overloaded, I activated tornado spin with less than a thought. The arc of my spear spun into a tight shield. Lightning crackled against metal.

"Argh!" Poe's assassin needle flew from his grip. He clutched his hand in pain. "You son of a—"

I triggered dash and rammed the point of my spear into his gut.

> Combo!
> You dealt 72 damage to [Poe]

The assassin's health bar sank to half as he rolled out of my range and scooped up his weapon. He was lucky my deadshot skill was grayed out or he would've been hurting even more.

"Poe!" I growled. "Up to your usual tricks. You ever considered tackling your problems head on?"

"I'm an assassin," he spat. "A rogue, just like you."

"Nothing like me."

He coughed blood and twirled his dagger menacingly. "I've read your forum posts, Talon. I've seen your skills: darkvision, sneak, subdue. Don't pretend you're on any path other than assassin. It's only that legendary weapon that makes you any different."

"Drop your weapon, I'll drop mine," I replied evenly.

He sneered and vanished.

I readied for an attack from any side.

Poe's disembodied voice carried over the wind. "See, I'm thinking that waste of a skill point you call tornado spin has a long recharge time."

I turned in a circle, waiting. He was dead-on about the skill cooldown. A full 2 minutes meant it was very nearly a one-and-done per combat encounter. If it hadn't been for my previous overloads, I could've surprised him with the separate spinshield skill. I almost drooled thinking about it. Unfortunately, that wasn't happening. I had no way of knowing when my skills would be available again.

Poe materialized behind me. "Boo!"

I dove away as his blade swept through my cowl. Reversing my spear, I came back for him, but he was gone. It was a helluva hide skill he had, no doubt aided by the assassin needle's +8 agility. It was the middle of a sunny day and he was disappearing in plain sight.

My intuition rang again. That combined with my supposition that he would once again attempt a backstab prepared me for a proper crossblock. As his needle rang off my spear, I returned a blow that stabbed his leg.

Combo!
You dealt 44 damage to [Poe]

He was gone before I could swipe again. I held my spear out and patiently waited for my dash timer to recharge. 5 more seconds.

"Tick, tick," taunted Poe. "The end is nigh."

My intuition warned me again. This time I sensed danger behind me and to my side. I hesitated long enough, confused by the changing danger notifications, that when Poe emerged from hiding right in front of me, I was caught completely off guard. The assassin jammed a knee into my elbow. I released the dragonspear as he shoved me.

> Agility Check...
> Pass!

I tumbled onto my back. He grinned and kicked the spear away. And then he admired it for a second. "A nice prize to add to my collection." He raised the point of his enchanted needle. "But first thing's first."

> **Lash:** *Sorry, Talon. Can't wait any longer. It's go time.*

I scowled as Poe hovered over me in a ready stance, savoring his victory. One good hit from his assassin needle would stun me and leave me nearly defenseless. I was counting on that overconfidence.

As Poe leaned over me, I chuckled. "Sucker." My dash recharged. I surged upward, past his hungry blade's guard, and jammed *my* assassin needle right through his chest, all the way to the hilt.

> Surprise!
> Stun!
> You dealt 48 damage to [Poe]

The bewildered assassin dropped his blade and stared at the identical dagger plunged through his heart. "H-how?"

I snickered and withdrew the needle from his chest. "I told you I could beat you on even ground." No longer propped up by me, the rogue crumpled to the dirt. "Impressive damage considering I didn't use a sneak attack."

"And you claim you're no assassin."

I wiped blood off the needle and returned it to my inventory. In its place, I drew another weapon. "You're right, it's not really my style. I think I'm gonna kill you with a blade worthy of your vaunted reputation."

Poe whimpered as I stuck him with my whittling knife.

> You dealt 3 damage to [Poe]
> [Poe] is dead!

> **Loot:**
> 27 silver
> [Tiger Claws]

Hey, now. Not only did the assassin lose his prized weapon before dying, but his random drop was a score. I finally had an upgrade to my regular climbing claws. I hastily scooped up the drops. Then I remembered.

"Lash."

I snatched the dragonspear and hurried around the guildhall. A large cluster of rogues bore down on Crux and the white knight. A yellow energy wall held reinforcements at bay, but only for moments at a time. Lash rolled heads and interfaced with the turret between swings.

Spent 2 DP: Turret repaired

With a free hand again, Lash re-equipped her body shield. Crux, mostly protected behind it, placed the second of three caltrops. The enemies in the area scattered.

I rushed forward as fast as I could. Lash's energy barrier cracked. Cutthroats lunged forward. I needed ten yards to get there, ten seconds for a tornado spin. Too far, too late. Bravo Team was engulfed by enemies.

Lash grunted mightily as blades penetrated her armor. The cleaver was ripped from her grip. She raised her black shield high and slammed it to the ground.

[Lash] used Shieldquake

The resultant shock wave knocked two thirds of the rogues off their feet. Lash was wounded, but she'd bought them enough time for the next step. Her eyes met mine. She could've gone for her cleaver. Instead, she barreled through the crowd in the opposite direction and repaired the second turret. Crux placed the final caltrops just before they were once again overwhelmed.

Sprinting full bore, I planted the spear and vaulted clear over their heads, landing on the far side of the caltrops with a weapon slam. I fought off several blades as the seconds counted down, refreshed turrets firing away in support, then I cleared the area with a tornado spin. XP gloriously rolled in as I came to a stop. A last batch of ten Brothers approached from the thoroughfare. I turned my head to check how many had breached Black Hat territory.

Two blades speared Crux's body as he attempted a retreat. Lash knocked the assassins away with her shield. She grabbed the thief and began dragging him to safety. More blades slashed the back of her legs. The knight tripped before she could reach the cleaver, but she heaved Crux forward as she fell. He dove for it, deftly scooping it up and tossing the heavy weapon back to her. The move left his back open to surrounding enemies.

Brothers in Black closed in on Crux like a pack of alligators. His health bar sank to 0 in less than a second.

I roared and dashed over the caltrops as the cutthroats converged on Lash. I bashed them away with my spear—one here, two there—but I was surrounded now too. Daggers came fast. My skill points were low and my main attacks were out of commission. Kicks knocked Lash's shield away. Blades hammered her plate. I killed another rogue as the turrets finished off two more, but the reinforcements were making it through, damaged but pressing for the kill. I put my back to Lash and resorted to crossblocks again and again to keep the baddies at bay, my skill points nearing empty.

"Get out of here..." drawled Lash, too weak to fully stand.

"FUCK THAT," I said, bashing knives away. "You've saved

me more times than I can count. You got our defenses back up and repeatedly put the lives of your teammates above yours. I'm not leaving you behind."

Lash grunted in agony. She must've had a torn Achilles tendon or broken leg or something—the combat log was too busy to catch everything. What was clear was that she wasn't going anywhere anytime soon, and I doubted I was strong enough to carry her. As the rogues fanned out to flank her, I moved to stab whoever got close.

Backstab!
56 damage

I whirled and struck my attacker.

Backstab!
62 damage

I grunted and swung again, preemptively killing the next enemy lurking behind me, but I couldn't hold out any longer. They had just enough people in place, after just enough attrition, that they'd gotten the better of us. It was gonna end. And Hadrian was still nowhere in sight.

I swung the dragonspear with increasingly wild attacks, fighting with heart and soul instead of tactics. It was all I had left. As I was backstabbed yet again, teary eyes scanned over the battling forces on the southern road. Scores of bodies, many clad in black but others from my side as well, littered the streets with abandon. Ogres charged through distant lines, and I smiled at the fact that our forces had the upper hand. They would continue fighting, even without me.

Somewhere across the haze of the battlefield, a blurry behemoth charged into my field of view, galloping right at me, and I blinked.

[Izzy] cast Icicle Blast

Missiles rocketed past me, cascading into the floor and the enemies behind.

[Glinda] cast Minor Healing Aura
You are healed and instantly relieved of minor status effects.

Our health bars surged upward. My vision cleared and I saw a beautiful thing. Izzy and Glinda charging into the fray atop a powerful black stallion and one very-pissed-off mountain bongo. The pixie flipped off my magnificent pet and landed on her toes, slamming her staff back and forth. Bandit's horns crashed into a stream of assassins coming for me, hooves trampling any not quick enough to escape.

Glinda dismounted as Izzy and the turrets did mop-up duty. The priest cast a spirit buff and ran to our side. Lash ripped off her helmet and breathed in exhaustion, smiling from ear to ear. "Damn, you guys know how to make an entrance."

Despite being restored to full, I collapsed on the road beside her, laughing. "You are certifiably insane, Lash, you know that?"

"Takes one to know one." She tiredly reached for her cleaver, but there was no one left to kill.

"Look at the trouble you get into without me," said Izzy, helping me to my feet.

"Don't I know it." I gave her a hug and checked the battle map. "Don't worry. There's plenty of trouble left to come. The Whisperer is still amassing forces on the thoroughfare."

"He hasn't even shown his face," complained Lash. She salvaged Crux's gear and gave his fading body a solemn nod. "The kid did good."

I gritted my teeth and clapped her white pauldron. "For a pacifist."

I rubbed Artax's neck before shooing him to the sidelines. He didn't need to be involved in this battle. Bandit stuck close to me as we moved down the street to support the others. Somewhere during our reprieve my overloaded skills returned to active duty. Good thing as there was still plenty of fighting to be done. From here on I resolved to be more judicious with my use of overloads.

Glinda frowned at the battle-scarred terrain. "So everything so far has just been Hadrian's opening salvo?"

"If the defense map is any indication." It was worrying to me how completely Hadrian was able to reinforce his numbers.

Lash looked the two over. "Where did you ladies get off to, anyway?"

Izzy shrugged. "It was some kind of teleportation spell. Stuck us out in the boonies. Somewhere random, I think. It wasn't dangerous except for the pack of bandits outside the gates, but most of them were moving to the river north of town."

"The kraken controls the river gate," I explained. "The breach is feeding their army."

"And the shadowguards?"

"Still alive. Still protecting Hadrian."

Lash shook her head. "How are we gonna stop them?"

"Our vacation gave me a lot of time to consider that," said Izzy, "and I think that Void Orb spell requires both shadowguards to cast."

I nodded in revelation. "That's right. They worked together both times they used it. So if we kill one of them..."

Lash slipped her helmet back on her head. "Then we neutralize their superweapon."

Izzy pressed concerned lips together. "Not counting the titan."

Our rejuvenated group made easy work of the remaining rogues on the street. Glinda and Caduceus provided much needed support to the troops. Our low-level healer was dead.

Dune came sprinting back. "They're in the water!"

"Who is?"

"Undine!"

According to my display, we had two incoming enemy spearheads: those snaking down the river to the east and others filing into the ruins to our west. What little time we had to recover was almost up.

Grim silence overtook the battlefield. Rogues peeked out from rubble. Grips tightened on weapons. Scattered flames on the river surface dwindled as scaly bodies drew ever closer.

The third wave was about to begin.

1460 Command & Conquer

Errol and the pirates had the most experience against the undine. They drew hooked weapons and split to defend against the river incursion. The other half of the faction covered the street. I couldn't shake the feeling that thinning ourselves out was a losing strategy, but what else could we do when we were surrounded?

> **Talon:** *Kyle, any luck with those sockets?*
> **Kyle:** *Negative, Alpha Leader. The bone pearl just doesn't want to slot onto anything. I switched the dove pearl to the wind socket, but it looks to give the same functionality.*
> **Talon:** *Too late for messages to help us.*

I cursed.

> **Kyle:** *I have a theory, though. We're ignoring the dirt pearl. There's a chance it can notch over one of the other pearls.*
> **Talon:** *But then we lose our turrets.*
> **Kyle:** *We could slot the shale pearl back in there.*
> **Talon:** *We're way beyond choke points, Kyle. They're flanking us. Reposition the turrets. Two on the road and two on the riverbank.*
> **Kyle:** *Roger that.*

The shale turrets repositioned themselves. Despite being surrounded by superior numbers, there was something reassuring about having artillery on your side.

> **Errol:** *Here they be comin', Talon. Waves o' undine, crawlin' up the brick with nothin' but claws an' determination.*

Before I could respond, a charge signal went out in the ruins. Units of bandits rushed the line with wild abandon. There were more of them than I thought. Red dots clustered together on a map were difficult to count. Even worse, location markers said nothing of the enemy type. When several ogres rose from their ranks, I realized Hadrian had been saving his big mobs for last.

The next surprise came just as suddenly. Hordes of imps spilled into the streets. They were nothing, white mobs, not a challenge at all. So why had they been reserved for this wave?

The barbarous imps loped on hands and feet, quickly

overtaking their bipedal brethren. They poured into the street like a flash flood. As the turrets worked overtime to suppress them with shale, the enemy strategy became all too clear.

"Wait!" I called. "Hold off for the humans!"

Claws met steel as imps crashed into the line. Say what you want about noob mobs, but many of the Black Hats were low enough level to be shaken by the rush. As the trailing humans neared, I screamed, "Now!"

A line of grenadiers tossed destructive potions over the battlefield. Many of them were Kyle's stock of corrosive. Some had been purchased in shops or crafted by others. Isolated explosions harassed the incoming bandits and destroyed any semblance of order. Which was to say both sides of the conflict met with chaos.

Our weapons danced swiftly, taking out two imps for every human encountered. The initial wave wasn't enough to overwhelm our steely faction members. It hadn't been meant to. During our preoccupation with numbers, the enemy ogres went for our defenses.

"Protect the turrets!" Bravo Team moved toward one while Izzy and I took the other.

We engaged the enemy ogres while I ordered our ogre crew to take on the humans. I could've pitted like against like for a solid counter, but that would only incur losses on both sides. I needed my biguns alive to clear the smaller mobs away. Sacrificing chess pieces was fine only when you had extra to spare. Taking them on ourselves was the smarter play.

Ogres were far from invincible. Their power, however, was undeniable. The trick to fighting ogres was simple: don't let their meaty paws catch you. It was an easy enough task for experienced fighters either quick on their feet or equipped with good gear. The problem was our turrets didn't possess either.

Although Izzy and I engaged one monster, the other smashed the shale column off its base. It stopped firing, and it was only seconds before its absence was felt. Izzy froze the second attacker to the ground as I impaled it with a deadshot. A couple more skill combos finished off the pair without effort.

Imps had fallen by the scores. I watched Lash cleave the final ogre to the ground. Unfortunately, the damage was done. Our turret was destroyed and theirs hadn't fared any better. The fodder mobs had achieved their objective.

> **Errol:** *We can't keep 'em off the shore, Talon. If we don't pull away, we're goners.*

More bad news. I briefly considered repairing the turrets with our scant 8 DP, but the bandits rushing to flank us to the north and south changed my mind.

"Fall back!" I ordered. "To the center of Oldtown!" I repeated the order over brigade chat. Then I placed my fingers on my lips and whistled sharply. When Bandit cantered by I snagged her horn and swung onto her back. We rushed to the opposite front where Errol's men were retreating.

"Sorry, Talon. Thar riverbank's too dangerous. If they pull us in, we can't fight back." The shore was overrun with vicious undine. "Good news," added Errol, "is thems fish tails ain't what ye'd call efficient on land. They're advancin' mighty slow."

Watching the mermaids and mermen struggle over the grass

and dirt was surprising. When Trafford rushed from the tower and fired some shots their way, an idea sprang to mind.

"Trafford, we'll be overwhelmed if both fronts pinch us at the same time. The undine are slow—we have to make them slower."

His arquebus flipped in his hand as he reloaded it with powder. "Aye, that's an accurate analysis. What'd you have in mind?"

Errol spoke up. "Maybe caltrops will give the fish even more problems than humans."

"Try it," I agreed. "But also construction supplies. The lumberyard lines the river. So does the tower." I pointed to my map. "If you offload lumber and stone at these positions, it'll slow or even redirect the undine. They'll take the path of least resistance."

The old man's head swiveled from me to the approaching fish people. "That's a tall order, chief. And my strength ain't what it used to be."

"Don't get snippy, Trafford. Use Jixa's crew. They'll get it done in no time."

The buildmaster general's eyes brightened and he hurried off.

"Pirates, let's reinforce our people in the middle before they're surrounded by bandits."

A chorus of hurrahs resounded and they charged through Oldtown.

Talon: *Kyle, the turrets are down. With what we're fighting, I don't know if they're worth repairing. Give us some temp walls along the shoreline.*

I quickly explained my plan while I scoured for additional threats.

Kyle: *Cool. That'll let me try out my water-dirt combination.*

I watched him alter the socket layout.

Socket Manager

Feather:
Wind: Dove
Water: River -> Dirt
Earth: Shale

Unused: Bone

Walls erected between the mermen and myself. At the same time, the moved dirt pearl thickened the river with mud. The undine struggled and flapped their tails in the goop. Climbing the steep bricks from the shallow surface was now a slippery business, and I watched in satisfaction as the tide of undine was stemmed. Trafford and the ogres rushed by and unloaded supplies from the lumberyard. Makeshift obstacles added to the countermeasures. While the eastern front was far from neutralized, it was handily delayed.

I charged back to the central action, riding Bandit and using my spear as a lance. Errol's men had bolstered the defense and things were looking closer to even now. I wasn't sure if even was enough to stick this whole thing out when Hadrian hadn't even shown up yet. As always, it was up to the playmakers to save the day.

Barbed javelins of ice wielded by the frost mage mowed down cutthroats. The Scar of the Six Seas and his merry swashbucklers flung blood left and right. The white knight's cleaver arced through the air and leveled opponents, golden buffs turning the field to our advantage. The green ranger flipped this way and that, silver arrows punching their marks with unerring accuracy. The white witch and the good doctor traded off healing duties while the berserker and the barbarian tanked. I had never seen such precision and grace in a group effort, and I knew we had built something special.

Bandit galloped wherever we were needed, and no single enemy could withstand the might of my charging dragonspear. But our foes kept coming, and the battle map didn't give me any delusions that the wave was close to over.

> **Kyle:** *Oh ho ho, brother, you are going to LOVE me.*
>
> **Talon:** *What's up? I could use some good news right about now.*

> **Kyle:** *I finally figured what to notch the bone pearl into. I think it'll work, anyway, as long as you're cool with me taking the mud out of the river.*

A stream of undine were mazing through Trafford's labyrinth, caltrops stymieing their progress. The mud in the river was drying out fast, losing its effectiveness. I decided we could risk it.

> **Talon:** *Do your thing, jewelry man.*
> **Kyle:** *Done.*
> **Kyle:** *But seriously, bro, don't call me that.*

I chuckled as the river washed free, still stuck at shallow but water once again. The jolt of the transition actually washed some climbers upriver, and I wondered if alternating between water and mud was the optimal strategy. The shale walls lowered as Kyle removed the pearls. The ogres hurried to patch the defensive holes.

I was confident they had the problem well in their giant meaty hands. Much more worrying was the sudden rumbling from deep in the ground. All of Oldtown seemed to shake beneath our feet.

"Shit, Kyle. What'd you do?"

<table>
<tr><td>Socket Manager</td></tr>
<tr><td>Feather:
Wind: Dove
Water: River
Earth: Dirt -> Bone</td></tr>
<tr><td>Unused: Shale</td></tr>
</table>

So the bone pearl slotted over dirt. The tremors in the ground abruptly halted, leaving several fighters wondering what the earthquake had been about. Bandit reared on her haunches and nearly threw me when a skeletal hand ripped through the dirt.

> **Kyle:** *So... you know how the city's built on top of ancient catacombs?*

I pulled Bandit aside as more limbs pierced the ground. "What in the..."

One by one, the not-so-restful dead that resided in the tunnels below clawed their way from the ground around the barracks. Humans consisting entirely of bone limped over the battlefield. Some were naked, others wore tatters of cloth or armor. Their skulls were empty of emotion and their mouths and eyes full of dirt. In their hands were the rusty implements of death.

Any apprehension I had about the situation abruptly faded when a thousand-year-old knight smashed a mace into a fleeing bandit's head.

> **Talon:** *Kyle, remind me to give you a raise.*

I screamed encouraging words to any Black Hats unsettled by the scene. Bandit weaved through the undead unmolested as I bashed passing rogues aground. The skeletons were cruel and unrelenting fighters, moving slowly over terrain but striking with supernatural efficiency. Daggers scraped across their bones to little effect, all but neutralizing the invading army's weapon of choice. As more rogues fell to the ghastly reinforcements, Black Hats fell in line with their new compatriots. The dead were wholly on our side.

That was one way to turn the tide.

Brothers in Black scattered from the threats as best they could, but without a full retreat order they were only buying themselves precious moments. We combined spell and sword to slay as many as we could. The smart enemies mustered the courage to single out and gang up on targets. The even smarter ones used bashing weapons. Once a skeleton crumpled into disparate pieces that didn't reanimate, word was out that they weren't invincible.

As more and more skeletons rose from the dirt, our defense points ticked down. This obstinate army was a finite resource. However, as long as they indiscriminately slaughtered the enemy, the pool of DP refilled itself. We were holding at around 6 and I didn't foresee the flow of undead stopping any time soon.

Of course, mazing be damned, the undine did eventually

reach the conflict's epicenter. The stream was slow, but they were game changers just as much as the skeletons were. Despite losing their main advantage on the ground, the average mermaid was still more formidable than the average cutthroat. Their claws were sharper than daggers, their natural poisons worse than anything the rogues concocted.

I recalled the healers to deal with withering sickness as we engaged the undine. Stigg bellowed in glee and hit our group with a buff.

[Stigg] cast Berserker's Frenzy
For the next 30 seconds, your physical skills do not require cooldown.

We discharged our skills with abandon. The berserker overcommitted to his charge and got raked by black claws. Caduceus took care of him as he returned to safety. It was a glorious tag-team rage-in-the-cage mega-fight.

It was fun watching the skeletons engage the new mobs. The claws were slashing weapons and were thus weaker against bone, and the undine poison was pretty much useless against the dead. Still, the mermaids weren't as frightened of the mobs as the humans. They attacked in relentless groups that proved an effective counter.

Rogues had taken to attacking the barracks. I wasn't sure what their strategy was but figured I could deal with the damage later. As long as fewer men were attacking mine, I considered it a win. Especially since we now had our hands full.

A stray arrow caught Caduceus in the back.

```
Critical Hit!
Stun!
```

The attack had somehow managed a bunch of damage. Conan shoved her to safety and engaged a pair of mermen. His axe could only counter so many claws. They slashed him mercilessly while Caduceus was unable to heal him.

```
[Undine] dealt 33 damage to [Conan]
DoT: 15 dmg/10 secs
[Undine] dealt 37 damage to [Conan]
DoT: 15 dmg/10 secs
[Undine] dealt 31 damage to [Conan]
[Conan] is dead!
```

I slaughtered the pair a second too late. I only had time to salvage his property back to him before needing to retreat myself.

Lash scowled as she hung Caduceus over her shoulder, retreating as well. "Come on!" The knight slammed her shield into the ground to trip up her pursuers.

Stigg dutifully followed, protecting her back. From my seat atop Bandit, I didn't see Izzy anywhere. I had taken some poison myself and was finding the swarms of enemies dizzying. I swung the spear and charged Bandit ahead to clear a path for the others.

The crowd of rogues parted. At first it was fear but, as my head swam, it was no longer panic. They were the Red Sea, parting unnaturally, and my poison-riddled determination galloped me forward into it. Before I knew it, a single figure stood fixed in my path. Hadrian. My surprise contorted to hate, my knuckles whitened on the dragonspear, and the shadow crashed into me before I ever saw it.

Air rushed from my chest as I banged on the ground. Shadowy fingers scraped the bongo as she tried to defend me. Somehow I'd managed to keep my grip on my weapon. I blinked back shell shock and sat up.

Stigg rushed past me without hesitation, wooden staff spinning toward Hadrian. The Whisperer stood in place, the second shadowguard clinging to him like a coat. The berserker's attack whiffed as Hadrian appeared behind him, countering. The third assassin needle made a reappearance and pierced the red robe.

Backstab!
Savage!
[Hadrian] dealt 197 damage to [Stigg]
[Stigg] is dead!

Dune roared in the distance. A silver arrow zipped by my head. Hadrian's shadowguard snatched the projectile in midair, inches from the Whisperer's heart.

The other shadowguard didn't wait. It lunged for me. I dashed to the side as Lash twirled her cleaver and dealt it a glowing-yellow body blow. I readied a deadshot as a pair of undine joined the fray. As I fended them off, a notification came through.

> Barracks suffered catastrophic damage
> Barracks is destroyed!

Icicles barraged Hadrian's back. The shadowguard-turned-armor winced away from the magic, angering Hadrian. He rushed between rogues to use them as body shields.

I braced a crossblock against the shadow.

> 22 damage

The combined jabs and poisons were starting to take their toll. Lash once again hit the shadow demon. She and Izzy were probably the best we had against them, and they were barely enough, especially since the bodyguards had apparently healed some since our last encounter. The wraith struck and grooves opened across her white breastplate.

The physicker swooped in with her holy rod.

> [Caduceus] cast Greater Holy Light
> *For the next 30 seconds, you have the ability of Greater Regeneration.*

Nearby Black Hats enjoyed surging health bars. Caduceus had found one of Haven's earlier relics, holy based even though she was a woman of science. Hey, I wasn't complaining.

"The healers!" screamed Hadrian. "Kill the healers!"

The shadowguard plastered to him immediately obeyed. It

peeled away and dove past Lash, still engaged with the other. I moved to intercept but it vanished.

> Critical Hit!
> [Shadowguard] dealt 87 damage to [Caduceus]
> [Glinda] cast Minor Healing on [Caduceus]

Although it wasn't a major heal, it got the physicker out of immediate danger. The added regeneration returned her to full in short time.

The shadowguard snarled and twisted around. Both it and the one engaged with Lash snaked to the incoming white witch and decapitated her before she saw them coming.

> [Glinda] is dead!

More determined than ever by their success, the shadowguards doubled up on Caduceus, just getting to her feet.

> Shock!

With greater regeneration, the damage was less critical than the shock, which would prevent Caduceus from using skills for a full minute. I put myself between Caduceus and the shadows and gritted my teeth.

Damn it. Kyle's selfless move with the kraken had jump-started Oldtown's defense when we'd needed it, but we were feeling the repercussions now. We lost the mirror shield and, more vitally, the bishop's gauntlet that we needed to take on the darkness.

I stood my ground anyway. A well-timed tornado spin, overloaded of course, fended away the first set of attacks. Izzy erected a wall of ice to protect the physicker's flank. Still, the shadows wouldn't stop coming. Lash struck one in the back as the other went for the medic.

Errol fucking Oates galloped over on Artax's back. The war horse trampled rogues in his path. The pirate flipped head over heels in something closer to showmanship than combat, and buried his rapier into the shadowguard.

> [Errol] dealt 34 damage to [Shadowguard]
> (260/600)

The shadow slashed back.

> Leg Break!
> [Shadowguard] dealt 67 damage to [Errol]
> DoT: 30 dmg/15 secs

Lash pressed in with a spinning cleaver, backing the demon off Errol. Unfortunately, the other one had a clear shot at her back.

> [Shadowguard] dealt 45 damage to [Lash]
> DoT: 30 dmg/15 secs

Errol dropped to his knees, winded. Unlike Lash, he'd been out of range when the regeneration buff went off. A brave mermaid caught him across the neck. I buried the dragonspear between her scaly breasts.

The pirate breathed harshly as Caduceus crouched by his side. "Just 20 more seconds till my shock wears off," she said. "Then I can heal you."

"Darlin'," breathed the mortally wounded pirate, "I ain't gonna make it that long. But I thought ye should have this." Errol pulled a gaudy helmet from his inventory, handed it to the physicker, and said, "A pirate captain oft be surrounded by lethal ladies. Of 'em all, yer my favorite."

[Errol] is dead!

Grom scratched his head in befuddlement. "Oi, should we tell the cap'n she's gay?"

Caduceus stared at the full helm in grim reverence. It was made out of steel, with a crosscut slit on the face, horizontal over the eyes and vertical down the center. Atop the helmet rested a bronze cross, large and iconic like a hood ornament. We may not have had Bishop Tannen's glove, but we sure had his helmet.

I defended Caduceus from the shadow and undine as the other shadowguard punched through Lash's chest.

Critical Hit!
[Shadowguard] dealt 80 damage to [Lash]
DoT: 30 dmg/15 secs

The shadow, though faceless, managed a cruel grin. Unconcerned with her fate, the white knight ripped her cleaver upwards, a blaze of yellow tearing through her foe.

Deathblow!
Critical Hit!
[Lash] dealt 67 damage to [Shadowguard] (193/600)

I fended off one last attempt at Caduceus before she slipped the helmet onto her head. For the faintest of moments, an orb of silence seemed to surround us. Then a shock wave flashed from her body. Golden light shone through the darkness. The frantic shadowguard immediately called off its attack. The one engaged with Lash withered away, but a shield wall cast behind it caught it in place.

I dashed to the white knight's side and comboed the stuck shadow with a deadshot.

Combo!
Critical Hit!
You dealt 41 damage to [Shadowguard] (152/600)

Somehow, the holy light exposed the withering demon to greater damage. While the shadowguard was pinned by a cleaver and the dragonspear, the frost mage summoned a stalagmite of ice from the ground.

Critical Hit!
[Izzy] dealt 36 damage to [Shadowguard]
(116/600)

Caduceus stepped close to the interlocked struggle and, for the first time, a pair of white eyes illuminated on the demon's face. They opened wide with fear. The physicker rested one hand on the dying knight's shoulder and instantly restored her to full health. She plunged another into the shadowguard's chest. It exploded in a rain of sparks and ashes.

[Shadowguard] is defeated!
225 XP awarded

Dune stopped at our side, blue flames washing over his body as he hit level 9, gifted full health and spirit. He raised his longbow, two arrows simultaneously notched.

Hadrian's eyes were fixed on the spot where his shadowguard had been. Motes of dark and light swirled and dissipated. The other bodyguard shied away to shield its master. Caduceus stood tall and swiveled her bishop helmet to the Whisperer.

Dune released his arrows. The shadow armor caught one. The other punched into Hadrian's gut. The wraith hissed and pulled him backward through a growing crowd of cutthroats.

"Don't let him get away!" growled Lash, rushing headlong into the fray. The ranger notched arrows and offered support as Caduceus pursued. I held back, blinking, scanning the battlefield of marauders and assassins and mermaids.

Something was wrong. "There's too many of them."

My map confirmed the fact. The final swell of enemies was rolling in. Somehow, the Black Hats were vastly outnumbered. Our ranks were dimming alarmingly. I scoured various status screens.

Black Hat Headquarters

Level: 2
HQXP: 4 / 8

HQR: 0
Daily HQR Production: 14
DP: 14

Current Buildings
Guildhall
Brothel
Lumberyard
Vault

Destroyed
Barracks

The destruction of a building lowered our headquarters XP to 4, but that was still enough for level 2. Our HQR production wasn't affected. Our defense points, however, seemed unusually high at 14.

> **Talon:** *Kyle, we have plenty of DP. Why aren't the skeletons respawning?*
> **Kyle:** *Sorry, was working on that. The troop barracks was serving as the spawn point. They hosed us by destroying it.*

I was angry with myself for not catching on to the enemy strategy sooner. Headquarters defense was still new to me. I was wet behind the ears. Hadrian, not so much. The way he'd attacked the turrets and the barracks, he'd had this all planned.

> **Kyle:** *Check this out, though. We have one other building the skeletons can spawn at. The brothel. Which makes sense 'cause it's a respawn point too.*

The ground rumbled for a moment and I grinned. Defense points ticked down as bony fingers once again clawed from the ground. Only this time, the skeletons that emerged beside the brothel were clothed in garter belts, candy heels, and crotchless panties.

> **Talon:** *Dude, did you just raise an army of skeleton whores?*
> **Kyle:** *Um... Maybe they're themed to the spawn point.*

I watched (without judgment) as a bony tramp clamped her

legs around a rogue's face for a quick mustache ride. Another ripped off a lacy bra and squeezed it around an assassin's neck. These ladies were real pros, and they weren't even charging for their services.

With reinforcements once again flowing freely, the battle was looking more winnable. With only fifteen Black Hats left standing, that was no small thing. I snagged Trafford and Jixa and pointed to the spawn point. "You guys protect that brothel with your lives. Keep it repaired no matter the cost."

"What a glorious death," snarked the old man. "They'll sing songs about me."

"Good luck," I told him. "I've been trying to get the pirates to sing about me for days."

They went to business. And with the obstacle work along the shoreline completed, it was great to have the ogres back bashing heads. I didn't hold back either. I dove headfirst into the action, content to take a break from management duties and have a bit of rip-roaring fun.

The last burst of enemies was vicious. With their barracks strategy a success, they went full-on at the brothel. It received extensive repairs until our defense points hovered at 1. The undine swarmed the ogres, treating them as giant pincushions, sticking them with so much poison it hurt to watch. Skeleton hookers took on the mobs with dead stares and both sides incurred heavy losses. The battle was winding down as soldiers in both armies fell. I found Bandit on the fringes of the action and rode her outward, searching the battlefield.

The Whisperer had retreated to the riverbank, a bullet of shadow effortlessly weaving past caltrops and walls. This frustrated Lash mightily. Dune took potshots where he could. Many missed their mark but others did their job. It was clear the arrows would be more effective when Hadrian was otherwise engaged. Luckily, Caduceus was keeping the good guys healthy.

The mountain bongo's thick hooves safely charged through the caltrops. Bandit hopped a pile of lumber and I speared Hadrian with a deadshot.

[Hadrian] used Shadowslip
Graze!
You dealt 27 damage to [Hadrian]

Despite the partial dodge, the force of the blow powered him to the ground. Hadrian clawed at the wet mud and laughed. I twirled the dragonspear in hand as Lash and the others stepped to Bandit's side, weapons drawn.

An amorphous body lifted from the river on a slew of tentacles. The hulking mass slapped the mud with a heavy squelch, shaking the ground. The kraken bared a throatful of teeth in a blistering roar. Hadrian snuck to the side as he revealed his last trick: the titan was still in the fight.

1470 Big Game Hunter

Articulated tentacles swung with fury, dealing hundreds of points of damage. Despite having the foresight to crossblock, the blow knocked me clear off my mount. Another smashed clean through Lash's energy shield and bashed her to the ground. Dune shoved Caduceus clear as another tentacle took his legs out with a crit. Even Bandit was smacked hard.

Artax rushed in and kicked the tentacles away. There were too many to take on. The kraken cracked the horse's back. Bandit drilled her horns into the titan, but it was too late. Artax was dead. For her effort, a thick appendage wrapped up the bongo's large body and thrust her aside like a play toy. She crumpled against the mighty stone of Dragonperch, screams of agony rattling my senses.

Bishop Tannen's helmet bathed the area in golden light.

[Caduceus] cast Salvation

Everyone in the immediate vicinity and still alive was

restored to full health. The physicker chugged a spirit vial for a refresh. "They're not giving me much anymore," she reported. "I don't have a lot of juice left."

"We need you alive," stressed Dune. "Take on the shadowguard, not the kraken." The physicker gritted her teeth and nodded.

Bandit whined in the distance. My heart broke as I realized she'd been out of range of the group heal. I couldn't break away to tend to her just yet. "Hold on, girl!" I cried.

I dashed clear of a smash attack. Dune nocked arrows and speared the titan. Lash buffed us with spirit boosters and defense bonuses. From behind, a barrage of ice crystals battered the kraken's side.

The god wasn't immune to damage, but its health bar had barely budged, down to 80% only because of the earlier river explosion. Still, even that remaining health accounted for a cool 16,000.

We backed away from another series of tentacle strikes. Hadrian hungrily spurred the kraken onward. It was fully in his control. He hugged its side and hid in its arms, a clown fish cuddled against an anemone.

"You did better than I expected," saluted Hadrian. "It's not often that I'm surprised."

Izzy joined us in backing away. My eyes ran over the battle notifications. Trafford was dead. Jixa limped toward us. Only Baz and one other ogre of our six were left standing. Besides a few scattered undine and rogues, the enemy was decimated. Only a handful of skeletons remained; our DP was at 0 and the diminished enemy count would prevent the accumulation of more. There weren't any low-level faction members left alive. Oldtown was a barren mess of destruction.

I gazed up at Dragonperch, the shining statue of Magnus Dragonrider a beacon glinting in the sun. Beside the great tower was a petrified titan on its knees, a tribute to the hearty defenders of Stronghold.

I scanned the clouds and blue sky above, thinking right now was a damn good time for salvation.

Arrows and stone peppered the kraken's back. Townsfolk from Hillside were attacking the invading beast. A rock narrowly missed Hadrian's head. The shadow armor swirled to the side, exposing itself. Caduceus jumped forward to take advantage of the distraction.

A tentacle plucked her from the ground. I slammed the arm with a deadshot, but it only loosened its grip. A silver arrow hardly did more. Caduceus tried to break away but the suckers had her. The cross on her helmet flared. The kraken roared and dropped her, singed tentacle still smoking.

Before Caduceus could retreat, another appendage swept into her head. It knocked Tannen's helmet off and snapped her neck in one blow. Our last medic bounced to the ground, dead.

"Do you feel it?" taunted Hadrian. "The creeping doom? The final death knell to your pitiful assault?"

A deafening screech tore through the air, not from the kraken but from high in the sky.

"That's funny," I said, a smile overtaking my face. "I was about to ask you the same question."

The Whisperer's head snapped to the sky. The hairs on my arms and neck stood on end as a black dragon streamed overhead. A deluge of acid cascaded over the titan. Dune salvaged his teammate's gear and jumped away. Izzy pulled Lash clear. Hadrian caught a splash of the dragon breath and recoiled. He slipped, head bouncing on brick as he splashed into the Albula river.

With the group free from immediate danger, I sprinted to Bandit and fed her a healing potion. "Heh, this reminds me of the day I found you." The pain in her eyes washed away and the bongo licked me mercilessly. "You're welcome, girl. Now do me a favor and stay away from the giant sea creature." She hopped to her feet and tried to follow me back. "No. BAD girl. NO sea creatures!"

The bongo snorted.

Jixa stopped at my side, panting. "Tentacleses. Lots and lots of big tentacleses."

I winked at the goblin girl. "I promised you an honest day's work, didn't I?"

A pair of skeletons with purple wigs slogged behind, the last of the two armies.

As I turned to engage the titan, a slip of shadow appeared on the riverbank and Hadrian solidified, miffed. "What is this?" he demanded.

I couldn't help but laugh.

His face reddened in anger and he approached. "What did you do?"

I kept my distance because of the shadowguard he wore around his shoulders, but I taunted him nonetheless. "Don't you see? Your faction is decimated. Your goblin army stuck outside the walls."

"I am far from defeated," he spat. "I ransacked your headquarters. There's a titan in your city. Why are you laughing?"

As if the dragon swooping overhead wasn't enough explanation, I spelled it out for the cocky son of a bitch. "I'm laughing because Hadrian the Whisperer, the machinist, the great puppeteer, fell for my plan hook, line, and sinker."

His eyes narrowed.

"That's right," I said, "*my* plan."

He scowled.

"You stand here thinking you've snuck a Trojan into Stronghold, believing every step of your grand conspiracy has come together for this single moment. Well, I admit, Lucifer and I didn't know who the interloper was. We chatted long and hard about the identity of Haven's usurper. I'll be honest: you didn't even make the short list. It was a masterful deception you worked. *But you never considered mine.*"

Hadrian visibly shook. "Preposterous."

"How do you figure? I've drawn you out into the open. Obliterated your forces and backed you into a corner."

"A titan is never backed into anything."

The kraken pressed forward with renewed tenacity. It lashed out at Izzy and Dune while slithering toward the white knight. It took everyone on at once because it could.

But it shied away when the dragon swooped past. My faction mates were paper cuts. The claws of a dragon were a threat, even to a god. Nightwing raked bloody grooves into defending appendages and both beasts roared with elemental fury.

Tornado spin was my only skill disabled from its last

overloaded use, so I was cautiously optimistic about my chances against the shadowguard. Especially since I now had the clearest shot at Hadrian since this whole mess started. The dragonspear rocketed to its target. The shadow bent the glancing blow away.

> You dealt 27 damage to [Shadowguard] (358/600)
> Graze!
> You dealt 9 damage to [Hadrian] (136/175)

I activated crossblock before the shadow swiped back. As before, it was able to break through the parry.

> 22 damage
> Health: 253/300

"Dune!" I called.

An arrow sailed our way. The shadow batted the silver down with minor damage. It gave me an opening to strike again. I hit Hadrian with a deadshot.

> You dealt 42 damage to [Hadrian] (94/175)

Aside from the shadow armor, the Whisperer was running pretty good defense. It was impressive seeing a level 7 like him compete. 125 fewer health points than I had. He hadn't avoided wipes in the past and was thus lower level than many of us. Then again, Hadrian had never been one for attention. Subservience had been his camouflage. Even now that his treachery was out in the open, he had shadowguards and titans protecting him.

Dune nocked another arrow but somersaulted away from the pursuing kraken. Hadrian phased out and reappeared several yards away. "What do you think you've accomplished?" he snarled.

"You can't teleport anymore," I realized. "It's not just an attack, it's how you phased through the Arena wall. It took both shadowguards to create those wormholes. You can dart around a bit but, in the end, you're stuck here."

"And so what? I'm here. The devil's dragon has no chance against a titan."

I chuckled. "I'm two-and-oh against citywide threats. You'd better hedge those odds."

Nightwing circled down to a clear spot on the ground. He wasn't huge—about the size of a school bus built like a snake— but he was just about the most menacing thing I'd ever seen up close. Everything about him was sharp and twisted, from his teeth, claws, and wing tips, to the jagged horns over his face.

Even Hadrian acknowledged the dragon fear.

"You're obviously not thinking this through," he hurried, slight anxiety in his voice. "Even if you somehow prevailed over insurmountable odds, what will you have accomplished? This is only a final battle if I destroy your headquarters. Uproot you from Stronghold. If you kill me, well, then what? I'll live to fight another day."

"Not if you get deleted by an angel," I said. "That's about as permanent as it gets."

"I haven't warranted their activation," he said smugly. "I

abide by the rules of the Golden Seven."

A calm voice cut through the battlefield—crisp and decisive and ever present. "There is more than one kind of angel, dear Whisperer."

The air beside me crackled and pixelated. Lucifer leaned on his witchwood staff, its quiet blue glow sparkling against the runes on his cloak.

"Wh... what?" he stuttered. "You can't be here. Not inside Stronghold."

"It gets better," replied Lucifer.

Two angels drifted down from the heavens, perfectly modeled images of man, chests puffed, garnished with flowing black cloth. The angels fixed on Hadrian as they lowered, solid black eyes unnerving even from a distance.

"The Fallen," he whispered.

"You had us going," I told him. "We really had no idea it was you. We weren't even sure if the usurper was part of Shorehome. One thing I did know is I couldn't let Oakengard continue the arms race. With them compromised, something had to be done that would attract the notice of every single resident of Haven. Get the usurper's attention. Force him into a premature reveal."

He shook his head. "You can't be in Stronghold."

A message flashed across my view.

Global Haven Alert:
The player Luc1f3r has broken the terms of service and negatively impacted the play experience for all residents. His contract is terminated effective immediately. Decimus has been dispatched to carry out the judgment.

The devil cocked his head. "Took them long enough."

The Fallen descended on Hadrian. "To me!" he cried.

The kraken bowled over my teammates and rushed to its master. Hadrian's shadowguard zipped him to the safety of the tentacles. The dark angels slowed their pursuit.

"Keep at him!" snapped Lucifer.

The angels attempted to obey, but kept hesitating. Something in their core programming was overriding their hacked directives. I remembered using a similar exploit to my advantage.

"They can't interfere with the titan," I told Lucifer. "He's too important a game object. Angels were created to restore balance to Haven, not to supersede it."

Lucifer growled. "Nightwing!"

The dragon kicked up clumps of turf as it charged forward. Nightwing stretched his neck toward reaching tentacles and belched a black spray of stomach acid. The titan's many appendages recoiled as both they and the shadow struggled to shield their master. The beast was so large it took the entire attack stream.

> [Nightwing] dealt 425 damage to [Kraken]
> (14,112/20,000)

Decimus appeared on the cloudy horizon, arms extended, each wielding a silver sword. Unlike the Fallen, his loose robes were white, including the strip across his eyes that made up his blindfold.

"There's no time," muttered Lucifer. "Move in before it's too late."

The devil charged ahead. Nightwing lunged, snapping a wiggling tentacle in his jaws while using claws to push away two others.

> [Nightwing] dealt 117 damage to [Kraken]
> [Nightwing] dealt 73 damage to [Kraken]
> [Nightwing] dealt 78 damage to [Kraken]
> (13,844/20,000)

The shadow attempted to counterstrike. Dune's arrows forced him to keep on guard duty. Izzy summoned missiles at will, but it was clear from her measured attacks that she was low on spirit. Lash's cleaver was nearly as massive as the lone tentacle she took on.

Lucifer entered the melee ahead of me. From a full run, he skidded black boots into a slide, ducking under a defending arm. He brought his dark staff up and into the titan's gaping maw. An explosion issued from the blue crystal.

> [Luc1f3r] cast Azure Ruin
> [Luc1f3r] dealt 1,001 damage to [Kraken]
> (12,589/20,000)

The mind-numbing shock wave threw my friends to the ground. The shadowguard flinched at the unholy light but shielded Hadrian from the shock. The Whisperer palmed the assassin needle and lunged for the kill.

Lucifer twisted his staff and deftly parried the backstab.

> [Luc1f3r] cast Cerulean Sword

A blue saber of energy extended two feet from the bottom tip of his staff. Before he could land a counter, a stray appendage forced him to defend himself. The sensitive suckers burned against his magic.

Nightwing chomped harder, but couldn't stifle a yelp. Three tentacles latched onto the black dragon's hind legs and body. His head thrashed and tore like an alligator with a fresh catch, but from where I was standing, Nightwing might've just become the prey. I focused a deadshot on the nearest appendage. Lucifer slipped out to safety and hacked at the kraken's grip too. Izzy and Lash focused on another arm. Against all the attacks and Nightwing's vicious thrashing, the titan was forced into a ravenous frenzy. Damage and pain were so plentiful they became meaningless.

"Let... go... of my dragon!" growled Lucifer. He focused his energy blade in what must've been some form of overload and cleanly sliced through a tentacle like day-old butter.

Critical Hit!
[Luc1f3r] dealt 749 damage to [Kraken]
(9,200/20,000)

I didn't know what to do. If Nightwing went down this early in the fight, it was all for nothing. The failure of the Fallen, the urgency of the Golden Seven... It was something we hadn't anticipated.

I charged the kraken, planted the dragonspear in the dirt and vaulted up and over its numerous defenses. I swapped out my weapon for my upgraded climbing claws mid air and landed hard on the behemoth. Instead of simply hanging on, I swiped at the sea monster's rubbery skin, tiger claws gashing deeper and deeper.

Skill Evolution!
You learned Claw Handling

I wasn't sure if I'd just pioneered a new weapon type, and I didn't care. My goal was much more than the meager damage I was inflicting. I was going for enraging the distracted titan even more.

Baz and the other ogre joined in, each attempting and barely succeeding in wrapping up a whole arm to themselves. It was a temporary measure, and it was all we needed. Nightwing was down to one-third health, but with a final agonizing push, he ripped free.

Powerful hind legs flexed. Leathery wings unfurled. The dragon released a deafening screech as he triumphantly surged upward, daggerlike claws using the titan as a launching point.

Aided by a cloak of shadow, Hadrian sprang faster than a mousetrap. He lunged up, arm reaching skyward, and met Nightwing like a missile. The assassin needle slid into the dragon's underbelly.

Critical Hit!

[Hadrian] dealt 234 damage to [Nightwing]

[Shadowguard] dealt 145 damage to [Nightwing]

No longer guarding Hadrian, the kraken's tentacles were free to splay out in multiple directions. Lucifer hopped to safety, but Dune, Lash, and Izzy were all batted aside. I was thrown to the ground. Baz lay dead beside me, neck twisted so he faced backward. The other ogre was knocked into that which he feared most—not a sea creature but the sea itself. Even in the lowered river, he thrashed and panicked. Jixa hurried to help but a tentacle smashed her to oblivion, dead as a doornail.

But none of that mattered, because reaching appendages caught the flailing black dragon. Tentacle after tentacle wrapped him tight and squeezed his neck so that not even a screech, much less dragon breath, could escape.

With a bone-jarring twist of fate, the raging kraken crushed its foe for good and released a throaty cry of victory.

1480 Day of Defeat

The body of the great dragon shuddered and went still. Lucifer stared in idle shock.

"No..."

The maddened kraken heaved Nightwing down. I grabbed Lucifer and triggered dash, saving him from being crushed by the discarded body.

The last ogre was still attempting to scale the riverbank. Hadrian cruelly watched for a moment before plunging the assassin needle into the builder's neck. He turned to engage the two converging skeletons.

"This was not written," muttered Lucifer.

Izzy hopped a kraken tentacle. "Talon, Lucifer, on your feet! We can still do this!"

"No..."

I pulled the devil up. Tried to pull him away. "She's right."

"Release me."

Two sandals pattered to the dirt. Decimus pointed a sword that I knew from personal experience pretty much never missed. His voice rang out.

"Lucifer, you are in violation of the terms of service. You will be expunged from Haven."

The angel strode over and swung. The Fallen appeared out of nowhere. A golden cane caught the sword over Lucifer's face. Decimus arched an eyebrow above the blindfold and immediately swung his second sword. This blow was parried by a black scythe on the other side.

"Otho. Vitus. You should not be here."

The Fallen stared with emotionless black orbs.

"So be it," concluded the angel.

Decimus spun and struck both weapons with opposite hands. He kicked Vitus. Otho swung the scythe. Decimus ducked and flipped away. The dark angels pressed. Celestial weapons clashed against the dual wielder, each collision accompanied by a mini sonic boom.

Lucifer rested a hand on the matte-black scales of his fallen comrade. "Through your sacrifice we will survive."

Lash and Dune drew the kraken's attention as they retreated. Izzy tugged my arm. Lucifer's hand flashed and a blue glow overtook Nightwing's body. The dragon's scaly hide shrank until he was nothing more than a curled black snake. Lucifer held a blue gemstone in his hand.

The devil flushed as the Whisperer effortlessly cut down the last of the harassing skeletons. For those keeping score, that was the last of the Black Hat army.

Meanwhile, Decimus put on an impressive show, but against two of his own he was outmatched. As the cane butted his knee, the scythe painted a line of blood across his shoulder. The angel backed away calmly.

Global Haven Alert:
The player Luc1f3r has broken the terms of service and negatively impacted the play experience for all residents. His contract is terminated effective immediately. Longinus, Marius, Gaius, and Severus have been dispatched to carry out the judgment.

I blinked dumbly at the notification. That fleet of angels, combined with Decimus and the Fallen, counted for the sum of the Golden Seven. Never before had they all been activated at one time.

Izzy scowled. "They're rolling out the big guns."

"Then we need to hurry," said Lucifer with renewed vigor. He spun in his boots and marched toward Dragonperch.

Hadrian attempted to intercept. Lucifer whirled and deflected two blows with his staff, one from the assassin needle and the other from the shadow blade that followed. Another spin of the witchwood rapped the Whisperer in the gut.

[Luc1f3r] dealt 101 damage to [Shadowguard] (166/600)
Graze!
[Luc1f3r] dealt 16 damage to [Hadrian] (78/175)

Seeing the usurper so near death, I lunged as well. The shadow deftly knocked the dragonspear aside. Izzy hurled a javelin of ice. The living armor dragged its master back to the safety of the kraken. With the Whisperer in possession of the Squid's Tooth, the titan was a docile weapon. It stopped attacking to once again act as a personal shield.

Four blindfolded angels appeared in the haze on the horizon. Lucifer halted his pursuit of the Whisperer and frantically scanned our surroundings. In the end, he opted to run.

I charged after him. "What're you doing?" I dashed into his path and clamped his shoulders tight. "We're so close! Hadrian's almost dead."

"Do not forget yourself in the heat of the moment, Talon. Killing Hadrian is the great illusion. Death is but an escape unless he succumbs to the Fallen. The only way to accomplish that is to neutralize the titan."

"So you're giving up?"

"It's too late for that. I can't escape the city without Nightwing. The only path remaining is onward." He sidestepped and hastened to Dragonperch. Bandit shuffled nervously at its wall.

I fell in at his side. "Onward where? We need your power against the kraken."

"That's exactly what I mean to give you. Do you have the bit key?"

"What?"

"The bit key. I need it." Lucifer stopped. "Do you trust me, Talon?"

I swallowed. Ran my eyes over the ruins of Oldtown, the dueling angels, the usurper nestled within tentacle and shadow. "Hell of a time to ask for a leap of faith," I told him.

"Times like these are the only ones that matter."

I snorted in response to his endless wit. For better or worse, I'd tied my fate to Lucifer's. I wasn't going to abandon him just because he was down. I removed the golden cartridge from my inventory and handed it to him.

Saint Peter flickered onto the field of battle. "*That* will be quite enough," he decreed. Decimus, chest bloodied, backed away from the melee. The saint frowned, first at him then at the rogue Fallen. "I can't say I approve of them."

Lucifer waved an arm and Otho and Vitus joined the idle standoff.

Peter paged through several menus to get updates on current events. He eyed all active characters in the vicinity harshly, including myself. Part of me hoped he was here to save the day, but my practical side knew better.

"You found the link to Hadrian?" I asked. "From Loras?"

Hadrian stood firm within the titan's grasp, taking advantage of the break by chugging health and spirit potions. He didn't seem overly concerned with the saint's presence. As before, the kraken paused its offensive rather than risk the developer's wrath.

"Saint Loras is not here," answered Peter unequivocally. The saint's glare fixed on Lucifer. "A glitched persona cannot freely enter a hub undetected."

"But you've got to see it was Hadrian."

"I saw a bug in the game code, an unintended behavior—nothing more. Christian is looking into the matter."

Lucifer's expression softened. I completely deflated.

"You told him?"

"He's the owner of the company," said Peter. "Of course I told him." His eyes flitted to the bit key in Lucifer's hand. "It is a crime even to possess that."

The devil smiled evenly. "Look around, Peter. Nobody here is without sin."

"You should be ashamed of yourself. Of this farce. All that's been done for you, all that you..." The saint gathered himself and cleared his throat. "You shouldn't have that."

"You're gonna be happy that I do."

Peter didn't budge. "Let us end this here, *Lucifer*. Give yourself up. There doesn't need to be any more fighting."

"You don't care about me," countered Lucifer. "You care about angels fighting angels. It'll ruin your precious *game*."

"That's not true."

"You have only material desires, yet I act to defend my very being."

Four angels, newly arrived, set down on the ground beside the saint. Longinus, with an ivory trident. Marius, a bronze spear. Gaius whirled a mean marble hammer. Severus was the only angel besides Decimus with two weapons, small iron axes.

"I can call them off if you stand down," assured Peter.

"Spare the rod?" Lucifer sneered. "You would strip me of everything that defines me."

The saint frowned. "This. Isn't. You."

The statement was met with an indignant laugh. "Dearest Saint Peter, it is pride that will be your downfall. You don't control the angels any more than you retain control of Haven. You can't stop the angels because he won't let you."

"Who?"

"You're not the only active saint in the sim."

"Yes, I am. I—" Peter stroked his beard. "No, no, you speak of Loras again. I would be alerted to his presence."

Lucifer showed his teeth. "What do you think it is that you're feeling?"

The saint stepped back, a minor dither. I didn't see or hear anything out of the ordinary, but I did get a sense that something was now lurking just out of sight. My intuition skill? I checked Lucifer's hands to see what he was fiddling with. The blue gemstone from the snake's body.

Peter's mustache perked. "What... is... happening?" His body flickered out for a fraction of a second.

"What did you do?" I growled.

"Not I," said Lucifer.

Peter whirled around, looking for some unseen attacker. "Loras? Not in form but in function."

"How right you are," answered the devil, realization dawning across his face. "A Trojan. Not an entity but a programming routine."

Saint Peter jerked around. "This can't be! This—"

He snapped out of existence again. This time, he didn't come back.

Hadrian chortled. "Well, I thought he'd *never* stop talking."

With the suppressing presence gone, all five of the untainted angels came for Lucifer.

1490 Power Stone

Otho and Vitus snapped into action. Scythe and cane blurred against the host of angelic weapons. Holy and unholy clashed in a barrage of sight and sound.

"We're out of time," said Lucifer. "The saints have been compromised." He rushed to the base of Dragonperch. "Do you trust Bandit?"

"What?" I asked. "Of course. She's my pet."

"Yes, but do you trust her absolutely? With your life?"

As we converged on the mountain bongo, I patted her shoulder. "No question."

Lucifer nodded and placed the blue gemstone on her forehead, the capstone to the V of her horns.

"What is that?"

"The enemy utilizes a Trojan virus, but we have a Trojan horse. Or bongo, in this case."

As the crystal floated in place, he brought his staff around and pressed the magical azure tip to Bandit's head.

"What are you doing?"

"I'm hacking her asset ID. Dragons don't exist in the world yet—you know that—but some facets of them have been created.

The only way to instance them is to piggyback off an already existing asset."

Clever. Sneaking one asset in with another. A Trojan horse indeed.

An ivory trident came at Lucifer's head. He whipped around and countered the blow with his staff. Vitus hooked Longinus, cane around arm, and pulled the angel back into the scrum.

While Bandit was disconnected from Lucifer's power, her legs wavered. I braced her large body and examined the gemstone on her forehead.

[Dr5g0nsh5rd]
Deep-blue crystal shard.

Lucifer returned his staff's stone to the shard. Strength surged through Bandit. She recovered and stood straighter, but the angels kept coming.

Severus kicked Otho's leg out and lunged for Lucifer. The witchwood staff parried one axe, then two. The angel caught Lucifer with a knee to the stomach. He spun, axes becoming blurs. I moved to parry but he was too fast. The first axe chunked a cut from the witchwood. The second blade landed square onto the heart of the gemstone.

The power core of Lucifer's staff spiderwebbed. A small explosion forced us all aground. Bandit faltered on shaky legs. Lucifer skidded away in the dirt, disbelief painted on his features. Severus, who'd taken the brunt of the explosion, recovered a dropped axe and faced Lucifer. Otho and Vitus walled Lucifer off as he backed away.

"I'll do it myself!" shouted Hadrian, crouching on a low tentacle and pointing. "Get him now!" The kraken approached Lucifer's back.

"I'm sorry, Talon. My power... it's unstable."

My efforts to prop Bandit up failed and she collapsed. She hit the floor with a whine. Blood snorted from her nose.

"You've got to save her!" I said. "Finish whatever you were doing. Or undo it."

"I can't." The blue crystal on his staff began sparking and emitting stray beams of energy. It took great effort for him to contain it.

"The last of your magic!" I cried. "Use the last of your magic to save her!"

"It's your turn to pick up the battle. Remember, I chose you for a reason."

"But I can't save Bandit! I'm not a hacker!"

"No, Talon, you are much, much more."

Lucifer clenched his jaw as the kraken bore down on him. While he no longer had the magical saber extending from his staff, the blue crystal at the top was surging with energy. He waited stoically, channeling the power and gauging the sea monster's stride, before launching into a sprint. Lucifer hopped a tentacle, somersaulted under another, dove away from a crushing attack, and jammed his weapon down the kraken's throat.

[Luc1f3r] cast Azure Ruin

Azure Ruin overload!

[Luc1f3r] dealt 3,003 damage to [Kraken]

(5,473/20,000)

The raw unbridled might of the explosion rocked the titan backward and knocked Hadrian aside. The sound of the kraken's wail was deafening. The beast smacked his appendages together in a mighty clap. Lucifer escaped the danger with an impossible series of twirls and flips.

He wasn't, however, completely unscathed. His prized witchwood staff no longer held a crystal at its head. Glittering blue rain sparkled around him as he retreated.

Beside us, the battling angels were a mesmerizing sight, each string of strikes and parries a miracle of speed and precision. The Fallen must've been boosted somehow because they'd so far held their own against five of their brethren. As Lucifer backed away from the kraken, Decimus nodded his way. Marius and Gaius broke off.

"I've done what I can, Talon," said Lucifer. "I'm sorry it wasn't enough."

The marble hammer came down. Lucifer pixelated and disappeared. The blindfolded angel turned slowly in disbelief.

I sprinted to block the other angel's path. "Stop," I pleaded. "He's not what you think he is."

"This does not concern you, resident." Marius rammed his spear to the ground. A shock wave of energy burst outward and rattled Lucifer's defenses. His blurred form sparked and appeared several yards away, running north. Both angels turned and followed.

Out of frantic desperation I activated deadshot. The skill points expired with an error sound. Offensive skills couldn't be used against angels. There was practically no recourse against them.

Hadrian returned to his perch on the kraken. Seemingly satisfied with the angels giving chase, he refocused his attention on us and lumbered over. I wanted to help Lucifer, but didn't know what I could do. Behind me, Bandit whimpered, attempting and failing to stand. I couldn't leave the girl. She was helpless.

I set my jaw and stared down the titan. We'd managed considerable damage thus far, just about three-quarters of its total health. A valiant effort that proved the beast was far from invincible. I just wondered if we were up to finishing the task.

> [Lash] cast Warrior Spirit

Our spirit points refilled. The buff was much more than raw resources, though. It was that little bit of morale needed for everyone to join together in the struggle at hand. I cocked my head in thanks. It was a start. Good to see Izzy getting some juice too.

"We can fight this thing," I asserted. "All of us—what's left of us—together."

Dune and Lash flanked the titan's back. Izzy stood to the side, between the angels and the kraken. I crouched beside Bandit and scrubbed her cheek, sorry I'd already used a healing vial on her.

"Don't worry, girl. If we die, we die together."

Between hyperactive breathing, she blinked and fixed on me, strangely prescient.

In the shadow of Magnus Dragonrider, I rose and pointed the titanslayer at the great beast.

With Marius and Gaius in pursuit of Lucifer, the collision of angels was taking a nasty turn. The golden cane of Vitus smacked an ivory trident away. Longinus was slow to recover, because a blink later Otho's black scythe caught his cheek. Decimus smacked the killing blow away. Severus' axes flashed and caught Otho's back. Vitus hooked one axe and sent it clattering against stone. Otho kicked Decimus. As Longinus stabbed his trident, Otho sidestepped. Vitus caught the three-pronged weapon with his cane and jerked it aside.

Severus, disarmed of one axe, moved to parry the strike. His axe smacked the golden cane away, but he failed to account for his brother's weapon. The commandeered trident sank into his chest.

Severus faltered. A wild axe swing missed its mark. Otho used the opening to bury his scythe into his exposed back. Severus went stiff. Seams of cruel light cracked across his flesh. He opened his mouth wide and pure energy burst from his body a second before he exploded. When we recovered from the shock wave, he was gone.

One of the Golden Seven was no more.

I didn't have the acrobatics of Lucifer, but I was no slouch. As the kraken neared, I dashed up Dragonperch, transitioned to a wall run higher along the ancient bricks, and vaulted out and over the kraken's reach. I bore down like a guided air-to-ground missile. While the kraken's maw was out of reach, I had a clear shot at the top of its head.

Despite a wash of shadow slowing the blow, the dragonspear punched into the kraken's body.

```
Combo!
Critical Hit!
You dealt 234 damage to [Kraken]
(5,239/20,000)
```

My teammates charged the titan's exposed backside.

```
Surprise!
[Dune] dealt 124 damage to [Kraken]
[Lash] dealt 147 damage to [Kraken]
[Izzy] dealt 176 damage to [Kraken]
(4,792/20,000)
```

A meaty tentacle knocked me to the ground.

```
110 damage
Fall damage!
17 damage
Health: 126/300
Stun!
You are stunned. You may not use skills, move,
or attack for 20 seconds.
```

The dragonspear rolled on distant grass.

The kraken spun on a dime, a series of tentacles trailing its body in a beautiful spiral of destruction. Izzy was out of range and Dune successfully recoiled from harm's way. Lash planted her heavy shield and spun in a circle, deflecting the swinging wrecking ball in an astounding show of power.

Only the kraken's other tentacles followed close behind. They rammed Lash across the grounds. The white knight landed with a crunch, helmet jarred loose and bouncing in the grass. Her painted eyes squeezed in pain.

```
Arm Break!
[Kraken] dealt 220 damage to [Lash]
```

My vision was a haze. I tried to shake off the sluggishness but it was suffocating. I watched in horror as Izzy and Dune moved to protect Lash from the kraken's raging fury. They both took heavy hits. Lash couldn't hold a weapon. She was only spared by retreating with the others. It became a game of cat and mouse, with one of the three putting themselves in danger to save the other two. Hadrian grinned in anticipation from his bestial perch.

My stun wore off, but the swimming in my head didn't.

Venom filled my blood. I loathed the thought of seeing more of my teammates struck down, but I had only rancor for the cause of this destruction. My vision went red. With the dragonspear in the grass, I realized I'd subconsciously palmed the next best weapon in my inventory: the assassin needle.

Was that what Lucifer had seen in me? The same potential

afforded by Saint Peter? I propped myself up on wobbly hands and knees, tunnel vision zeroing in on Hadrian. I hated him more than anything. If I could suddenly end him, his hold on the kraken would evaporate. Maybe the titan would be easier to defeat when left to its baser instincts.

I opened my player menu and scrutinized the choices laid out before me.

Ghost, the runner.

Pathfinder, the min/maxer.

And, of course, the ultimate in killing efficiency: Assassin.

I could do it right now. Select the title and look for an opening. I had the weapon that, if well timed, could end this. Maybe it wouldn't save my friends, maybe it wouldn't defeat the kraken, but I could find a way for my blade to beat the shadow to Hadrian's heart.

Was that enough, or did I want something more than that?

What had Lucifer said to me? I wasn't a hacker, I was much, much more.

A few yards away, Bandit whimpered and kicked in the dirt. The girl was in pain and peril; I was having a hell of a time figuring out how to save her from either. But as my eyes met hers, something inside me fluttered. For the briefest of moments, there was a crack in my resolve. My enmity dissolved. My burning city, the invading rogues and undine, the blind angels and the absentee saints—I'd been focusing on all the wrong things.

I wasn't doing this for the carnage, the power, or the applause. I was doing it for Lash, bones broken and still fighting. For Izzy, damaged and hurt in more ways than one, and still a tougher badass than I'd ever known. For Dune, the stoic friend who never made a big deal about always being there in support. There was Kyle, and Trafford, and Errol, and a ton of other people who were here because they all believed in me. And yes, that trust was even shared with a stray mountain bongo who'd followed me home one day.

Choosing assassin was the coward's way out.

I blinked at my screen. Faced Bandit. I dropped the assassin needle and put my palm on her rough fur, felt her ragged breaths.

There was a time when Saint Peter was surprised I'd taken her as a pet. When Lucifer saw me using skills in unintended ways. When I dared defy the very angels and titans themselves. There was even a time, very recently, when I had refused to accept the paltry legendary abilities presented to me. I'd taken action, used the knife handling scroll, to afford myself another choice, and even then I defied the programming.

Lucifer's words. I wasn't a hacker. I was more than that. I was a developer. I was an evolution.

Hadrian finally grew weary of chasing my teammates around. He'd hurt them all, with nary a scratch to show for it. Catching me kneeling by my pet, he grinned with predatory hunger. I wasn't strong enough to carry Bandit away. The kraken spun and came for us. Hadrian knew I couldn't leave her.

I climbed to my feet empty-handed. Faced down the charging behemoth. Adrenaline surged through my body, causing me to visibly shake. I leaned down and rested my palm on Bandit's head. On the dragonshard. The energy from my body seemed to feed the crystal.

I don't know if it was willpower, a guardian angel, or pure, dumb luck, but a fourth option appeared in my legendary ability menu: Dragonrunner.

With a flash of blue, Bandit shuddered. Bones popped and skin stretched unnaturally. Her fur didn't follow suit so it left her with thick leathery hide. Spiny nettles protruded from her shoulders and back. Eyes went yellow and already massive horns elongated. Large, membraned wings burst from her back and a spiked tail grew from her body. As the mountain bongo's jaw lengthened, she bared a string of razor-sharp teeth.

The girl retained her chestnut-brown color, iconic cream body stripes, and V-shaped horns, but besides that, she was nothing like the old Bandit. My pet was now a hulking dragon twice the size of Nightwing.

She opened her mouth and released a waking roar of thunder that shook Oldtown. Then she breathed in and spat a beam of light that blasted into the titan's body with pure elemental wrath.

> [Bandit] dealt 2800 damage to [Kraken]
> (1992/20,000)

The point-blank discharge upheaved the massive behemoth. The kraken flailed and upended, throwing Hadrian and the shadowguard. Bandit's colossal paws pounded the dirt beside me. She pounced on the mass of tentacles and blubber like a dog finally catching a car and finding it unworthy. Claws raked deep as she shoveled teeth into the quivering body, dealing epic damage.

Lash buffed us with a war cry. Dune nocked multiple arrows and fired. Izzy hooked icebergs around the beast so it couldn't wiggle away. I recovered my dragonspear between dueling angels and overloaded dash and deadshot for a savage blow.

The notorious kraken never stood a chance.

1500 Altered Beast

Brothers in Black Reputation -999 (MAXED)

The dead titan collapsed under its own weight. Blue flames washed over Lash with muted sound effects, healing her broken body. The white knight finally matched my level. I wasn't surprised.

What did take me off guard was a similar effect consuming Bandit's dragon form. Despite pets not having visible progression markers or consuming XP as far as I knew, Bandit had leveled up.

Hadrian, on the other hand, tripped to the ground. A curved horn of bone the length of his arm bounced from his possession. The Squid's Tooth. The embattled Whisperer crawled on his elbows to recover it. The loose item vibrated in the dirt and spun, faster and faster, until it fractured and exploded, pieces ejecting into nothingness.

Beside us, a rumble came from deep within the kraken's belly. Even the angels stopped to watch as the husk of the leviathan chunked into squishy pieces of blubber that bounced away. I picked a couple of them.

Loot:
10 silver bars

Loot:
[Atlantean Anchor]

As we emptied the blubber chunks, they faded away. There was plenty to go around, including what we set aside for fallen faction mates. But loot distribution wasn't the biggest problem we had left to address.

Izzy, Dune, and I converged on the spymaster as he regained his feet. Most of us were battle worn, but his monster was gone. He backed away, head swiveling from one angry threat to the next. The shadowguard snaked over his body and sneered.

Hadrian the Whisperer turned and ran.

Dune launched an arrow. Even in retreat, the shadow armor blocked the attack. My pursuit was stalled as an angel's ivory trident landed at my feet with a rumble. Vitus was thrown into Izzy and they both face planted to the ground.

Seeing his opening, Hadrian attempted to slip by Lash as she searched for her lost helmet. A tactical error, since the level up had fully healed her arm. Her giant cleaver swept the Whisperer off his feet. If it hadn't been for his shadow armor, he'd be missing a leg.

"You're weak," spat Lash, charging up her weapon.

Hadrian scurried to his feet and bolted for the river. The white knight hefted the weapon overhead and spiked it down. The blade glanced off Hadrian's side. The force of the blow drove the cleaver downward and embedded it deep in the muddy bank.

The shadowguard stretched as it attempted to cross the river. Instead of fully blinking out, it turned in confusion as the glowing sword pinned a piece of it to the ground. The shadow yelped and slowed its crossing.

"No!" snapped Hadrian. "Get me all the way!"

Longinus bowled by me as he rushed to pick up his trident. Bandit reared and readied for a fight. I tugged her neck to keep us clear until I could help Izzy up. As we shied away from the encroaching angel skirmish, Bandit grumbled a warning their way.

"Leave them be, girl. They're more powerful than they look."

She snorted, unimpressed.

Longinus reached for his weapon. Vitus hooked the golden cane around his enemy's neck and stopped him short. Decimus swung in. Still hooked around Longinus, the cane parried one of Decimus' swords. The other blade of silver bit into the fallen angel's gut.

Otho lunged to save his dark brother. The black scythe cracked against a silver sword. Vitus pulled away from Decimus and twisted his cane. Longinus brought his trident around, burying the tips into Vitus' chest. Enraged, Otho shot around and took Longinus' trapped head clean off.

The resounding explosions of force buffeted and blinded us. When the light cleared, two more angels had been slain. Only Decimus and Otho were alive.

To the dismay of the shadowguard, Hadrian forced his way across the Albula. Izzy summoned a wall of ice beside the cleaver. The magic tore the shadow back to us, now separated from its master. On the far side of the drained river, Hadrian sprinted away while Dune took potshots at him. The shadow demon, abandoned yet loyal, managed to stretch enough to knock the arrows down.

> **Talon:** *Kyle, we need your gauntlet.*

From the roof of Dragonperch two hundred feet up, Kyle released the holy item. It bounced on the mud beside Lash, who was all too happy to equip it. Still helmetless, she tested the fingers of the fitted glove before showing her teeth and beating the shadow back to wherever it had come from.

Instead of sticking around for the show, I willed the doors of Dragonperch open on a hunch. I hurried into the tower, keeping an eye on my notifications.

> Holy weakness!
> [Lash] dealt 88 damage to [Shadowguard]
> Holy weakness!
> [Lash] dealt 78 damage to [Shadowguard]
> [Shadowguard] is defeated
> 563 XP awarded

> **Loot:**
> [Void Pearl]

I opened the ground-floor armory and grabbed the dusty saddle. It didn't slot into my inventory so I lugged it outside by hand. When I applied the item to Bandit, it auto-equipped.

> **Izzy:** *Kyle, fill this river back up before Hadrian gets away!*

The dragon saddle fit Bandit's beast form perfectly. I smiled like a kid as I pulled myself up and onto the worn leather seat.

"Go get him, girl."

Bandit zeroed in on Hadrian, now escaping into the busy neighborhood of Hillside. Her body snaked to her prey as my eye caught the standoff between the final two angels. Decimus was cut and bloodied. Red soaked his white garments. One-on-one against a hacked Fallen, I wasn't optimistic about his chances.

Otho's head jerked aside, alarmed by some distant emergency. Instead of engaging Decimus, he pointed his scythe to the air and took off. The blindfolded angel immediately pursued.

Decimus wasn't the last of the Golden Seven. Marius and Gaius had given Lucifer chase. He must've been in trouble if Otho was hurrying to his aid.

Bandit loped toward the river and bounded high into the air. Powerful wings beat as we took flight. Internally, I struggled with everything that had happened and what needed to happen next.

I couldn't accept the sacrifice.

"Can you get him from here, girl?" I asked through the whipping wind.

The dragon's body banked as she adjusted to the position of her target. The Whisperer hurried to lose himself within the populated neighborhood of Hillside. From this distance, he appeared more unremarkable than ever. Just another frightened man scrambling all too slowly for his life. Before he could make it to cover, Bandit stretched toothy jaws. A focused beam of light consumed Hadrian.

I jerked the reins sharply away from the attack.

"Whoa, there! We don't wanna kill him."

Hadrian collapsed in a sputtering heap. He was still alive, but barely.

> Oldtown has been successfully defended!
> 3 HQXP awarded

As we veered away, my allies crossed the filled river on a makeshift bridge of ice. Izzy was the first ashore.

> **Talon:** *Make sure to keep him breathing.*
> **Izzy:** *Aw, no fun. Can I at least stick mermaid claws under his fingernails?*

Yeesh, remind me never to piss off the frost mage. Hadrian

lay on the ground, stunned. The combat log confirmed he wouldn't die yet. The warrior in me was disappointed, but things had gone according to plan. At least in part. With the Whisperer defeated and subdued, there was one last thing to take care of.

Bandit cracked across the sky like lightning, hot on the heels of the angels.

1510 Final Fight

The angels were swift flyers but they remained low to the ground. Having made it north out of Oldtown, Stronghold's impressive buildings became obstacles they needed to slalom. I urged Bandit to gain altitude and give us a dragon's-eye view of the city.

Unsurprisingly, Stronghold was sealed. Watchmen crowded the gates. Legionnaires lined the battlements and stood in formation outside the walls. I couldn't believe the army was actually on the offensive. Along the distant tree line, a reduced goblin horde beat war drums.

In hindsight, I figured it all for a diversionary tactic, a way to occupy the city watch during our little tower defense. But part of me couldn't dismiss the siege that easily. If I were a betting man, I'd wager General Azzyrk was awaiting a signal from Hadrian to make a move. It was a signal that would never come.

Although the west gate was the one closest to Oldtown, it was also the busiest point of defense in the city. Lucifer wouldn't be able to use it to escape. I flew past, eyeing the alleys between structures lining the Circus. A flash of white robes chasing black. I'd spotted Decimus and Otho.

"The north river gate," I concluded. It was broken and no longer in need of defense. Bandit snorted through her mighty dragon snout and closed with the ground. She swooped along Stronghold's outer wall on a vector to beat the angels to the river.

I leaned forward in the saddle, muscles taut. Lucifer had risked it all for this showdown. He hadn't just offered his support, he'd sacrificed Nightwing, the Fallen, the dragonshard. He'd even put his very existence on the table, a risk of deletion, living or dying by the draw of a single hand.

It was a heck of a poker play. Hell, the recent months had been an intricate chess gambit, perfectly executed until the end. Except... were we at the endgame yet?

As Bandit sailed toward the river, I frowned and scanned the well-guarded capitol buildings at the head of the Forum. Lucifer's request for the bit key had bothered me. What would a gold cartridge have to do with embedding the dragonstone on Bandit's forehead? Unless it was for something else.

I pulled the reins. The mountain-bongo-turned-dragon diverted away from the wall and toward a new target: the Pantheon. It was a risk, a loss of valuable seconds, but it had to be done. As we dove low, rows and rows of centurions and legionnaires gazed upward. As promised, Saint Peter had wisely defended the Pantheon from intrusion. The city itself was safe, at the cost of inaction by the city watch. They were rightly daunted by dragon fear, but they knew my face well.

Amid the distraction, a jumble of pixels glitched up the stone steps of the column-lined portico. The invisibility function was less effective than usual, as if Lucifer's hacked code had been compromised by the angels. The imperfect deception was more than adequate considering how many eyes were on me.

As expected, none of the angel statues were fixed atop their Pantheon perches. Three of the columns lining the entrance walkway now lay toppled, the angels and their housings permanently destroyed.

Marius and Gaius silently drifted a yard above the ground and entered after Lucifer, unmolested by the city watch. Bandit touched down between the army, large feet climbing the stairway but pausing at the summit. Her hulking mass couldn't squeeze between the portico columns and entrance.

I begrudgingly dismounted. I felt downright invincible on her back, but it disconnected me from the action. I needed to get inside.

"Don't stop the other angels from coming in," I told her, rubbing her chin. Stray hairs gave way to leathery hide but the motion, even if exaggerated in length, felt natural. The massive dragon purred and wiggled an ear.

Having the reassuring trust of the stationed soldiers, I drew the dragonspear and sprinted inside. The inner portico was quiet. I hurried to the doorway and zoned into the rotunda.

Lucifer fended a bronze spear off with his cracked staff. He blinked to the side as a hammer smashed the floor.

"Stop this!" I yelled.

Behind me, Otho entered and intercepted Gaius like a comet. The angel dropped his marble hammer as they slammed into the far wall. Lucifer parried another spear strike—impressive considering Decimus had always auto-hit me. Then again, while Lucifer wasn't the oldest player in Haven, he'd taken advantage of a trick, long ago moving his profile to the permanent servers. No one knew how many wipes he'd avoided; his hacked name tag forever obscured a level.

The most powerful player in the afterlife was one thing, but it was only a matter of time before the reality of going one-on-one against an angel set in. Bronze spear clashed against witchwood over and over. The angel's weapon was faster. The spear tip gouged the devil's side as Decimus entered the rotunda.

The strike was a costly one, but it gave Otho the opening he needed. He blasted off the wall and buried his scythe into Marius' back. The angel screamed and collapsed as white light overtook him. Outside, another pillar crumbled to the street.

Decimus charged in and swung. Otho's scythe blocked the downward slash, but the dual-wielded upswing struck true. Decimus cleanly sliced off Otho's arm at the shoulder. The black scythe clattered to the tile. Otho bounced against the wall, black eyes blinking with cold calculus at his stump.

Gaius broke away from the stone wall, rock crumbling from the impact crater. He recovered his hammer and stood over Otho. Decimus turned, blind gaze lasering on Lucifer, who stood at the Oculus typing away. Beside him, the gold cartridge rested in the terminal slot.

"I hope you're right about the saints, Talon. They're our only chance."

Decimus stepped onto the altar. "Lucifer, you are in violation of the terms of service. You will be expunged from Haven."

The devil's finger loudly rapped the Enter key. Saint Peter stumbled into the room and flinched at the sudden transition. Decimus raised his sword in execution.

"Stay your hand!" cried the community manager.

Decimus didn't turn his head or break away. He simply froze in place, silver sword gleaming in the light of the Oculus.

Saint Peter hastily took in his surroundings and determination overtook his features. He stomped to the Oculus and retrieved the bit key. The broad ray of light shining from above blinked and dimmed slightly. As he folded the gold cartridge into his robe, Peter studied Lucifer with a haggard gaze.

"You hacked the game... to save the game."

The devil nodded curtly.

"We have Hadrian in custody," I added. "We fended off the assault on Oldtown, defeated the kraken, and exposed the plot to usurp Haven."

"And what good is exposure?" asked a cruel voice. Another cream-colored robe striped with maroon blinked into the sanctified room.

"I don't know how he's doing it," said Lucifer. "A virus, I believe. I can't root it out of the system, but I was able to release its hold on you."

Saint Loras glowered at the freed saint, the stalled angels, and the apparent victors. He was especially disgruntled to find me still breathing.

"Exposure is everything," I replied. "The people have seen what you've done."

"And so what? Stronghold fends off another assault for the time being, but Shorehome and Oakengard have already fallen. The core city stands alone and outnumbered. You're too late to save it."

"If that's true, why bother showing your face? It's risky opening yourself up to the hub."

Loras shrugged. "It is my mission. Decimus!" The false saint pointed to Lucifer. The angel took a breath of air and tensed his raised arm.

"Halt!" commanded Peter.

Decimus froze in place. Loras grumbled and raised curled fingers toward Peter. Lightning shot forth. The old man countered with lightning of his own.

"You can't hurt me, Loras," said Peter coolly. Loras reddened and called off the attack. Peter dusted his robes and cleared his throat. "But your disdain is interesting. Who are you? I'm guessing you have a remote operator. You're not still Larry, are you?"

"That fool?" he spat. "He almost junked the whole operation."

"Whoever you are, it was a mistake coming here. As a remote, your control priority is subservient to mine." Saint Peter twisted his hands to access developer sub menus. "It's just a matter of isolating the control module and..." Saint Loras grinned. Peter jutted his lips out. "I don't understand."

"And why would you?" Loras wicked sweat from his short black hair. "You think I'd come to Stronghold if it was that easy?"

Peter stuttered. "But this is impossible. You're not responding to the network."

"Talon," said Lucifer, "use your developer menu."

My brow furrowed. "I can't."

"Now," he urged.

I tried to access it.

```
DEVELOPER CONSOLE
>> STATUS
>> LOCKED
```

"Whoa, it opens. Except I'm locked out."

"What?" Lucifer double-checked the console.

I tried typing common commands at the prompt. "It's not working... We enabled it on both ends. It should be accessible. Wait—"

I swiped to the Everchat menu and saw the notification from Tad. I hailed him. He picked up almost immediately. "Talon! I've been trying to reach you."

"Been a little busy. We got Hadrian. Loras is with us."

"The developer menu..." urged Lucifer.

"Right," I said. "I'm still locked out of the dev menu."

"Is this him?" asked an off-screen voice. Tad Lonnerman nodded. "Let me see." Tad handed his camera over. A man with blond hair and blue eyes assumed the Everchat interface. "Hello, Tad. I mean, Talon, I suppose."

I blinked. "You're Christian Everett."

"Unfortunately."

Lucifer stepped off the altar and approached. His voice broke. "Daddy?"

Christian tensed. "Lucy? Is that you?"

Lucifer ran to my side. His face shuddered as he gazed on the Everchat window. "It's been so long."

Christian smiled longingly. "Oh, honey, I see you're still

hacking my world."

"Don't hate me."

The CEO's voice cracked into a nervous laugh. "On the contrary," he said softly. "I finally understand what you've been up to this whole time. I've been blinded by my own vision." Christian turned the camera to a dusty external hard drive on his shelf. "I've kept it the whole time. No longer hooked up, of course, no longer housing your mind, but I kept it. Without word from you, it was the only thing I had left to comfort me."

Though the angels wore blank expressions, Loras was shocked. I was too. Lucifer was the CEO's daughter. It explained so much, yet raised just as many questions.

"You should have said something," I chided Peter.

"I couldn't tell anyone," said the saint. "She was a child. It was immoral—illegal now. She couldn't have known what she was signing up for. We put age minimums in place to prevent this from ever happening again."

"She was the only shred of family I had left!" cried the bereft CEO. His head shook frantically. "Haven was to be our home. A place we could finally be happy, devoid of the harsh realities of what we call life. No sickness, no disease. The afterlife would be better, would be forever. Finally, I could use my love of games and computers to help my family. My beautiful daughter." He stared at her and tears welled in his eyes. "You were the last to die, the first to make use of the technology. You were the only one I could save."

Loras callously sniggered. "I should've known you had a seed in the system the whole time."

"Be quiet!" snapped Peter, gesturing toward the rogue saint.

Loras stiffened.

I was still stuck on Lucifer's identity. "But the devs have constantly tried to delete her," I said.

"The hacked construct," said Christian. "Never my daughter."

Loras fought off Saint Peter's attack. "A useless gesture. You previously proved we can cancel each other out."

Lucifer's face went rigid. "The dev menu. We need the dev menu."

On the other end, Tad explained to Christian what we'd done. Loras interrupted on ours.

"What would that do, give you the power of the saints? So what?"

"No," cut in Christian. He focused on me. "Talon, you're different. You're a developer—they're just along for the ride. You have access to the source. As big a responsibility as saint mode is, developers within the game are something greater."

Loras twisted his face and swiped his hands. The Everchat interface winked out.

"No!" I snapped. "How do I access the dev menu?"

Saint Peter rapped invisible options and the interface flashed back on. Christian was talking, but the audio popped in and out.

"Menu... in the... first-time access."

"What?" I asked. "How do I open the menu?"

"Access... password is..."

The screen pixelated and blinked off again. As Peter and Loras struggled, a notification popped up.

Everchat connection terminated

"Get him back," prodded Lucifer.

I hailed Tad again. The saints swiped through invisible menus in an invisible war, fingers attempting to outrace the other. The Everchat signal connected and dropped multiple times.

"Decimus," pressed Loras.

The angel took a single step forward. Lucifer backed away.

"You will... hold," countered Peter through gritted teeth.

The angel complied. As far as I knew, saints couldn't activate the Golden Seven or choose their targets, but it appeared they were able to influence whether or not they carried out their judgment, at least temporarily.

Amid the struggling saints, my Everchat hail was once again canceled. "It's pointless," I told Lucifer. "The saints are just canceling out each other's moves. Neither one is making headway against the other."

Lucifer approached my side. "A stalemate favors Loras. I'm not in imminent danger of being deleted, but there's no way we'll keep a signal long enough to talk to my father."

"But we need the password to activate the dev menu."

"So it would appear." Lucifer pulled away, lowering his hood. His hands rested on the split head of his staff where the blue gemstone had resided. Whatever leftover energy still under his control thrummed, much more muted than before. "What did he say about you? Developers within the game have the potential to be greater than the saints..."

I grumbled. "What's greater than a saint?"

"A savior."

I rolled my eyes.

"I know you hate that label, Talon. When I mentioned it last, I was referring to my father entering Haven. If he's to be the second coming, maybe you're the first."

"Come on," I spat. "For just one time, stop speaking in riddles."

The devil flashed his teeth. "I know the password: iddqd."

I arched an eyebrow but didn't object. I quickly typed it into the developer console.

```
DEVELOPER CONSOLE
>> STATUS
>> UNLOCKED
>> MENU ENABLED
>> _
```

"I got a cursor! But..."

"My father's favorite game was Doom," explained Lucifer. "Primitive by all accounts, yet through his passion I was well acquainted with it. He called the community team's loadout saint mode and I figured, why not use Doom's god-mode cheat to counter it?"

Loras grunted in anger. Lightning arced from his fingers and sprayed us. Lucifer was forced behind his witchwood staff. Peter intervened, striking out with lightning of his own to shield me.

He wasn't fast enough.

Energy bolts popped against my flesh. I shuddered under the assault as Peter's shield took over. Air rushed through my lungs, my body threatened to shut down—but I noticed a funny thing about the attack's aftermath.

I didn't feel pain. There was no damage notification. I mean, I didn't feel invincible. My health wasn't even maxed after the previous battle damage. But a community team defense mechanism was ineffectual against me.

God mode.

I swiped back to the Everchat screen, somehow confident I could override Loras' signal intrusion. Then I cocked my head and wondered if that was even necessary. I opened the developer console. A cursor blinked, awaiting my input. I populated it with a thought.

`>> saints_`

I blinked at the menu that suddenly sprang up. It listed Saint Peter and Saint Loras, with options enabled for whoever was selected. I was overwhelmed with the implied significance. Never again could outside forces dictate internal Haven policy. That's the world Christian had envisioned. An independent one, free of the business realities of the analog sphere.

I used the menu to isolate Loras.

The rogue saint's face flushed. "What are you doing?"

"Maybe Lucifer's right about a virus," I said. "It doesn't list you as having an operator."

"That shouldn't be possible," assured Peter. "If there's a virus in the codebase, he might be able to operate a saint remotely without a record."

"Anything's possible, but you're the one who said he had no network response." I dug deeper into his status. "No packets are being sent. It's almost as if he has no connection to the outside at all. Like he's an AI."

"Now that *is* impossible," concluded Peter. "I know enough about programming to confidently say saint avatars have no behavior state machine. There's no logic at all, no fallback governance. Without an operator the saints aren't instanced."

"Get out of there!" frothed Loras. "Decimus, I'm ordering you to carry out your edict."

With Saint Peter countermanding him, the order was useless.

"If you're still bound by operator logic," I mused, "and nobody's behind the wheel, I wonder what would happen if I logged you off."

"No." Loras recoiled and waved an arm. I revoked his access. His attempt to teleport away was suspended. His eyes widened. "No."

I went to the bottom of the menu and kicked him from the world. Saint Loras was booted from Haven with barely a whimper.

Everyone in the rotunda waited a few moments before allowing themselves a breath. The silence proved the point. The battle for the city was over.

1520 Final Lap

We strolled down the grand portico stairs. Bandit waited on the road, reverted back to bongo form.

"Hey, girl," I said, patting her neck. "I suppose even legends deserve a rest."

She wagged her tail and let out a toot of noxious gas. I laughed and shoved her backside away before I passed out. She was a big cutey in her normal form, but I'd take on dragon breath over bongo farts any day of the week.

Approaching through the Forum were Izzy, Lash, and Dune. They kicked Hadrian ahead of them, arms and legs bound just loose enough to allow transport. The legion of soldiers parted and surrounded the incoming group. There'd be no escape for the great Whisperer of Shorehome. It was hard to think of a more satisfying conclusion to his story, but I would damn well try.

Behind me, angels rose to their lofty perches, Gaius on his Corinthian column and Decimus on the summit of the portico roof. The only other column not reduced to rubble had a decisive crack running up its length. That one belonged to Otho. Strangely, the wounded angel was absent.

Lucifer smiled conspiratorially as he approached with Saint Peter.

"I can take him from here," announced the white robe.

Izzy shoved Hadrian forward.

"I'll give escort if you don't mind," said Lucifer, silver runes twinkling on a field of black. "He needs to be on suicide watch. We wouldn't want him having an unfortunate accident and respawning to safety."

Hadrian growled as the two dragged him away.

It was strange, after everything, to see Lucifer waltzing around Stronghold as a normal citizen, accompanied by a saint of all people. I didn't believe in miracles and I suspected the hacker was due a reckoning. There was too much bad blood for someone, somewhere not to catch up with him. Still, Saint Peter finally believed in Lucifer's intentions. That was enough to postpone final judgment. For a time, anyway.

"Warden Jorah is a good man," I called out to them. "Tell him to give Hadrian the VIP treatment."

Hadrian flushed against everyone's laughter. If he was angry now, he had another thing coming. The spymaster was due to find out just how many people he'd crossed in his quest for godhood.

"If that's not a happy ending," said Dune, "I don't know what is."

Izzy punched his shoulder. "It wouldn't have been so happy without your backup."

He shrugged. "XP is XP."

I shook my head. The ranger couldn't take a simple compliment. I decided to put him on the spot. "Your people fought selflessly, Dune. You should all be proud."

"As should you," he returned without an ounce of wit. "You know, Talon, you're starting to make joining the Black Hats look tempting."

"The offer's always open."

He nodded. "Maybe I'll finally take you up on it. I need to talk to my people first. Stigg likes his freedom, and Caduceus would kill me if I didn't consult with her."

Lash laughed. "I'd say she earned that right. Bitch was a badass out there."

"From one badass to another," he replied with a charming smile. He flashed one last look at Hadrian being taken away and said, "I guess my work here is done." The ranger twirled his green cape and headed off.

Bandit trailed a short distance as we strode through the marketplace. After some jawing with Izzy, Lash drifted behind to get a better look at the bongo, now wearing a downsized dragon saddle. The physical transformation had been amazing. Everyone had questions. I only wished more Black Hats had been alive to witness it. Then again, I was sure the gossiping duo of Lash and Dune was sufficient to kick-start the legend. I was happy Bandit was getting a bit of the spotlight, too. Maybe we'd finally get that song.

"By my count," said Izzy suggestively, "that makes two titans you've brought down."

"*We've* brought down. They were both team efforts. Especially this one."

"True enough." We walked for a moment in silence before the frost mage cleared her throat. "You know... I hate to bring it up... But if we're going to war with Oakengard, it occurs to me that we still haven't seen or heard from their titan yet."

"You are *not* gonna bring me down to reality right now."

"What?" she asked with an innocent shrug.

"You know what you're doing. Keeping me focused. Preventing my head from swelling."

"*Trying to,* anyway." She chuckled.

I eyed her sharply.

"Hey, you said it."

I bumped my hip into hers to gently knock her aside. "Well, from one badass to another, I'm gonna celebrate this win. This was about good overcoming evil, breaking the chains of oppression, and refusing to kowtow to greed."

Her lips pouted. "Cheeseball."

I scoffed. "Buzzkill."

She broke into a grin. "Romantic."

I looped an arm around her shoulder and bent her low. As our lips met, she chuckled and kicked a leg into the air with decadent flair.

"Get a room," grumbled Lash, stomping by.

Izzy righted herself and straightened her robe, suddenly the paragon of modesty.

I sighed. "I'm surrounded by people who don't know how to have fun. I wish Kyle was here."

Bandit hoofed by with a snort.

Instead of heading straight into Oldtown, we stopped at the west gate. Legionnaires filled the battlements above. I pressed through the troops and called for them to open the double doors. Then I suddenly had a better idea.

```
DEVELOPER MENU
>> city watch_
```

Amazingly, army controls populated right before me. With several swipes and not a word, I recalled the troops to the city.

Izzy noted my hand gestures with interest. "What're you doing?"

"Have a look for yourself."

"I don't see anything."

I bit my lip. Some of the saint menus had been invisible to me too. It seemed special developer menus were for authorized eyes only.

"The army's still out there," I explained. "They're readying a defense, but I called them back in."

Lash widened black-lined eyes. "You can do that?"

"I guess I can now. I admit it's pretty crazy, even for me."

The great gates heaved open. City watchmen moved aside as legionnaires marched through. A centurion broke away from the head position and met with us.

"Good to see you're safe," said Gladius. His gold helmet swiveled as he surveyed the returning legions. Then he frowned and turned to me. "I'm sorry about not being able to intervene against Hadrian. Without explicit direction from the saints, we're not supposed to stray from our mandate to protect the city, and we're not supposed to assist in PvP wars."

"It's alright," I told him. "I suspect the Whisperer had long ago prepped his pieces so things would play out this way. He still has a few tricks I'd like to learn about."

"And what of the goblin horde?" asked the soldier.

"Azzyrk's army is small, and I don't want to get drawn into anything unnecessarily. Stronghold's been through enough today."

"They may force the issue."

"Maybe, but we still don't know their purpose here. With their numbers, there's no way to successfully storm the gates. I doubt they're here to give up their lives so easily. Hadrian's too careful for that. There has to be a bigger picture. I'm hesitant to act before we discover it. This could be an elaborate trap."

The head of the city watch nodded. "You might be right..."

"Let's give it some thought. For now, we've got a city in need of attention. We're getting a new addition to our humble jail. We need to draft strict security procedures."

"Understood." Gladius turned to his troops. As he directed them through the road he gave follow-up orders. "Keep watch on the walls. I want hourly reports on enemy positions. The north river gate has been secured but we'll need a team on permanent repairs. The rest of you will transition to cleanup, including a full dredging of the river. Stronghold needs us."

I marveled at the coordinated effort of dozens of troops. The city watch was an interesting asset. Invaluable, no doubt, but as NPCs and, more specifically, city guards, there were a lot of rules and hangups to their powers. With the new developer console, I wondered if I finally had a way to cut through the red tape.

After all, we'd need every advantage we could get. The undine forces may have fled but Prince Navoo would be back, the city was surrounded by a raving goblin horde, Hadrian's bandits were alive and respawned somewhere, Cleric Vagram was still on the run, and I didn't even want to think about the Oakengard army deciding to mobilize.

Together, we were powerful, but Stronghold wasn't the only unified force out there. We had to get better at this, and fast, because the stakes kept getting higher.

With the conflict ended, the last surviving Black Hats returned home. Oldtown was more ruinous than ever. After everyone had died, it was also depressingly empty. My heart hurt to look at it. Everything we'd built over the last month. Bodies still littered the streets, ashes mixed with blood in a hellish nightmare of destruction. Our shiny guildhall that was supposed to have its grand opening tonight wasn't so shiny. The other structures had fared worse. The barracks, completely destroyed. The brothel was in bad shape. Thankfully, Trafford's last stand had held it up. That saved the hassle of a lot of faction mates respawning elsewhere. A guild needed a heart for members to regroup and lick their wounds. Ours just happened to abound with bouncing boobs and wagging dongs.

"I need to check on Bravo Team," said Lash. "Crux should be in there." A grim expression overcame her. "Hex is still missing."

"We'll get her back," said Izzy.

I nodded with heartfelt determination. "And Grimwart and whoever else has fallen victim to Hadrian's plans. We'll get everything back to normal."

Lash clenched her jaw. She agreed with the sentiment but stopped short of inheriting our optimism.

I swallowed uncomfortably. She was ready to leave but stalled as I prepared to speak. "Lash... I know I've been tough on you lately." I licked my lips. "I know we don't always agree on the best course of action. Sometimes, you're right."

She snorted. "No worries, boss. I say what I think and don't pull punches. I'm never gonna change that."

"And I'd never want you to. Having someone to butt heads with keeps me honest. You've proven yourself over and over again. You risked level 10 today, multiple times, and that kind of XP is hard to come by. You'll always have a place in Oldtown."

She snickered. "Don't get all sappy on me, Talon. We know each other well enough by this point. Been through hell and back together. 'Nuff said."

She held out her hand and I clasped it tight. Bitch had a helluva firm shake. When she pulled away, she saluted. Her armored boots spun in the dirt and she headed into the brothel.

"Wow," said Izzy. "Looks like you two are no longer frenemies."

"I'm sure she's just in a sentimental mood."

Izzy's eyes twinkled as she studied me. "Hard not to be in a moment like this."

"And now that we're finally alone..."

I leaned down to kiss her. Inches away, her eyes went to full alert. "You're right! What was I thinking?"

I cocked my head.

Izzy's eyes widened in alarm. "Look out!"

The pixie pointed behind me. I spun around on a dime, drawing the dragonspear and readying for whatever was coming.

A lonesome breeze wafted over the midday ruins. There was no one here. Like I'd said, we were alone. When I turned to question Izzy, she was running from corpse to corpse, salvaging faction gear and looting mobs. A step ahead of me.

"You little..."

I broke into a sprint and collected what I could.

Given the makeup of the invaders, we recovered a pile of rogue gear and ocean resources. I would sort through it later and add the cream of the crop to the armory. Lots of people had fallen for this victory, and I wasn't about to gank it all for myself. Most of it was solid equipment for an army, but only a few items stood out.

For one, the Squid's Tooth was gone. I had known as much—we'd witnessed it shatter—however, I was hoping it could still be recovered somehow. As a special boss, I wasn't sure whether the kraken would respawn. If the statue of Orik was any measure, titans could never be completely erased from Haven. The only way to guarantee safety would be to acquire the soulstone, if it still existed.

Second was the Atlantean anchor. That bad boy was already

in my inventory.

> **[Atlantean Anchor]**
> Ancient ship anchor for mooring to unexplored depths.

As with the dusty saddle, the description was ineffectually vague. Given what I'd learned thus far about the afterlife, the obtuse utility signified the item was either completely worthless or a priceless artifact. I added it to my list of things to research.

Finally, one of the shadowguards had dropped a void pearl. My whole body tensed with excitement when I imagined the possibilities. Void magic seemed to create black holes and allow shadow walking. I only hoped Kyle could slot it into Dragonperch somewhere.

When the field of battle was finally cleared of loot, we wandered back to the tower. I checked the headquarters and faction screens to see what we still had left after it all.

Black Hats

Faction Level: 2
Members: 60 / 100

War
Catechists
Brothers in Black

Armistice
Pagans

We hadn't lost any members, but we did pick up the burden of a new war. If we were lucky, our victory would attract wide-eyed adventurers to the cause. Regardless, it would be a bit before the faction gained enough members to level up.

<table>
<tr><td colspan="1">

Black Hat Headquarters

</td></tr>
<tr><td>

Level: 2
HQXP: 7 / 8

</td></tr>
<tr><td>

HQR: 0
Daily HQR Production: 14
DP: 1

</td></tr>
<tr><td>

Current Buildings
Guildhall
Brothel
Lumberyard
Vault

</td></tr>
<tr><td>

Destroyed
Barracks

</td></tr>
</table>

The 3 headquarters experience points we were awarded for winning the battle were huge. Once we rebuilt the barracks, we'd hit level 3. That meant more HQR and more development. Unfortunately, our resources were tapped empty for the day. Besides that, every single one of our builders was on 24-hour lockdown.

Those were fine reasons for a day off.

Tomorrow, we'd rebuild the barracks. After that, my whole

outlook on headquarters construction would change. I'd never considered the tower defense capabilities of placements before. I'd need to think more strategically about Oldtown. With a new set of builders, the sky was the limit. It almost made me envious of peace time.

Almost.

As we approached Dragonperch, the great door heaved open. Instead of receiving a hero's welcome, Trafford blabbed away.

"There you are, Talon! I don't know if you're a rabbit's foot or a broken mirror, but my heart can't take this kind of heat every other week! I'm an old man. I deserve to retire."

I chuckled and started up the winding stairs. "I thought you had a soldier's soul, Buildmaster General?"

"No more generaling for me! I'm through with the army. Give me lumber and stone any day. Now that I have a talented crew backing me up, I'll stick to being a plain old-fashioned buildmaster, thank you very much. Beats being gutted by a mermaid!"

As we passed the kitchen floor, we caught Errol in the middle of a seafood gumbo recipe. Completely oblivious to our presence, he belted out an original tune.

"Old man Trafford's his name,
An' grumpin's his cause.
He runs a welcome shop
That don't tolerate slack-jaws.

They call him an old man.
They call him a crank.
He released tenfold oaths
'Gainst that mermaid skank.

When Trafford stands ground
One truth will resound:
Whether sober or plastered...
He's a miserable bastard!

A passable builder,
A swordsman quite awful,
But where would we be
Without our fine brothel?

Topless an' curvy
With a mean set o' claws.
Undine stabbed his heart through
And snipped off his balls.

When Trafford stands ground
One truth will resound:
Whether sober or plastered...
He's a miserable bastard!"

Izzy and I snorted down laughter. "No wonder you're retiring," I told Trafford. "On the bright side, you're famous now."

"I'm too old for this shit," he grumbled. The buildmaster made a dejected U-turn and headed for the underground grotto.

After he was out of earshot, I turned to Izzy. "Pirate ditties are surprisingly intricate."

Her eyelashes fluttered. "I just hope there's not a verse about sexy fish parts."

My face scrunched in disgust as she climbed ahead toward her room. "He wouldn't..." After a second's hesitation I peeked into the kitchen.

Errol put an opened oyster shell to his lips. "Now the trick, ya see, is t' treat that pearl as gently as a flower."

I hurried upstairs when he started making egregious sucking sounds. "Pirates..."

I found Kyle exactly where I knew he'd be, lounging on the couch watching RoboCop. The original, of course.

"Bro, this is hilariously amazing. Exhibit A in the case against CG blood effects. Look at that! Chunkier than Ragú."

I stifled a reproach. Kyle wouldn't be Kyle if he took anything too seriously, even a world-ranging conspiracy to control Haven. He noticed the look on my face.

"What?" he asked. "It's not like Hadrian the Wankerer got away. I deserve some R and R."

I chuckled. "That you do, Kyle."

He was so into his downtime I decided to save the news of the void pearl for later. I kicked his foot instead. He scooted over and I plopped down on the couch beside him.

"Did you get to the part where he shoots the guy in his junk?"

"Almost there, bro. Almost there."

We watched the gorefest for a bit, laughing and alternating between mimicking the over-the-top deaths and RoboCop's slow walk. It was the little things in life, and apparently the afterlife, that made everything worth doing. What good was winning if there was nothing to fight for?

"Man, I forgot what a masterpiece this is," I said. "Maybe I should play it at the grand opening of the guildhall tonight."

Kyle paused the movie and turned to me. "Bro, the whole clan's on 24-hour lockdown, including the brewmaster, and Oldtown's a wreck. We gotta postpone the party."

"I know. We'll do a real grand opening tomorrow night, but I wanna make an appearance today. We plastered flyers all over town. We need to show people we're reliable, prove that we mean business. After our overwhelming victory, the place will be packed with new recruits. Just you wait. All of Stronghold will be talking about us!"

His face didn't mirror my excitement. "I suppose. It's just a bummer. Why are evil conspiracies always cramping my style? It ain't easy being a player."

I smirked. "Don't hate the player, hate the game." His eyes narrowed. "Wait, that doesn't make sense. How about, hate the player, *not* the game? But not all players, of course. Only trolls. And I don't consider Haven a game anymore. It's—"

"Bro," he cut in. "You seriously need a beer."

"That's what I've been trying to say."

That night, I was in the middle of my sixth fancy tankard on the unmarred bar top. I sighed at the abandoned guildhall. I knew the lockdown would prevent respawned Black Hats from attending, but I'd really thought curious town residents would at least pop in to congratulate the victors.

Then again, it was entirely possible that partying with the Protector of Stronghold would insert oneself into the middle of an assassination attempt or, saints forbid, another titan outbreak. Then there was the goblin horde. They still skirted the tended land pounding war drums with aggravating vigor. I supposed, in the end, people didn't really feel safe straying from their usual routines tonight.

I filled the time by absentmindedly browsing the Haven Live Feed.

> **Lash** marked herself safe during **The Incident At Oldtown**.

I rolled my eyes. The white knight may not have been present but she was doing her own form of publicity. At least the news was spreading. Today was a day of fear and relief. The celebration and accolades would come tomorrow. I could live with that.

My breath eased as I settled into the lonely mahogany tavern. Quiet was good. Besides, I was in good spirits over finally deciding a name for the place. After Hadrian's inexhaustible assault, the pub would be known as the Last Stand.

The door opened and Izzy walked in. "Still here?"

"Yes. Have a drink with me."

She hopped up and planted her butt on the bar beside me. "I'll pass. You know I prefer my drunken debauchery in moderation. Besides, there's no one here to run the microwave. I'm saving myself for the real grand opening tomorrow."

I leaned my arm in her lap and rubbed her thigh. "Saving yourself, huh?"

She batted mischievous eyelashes.

I rose to my feet and slid my tankard aside. "I suppose there's a plus side to being absolutely alone. It occurs to me the guildhall has not been officially christened."

She looped a leg around to straddle the bar, laughing and leaning back as I climbed over her. "Not so fast, Talon. What kind of girl do you think I am?"

"Rough and demanding." I bit her earlobe.

She shivered under my kiss. "You got me there. But... speaking of demanding..." Izzy slid up the bar so her inner thigh brushed my cheek. Her fingers ran through my hair.

"I guess I walked right into that one," I said with a smirk. I reached my hand up her robe and grabbed her underwear, fingers slipping against the waistband.

Izzy craned her neck. "What are you fumbling with down there? It's not a bra strap."

"I..." My head sagged into her crotch. "This isn't a private zone. Underwear doesn't come off here."

She blinked several times, then dropped her head on the bar. Her whole body shuddered up and down. At first I thought she was going for a dry hump, but she broke into hysterical laughter. I couldn't help but join in.

"So much for players being masters of their fate," she said

wryly. "Isn't there something you can do about this with the developer menu?"

The front door opened again and Izzy and I sat at attention. A familiar man stood in the doorway, looking around and obviously confused.

My jaw dropped. "You're—"

Izzy pinched my side.

"A restaurant host," I finished. "Funny, we were just talking about Gordon Ramsay the other day."

"That hack?" [Tony B] frowned at us. "What's going on here? I mean, there's bar service and then there's *bar service*."

Izzy pulled her robe lower and hopped to the floor. "Nothing's happening. Come on in."

"No reservations?"

"Very funny."

The newcomer entered and appraised the guildhall. "What a gyp. The flyer said there'd be Hot Pockets."

"I'm not sure we have the culinary muscle to pull that off." I spun from the bar to the back floor. "You're a new player, right?" I poured him a beer and placed it next to mine. "How about a drink?"

Any misgivings he had dissolved at the sight of the tankard. "Well, these may be parts unknown, but I always say do as the locals do.' You know, there's no better living than spending time with friends, sharing a meal, kicking back, and letting loose."

I retook my stool and grinned from ear to ear. "Brother, you said it."

1530 Alone in the Dark

I followed Warden Jorah down the chiseled staircase and into the murky depths.

It was a new day of calm in the city. While Oldtown residents were eagerly waiting out the last few hours of lockdown, I'd decided to get a jump on strategizing the faction's next course of action. Grimwart and Hex were still missing, General Azzyrk and Cleric Vagram weren't going away, and my concerns over Oakengard weren't alleviated after the destruction of Saint Loras. Which all meant it was as good a time as any to visit the Stronghold jail.

The grounds were surprisingly large given that actual prisoners weren't commonplace in MMOs. The main jail building served as a guardhouse with minimum security rooms. There was a greater jail yard and cell building. We were now beneath that, in the dungeon. Cell after empty cell, all seemingly for nothing. I chalked it up to a canceled feature by sadistic game designers.

The city watch wasn't taking chances. A well-armed unit of

guards monitored the building entrance. Roving patrols watched the perimeter. Underground access had a redundant gate for extra security. It was decidedly impregnable.

Chadwick was down here, snatched by the watch from his own lockdown. I wasn't sure what would happen to him yet. It was cruel to lock a player away in the afterlife. Then again, it wasn't any different for mobs and NPCs anymore. Chadwick was a bad guy who'd opportunistically taken advantage of residents during the attack. He needed to pay for his crimes.

Nooner, to his credit, had actually assisted in the town's defense. He'd employed his peculiar brand of hooliganism, of course, but it was more than I could say for Chadwick. So Nooner was still a free man, able to rebuild his empire in the absence of his rival. I recalled Papa Brugo's words about men like him. Give him enough rope to either control him or let him hang himself.

At the end of the hall was a large wooden door that opened to a solitary confinement cell. It was a dark place, without a window or much room to maneuver. Hadrian, the level-7 spymaster, sat in a special chair that shackled his arms and legs in place. The extreme measures were the only way to prevent the usurper from taking his own life.

"This is it," announced Jorah. "Prisoner one one seven, Hadrian the Whisperer. He's all yours, Protector of Stronghold."

The man in darkness spat. "Why don't you execute me and get it over with?"

I snorted. What could you do to the worst of the worst in an MMO? You couldn't put them to death. Bishop Tannen had used executions as a public show, but they wouldn't gain us anything here.

"So you can respawn in Shorehome? Reestablish your power base?" I shook my head firmly. "That's not gonna happen. Otho's missing and Decimus won't activate without proof. We may not be able to get the angels to delete you, but give us time. We'll figure something out."

"You can't keep me here forever."

I worked my jaw. If Hadrian had only ever uttered one ultimate truth, it was that. Forever was a long time in the afterlife. The only guarantee of endless confinement would be escape. Eventually.

"The goblin horde isn't attacking," I remarked. "They don't have the numbers, and they don't want to die."

"Why are you telling me this?"

"Because I know you sent them. That's what you do, isn't it? Get your hooks into people. Have them do all the dirty work while you slink around in the shadows." I leaned into the bound prisoner. "Tell me, how'd you manage to get to a saint? I mean, I understand paying off Larry on the outside, but once his cover was blown, you hacked an avatar and had it doing your bidding."

The corner of Hadrian's mouth crooked just enough to betray pride in the feat. "Are you asking me to incriminate myself? State that I breached the terms of service? How about instead I just send Decimus a personal invitation to my deletion?"

So the spymaster meant to keep his secrets. I hiked a shoulder. "Didn't hurt to try." I moved to the wall. The stone was cold and dry. "I had a chat with my contacts on the outside..."

"You place too much faith in the developers."

I caught the twinkle in his eye that confirmed it. It was a certainty for me now; I just couldn't prove it.

Hadrian was the Trojan. Somehow he'd amassed the power to influence game mechanics and characters around him. A hard man like Brugo shouldn't have been so easy to outplay. The kraken should've never surrendered to being so docile. Hadrian had controlled them somehow. NPCs, titans, even the saints—none had stood against him. Even now, in defeat, his confidence was supreme.

I moved to the door and stared him down. "I know it's you. The ghost in the machine. The threat to both Kablammy and Haven."

The prisoner didn't say anything. He just stared at an empty spot on the floor and grinned.

"I'm gonna find out how," I swore. "I'll scour the codebase and the history logs. I'll become intimately familiar with the corporate playing field, uncover all the actors with a stake in Kablammy's future. I'll comb the countryside for every enemy you have. And I'll raze Oakengard to the ground if I have to. One way or another, your schemes are gonna come crashing down hard. And when they do, if you happen to be at the center of all the debris, well..." I shrugged. "Don't say I didn't tell you so."

I shut the door behind me, leaving the spymaster to the solace of his shadows.

-Finn

Character Sheets

Talon		Level	10
Class	Explorer	XP	90313
Kit	Scout	Next	113400

Strength	18	Strike	390
Agility	24	Dodge	450
Craft	6	Health	300 / 300
Essence	10	Spirit	255 / 255

Coin	
Silver	417
Plates	2
Bars	4

Skills	1
Spear	3
Crossblock	3
Deadshot	3
Tornado Spin	1
Spinshield	1
Knife	1
Claw	1
- - Dragonrun - -	
Awareness	
Exploration	
Tracking	
Darkvision	
Intuition	
Survival	
Navigation	
Cartography	
Traversal	
Dash	
Vault	
Wall Run	
Scale	
Stealth	
Sneak	
Subdue	

Reputation

Reputation	
Pagan	-600
Crusader	-200
Catechist	200
Wildkin	0
Brothers in Black	-999

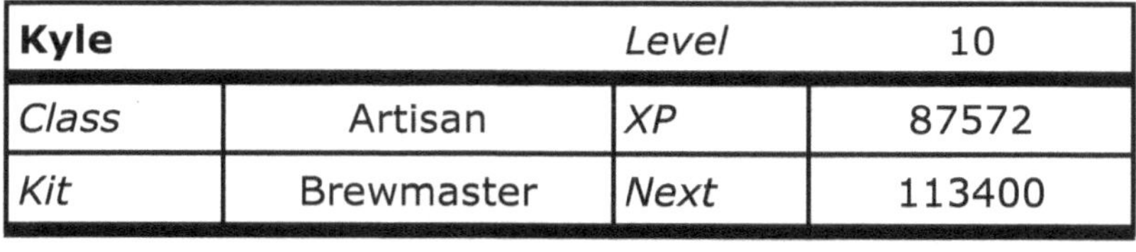

Kyle		*Level*	10
Class	Artisan	*XP*	87572
Kit	Brewmaster	*Next*	113400

Strength	22	*Strike*	355
Agility	5	*Dodge*	185
Craft	20	*Health*	245 / 245
Essence	10	*Spirit*	217 / 217

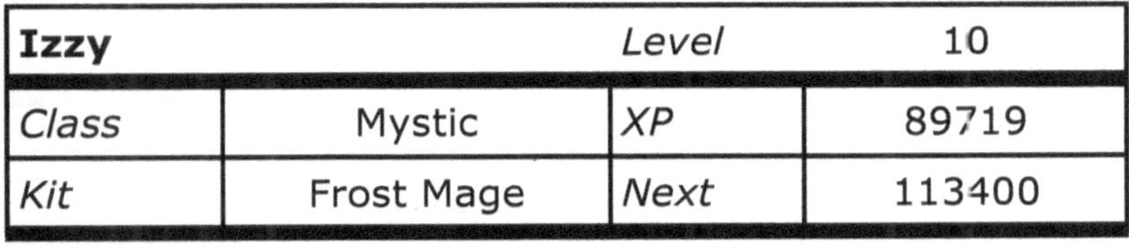

Izzy		Level	10
Class	Mystic	XP	89719
Kit	Frost Mage	Next	113400

Strength	9	Strike	220
Agility	17	Dodge	300
Craft	6	Health	175 / 175
Essence	25	Spirit	440 / 440

Haven Live Feed

Lash marked herself safe during **The Incident At Oldtown**.

Glinda

Glad one of us made it!

Conan

Go Bravo Team!

Lash

It was a group effort. I'm proud to fight alongside you all. Even **Crux**.

Crux

It was exhilarating, I'll give you that.

Kyle

Good job with that bishop gauntlet! Speaking of which... you mind giving it back now?

Lash
I would but I'm too busy figuring out what to do with all this XP. Sorry, I shouldn't mention that around you guys.

Kyle
No worries. I rejoined the party and got XP too.

Conan
What!?! You can do that? Why didn't anybody re-invite us?

Glinda
Paging **Lash**.

Lash marked herself **Away on Vacation**.

Saint Peter
I'm elated to see everyone safe and sound. Truly. But if I may burden the Black Hats with a single request... Is it too much to ask that we go through the next week without threatening the sanctity of the simulation?

Talon
Sorry, Pete. That's up to Oakengard.

Kyle
We got a man and woman down.

Saint Peter
I just don't want to see Haven become a player battleground.

Lucifer
If I'm not mistaken, a saint was pivotal to the recent theatrics.

Saint Peter
Allegedly!

Saint Peter
...

Saint Peter
You guys really aren't gonna throw me a bone, are you?

(Sponsored Content)
Meet <u>real mermaids</u> in your area.

Dune
Risky click of the day.

Chadwick

If anyone has a moment, I'd appreciate a visit to my Kickstarter page to fund my legal proceedings.

Drummond

You realize you're asking for money from people you've robbed.

Nooner

Ha! If yer so desperate you can sell me that pack animal business you stole.

Chadwick

I built that operation from the ground up!

Nooner

Scratch that. I'd rather wait till yer late on rent. I kin make a killing after yer holdings go into overexposure.

Drummond

I think you mean foreclosure.

Nooner

I meant what I said, banker boy!

Caduceus

I never thought I'd say this, but death lockdown isn't half bad. I finally get to kick my feet up.

Stigg

You've been doing a lot of that in the brothel lately.

Caduceus

Jealousy doesn't suit you, my Viking brother.

Domino Finn invites you to join his Facebook group (facebook.com/groups/DominoFinnFans).

Talon changed his relationship status to: Seeing someone.

Izzy

Okay, fine. I've made you sweat long enough.

Talon

Wanna sweat some more?

Errol Oates

Poll: Vote fer the subject o' the next pirate ditty.
- Talon, fearless leader o' the Black Hats, defeatin' the mighty kraken. [17%]
- Talon, fearless leader o' the Black Hats, finally consummatin' his relationship. [83%]

Trafford

Yes times a million. Move on to another flavor of the month.

Dune

What's this I'm hearing about for the very first time ever? JK Kyle told everyone.

Kyle

What can I say? This place is like high school.

Talon

Sighs This is my life now.

Gladius

Anyone happen to see a stray Fallen named **Otho** around? (Description: standard angel wings, solid black eyeballs, missing one arm.) Asking for a friend.

Talon

Anyone else think these author ads are a little out of control?

Errol Oates

I posted the first verse o' the new song on me SoundCloud. I entitled it: The Dainty Little Girl an' the Purple Pixie.

Baz

HA HA. FUNNY BECAUSE YOOMANS SO PUNY LOOK LIKE GIRLS.

Jixa

No laughses at boss man, Baz! He can't helpses his small hands.

Talon

Okay, guys. I can take a joke as well as the next man, but— Hold up. Since when could NPCs and mobs post to the live feed?

Errol Oates
Beats me.

Baz

WHAT IS LIVE FEED? BAZ HUNGRY. GO EAT HORSE.

Artax
Nickers

Bandit
Growls

Kraken
BLABOOBLARRGHH!!!

Creature Wiki

Dirt Beetle	5 HP	25 XP
Weed Snake	6 HP	40 XP
Pack Rat	8 HP	40 XP
Swamp Toad	15 HP	60 XP
Wild Hog	19 HP	90 XP
Imp	30 HP	150 XP
Devil Badger	45 HP	175 XP
Kobold Handler	38 HP	200 XP
Kobold	45 HP	250 XP
Goblin	55 HP	300 XP
Wildkin	65 HP	310 XP
Walking Dead	50 HP	300 XP
Rogue	60 HP	300 XP
Gangster	60 HP	300 XP

Bandit	80 HP	325 XP
Cutthroat	100 HP	350 XP
Assassin	140 HP	500 XP
Blackwood Prisoner	85 HP	360 XP
Mother Pack Rat	85 HP	400 XP
Undine	100 HP	375 XP
Goblin Warlock	100 HP	400 XP
Goblin Captain	120 HP	600 XP
Goblin Assassin	200 HP	850 XP
Cannonball Crab	150 HP	700 XP
Sandworm	200 HP	750 XP
Boggart Witch	200 HP	1200 XP
Keeper	225 HP	600 XP
Great Sandworm	325 HP	1100 XP
Ogre	300 HP	1200 XP
Keeper Brute	375 HP	1400 XP

Troll	240 HP	1800 XP
Shadowguard	600 HP	4500 XP
Kraken	20k HP	25k XP
Orik	100k HP	100k XP

WIKI SEARCH: dragons_

[Nightwing]
Brave and terrifying dragon who gave his life to
defeat Hadrian and the kraken.

No other entries found...
  Create New Entry?

About the Author

I'm Domino Finn: game-developer-turned-fantasy-author, media rebel, and product of my generation. (Where in the world is Carmen Sandiego?)

Afterlife Online will be back. Join my reader group (http://dominofinn.com/newsletter/) to get the first word on sequels, cover reveals, and other DLC.

Help Trojan level up. Post an online review, mention it on reddit and social media, and help spread the word.

Finally, don't forget to keep in touch. You can contact me, connect on social media, and see my complete book catalog at DominoFinn.com.